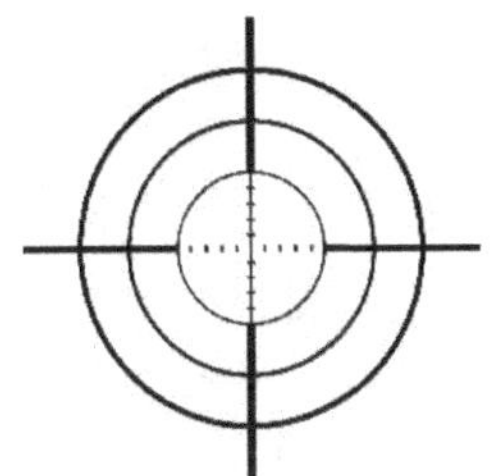

—ONE—

After almost two hours crawling through the impossibly green native undergrowth and over the crest of a hill overlooking the target's estate, the sniper settled into a hollow between two trees. His chameleon ghillie suit made him practically invisible to human eyes beyond a meter or two, and its built-in shielding hid his life signs from sensors. He was, essentially, the invisible man. Even his weapon, a long, heavy railgun masked by the same chameleon coating as his suit, wouldn't register until he powered it up seconds before taking a shot. The sniper opened a bipod attached to the barrel's casing two-thirds of the way back from the muzzle and settled into the most comfortable firing position he could find.

Mission Colony's reddish sun hung directly overhead, but here in the foothills west of Ventano, the star system's capital, a gentle breeze wafting off distant snow-capped peaks kept the ambient temperature pleasantly cool.

Neither the mansion, nestled at the bottom of a pleasant glen, nor the dozen human beings enjoying a lunchtime drink on the stone patio cast much of a shadow. At this distance, the sniper's unaided eyes weren't capable of making out individual features, but he knew which one was his target.

It had to be the man at the center of the group, basking in the adulation of his flock, though the sniper knew better. These were not followers but financiers and bureaucrats who worshiped power. True radicals of the sort who enlisted in the Freedom Collective's ranks would never receive an invitation to lunch with their supremo at his partner's country manor. Otherwise, they might discover his revolutionary zeal found sustenance in the trappings of wealth.

Unfamiliar scents tickled the sniper's nose while equally alien sounds produced by local wildlife unconcerned with his presence filled his ears. He flipped up the covers on both ends of the telescopic sight sitting atop the railgun's receiver. Its unpowered optical array, a design virtually unchanged over the centuries, was as undetectable as the rest of his equipment, a low-tech solution to the high tech surveillance sensors blanketing the glen.

He settled his cheek against the stock and pulled the butt plate into his shoulder, merging body and weapon into a single, steady organism, half man, half machine. The sniper's right eye lined up with the scope and distant, blurry faces became crisp, clear, and identifiable. Though the sniper's hide was over a kilometer from the mansion, it seemed as if he might reach out and touch its walls.

The bearded, smiling man standing at the center of the circle, champagne glass in hand, was indeed Gustav Kerlin. He was a rabble-rousing politician, the leader of the Mission Colony Freedom Collective, as well as a fake revolutionary and a scumbag who liked to bed the underage children of his followers before passing them around a circle of like-minded deviants. And those were the least of his crimes, but his political connections and his partner's money ensured complainants remained mute. Kerlin laughed at an

HARD

STRIKE

Decker's War — Book 7

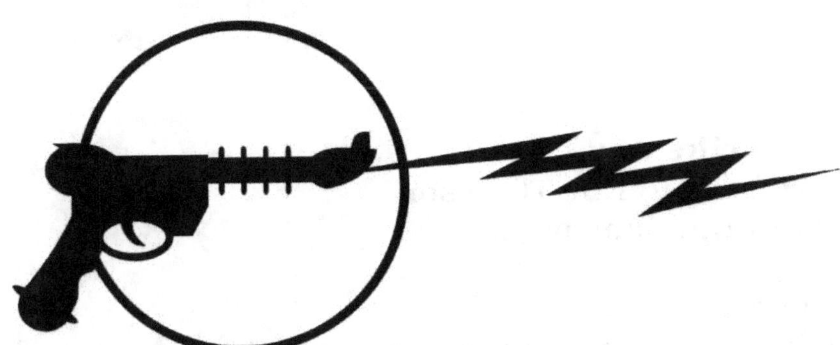

ERIC THOMSON

Hard Strike
Copyright 2019 Eric Thomson
First printing January 2019

All rights reserved.
This book, or parts thereof, may not be reproduced in any form without permission.

This is a work of fiction. Names, characters, places, and incidents either are the product of the author's imagination or are used fictitiously, and any resemblance to actual persons, living or dead, business establishments, events or locales is entirely coincidental.

Published in Canada
By Sanddiver Books
ISBN: 978-1-989314-07-4

unheard comment and took a sip of his amber, bubbly drink, imported from Earth at exorbitant cost.

The sniper rested his aim on each of the men and women surrounding Kerlin in turn though he was unable to name the three facing away from him. Those he could identify represented everything Kerlin railed against in his incarnation as a radical reformer and a man of the people, making a lie of his claim to serve downtrodden, economically disadvantaged settlers denied full self-rule by an oppressive Colonial Office.

In an ideal universe a liar of that caliber shouldn't prosper, not when his followers were about to cross the line between legitimate dissent and political violence on a scale unheard of in these parts.

He settled the scope's crosshairs on Kerlin once again and felt an unexpected jolt of pleasure at holding the man's life in his hands. Kerlin represented everything the sniper hated. He steadied his aim on Kerlin's prominent nose, took a deep breath, and flicked on the railgun's power pack with his right thumb. As he felt the weapon come to life, he released half of the air in his lungs and gently pulled on the trigger.

The railgun expelled a tungsten dart, smaller than a baby's finger at almost ten times the speed of sound. It left a flat crack in its wake, like a branch snapping underfoot. Kerlin's skull exploded before the sniper was able to blink, showering the other attendees with bloody bone shards and glistening gobs of liquefied brain matter. The sniper kept his aim on the target to confirm the shot.

Nothing remained above Kerlin's jawline, as if someone had sliced off half of the politician's head. Without warning, his body crumpled to the ground.

The others seemed rooted to the spot as they processed what just happened. Then, the first distant screams reached the sniper's ears and what had been a quiet pre-lunch drink turned into a mad rout, a scramble for cover. The sniper zoomed out his scope in an attempt to identify the three who moments earlier had their backs to him.

One face, in particular, caught his attention, and he mentally swore. That woman's presence could imperil his escape and the next phase of the operation. He briefly considered firing a second shot to eliminate the risk, but decided it was best to stay within the agreed-upon parameters. Bad enough he might face a police presence earlier than planned.

With little regard for stealth, the sniper rose from his hide and headed back into the nearby hollow where a carefully hidden speeder waited. He disassembled his railgun and stowed the parts in its pack as he moved through the forest. By the time he reached the small ground effect vehicle tucked between the roots of a giant fern-like conifer, the distant howl of police sirens filtered through the treetops.

He stripped off his ghillie suit and stuffed it in the railgun pack, then retrieved civilian clothing from the speeder and completed his transformation back into an ordinary colonist. Though he would prefer to keep both weapon and suit, they weren't traceable and being found in his possession if the police stopped his speeder would compromise the entire operation.

He shoved the pack under a bush and spread rotting organic debris over and around it. A determined search would uncover the cache, but by then, Major Zack Decker and his partner, Commander Hera Talyn, would be long gone. Or so he hoped. After one last glance around, Decker climbed aboard the speeder and threaded his way through the trees to a hidden animal track. It led further west until crossing an old logging road that dated back to the Shrehari occupation almost eighty years earlier.

Judging by the strength of the emergency response team sirens, they were virtually at the late Gustav Kerlin's mansion, which meant the chase would soon be on. And these hunters wouldn't be militia or planetary cops. Mission Colony, as befitted a planet under federal jurisdiction, was policed by the Commonwealth Constabulary itself.

Decker reached the logging road without his military-grade battlefield sensor warning him quasi-invisible surveillance drones deployed by the Constabulary to blanket the area had spotted him. The assassination of a firebrand political rabble-rouser might not demand an all hands on deck scenario in these troubled times, but rank has its privileges.

The commanding officer of the 24th Constabulary Regiment — Mission Colony's de facto chief of police — was one of the three whose faces he identified moments after Kerlin's head vanished in a pink and gray mist. An unplanned complication, but it was too late for regrets, and absent specific direction from HQ, none of Decker and Talyn's business.

Assistant Commissioner Kristy Bujold keeping company with someone like Kerlin and his backers was a problem for the Constabulary's Professional Compliance Bureau, and it frowned on the sort of direct action preferred by Naval Intelligence's Special Operations Division, especially assassinations. But if she was up to no good, he and Talyn could expect Bujold to throw the full weight of her police force into the investigation. And Kerlin's death was only one phase of the operation.

After a few minutes, the distant sirens died away and Decker allowed himself to hope he was still beyond the Constabulary's ever-growing search area when he saw the logging road's unmarked junction with a country lane. The latter meandered through half a dozen small valleys, each with farming settlements, before it left the foothills and connected to the main east-west highway linking Ventano to its agricultural hinterland.

He'd chosen his escape route based on the fact it didn't connect with the road leading to Kerlin's manor until just before the highway, but Decker's luck ran out at the same time as the country lane just the same.

A pair of dark blue Constabulary patrol skimmers, civilian versions of the combat cars used by every military and paramilitary force within the Commonwealth, blocked the intersection. His rental vehicle could generate enough lift to jump over them, but anyone evading the checkpoint would immediately turn into a suspect and become the target of every police aircar in the vicinity. Decker slipped the battlefield sensor into his pocket and slowed to a walking pace.

A square-faced man with sergeant's stripes on his gray police-grade armor waved him to the side of the road while two more assumed covering positions to each side. Decker knew that at least one of the combat cars would aim its gun turret at him. Though they carried only twenty-millimeter dual cannon, they could shred his speeder in a matter of seconds. Right now, however, he knew targeting sensors were giving him the once-over. A good thing he'd ditched the railgun. It would have stood out on their screens like a Sister of the Void at a sex workers' convention.

As the sergeant approached, Decker dropped the driver's side window and gave him a quizzical look.

"Are the damned boneheads back?"

"Just a routine traffic check, sir." His tone was polite and professional. "May I see your ID and your vehicle's registration?"

"Certainly."

When Decker reached into his jacket's inner pocket, the sergeant asked, "Are you armed by any chance, sir?"

"Yes.   I'd be a piss-poor security consultant if I weren't."

"Is that your line of work," the sergeant waved a reader over Zack's proffered identity wafer, "Ser Corbin Peel? Private security consultant? Or should that be mercenary? You're not a resident of Mission Colony."

"Call it what you want, as long as my clients call themselves satisfied." Decker grinned. "And so far I've heard no complaints." He tucked his ID wafer away again and offered the rental's registration.

"Please show me your weapons."

"No problems. I carry a blaster in a shoulder holster and a dagger strapped to my forearm, both on the left side." Decker raised his hand in a slow, exaggerated motion and pulled his jacket aside.

"What the hell is that?" The sergeant asked in an incredulous tone. "A hand cannon?"

"Standard Shrehari issue sidearm. I took it in a raid when I was in the Service." He released his jacket's lapel and pulled up its left sleeve. "Marine Corps dagger."

"You were in the Corps, Ser Peel?"

"Twenty years before moving to the private sector."

"Are you carrying a copy of your service record, by any chance?"

"Sure." Decker fished a second wafer from his pocket and held it out for the constable's reader.

"Pathfinders? I'm impressed." He looked up at the Marine.   "Tell me, what business does a security consultant have in the foothills? It's nothing but farms and logging operations."

Decker shrugged.

"Do you ever wake up in the morning with an urge to get out of town, breathe clean air, and see unspoiled nature?"

"Can't say that I do, Ser Peel."

Before Zack could reply, the sergeant tilted his head to one side in the unmistakable gesture of someone listening to his earbug. After a few seconds, he said, "Please stay where you are." Then, he turned and gestured at his constables.

Both patrol cars cleared the intersection moments before a lightly armored and more luxurious staff skimmer, also in police blue, came barreling down the road from Kerlin's mansion. Decker caught a glimpse of Bujold's ashen face through the rear window as it passed through, headed for the main highway. Now *that*, the Marine thought, was one unhappy assistant commissioner.

Maybe his partner should send word of Bujold's dubious associates to her friend who was in charge of the Rim Sector's Professional Compliance Bureau. If internal affairs latched onto her scrawny ass, the 24th Constabulary Regiment's commanding officer would find an even better reason to look like death warmed over.

The sergeant walked back to Decker's car.

"You're free to go, sir. Thank you for your cooperation and enjoy the rest of your day."

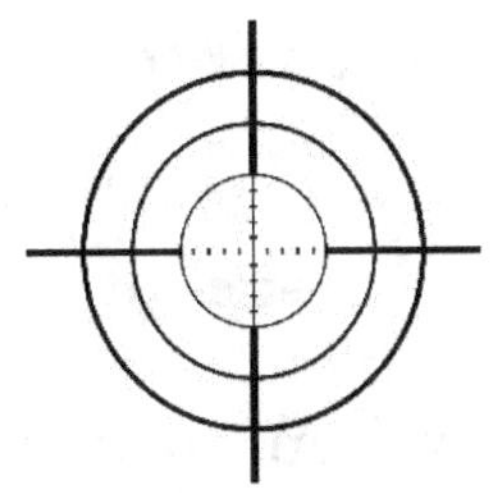

— TWO —

A thirty-something man emerged from one of the rundown apartment complexes bordering a shabby little city park. He looked around nervously before setting off toward downtown Ventano at a rapid pace. Pasty-faced, unshaven, and wearing shabby clothes, he differed little from the other residents of an area inhabited mostly by idlers living on government benefits, small-time criminals and every other example of life's losers. But a set of eyes, carefully hidden behind polarized sunglasses, tracked his progress.

Moments before the man vanished around the street corner, a grandmotherly woman in a broad-brimmed hat rose from the park bench nearest to the apartment and set off in pursuit, careful to avoid attracting his attention.

Osric Floros wasn't a complete beginner in the art of fieldcraft. He knew how to check for tails, but she'd been doing this for decades, while the man's shift from merely spouting radical rhetoric at the Ventano University's Faculty of Political Science to carrying out direct action was more recent. So recent, in fact, he did not notice her brush by him at a crosswalk and attach a minuscule listening device to his jacket.

It had a limited range and a short lifespan but would suffice for her immediate purposes. A more experienced and more paranoid revolutionary gripped by dread after hearing of his leader's assassination might have noticed the brief contact.

The old woman followed him to a more upscale apartment complex. When an unseen tenant admitted him through the ground level door, she found a small cafe with outdoor tables on the opposite side of the street, half a block away. She ordered a cup of tea from the holographic menu that popped up the moment she sat, then touched the frame of her glasses. A small red dot appeared on the inside of the left lens, indicating her listening device and the man to whom she'd stuck it were on the apartment's third floor. She tapped her right ear lightly with an extended index finger and immediately heard voices.

"Why are you here?" A harsh voice, oozing displeasure asked.

"Someone assassinated Gustav." The revolutionary's voice quivered with anguish. "We received word through the cell network fifteen minutes ago from our comrade who watches over his personal security. He told me how to find you."

Silence. Then, "Where did it happen?"

"At a country retreat that friends of the Collective made available to him."

The woman smirked. Kerlin, like most of his sort, thought nothing of lying to naïve supporters while enriching himself and his closest friends at the same trough as those he purported to oppose. He saw political radicalism as a means to achieve power and accumulate more wealth, not a way to improve the lot of ordinary citizens.

"How did it happen?"

"No one knows. Gustav was having drinks with friends on the patio when his head literally exploded. Our comrade heard nothing to indicate a shot. The Constabulary's emergency response team was arriving when our comrade called."

A fond smile replaced the woman's earlier expression of disdain. Her partner scored a clean kill. Perfect.

More silence. "Railgun."

"Pardon?"

"The assassin used a railgun. A professional's weapon. Soundless, but the darts it fires are capable of causing indescribable trauma to a human body from a great distance. The police won't find him — or her."

A pleading tone entered Floros' voice. "What do we do?"

"Lie low. Don't attract attention, lest you end like your boss. And never contact me again. Ever. Now leave and forget this address."

"But—"

"Someone just declared war on the Mission Colony Freedom Collective, and it's one you won't win. Not against ghost snipers able to kill at will. Step back and wait. In six months, or a year or even five, when whoever killed Kerlin thinks your movement died with him, it'll be time for resurrection. Under a new name. The revolution will happen, but it's been postponed."

She picked up a gasp, then a door slam, followed by muttered imprecations. But Floros was no longer her immediate concern. He'd served his purpose and could wait until later. She wanted the man to whom Floros just spoke, the offworlder who'd met with Kerlin on a dozen occasions over the last two weeks. Each time it was under security tight enough to prevent her from identifying him, let alone listen in on the conversation.

Commander Hera Talyn drained her tea, strolled back toward the apartment complex, and studied it from all four sides. The unit in question was on the third floor. Judging by the angle, it was centered and faced the boulevard. She could make out three duplicate window groupings, indicating three units and that meant her target occupied the middle one.

Talyn expected him to bolt, now that the Mission Colony scheme was on the verge of collapse and Floros had compromised his location. It didn't give her much time. She scanned the front door and found it festooned with the usual security measures — sensors, video pickups, high-grade remote locks. One entered only with the right credentials or by invitation.

Shortly after she finished her study of the front entryway, a woman approximately Talyn's apparent age crossed the street, making a beeline for the building's door. She seemed distracted as if in a hurry and Talyn, who'd been prepared to wait for just such an occasion, closed the distance between them while remaining at the edge of her peripheral vision.

The woman stopped short of the entrance and waited until the door opened with a faint whoosh after scanning her credentials. Talyn crowded in behind her with a reassuring smile that signaled she belonged here. The agent's harmless appearance drew nothing more than a preoccupied, somewhat distant glance but thankfully no questions. Talyn loitered in the lobby until she was alone before taking a lift to the third floor.

Eight apartment doors lined the hallway, three toward the building's front, three toward the back and one at each end. Talyn found the middle unit and scanned it. One life sign registered. It was moving briskly between rooms, showing the offworlder was either packing or wiping away any evidence of his temporary tenancy.

If news of Kerlin's assassination had spooked him, so much the better. She studied the apartment door's locking mechanism and found it to be of the same high quality as that used on the building's main entrance. It was impregnable without making a lot of noise or a big mess. Or both. Talyn removed her glasses, pushed her hat back to expose an elderly face wrinkled like a dried apple. She touched the call button and stepped back so the mysterious offworlder could examine her via the security camera.

"What is it?" A voice made familiar by her listening device asked through a hidden speaker.

"Gustav's wife sends her sorrowful greetings. I come with a vitally important message concerning business matters following today's tragic events."

Silence greeted her unexpected reply. But curiosity won out, and he opened the door. Talyn found herself face-to-face with a man of uncertain age and ethnic origin, of middling height and weight, with brown hair and eyes. Unremarkable in every aspect, someone easy to miss in a crowd but for the gun pointed at her midriff. He waved the weapon to one side.

"Come in." When the door closed behind her, he asked, "Who are you and how did you know where to find me?"

Instead of answering, Talyn shook her right arm, releasing a needler hidden under the loose sleeve. It dropped into her palm, and before he could react, she raised it and stitched his cheek with knockout darts. A look of pure astonishment overcame him. He crumpled to the floor like a sack of wet seaweed, felled by the fast-acting narcotic.

Talyn dragged him to the bedroom before tying his wrist and ankles with virtually unbreakable plastic restraints. She found rolled socks in the open travel bag sitting on an unmade bed and shoved them in the man's mouth. A search of his pockets produced anonymous cred chips, a rental car keycard, and an ID wafer identifying him as Alek Mannsbach, forty-two, Cimmerian citizen.

Talyn emptied the bag and searched it as well, but without coming across anything of interest. She then searched the apartment, with similar results. Other than the blaster, a standard model easily obtainable throughout the sector, there was nothing to distinguish Mannsbach from an honest citizen.

Talyn pulled a cheap-looking civilian communicator from her loose, pajama-like tunic and switched it on. It hooked into the local net almost at once. After a brief internal debate, she entered the authorization code activating the communicator's encryption ability, turning it into a naval grade unit able to confound even the most sophisticated police surveillance algorithms.

"What's up?" Decker's voice asked a few seconds later. "And why are we secure?"

"I have the offworlder."

"And I iced Kerlin."

"So I understand. The plan worked."

"With one wrinkle. Assistant Commissioner Kristy Bujold was among those spattered by Gustav's liquefied brain matter."

"Oops."

"Yeah. The police response time was much shorter as a result, but I made it through the cordon. Barely. HQ needs to know about her being chummy with Kerlin."

"We'll figure out the ramifications after interrogating the offworlder. Where are you?"

"I'm about to cross the city limits."

"Return the rental and join me at 1251 Fourth Avenue, apartment three-oh-seven."

"Will do. Give me thirty minutes."

Talyn cut the link. Their brief conversation would be flagged as suspicious once the Constabulary analyzed communications in search of Kerlin's killer, but only because it was scrambled nonsense impervious to decryption efforts.

Better that than hearing her give Decker the address. She glanced at Mannsbach and wondered how long it would take her to break him.

"Are you conditioned, my friend?" She murmured, eyes tracing the contours of his face. "Will you give me a chance to practice the dark arts, or are you the type to blubber at the first hint of pain?"

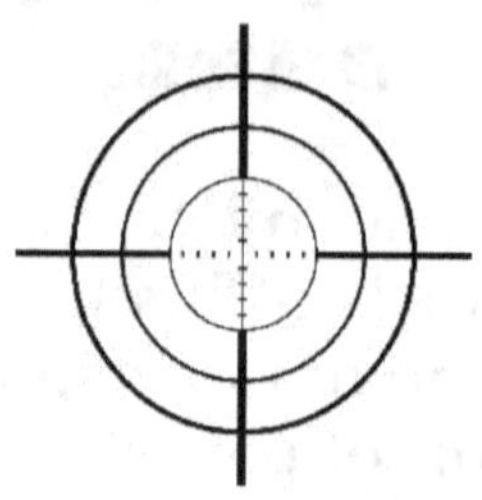

— THREE —

"Where's your gear?"

Decker, eyes scanning the sparsely furnished living room, shrugged. "I left it in the forest, hidden under a bush."

"They'll eventually find your cache, and we can't afford to go back there."

"Considering I ran into a Constabulary roadblock complete with armored patrol cars, it was just as well. They'd have detected the railgun."

Talyn nodded once.

"Fair enough. What about Assistant Commissioner Kristy Bujold?"

"Laughing and sipping champagne with the other assholes. She had her back to me before the shot so I couldn't know."

"Are you sure it was her?"

"Not a moment's doubt. While I was at the roadblock, Bujold's staff car came speeding down the road from Kerlin's cottage. She was in the back seat, wearing the face of a woman whose career might vanish into a black hole."

"Meaning we can expect Bujold to make hunting Kerlin's killer a matter of self-protection."

"Too bad the gray-legs are out of bounds. Otherwise, we might do your internal affairs friend a solid by exposing Constabulary corruption around here. I'm sure the Chief Constable will take a dim view of a regimental commander socializing with wannabe revolutionaries. Where's our customer?"

"In the bedroom. The ID he was carrying make him a Cimmerian by the name Alek Mannsbach. Forgettable face, the kind that works well in our professional circles, but he didn't show the level of paranoia that should come with it." Talyn recounted how she'd tailed Osric Floros and talked her way into the apartment before taking Mannsbach prisoner.

When she finished, Decker let out a dismissive grunt. "Sounds like he hasn't lost his amateur status yet. I doubt he'll be conditioned."

Talyn made a disappointed moue. "That's what I figure. Shame. It's been a while since I enjoyed a good interrogation challenge."

"We do it here?"

"Unless you can tell me how we might transport him to the safe house without attracting notice."

"Then we need to start now. If Bujold's criminal intelligence folks are combing the communications net, they'll find our encrypted call, and she'll order them to search for the source. Last I checked they can narrow it to a fifty meter radius. Granted, this is a high-density area. Or as high-density as it gets in Ventano, but still. How long until Mannsbach wakes up?"

"On his own? Twenty minutes. But I'm carrying a full kit."

Decker walked over to the bedroom door and stuck his head through for a glance at their prisoner. Then, he checked the apartment's other rooms. "It's not an ideal place. Where do you want to do it?"

"On the kitchen table. Put him on his back and tie his limbs to the legs."

"You intend to use waterboarding?"

"No, but it's the most uncomfortable position we can manage under the circumstances and the hardest one to struggle against."

"True." Decker returned to the bedroom, picked Mannsbach up by the shoulders, and dragged him across the apartment to the kitchen. A few minutes later, he said, "You can wake sleeping beauty now. He's not going anywhere."

Talyn entered the kitchen and slowly walked around the marble-topped, stainless steel table, studying Mannsbach from every angle, stalked by her reflection in the shiny white cabinets covering three of the four walls. She stopped and gestured at their prisoner.

"Cut our friend's clothes off, please."

"Is this about to turn kinky?" Decker produced his dagger and sliced through Mannsbach's shirt, trousers and underwear, baring the front half of his prone body.

"He's not my type, honey." She pointed at a small tattoo on his left breast, above the nipple. "Tell me that's a stylized spiral galaxy surrounded by a wreath of stars."

"Okay. It's a stylized spiral galaxy, surrounded by a wreath of stars. If it were just a galaxy logo, I'd wonder whether Deep Space Foundation employees were required to prove their loyalty by etching its symbol into their skin. Careless to wear distinctive body art when you're working undercover, unless it's designed to misdirect people like us in case we put him in this exact position, which I find unlikely. And since removing a tattoo that size is a five minute procedure..."

"You of all people would know." Talyn leaned over to examine the mark more closely, then straightened and pulled a small pouch from her tunic. "Time to ask Alek about it."

She applied a thumbnail-sized dermal patch over Mannsbach's carotid artery, stepped back, and gestured at Decker to join her.

"Let's stay beyond his peripheral vision for a bit."

As they watched, the Cimmerian worked his jaw as if fighting a dry sticky mouth. His right eyelid fluttered open, then snapped shut again under the glare of the ceiling light. His shoulder and thigh muscles quivered as he tested the restraints. After half a minute, both eyes opened. They stayed that way while his head pivoted from side to side before lifting to glance at his feet.

"What the fuck," he croaked in a weak voice. "Hey. Old woman. Where are you?" His tongue darted out to lick dry lips. "What the hell do you want?"

He must have sensed Talyn and Decker's presence because he struggled to see over his shoulder but in vain. After testing his bonds again, Mannsbach relaxed.

"Okay. I know you're there. What do you want?" His voice was stronger now that the dermal patch flushed away the last dregs of Talyn's knockout drug.

Neither of the agents replied or made a sound. They possessed the patience of interrogators trained to let their subjects work themselves into a state of nervous tension if not outright fear. Almost ten minutes passed before Talyn drew a stiletto from a forearm sheath similar to the one Decker wore. She stepped closer to Mannsbach and, reaching over his head, gently ran its tip across his lips, careful to avoid breaking the skin.

"Hello, Alek," she said in a throaty voice at odds with her matronly disguise.

"Who are you?" He asked uncertainly.

"She who holds your life in her hands. Tell me, are you conditioned against interrogation?"

With the stiletto once more beyond his field of vision, Mannsbach turned his head from side to side, searching for her. "What do you mean?"

"My question is simple, Alek. Are you conditioned? It's important you answer truthfully because your life is at stake."

Mannsbach seemed to hesitate for a second, before saying, "Yes, I am."

"Really?" Talyn ran the stiletto's tip up his cheek until it hung a few millimeters over his right eye. "You're not a good liar, Alek. In fact, pretty much everything about you is sub-par for a man playing footsie with volatile maniacs like the late Gustav Kerlin."

She walked into his field of vision and stared him in the face. "One last time. Are you conditioned against interrogation? Because if you are, I'll use more extreme means to get answers."

She ran the stiletto's tip along the inside of his right thigh, across his genitals and along the left leg.

"The average human male can generally survive non-surgical castration and even the amputation of his penis. Of course, the pain is excruciating and the psychological effects devastating. But even partial castration, by making a small incision and reaching in helps loosen tongues imprisoned by conditioning."

Fear lit up his eyes.

"Okay, okay, you crazy bitch. I'm not conditioned. What sort of psychopath are you?"

Talyn's soulless smile turned her wizened face into a demon's mask.

"The sort who always gets what she wants."

She removed the antidote and pressed a fresh dermal patch on Mannsbach's carotid.

"You're about to feel giddy. Silly, even. Don't fight it. Go with the flow. Answering my questions will bring you pleasure."

Talyn ran her fingers gently along his jawline and leaned over until her lips almost met his. He tried to turn his face away in disgust, but she grabbed his chin and forced him to stare into her eyes.

"You and I will have so much fun, Alek."

Talyn stepped away and studied his face for signs the drug was taking hold. After only ninety seconds, she glanced up at Decker, still standing quietly beyond Mannsbach's life of sight, and nodded.

"What's your name?" She asked in a gentle, friendly tone.

His jaw muscles worked again as if fighting back an unstoppable urge to speak.

"Alasdair Malter." He spat out the name.

"Which star system do you call home?"

"Cimmeria." A goofy smile suddenly lit his face. "Not bad, right? Alek Mannsbach — Alasdair Malter. Can't accidentally mess up when initialing something."

"Nicely done, Alasdair."

"Thank you," he replied in a bright voice.

"What does the tattoo on your left breast represent?"

A sly expression lit up his eyes. "Now that would be telling."

"You'd make me ever so happy if you explained its meaning."

"That is a stylized spiral galaxy surrounded by stars, but tell no one."

"Does it symbolize something important? An event in your life, perhaps?"

Malter giggled.

"It represents an alliance of star systems. Can't you tell?"

"I'm not as smart as you are, Alasdair, so please humor me. Is this alliance of stars an organization or an idea?"

"Oh, it stopped being just an idea months ago. You'll find out soon enough. We're growing." He chortled with pleasure.

"I'd rather find out now. Tell me about this organization. Does it have a name?"

His eyes narrowed while his lips pursed as if he was about to reveal the secret of eternal life.

"It's called the Democratic Stars Alliance."

She glanced up at Decker who shook his head.

"What is its goal?"

"To rid Commonwealth worlds of their plutocratic rulers and bring humanity together as one big family, without the regressive sovereign star systems nonsense."

"Sounds like a noble endeavor. Who were you meeting here on behalf of the Democratic Stars Alliance?"

"Gustav Kerlin, the leader of the Freedom Collective."

"Why were you sent to meet with Gustav Kerlin?"

"The Democratic Stars Alliance wants his organization to join it."

Talyn saw Decker gaze out the window from the corner of her eyes but kept watching Malter. When he turned back, she glanced up and saw his fingers dance in the sign language taught to Naval Intelligence field operatives.

Police outside. Looking for source of encrypted transmission? Your communicator's disabled? Mine is.

She nodded once.

"Why does the Democratic Stars Alliance wish to absorb Kerlin's Freedom Collective?"

"So that our movement establishes a strong presence on Mission Colony."

"And once it's done so, what happens?"

"We take control. Just as we will elsewhere in the sector." Malter giggled again. "And beyond."

"Did you meet only with Kerlin or were there others?"

"No." Malter shook his head vehemently. "Kerlin wanted to keep this to himself. His security chief was nearby, but unable to listen."

Decker gestured for her attention again.

Police watching this building. Time to wrap up.

A spasm shook Malter's body as his face twisted in pain. The battle between his inhibitions against revealing too much and his drug-induced loquaciousness was reaching a critical stage. He would either become catatonic or suffer cardiac arrest if she didn't administer the antidote within the next few minutes.

"One more question. How were you supposed to convince Kerlin that merging his Freedom Collective with the Democratic Stars Alliance would help him?"

"Money, an advance now, with regular payments in the future. And the offer of a gift to help him advance the cause," Malter answered reluctantly from between clenched teeth.

"What was the gift?"

A strangled laugh broke through the increasingly frequent spasms. "Mayhem. A whole damned kilo."

Talyn glanced up at her partner again and saw an alarmed expression on his face.

Ask him if he handed the gift over to Kerlin.

"Did you give Gustav the Mayhem?"

"Yes." A more violent spasm shook the entire table.

Decker made a cutting gesture, telling her to stop. She tore off the second dermal patch and applied a third, loaded with a counteracting drug. The spasms immediately lost their intensity but didn't subside entirely.

"Why do I think you know what he was talking about, Zack? Mayhem is a strange word to use in this context."

"It's also the nickname for an explosive compound so highly classified, even knowledge of its existence within the Fleet is severely restricted. Never mind it takes a flag officer's permission to even draw a single gram from one of the few ammunition depots in the Commonwealth allowed to hold the stuff." Decker's eyes were drawn to Alasdair Malter. "I think we're losing him, Hera."

"Cardiac arrest. I applied the antidote a few seconds too late. He'll need medical intervention."

"We can't afford to attract attention, not if there are even a few atoms of the devil's compound loose on this planet."

She stared at him in surprise for a few seconds.

"I'm surprised at hearing you, my conscience, recommend I kill him."

"We need to find the Mayhem before it turns Ventano or any other city on this planet into a smoking crater. Besides, as far as I'm concerned anyone trafficking the stuff forfeits his life."

Talyn removed the antidote patch and pulled a subdermal injector from her pouch.

"Last chance."

"Do it." He looked out at the street again. "Tell me this place has a hidden back door."

"Sorry. But there is an underground garage." She pressed the injector against Malter's neck. "Done. And I found a rental car's keycard in Alasdair's pockets, so it stands to reason he's using this unit's space in the subbasement."

The Cimmerian twitched one last time and then lay still. She pressed her fingers against his carotid.

"He's dead."

"And we're leaving a murder scene for the Constabulary to find."

"Hopefully not until they get search warrants for every unit in this building. Now tell me about this Mayhem."

Talyn picked up the discarded patches and tucked them back into her pouch, which vanished inside her voluminous tunic. While Decker spoke, she removed her facial disguise and changed from a ninety-year-old matriarch into a woman forty years younger.

"As I said, it's an unofficial nickname — MAximum Yield High Explosive Mixture — but the official designation is MHX-19. The guy who invented it had a warped sense of humor. He came up with the formula to circumvent the ban on detonating nuclear weapons in an atmosphere."

When he saw the questioning look on her face, he said, "MHX is neither antimatter nor nuclear. However, a hundred kilos of the stuff is enough to scour several square kilometers of a planet's surface to bedrock while presenting a visual detonation signature almost identical to an antimatter explosion, but without a nuclear bomb's radiation burst, meaning it's clean. The Army and Marine Corps have little use for Mayhem. It's too powerful and presents an excessive risk of collateral damage. And because making the compound is brutally expensive, the Navy prefers cheaper nuclear warheads for its missiles. That single kilo he mentioned would be enough to wipe out the entire government precinct. This is serious business, Hera."

"Can't say I ever heard of it."

Talyn shrugged out of her tunic, turned it inside out, and pulled it on again, replacing the brightly colored floral pattern with a more sober dark blue.

"The only reason I know is because I'm a Master Gunner. We're sworn to secrecy before they tell us about the stuff."

Talyn scoffed at him. "Charming."

"Hey, I didn't invent that devil's mixture, and I never used it. But I saw what it did to the proving grounds on Caledonia. If the Freedom Collective's radical nut jobs have Mayhem in their possession, we're looking at a mass murder waiting to happen." He glanced out the window again. "Where does the underground garage emerge?"

"At the back."

"Let's find Malter's rental and try it."

"How about we sanitize the scene first? Take the rest of his clothes off and put him in bed. I'll clean up the kitchen and dispose of the evidence. It won't fool a decent criminalist, but if we can make the cops think he died in bed, if only for a few hours..."

"Don't forget to take his ID and weapon."

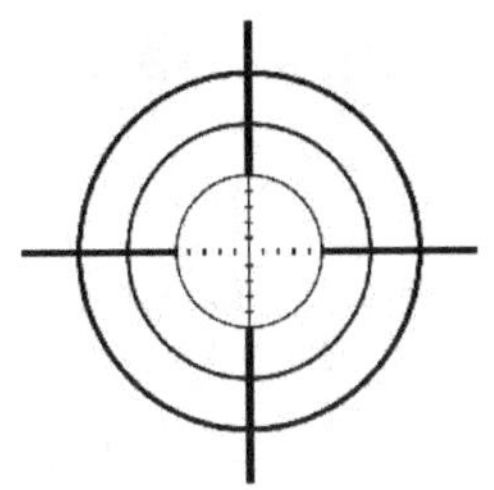

— FOUR —

They reached the underground garage without meeting another soul. Finding Malter's rental proved easy. The economy ground car, white, angular and practical, sat in a private stall marked 307, and opened its doors at their approach, sensing the keycard in Talyn's hand. She slipped in behind the controls while Decker took the passenger seat. The car backed out of its stall at Talyn's touch and silently made for the ramp leading to ground level. An automatic door dropped at their approach, allowing late afternoon sunlight to spill over the concrete floor. They emerged into a side street and saw a pair of gray-uniformed constables by the apartment building's rear exit, heads bent over handheld scanners. Both looked up at the car as it passed, but made no attempt to stop them.

"Take us to the rental office," Talyn said when they reached the corner. "Ser Mannsbach asked us to return this unit since he no longer requires it."

"Acknowledged," the artificial intelligence driving them replied in a soft, androgynous voice before turning left onto Fourth Avenue, which was already filling with workers headed home. Noticeable among them were a half dozen more constables with scanners on the sidewalks around the apartment building's front door.

Decker wanted to comment about them waiting for another call from the mysteriously encrypted communicator then remembered at the last minute their car's AI might record everything. And once the police found Mannsbach/Malter's body, they'd trace his rental back to the agency and find out about the two mysterious individuals who returned it. Once parked in the agency's lot next to the Ventano spaceport, Decker and Talyn climbed out, leaving the keycard behind and walked away.

"We need to change faces again," she said leading them to the nearest public transit stop. "But once we're at the safe house."

"What about tracking down the Democratic Stars Alliance's gift of death and destruction? Why waste a fresh set of identities if we plan on knocking a few more heads?"

She was silent for a moment, then nodded.

"Agreed."

"In that case, I suggest we pay our little buddy Osric Floros a visit right away since he was the late and unlamented Gustav Kerlin's chief of staff for rabble-rousing affairs. If he doesn't know where Kerlin took the stuff, he'll surely be able to point us at someone who does."

"That mention of Mayhem really has you spooked."

"You better believe it. And I don't scare easily." Decker paused, and then asked, "How come we never came across this Democratic Stars Alliance before today, if it's been around for a few months already *and* recruiting radical groups all over the Rim Sector?"

"Since Admiral Kruczek's inquisitors probably didn't winkle out every last Black Sword traitor in the Naval Intelligence Branch, I suppose someone working a political analysis desk is sitting on the news so operatives like us don't interfere in the DSA's expansion."

"A few cockroaches always escape the most thorough fumigation. Once Ulrich hears of this, I'm sure the inquisitors will find out who kept the information from working its way into the threat matrix. Would I be wrong in thinking this DSA could be the Coalition's newest ploy to advance its ambitions? How did the late Alasdair Malter put it? Get rid of so-called plutocratic rulers and unite human worlds into one entity without interference from sovereign star systems?"

"He used more flowery language, but that's the essence. And yes, I agree, it sounds like the Coalition found a new trick. Since co-opting legitimate governments hasn't worked so far, why not replace them altogether without worrying about niceties such as free and fair elections, or the will of the people?"

Decker grunted. "And once Coalition-controlled assholes like the Mission Colony Freedom Collective and their spiritual siblings on other worlds take over, goodbye star system independence. It's a pretty solid theory, especially considering they might be in possession of the most dangerous sub-nuclear explosive substance known to humanity, one which should never end up in unauthorized hands. Think of how many safeguards failed if a few kilos of it ended up in the Freedom Collective's arsenal. The Mayhem has to come via Black Sword traitors in the munitions control system, and since Black Sword belongs to the Coalition..."

A silent, half-full bus pulled up before Talyn could reply. They climbed aboard and spent the entire trip in silence. Back in the downtown core, Talyn took them on another public transit line which passed near Osric Floros' home. So far, the ubiquitous newscasts running on public displays made no mention of Alasdair Malter, better known as Alek Mannsbach. Decker questioned whether the Constabulary would, in fact, carry out a unit-by-unit search of the dead DSA emissary's building since there would be no recurrence of the encrypted transmission.

"I didn't notice," Decker said as they sat on the bench occupied a few hours earlier by an old woman wearing a loose tunic with a bright floral pattern, "but was Alasdair's apartment properly sealed?"

"Why?"   Talyn asked from behind her polarized sunglasses.

"Just wondering how long it'll take for the neighbors to notice the stench of a decomposing body."

"Does it matter?"

He gave her a half shrug.

"I suppose not. What's the plan with Osric?"

"How would you like to become a DSA goon?"

"And beat the sniveling little revolutionary wannabe to a pulp? Sure, but I don't think it's what you're planning."

"I'm not. How about this for a scenario? I'm Alek Mannsbach's superior and I've been watching the deal with Kerlin from a distance, ready to step in once they consummate it. You, Big Boy, are my bodyguard. Since Kerlin's dead, I'm taking over from Alek, and my first order of business is to recover the so-called gift."

"And my job will be to convince Osric that cooperation is a good idea."

"I'd rather not carry out another chemical interrogation and risk leaving a second body with drug-induced cardiac arrest. Osric looks less healthy than Alasdair did, and you saw what happened to him."

"He must have suffered from an underlying cardiac weakness, but since we don't have access to a properly equipped interrogation facility where we can test our subjects beforehand, you won't get any arguments from me." A pause. "We use our current cover IDs?"

"Yes." She stood. "Come, Ser Peel. It's time we introduced ourselves to Floros. He lives in unit two-twelve."

In contrast to the Fourth Avenue apartment building, the entrance security measures, weak to begin with, were inoperative. They met no one in the lobby or inside the dingy, plastic-coated concrete stairwell and emerged on the second floor unseen and unheard.

Talyn removed her sunglasses and pushed her hat back to expose her face, hoping Floros would open to an inoffensive, reasonably attractive woman not much older than he was. In their study of his habits over the previous week, Decker and Talyn saw no love interest of either gender, but enough evidence to show he was partial to women. It might make him more amenable to cooperating with one showing up on his doorstep.

She knocked on the door panel marked two-one-two.

"What do you want?" A querulous voice asked after almost a minute. Talyn recognized it as belonging to Kerlin's link with the radical community.

"My name is Sherri Zadeck, Ser Floros. Alek Mannsbach is one of my people. You informed him of Gustav's death, an unfortunate event which changes things, such as the agreement Alek previously discussed with him."

"How come I never heard of you?"

"You weren't meant to. But when Alek informed me of your visit earlier this afternoon, I took the lead. This is probably something we shouldn't discuss via intercom where anyone on the floor can listen. Perhaps we might continue this conversation in the privacy of your apartment."

"Who's the gorilla with you?"

"My bodyguard. Useful, but of no consequence other than ensuring nothing untoward happens."

A soft clicked followed by a louder squeak, and the door slid aside to reveal the shabbily dressed, unkempt, and wild-eyed former academic.

"Come in," he said with apparent ill grace.

Talyn, immersed in her role as a DSA grandee, looked around with a disdainful expression as she brushed by him and sniffed, "How cozy."

Floros stared up at Zack as the Marine followed his partner into the apartment. He winked at him and said, "Don't mind the boss. She's more the sort to enjoy Gustav Kerlin's country home than the humble abodes of his followers."

"I heard that, Corbin. Take heed you don't annoy me too much. Bodyguards are a cred a dozen, even big bruisers like you."

Decker smirked at Floros. "Of course, Sera Sherri."

A distinctly nonplussed Floros followed them into his own living room.

"What may I do for you?"

"You're aware of Gustav's negotiations with Alek?" Talyn asked.

"Yes. Alek invited us to join the Democratic Stars Alliance as the movement's Mission Colony affiliate. He promised us funding and support if we adopt your organization's policies."

"Who takes over now that Gustav's been murdered?"

"His partner, Eva Cortez."

Decker and Talyn exchanged a covert glance at the unexpected news. They knew Cortez was one of her late husband's enablers, if not accomplices, but becoming the most public figure of Mission Colony's radical movement? Or was her role to be a mere figurehead?

Floros must have seen their reaction because he said, "You need not worry, Sera Zadeck. Eva is just as committed to the cause as Gustav. Some say she's even more ruthless in her pursuit of our ideals."

"Then I should meet with her at the first opportunity. Where is Sera Cortez right now?"

"Still at the country house where Gustav was killed, I suppose."

"Whose country house would that be? Surely a man of the people like Ser Kerlin didn't own a plutocrat's real estate portfolio."

The man shrank back at her acid tone, and he shook his head with vehemence.

"No, of course not. It belongs to a progressive corporation that supports our movement. The owners placed it at Gustav and Eva's disposal so they can host friends, backers, and supporters in complete privacy. You understand we're viewed with suspicion by the colonial government and often placed under illegal surveillance."

"Something with which we're intimately familiar, Ser Floros. Can I assume our gift to the Freedom Collective is now in Eva's hands?"

"I wouldn't know. Gustav kept the details of his negotiations with Alek closely held. I assume Eva has it, but only she or Piet Yorik, Gustav's chief of security, can answer that question."

"And Yorik is at the country house as well, no doubt."

"He is. Pardon me for asking, but why this concern about the gift?"

"With Gustav's assassination, I must make sure it does not fall into hands inimical to the DSA and its allies."

Floros seemed unconvinced. He scratched his beard and said, "I see. You'll need to speak with Eva, seeing as how she's in charge now."

"How can I reach her? Or could you contact Eva for me, pass on the DSA's condolences and let her know I took over the negotiations from Alek? I'd appreciate an hour of her time as soon as possible, considering Gustav's death is bound to bring intense police scrutiny neither of us can afford. Will you do that for me, Osric?"

An engaging smile tugged at Talyn's lips.

"Okay." He still seemed hesitant, but she didn't push any further. "How can Eva or I reach you?"

Talyn produced her communicator.

"I'll give you my calling code. You or Eva can reach out to me at any hour, day or night." She stood. "Thank you, Osric. I know you still need to deal with your grief at losing a charismatic leader such as Gustav, but the inexorable march of political reform waits for no one."

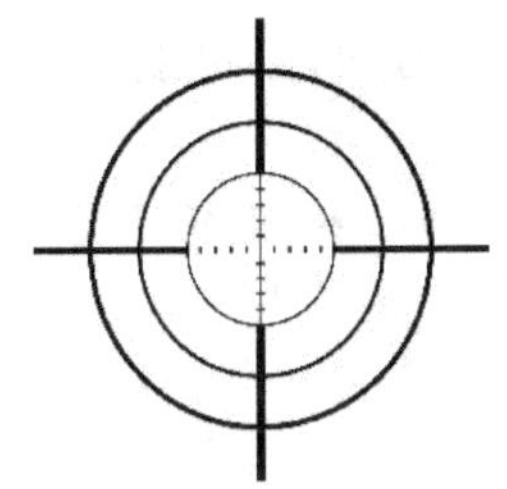

— **FIVE** —

"How is it even possible?" Eva Cortez, a long-haired brunette with smoldering brown eyes and the smooth, olive-skinned face of a woman twenty years younger demanded for the umpteenth time as she paced the living room to work off her rage. "How could a sniper get close enough to murder Gustav without triggering the security perimeter or alerting your people, Piet?"

The clicking of high heels on polished marble died away when Cortez stopped to stare at the silent chief of security, a hulking man as muscular and square-faced as she was svelte. His shiny, pale dome glistened with perspiration, as did his upper lip. She had been raging ever since the last of the shaken, and in some cases, terrified guests left after giving their testimony to the Constabulary investigators.

"I can't tell you more than what you already know, Eva. Not until my people finish searching the far end of the glen. A trained sniper with a railgun capable of firing darts at almost ten times the speed of sound could easily find a hide beyond our perimeter. In the hands of an expert, maximum range is dictated by the quality of the optics used, and I say optics because we would have detected active target acquisition. The killer went strictly low tech to stay invisible. Our security perimeter registered the power spike when he fired, nothing more, and it was so brief the sensors weren't able to triangulate. This guy's a pro."

"Guy? Why couldn't it be a woman?"

"I meant guy in the generic, Eva. Don't hassle me because of my choice of words. Not today." Piet Yorik squeezed the bridge of his nose to disguise his increasing irritation with Eva's temper. The conversation had been spinning in circles ever since they found themselves alone. "This was a well-planned and executed hit. I'm ready to bet my next year's pay the Constabulary won't catch him — *or her.*"

"Was it personal or political?"

"How the hell should I know, Eva? Gustav's habits made him personal enemies all over the place. Could be one of them decided enough was enough. I warned the both of you this could happen if he didn't put a brake on his appetites. But railgun firing pros like our sniper, they're expensive, much too expensive for folks holding a personal grudge against Gustav. For one thing, I've never heard of any on Mission Colony, so he, *or she*, is almost certainly an offworlder, which ups the cost even more."

"Political, then." Cortez resumed her pacing, and Yorik winced as the click of heels once more assaulted his ears. "The *cabrons* running this place have access to that kind of money. It'll make tossing the colonial administration out on its ass that much sweeter. Do you think they got wind of our timeline and that's why they killed Gustav? To stop the inevitable?"

Yorik let out an audible sigh. "I'm not the one to answer that question, Eva. Ask the Collective's governing council."

She whirled around and speared him with furious eyes.

"Those incompetent fools? People who actually believe the radical bullshit we're peddling? Please. I'm asking for *your* opinion."

"Okay. You want my opinion. Here it is. Whoever put the hit on Gustav isn't local. As I said several times in the last hour, the sniper is a consummate pro. An incredibly expensive pro. You need serious money to hire someone like that, and you need contacts to find him. I can't think of anyone in the colonial administration with the right connections or enough guts."

"If not a local, then who?"

"Stop asking me questions I'm unable to answer, Eva. Gustav's ambitions were bigger than Mission Colony. Perhaps he fell afoul of people with a reach that encompasses the entire damn Rim Sector if not the Commonwealth itself and we don't know about it. You of all people should remember how secretive he was. Just look at how he kept almost everyone out of the talks with this Democratic Stars Alliance."

"Then what happens now? Do I spend the rest of my own life waiting for a railgun-equipped pro to turn my head into a pink mist?"

Yorik answered with a weary shrug.

"There's no point in dwelling on it at the moment. Instead, you need to think about asserting control over the Collective before nightfall. One or two of the governing council idiots might think their time to lead has come. Leave the investigation to the Constabulary. Assistant Commissioner Bujold will make sure her people do a thorough job while seeing that Gustav's secrets are buried with him."

A smile briefly lit up Cortez's face. "I know she will."

"Which means we need not worry. I suggest you declare yourself Gustav's heir and concentrate on picking up the talks with Mannsbach."

"Unlike Gustav, I remain unconvinced we should hitch our fortunes to a group no one knew of until a few months ago."

"That's because you're not aware of certain things yet, Eva."

"Then make me aware."   She stopped to face him again.

"I watched Gustav's back during every meeting with the DSA man. He wanted no one else with him. I didn't actually sit in on the discussions, but Gustav told me enough afterward to understand what they're offering is a shortcut to your ambitions."

"What sort of shortcut?"

"One that'll make our beloved colonial administration beg the Freedom Collective to form this star system's next government."

A finely arched eyebrow crept up. "Oh?"

Yorik suddenly tilted his head to one side in the unmistakable gesture of an earbug wearer receiving a call. He raised his right hand to still her next words.

"This is Yorik."

After almost a minute, he asked the unseen caller, "And you're sure they're legit?"   Another pause, followed by a grunt and a frown. "Okay. Let me speak with Eva and get back to you." His head returned to the vertical. "That was Osric. Another DSA emissary came out of the woodwork not long after he told Mannsbach about Gustav's assassination. A Sherri Zadeck. She was with a gorilla by the name Corbin, last name unknown. This Zadeck claims to be Mannsbach's boss, and she said considering this morning's events, she's taking over the talks about our merger with the DSA."

Lines creased Eva's smooth forehead.   "Sounds strange. Her name is new to you, right?"

He nodded.

"First time I'm aware of this Zadeck's existence."

"What do you think?"

"She knew where to find Osric, she knows about Gustav's negotiations with the DSA, most importantly, she knows about the gift Mannsbach gave Gustav, meaning—"

"What gift?"

"That's what I was about to tell you when Osric called. Only Mannsbach, Gustav, and I are aware of its existence."

"Which indicates Zadeck's legit."

"Could be." A dubious expression creased Yorik's face. "But a new actor appearing out of nowhere hours after a pro whacks Gustav? In any case, she'd like to meet with you, and she seems worried about who's in control of the gift."

"Do you think I should? And will you tell me about this damned gift before I reach down your throat and yank out the answer?"

Yorik raised both hands in a restraining gesture.

"Relax, Eva. We'll take this one step at a time. Things are moving too fast for my taste, and that means they could spiral out of control. Let me think for a moment."

She scowled at him, lips compressed into a fine line.

"Okay," he said a few moments later. "First, the gift. Mannsbach brought us a kilo of the most potent conventional explosive ever invented. It's called Mayhem - MAximum Yield High Explosive Mixture. He said one kilo is enough to take out the government precinct and part of downtown Ventano. It's so highly classified by the Fleet, even most members of the Armed Services don't know about it."

"One kilo to take out downtown? Bullshit, Piet. A kilo of fissile material, maybe, but a sub-nuclear compound?"

"No bull, Eva. Remember the day before yesterday, when Gustav and I took the aircar for a run to your family's unexploited claim in the Cabrera Range?"

"Sure."

"Mannsbach came with us. He scraped a few grams of the stuff from that kilo block and stuck it against a detonator. Congratulations, the Cortez family now has a new clearing at the bottom of the Vittoria valley. You might remember I don't impress easily, but I was impressed when I saw the explosion. And a little scared. The thought of a radical organization like the DSA owning enough Mayhem to give it out in kilo blocks on spec as a recruiting bonus terrifies me when I think of how hard it must be to steal from the Fleet. These are serious folks with the sort of reach that keeps counterintelligence analysts awake at night."

A thoughtful expression replaced her earlier frown.

"Why do I get the feeling if we don't join this DSA, they'll simply take back their gift and find more willing partners? Perhaps they might even help those more willing partners sideline the Freedom Collective."

"Because you're no dummy, Eva. And the idea they might recover the Mayhem if we back away from the deal speaks to there being more DSA members than just Mannsbach on the planet. It makes sense they'd send someone like the gorilla Osric mentioned, for instance. But I think it might be a justifiable breach of our agreement to keep radio silence if I called Alek to obtain corroboration on his boss taking over."

She chewed on her lower lip for a few seconds.

"Wouldn't Zadeck perceive that as insulting?"

"I'm sure she understands the concept of trust but verify. Considering the turmoil we're experiencing... For what it's worth, Osric gave me a pretty good description of them."

Cortez squared her shoulders.

"Do it."

She went over to a set of French doors overlooking the patio where, a few hours earlier, someone had assassinated her husband. The mansion's cleaning droids had done an excellent job scrubbing away every last trace of blood and gore after the Constabulary's crime scene investigators finished their work.

But her mind's eye still saw everything as it was in those awful moments after Gustav's head vanished in a bloody haze, and the formless rage flowing through her veins flared up again. How dare they — whoever that might be — kill him and upset their plans? She promised herself to find the perpetrators and exact a vengeance so awful it would cement her place as the Collective's supreme leader, and Mission Colony's next first minister.

"He's not answering," Yorik said, snapping Eva back to reality. She turned to face him. "But his communicator is live."

"Perhaps Zadeck ordered him to avoid speaking with us now she's assumed the lead."

"Could be."

"You sounded a little funny there for a moment, Piet. What gives?"

"I can't shake the fact Zadeck's sudden appearance, hours after Gustav's death, is somehow not quite right."

"Yet if Alek Mannsbach isn't willing or able to speak with us anymore, I see little choice but to meet with her. The sooner, the better, in fact."

"Any preference where? Gustav used the beach house."

"Here. I don't want to drive all the way out there today. Besides, nosy neighbors can't see who is coming and going here."

"Or coming and not going?" A knowing smirk lit up Yorik's face. "Maybe you should invite Zadeck for the evening meal."

"Good idea."

He pulled a communicator from his pocket and stroked its screen. Moments later, he said, "Sera Sherri Zadeck? My name is Piet Yorik. I was the late Gustav Kerlin's security chief, a role I now carry out for his widow Eva Cortez." Yorik paused. "Yes, Sera Zadeck, a tragedy, but you're correct. Life and the movement must go on. We can mourn after freeing Mission Colony from the plutocratic oppressors."

He rolled his eyes theatrically. "Osric Floros tells me you wish to meet with Eva." Pause. "Indeed. Eva would like to invite you and your associate to dine with her tonight at the country house." Pause. "She'll be glad to hear it. At eighteen hundred hours? Great. I'll send the coordinates momentarily and tell my people to expect you and Ser Peel. Until then. Goodbye."

Yorik tucked away his communicator.

"Done."

"What did she sound like?"

"A woman. Low voice, almost husky. Pleasant, but with a hint of steel." He shrugged. "Hardly enough to form an opinion."

A discreet knock on the door still Cortez's reply. "Come," she said instead.

One of Yorik's men, a younger copy of the security chief, just as bald and barrel-shaped, stepped in. He carried a shimmering pack in his right hand, one Yorik immediately recognized as covered by a chameleon camouflage exterior.

"We found a faint track at the far end of the glen, a little over a kilometer away, where the trees close in and followed it over into the next hollow. It led to where a small ground car, probably a two-person speeder, was hidden at some point earlier today." He held up the bag. "Someone tucked this under a bush. There's a ghillie suit and a railgun inside. A seven-millimeter Falkenberg Longbow Mark Five with a Hammer Optics high-powered scope. Top of the line stuff, boss. Worth almost thirty thousand creds on the legal side, a hundred thousand on the black market. It has to be our sniper's weapon. No one throws away something like that because they're too tired to carry it."

Yorik pointed at a sideboard.

"Lay everything out for me."

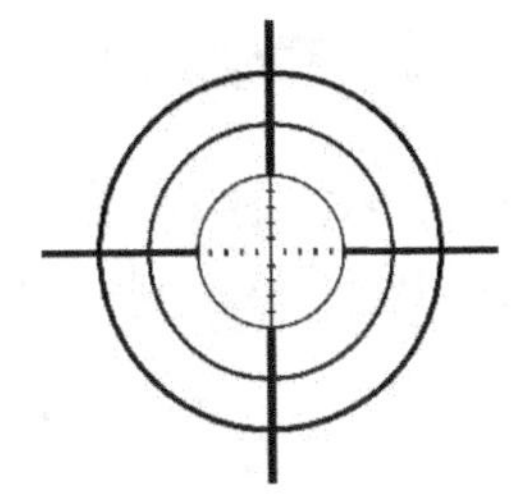

— SIX —

"We'll need a fresh rental car," Talyn said after shutting off her communicator.

"That's what I figured." He nodded at a passing bus. "Public transit doesn't quite make it out that far, and definitely not up the road to Kerlin's private retreat. Or rather Cortez's now. It'll be interesting to study my hide from the target's perspective."

"We should also buy more appropriate clothes. Or at least I should." She swept her hands along the front of her loose tunic. "This hardly screams senior DSA emissary."

"While my getup screams bodyguard to a senior DSA emissary?"

She glanced at him and made a face.

"I suppose not. Rental car, clothes shopping, then back to the safe house."

Less than two hours later, Decker and Talyn, wearing elegant but understated dark business suits, pulled up to the country house's front gate. A pair of toughs in black tactical wear carrying plasma carbines stepped out into the roadway. One kept them covered with his weapon not entirely aimed at their vehicle's windshield while the other cautiously approached the left side, motioning at Zack to lower his window.

"Sherri Zadeck and Corbin Peel to see Eva Cortez."

"You got ID?"

Decker held out a pair of wafers for the guard to scan. Once the man did so, he lowered his head and took a good look at Talyn.

"Are you armed?"

"Of course. These are dangerous times. Sera Zadeck and I each carry a blaster and a bladed weapon as your sensor no doubt told you just now."

The guard straightened and walked away while muttering in a voice too low for the Marine's ears. After a moment, he turned to his comrade and pointed at the gate. It slid aside soundlessly and the guard waved them through without another word.

"Want to bet they'll ask for our weapons at the big house, boss?" Decker asked as they wound their way along a narrow lane cutting through dense native vegetation, conscious that many eyes and ears were following their progress.

"No bets, Corbin. And try to remember I prefer you call me by my name. Boss is so—"

"Reactionary?" He grinned at her. "Retrograde? Retarded?"

"Enough." She raised a restraining hand. "Try to keep your dubious sense of humor under control once we arrive. I doubt Eva Cortez and her people are in a mood to jest after what happened."

"You won't hear a wrong word out of me, Sherri."

"I'd better not. It's important we convince Cortez to follow Kerlin's lead and join the Alliance. Ah!"

They emerged from the primeval forest into the glen Decker knew from its opposite end. The country house, a stone-clad, copper-roofed manor in everything but name sat in the center of a sculpted, park-like landscape littered with the color of native flowers, grasses, and shrubs.

Another guard, in the same black tactical getup as his colleagues, stood by the open front door and waved at them to park beside a luxury all-terrain speeder to the left of the broad stone steps. No sooner did they climb out of the car that a man almost Decker's size and wearing a suit eerily like his came out of the mansion.

"Sera Zadeck, Ser Peel, on behalf of Eva Cortez, welcome. I'm Piet Yorik, the head of security." He offered his hand to each of them in turn, testing Decker's grip for a few seconds before a fleeting smile crossed his lips. "I understand you carry sidearms."

"We do," Talyn replied.

"I'd be grateful if you left them at the guard desk immediately to your right upon entering. You're perfectly safe on this estate and Eva would rather only my men carry weapons after what happened this morning. Besides, I doubt the murderer will be back for an encore."

"How's that?" Decker asked as they followed him up the steps and into a high-ceilinged entrance hall paneled in various shades of wood.

Yorik gave him a sly glance over his shoulder.

"You'll see in a moment, Ser Peel. Kim here will take good care of your blasters and blades." He gestured at the guard sitting behind a console surrounded by video displays.

Decker's blaster earned wide-eyed stares from Kim and his boss. The latter let out a low whistle. "What the hell is that?"

"Shrehari, re-chambered for standard-issue fifteen millimeter disks." He popped out the magazine and power pack, and handed them, along with the now safe gun to Kim. Then, the Marine produced his dagger from the forearm sheath, flipped it, and presented the hilt to the guard still admiring the heavy alien weapon.

"Isn't that a Pathfinder knife?" Yorik asked, eyes narrowing with obvious suspicion.

Decker gave him a pleasant smile.

"Sure. Since you recognized my little friend, does that mean you were in the Corps?"

"Army. I was in the military police for twenty years before moving to the private sector. You?"

"I also did twenty but in the Corps, five as a Pathfinder before joining the dark side."

"Hence the war trophy blaster."

"Yep. Taken from the cold dead hand of a Shrehari corsair who forgot to duck."

"Impressive."

Decker shrugged dismissively.

"I was lucky, he wasn't."

"I'm sure Eva will want to hear the story."

They watched Talyn imitate the Marine, then Yorik led them into a carpeted corridor decorated with what Decker suspected were original artworks, and into the living room with its splendid views of the sun setting behind the Cabrera Mountains.

"Eva," Yorik said as a tall, slender woman in a designer dress turned away from the open French doors, "may I present Sherri Zadeck and Corbin Peel of the Democratic Stars Alliance?"

Cortez came toward them accompanied by the click of heels on marble and offered her hand.

"Welcome, Sherri, Corbin, I'm Eva. Since the Freedom Collective is at heart an egalitarian movement, we don't stand on ceremony around here."

"May I offer the DSA's and our personal condolences for your loss, Eva?" Talyn said as she released Cortez's beautifully manicured hand. "A terrible tragedy. I hope the person or persons responsible will be caught and punished before political assassinations become all the rage."

"I doubt the Constabulary will find Gustav's killer," Yorik replied. "His killing was an incredibly professional hit, carried out by a high-priced asset who's probably left Mission Colony by now."

"What makes you say that?" Decker asked in a neutral tone.

"Perhaps we can save it for later, Piet."

Yorik bowed his head toward his employer.

"Of course, Eva. Pardon me. Corbin is a fellow security specialist, and I was carried away. Can I offer everyone a drink? Sherri? What's your poison?"

"Gin and tonic, please."

Cortez smiled.

"A woman after my own heart. The same, please, Piet. And use the Mistassini Diamond. I'm sure Sherri would appreciate a sip of Earth's finest gin."

Talyn inclined her head.

"Mistassini Diamond? I'm impressed."

"It costs a fortune compared to the locally distilled stuff, but the difference in taste makes the expense of shipping it halfway across the Commonwealth worthwhile."

"And you, Corbin?" Yorik asked.

"My tastes aren't quite as refined. Whatever ale you have is fine."

"That would be the Ventano Bitter. Coming right up."

Yorik went to a sideboard and busied himself.

"I gather you never met Gustav?" Cortez asked Talyn.

"Sadly, no."

"Would you like to see where he was killed, while there's still daylight left?"

Cortez didn't wait for an answer. She turned away and made for the open French doors leading the stone patio. Talyn followed her out into a growing twilight underscored by hundreds of soft chirps.

"It seems so peaceful," she said.

Cortez kept her eyes on the dark shadows at the far end of the glen where Yorik's people found traces of the sniper's hide.

"It was our sanctuary from the stresses of bringing social justice to Mission Colony and inspiring our followers to keep up the fight against institutionalized plutocracy. We were hosting friends and supporters for lunch, people willing to help advance our dreams in any way they could, some of the most important people on the planet. Just as Gustav was about to propose a toast..." A strangled sob escaped her throat. "It was horrible."

"I can't begin to imagine what you must be suffering."

Cortez spun toward Talyn, eyes blazing with unrestrained fury.

"What I'm feeling is unrestrained hate, Sherri. Hate for the animals who murdered him, for their masters, and for anyone opposed to the Freedom Collective's historic undertaking."

She took a deep calming breath when she noticed Yorik approaching with a cut crystal tumbler in each hand.

"Mistassini Diamond and tonic." He handed them out and said, "Enjoy," before returning to the living room where Decker waited.

Talyn raised her glass and said, "If you don't object, I'd be honored to toast the memory of Gustav Kerlin and vow we will carry on his struggle until Mission is truly free?"

"How kind of you." A strained smile replaced Cortez's earlier wide-eyed rage as she imitated her guest. "To Gustav — not the easiest of men, but those destined for glory never are."

They took an appreciative sip, and Talyn said, "The Mistassini never disappoints." She waved her glass at the manor, now blazing with lights. "You're fortunate to own such a marvelous estate."

"This isn't ours. Friends of the Collective placed it at our disposal as part of their contribution to the cause.

Gustav preferred to live modestly, like most of the Collective's members."

"I'm sorry I never met Gustav. If you feel up to it, I'd love to know more about him." A faint smile touched Talyn's lips. "And about you."

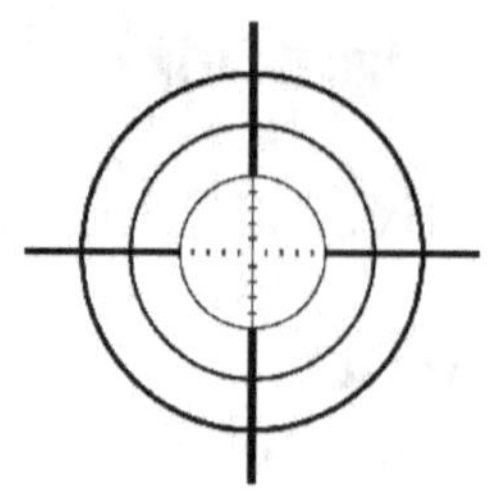

— SEVEN —

"Do you want this in a glass?" Yorik held up an amber bottle with a green label.

"Since the boss isn't looking, I'll drink it the way nature intended."

"Is she a stickler for protocol?"

"Nah. We kid around a lot. Yours?" Decker accepted the proffered bottle and uncapped it.

"Depends on her mood." Yorik raised his drink. "Skoal."

The Marine took a healthy sip.

"Nice. What are you having?"

"A whiff of the local whiskey. Eva calls it rotgut, but Gustav shared a daily dram with me." He raised his glass again. "Absent friends."

"Absent friends." Another sip. "And what is Eva's mood right now?"

"What do you think? She's itching to kill someone."

"She and Gustav were a tight couple?"

"Sure. As tight as it gets in their social circle." Yorik studied Decker with hooded eyes. "Tell me, are you simply hired muscle or do you believe in the cause?"

"Why?"

"Humor me, Corbin."

"The only cause I ever believed in was the Corps. Everything else is a job. Sherri pays me well, she's a good boss to work for, and there are side benefits to my employment."

"Are you willing to take a bullet for her?"

A lazy grin split Zack's face. "I'll make sure that round never gets fired."

Yorik chuckled.

"Okay. Understood. Why did you leave after doing twenty if the Corps was your cause?"

"Probably the same reason you left the Army. I didn't want to spend another ten moving from one boring duty station to another after my time in the Pathfinders was up. That and I found myself on the wrong side of an officer who made my life miserable."

"You were a noncom?"

"Sergeant first class, combat engineers. What about you? True believer or politically agnostic security professional? I can't see how a retired military police noncom would suddenly find meaning in radicalism."

"What makes you think I was a noncom?"

Decker tapped the side of his nose with an extended index finger.

"You and me, we're cut from the same granite."

"Hah." An amused smile relaxed Yorik's square face. "The old sergeant's network. Yeah. I was a staff sergeant back in the day, working patrol."

"You still didn't answer my question."

"Security professional, which doesn't prevent me from considering Gustav and Eva more than just employers."

"Understood."

"How are you with handheld weapons?"

"Pretty good. I took the preparatory classes for the Master Gunner qualification before deciding life would be sweeter in the private sector."

"Railguns?"

"Sure, though I'm no expert. The Corps uses them as sniper weapons, and I don't have the patience or the steady hands for it."

Yorik drained his glass then nodded at a connecting door.

"Follow me."

A familiar sight greeted Decker as he entered the cozy, mahogany paneled study, and it took every milligram of his training and experience to keep from showing even the slightest reaction. The bag he'd tucked under a bush one valley over sat on the small conference table like the embodiment of a murder accusation.

"Do you know what this is, Corbin?"

"No. A pack of some sort."

"This," he opened the top flap, "belongs to whoever murdered Gustav."

Decker cocked an eyebrow.

"Really? How can you tell?"

"Simple." Yorik reached in and pulled out the ghillie suit. "Top of the line chameleon wear. A civilian version of the standard Marine Corps issue." He shook it out and held it up by the shoulders. "Size extra-large. It would fit you nicely."

"Or you."

Yorik conceded the point with a brief nod.

"But that's not everything." He put the ghillie suit to one side and produced the railgun parts which he placed neatly in assembly order by the pack. "Falkenberg Armaments Longbow Mark Five, chambered for seven-millimeter ammunition, capable of propelling darts at Mach nine, complete with a high-end Hammer Optics scope, unpowered."

Decker let out a low whistle.

"That's a lot of money sitting right there. Are you telling me that's what Gustav's assassin used?"

"We backtracked the shot and found a faint spoor left by the sniper. It led us where someone parked a ground car about three kilometers from here. My guess is he ditched this stuff in case he ran into a Constabulary checkpoint." Yorik stepped back to give his guest a clear view.

"Makes sense." Decker walked over to the table, hands in his pockets and studied the disassembled weapon. "I guess we're dealing with a top-shelf pro if he not only uses a gun worth a hundred thousand on the black market but doesn't think twice about ditching it. He's unlikely to be local talent."

"That's what I think. Go ahead; feel free to touch the Longbow. Assemble it, if you know how."

"As much as I'd like to, I'll take a pass. That's evidence in a murder for hire." Decker looked up at a watchful Yorik. "I assume you intend to hand this to the cops?"

Yorik crossed his arms and leaned against the ormolu desk.

"Should I?"

A frown creased Decker's forehead.

"Isn't it the law?"

"You said it's worth a hundred grand on the black market. That's a lot of money."

The Marine shrugged.

"Do whatever you see fit. It's no skin off my nose. But kudos for finding the murder weapon. Too bad you couldn't trace the sniper any further."

"Who says we can't?"

"A pro who casually abandons something like that railgun? He's already on an outbound starship."

"I checked with friends at the spaceport, and only one ship lifted off since noon, bound for Cimmeria. Those friends sent me a video of the passengers boarding. There was no one big enough for the ghillie suit among them."

"Then your professional left this system as crew."

Yorik's eyes narrowed just enough for Zack to notice.

"I suppose it's possible. But my gut tells me our man is still on Mission."

"More reason to give the evidence to the cops. Their criminalists might find something that could identify the assassin. I'm sure a man of Gustav's stature had enough friends in gray to make analyzing the ghillie suit and gun a priority."

"If you say so." Yorik pushed himself off the desk and joined Decker by the table. "Were DSA affiliates or members assassinated elsewhere in the sector?"

"Not that we know of. This is likely a first."

"Because I'm wondering whether Eva shouldn't just say thanks, but no thanks to your offer of a merger, in case she becomes the next target."

"Again, no skin off my nose. I just make sure Sherri's happy and safe. She's in charge of politics. But if Eva backs out, we'll need you to return that kilo of MHX-19."

"It's not quite a kilo anymore."

"Oh?"

"Didn't Alek tell you he took a few grams off the top to prove its power?"

A gleam of skepticism briefly lit up Yorik's eyes.

Decker made a dismissive hand gesture. "He might have mentioned it to Sherri in passing."

"By the way, I tried calling Alek earlier this afternoon. He didn't answer."

"Really? He seemed fine when we last spoke not long after your man Floros told him of Gustav's untimely death."

"Spoke? Does that mean you didn't see him?"

"No. Our orders from home were to avoid personal contact. Alek sets the groundwork, and when the prospective affiliate is ready, Sherri takes over. That way if things don't work out..." Decker let the rest of his sentence hang.

"I see. He never mentioned anything about Sherri or you."

"Orders. The DSA likes to keep things compartmentalized. It's good security. We might find the Freedom Collective incompatible with our organization, in which case, no harm, no foul and good luck to you."

"You'd have left us with a block of Mayhem?"

Decker let a sly smile play on his lips. "No."

"And you'd recover it how?"

"I wouldn't. There's a remote-controlled detonator at the heart of the package. We get it back, or it goes boom and clears out half a square kilometer."

An appreciatively look appeared on Yorik's face, and he nodded.

"Nasty. I scanned the block myself and saw nothing. Not even a shadow."

"Of course not. Your sensor has no idea what it's looking at." When he saw his ruse give birth to a spark of uncertainty in Yorik's eyes, Decker's smile turned into a knowing grin. "And now you're wondering whether the Mayhem's current hiding place isn't too close for comfort. Somewhere on this property, perhaps? A word of advice. Don't expose the detonator without the disarming code. It's keyed to trigger a timer upon exposure to air or light, and then you'll live the longest two minutes of your life. Or the shortest, depending on your beliefs."

"Why tell me this?"

"So that if Sherri decides Eva's not her sort of people, we can part ways without unpleasantness. As they say, the DSA giveth; the DSA taketh away; blessed be the DSA."

A snort of derision. "I thought they said that about the Void."

"Perhaps the good Sisters are praying for our success."

"I'd never figure them for being radicals." The soft chime of a dinner gong echoed throughout the manor. "Time to rejoin our employers and enjoy a fine meal. It's one of the perks of working for the Mission Colony Freedom Collective's senior leadership."

"Very egalitarian, security chiefs and their principals breaking bread together," Decker said with a hint of irony in his tone.

"I don't ask questions and hear no lies." Yorik gestured toward the connecting door.

"What about the evidence?"

"One of my men will bag and tag it for the Constabulary. Maybe they'll find a DNA trace and link it to a known operator. Someone with a criminal or military record."

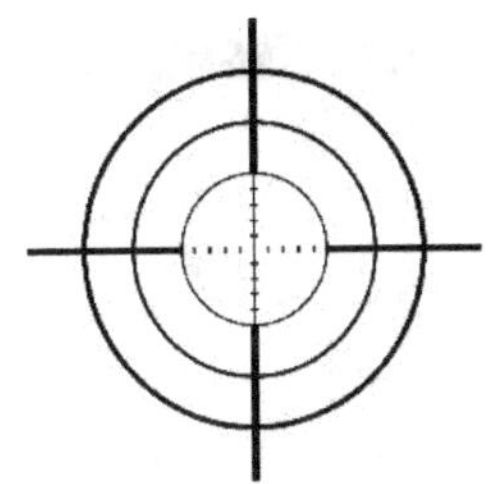

— EIGHT —

"I trust you enjoyed a good conversation between kindred spirits?" Cortez asked when Yorik and Decker entered the dining room.

"I showed Corbin what my men found earlier. He agrees with my conclusions."

"Excellent. If we're to become part of the DSA, it's important we see things in the same light." She gestured at the table. "Sherri, if you'll sit to my left. Corbin can sit across from you while Piet takes the other end of the table. Piet, please be a dear and serve the wine. It's a local vintage, but the better ones don't weather interstellar travel from Earth or Dordogne well enough to be worth the expense."

For someone who lost her life partner less than twelve hours earlier, Eva Cortez sounded overly cheerful to Decker's ears. But people react to tragedy in surprising ways. Yet the lively gleam in her eyes seemed more than a little fey.

"I'm sure it'll be fine, Eva." Talyn's voice seemed equally bright.

Yorik approached the table with a long, dark bottle.

"Would you like to taste it, Sherri?"

"I suppose I'd better. Corbin wouldn't know wine that's gone bad from dirty socks." She gave Decker a sardonic smile. "Right?"

"If you say so, Sherri," he muttered in a resigned tone. "See what I put up with, Piet?"

"I heard that, Corbin," she said in a singsong voice before sighing theatrically. "Good help is so hard to find, don't you think, Eva."

"But hard help is good to find," he replied with a smirk. "How much Mistassini Diamond was in those gins and tonic?"

"Never you mind."

Yorik splashed a mouthful of wine into Talyn's glass. She picked it up, studied its color, inhaled its aroma, and then took a small sip which she swirled around her tongue before swallowing.

"Very nice indeed, Piet. Thank you."

He half-filled everyone's glass before sitting at the foot of the table, opposite Eva, who raised hers and said, "To new alliances."

"Hear, hear," Talyn replied, imitating her. They drank, and then she asked, "What did Gustav share about his discussions with Alek?"

"Nothing." Cortez glanced at Yorik. "Gustav preferred to keep thing closely held until he was ready. But Piet told me about the DSA's gift."

"The Mayhem, yes. It is a blunt instrument, but then, sometimes forcing change requires bluntness when one faces entrenched interests."

"I warned Piet about the recall mechanism, should you not come to an agreement with Eva."

"Oh?" Cortez's sculpted eyebrow twitched in question.

"Apparently, there's a remote-controlled detonator at the brick's heart," Yorik replied. "Undetectable and tamper-proof. It requires a code to disarm."

"Why would the DSA do that, Sherri?"

"We'd rather keep such a precious and almost impossible to obtain substance for our affiliates. If you decline our invitation, then I would ask for the Mayhem's return, no hard feelings."

"And if we decide to keep it nonetheless?"

An evil smile twisted Decker's features. "Boom."

Cortez stared at him in disbelief. "You wouldn't."

"Lesson number one in understanding the Democratic Stars Alliance," Talyn said in a light tone that didn't quite hide the steel behind her words. "We make the best of friends and the worst of enemies. Ah, I see our first course is arriving."

Four housekeeping droids silently glided into the room, each carrying a delicate plate with an artfully plated variety of fish bites, including sashimi and smoked tidbits.

"Perhaps we can set business aside while we savor your kitchen's offerings."

As they ate, Decker and Talyn couldn't help but notice their hosts exchanging covert glances, as if trying to communicate silently.

"Is your entire staff automated?" Talyn asked between mouthfuls.

"Yes. Even the cook. Piet's men run the necessary errands, but food preparation, cleaning, and other household services are performed by droids. Using humans as domestic staff would clash with the Freedom Collective's values. Besides, the labor scarcity on a frontier world such as this makes automation more cost effective."

"And droids are good for security. They're less likely to talk out of school," Decker remarked before biting on the last morsel, raw native whitefish wrapped in seaweed.

"Or if they were properly programmed, unable to talk, period," he added after washing away the salty confection with the rest of his wine. "You should have taken over from Alek earlier, boss. I could get used to this."

"If you keep calling me boss, this will be your one and only fine dining experience for the rest of the trip."

At an unseen and unheard signal, the droids came back to remove empty plates and replace them with the next course, this time soup.

"Are there more lessons in understanding the DSA?" Cortez asked conversationally.

"We will do what's needed to win," Talyn replied between mouthfuls. "This is superb, by the way."

"Thank you. It's an old family recipe. And I agree, doing what's needed to win is also my modus operandi. I aim to become the next first minister of this star system and force the colonial government to leave."

"Was that also Gustav's goal?"

"Of course, and the moment I inherited his mantle as leader of the Freedom Collective, Gustav's ambitions became mine, though his assassination forces us to change parts of our plan. Nothing overly drastic, you understand, but our timetable will inevitably slip."

"Joining the DSA will without a doubt help the Collective achieve its aims."

"How?" Cortez studied Talyn over the rim of her glass.

"Money. As much as you need. Offworld political support and direct action resources to fight Colonial Office oppression."

A frown marred Cortez's smooth forehead.

"What do you mean by direct action resources?"

When he saw Talyn's mysterious smile, Yorik said, "People like Corbin and I, able to take players off the table as needed. Or perhaps rally the troops to give the governor and the current first minister severe heartburn."

Decker finished his soup with a slurp and sat back. "What Piet said. Our sort of direct action works on the idea that creating unstoppable chaos for the current administration will open the way for a savior, someone capable of uniting factions to stop runaway unrest and fear among the general population. Someone like you perhaps, Eva."

"And the Mayhem will help create this chaos?"

Talyn nodded once.

"Precisely. No politician wants to be the one who either caves to the demands of violent political militants or the one who doesn't cave and presides over a mountain of dead bodies."

"A no-win scenario."

"Which will pave the way for a new leader. Someone who can bring the militants to heel."

Cortez's hungry smile seemed surprisingly disturbing to Decker's eyes.

"And since this leader, this savior secretly controls them, it wouldn't be terribly difficult. I can envision such a plan with no difficulties."

Talyn and Decker exchanged knowing looks.

"Perhaps Eva will do even better than Gustav as our ally on Mission Colony," she said. "Alek expressed a few doubts about your late husband's commitment to doing what was necessary."

"Gustav had his weaknesses, like the rest of us," Cortez replied before taking a dainty sip from her wine glass. "But he would have become a fine first minister if not for that damned sniper."

"As I'm sure you will when the time comes."

Cortez noticed Talyn's use of the word 'when' instead of 'if' because a pleased smile creased her lips.

"I shall do my best."

"I don't doubt it, Eva. You strike me as an extraordinary woman, destined for greatness."

The four droids returned to place the main dish before them.

"Mission raised Kobe beef," Cortez said. "I hope you'll enjoy it as much as I do."

Without waiting, Decker cut into his filet steak and popped a chunk in his mouth. After an appreciative chew, he swallowed, said, "Sherri, if the Alliance needs a security liaison with our Freedom Collective friends, I volunteer."

"If Eva signs on, we probably should leave someone able to work with the Mayhem," Talyn replied in a thoughtful tone. "And Alek is needed elsewhere. Perhaps assigning you isn't such a bad idea, Corbin. A short-term deal, needless to say. You could train Piet and his people." She took a slice of meat and ate, eyes on Cortez, waiting for a reaction. "How soon do you intend to make your move, Eva?"

"We were close, a few weeks, before this morning," she replied, eyes flashing with suppressed irritation. "Now? I need to convince the Collective's governing council to grant me full powers before we can make a move. Many of them will see Gustav's death as a chance to realign our structure away from the centralized leadership model and back to the old, useless cooperative method, full of talk and devoid of action."

"We can help," Talyn said before taking another bite.

"How?"

"Corbin has a certain talent for thinning out recalcitrant herds." She glanced at Decker. "Don't you?"

"One of my many skills." He reached for the wine bottle and splashed a generous helping into his empty glass. "This steak is sublime. I'll thin out any herd you want if meat of this quality is on the menu once a week."

"What methods do you use?" Yorik helped himself to a refill as well.

"Depends on the target. I prefer to be subtle and make it look like a natural occurrence. It keeps the cops quiet and my employers happy."

"Who would figure a Marine Pathfinder turning professional hitman?"

Decker gave him a half shrug.

"It's a living, and I can't complain about the DSA's generosity."

"Did you ever thin out a herd via long distance, with something like what I showed you before the meal?"

"No. Not subtle enough. I'd rather no one figures out my work for what it is. That way the cops can't pin anything on me. A retired Marine gets nailed on gun-for-hire charges, he goes to a prison camp on Parth, and I'd rather not end my days fighting off bloodsuckers big enough to scare a Shrehari corsair. My tastes are much more refined these days."

He held up the last piece of his filet mignon, transfixed by a fork worth more than the average Marine private's daily rate of pay. "And this does me just fine. They don't serve steak in a penitentiary."

"But you have no problems working with murderously powerful explosives?"

"Piet, my friend, I'll teach you how to use the Mayhem in a way that'll scare this star system's ruling class. But you'll be the one setting it off. Or threatening to do so. You see, I'm big on plausible deniability, and so is my employer, the Democratic Stars Alliance. That way, if things go tits up, the authorities won't find any cause to crack down on us. You merely need a sacrificial goat when the time for direct action comes. Useful idiots like Osric Floros and his like should suffice."

A cruel smile crept up Yorik's face. "You're an evil man, Corbin Peel. I may begin to like you."

Talyn rolled her eyes at Cortez.

"And the male bonding begins."

"I also do light bondage." Decker gave Eva a wink. Her uncertain smile proved she didn't quite know what to make of his remark.

"Tone it down, Corbin."

The Marine put on a mock contrite air. "Yes, Sherri."

The cheese and dessert courses passed quickly, and they found themselves back in the living room for coffee. Full night had fallen while they were eating and the glen was pitch black outside, beyond a gentle pool of light bathing the mansion's stone walls.

"Where do we go from here?" Cortez asked after settling into a sinfully plush chair upholstered in dark red and crossing her elegant legs. "If I tell you I'm interested in allying myself with the DSA. Or should that be aligning myself?"

"Either word conveys the right meaning," Talyn replied. "But aligning would be more accurate if you're contemplating a long-term relationship. We would like to see the Alliance become this sector's dominant political force, capable of uniting human worlds in a common purpose. And after that? Bring the rest of the Commonwealth into our sphere and make humanity the strongest force in the known galaxy."

"An ambitious plan." Cortez nodded approvingly. "With opportunities for ambitious people."

"Indeed. But you and I need to develop an understanding. You asked where we go from here. How about we meet again when our minds aren't clouded by rich food and fine drink? A merger of this magnitude requires careful consideration because once consummated, it's difficult, if not impossible to dissolve without creating an ugly mess that serves no one. But time is of the essence."

"I agree. How about tomorrow?" She glanced at Yorik. "I suggest using the beach house where Gustav met with Alek."

"Provided Corbin can inspect the MHX brick Alek gave Gustav, I'm not fussy about location."

"Why inspect it?"

"Circumstances and players have changed due to intervention by a party or parties unknown, and until we come to a formal agreement, it remains in your possession as no more than a goodwill gesture. Corbin is one of the DSA's designated explosives experts. I need him to make sure whoever ordered Gustav's assassination can't get his or her hands on the Mayhem."

"I can assure you it's properly stored," Yorik said.

"No doubt, but I still want Corbin to see it. As you'll find out when we discuss specifics tomorrow, joining the DSA brings many advantages, including access to otherwise unobtainable weapons, munitions, or other equipment, but it also comes with certain obligations. Offering a senior Alliance emissary your full cooperation is one of them."

Yorik seemed unconvinced, but one glance at Eva told him she would override any further objections. He conceded with a tilt of the head.

"The beach house it is. I'll flip the coordinates to your communicator, Sherri."

"Shall we say ten hundred hours?"

"Agreed." Talyn finished her coffee and stood. "Since everything is settled for now, Corbin and I will stop intruding on your grief and return to Ventano. Thank you for your hospitality, Eva."

Cortez uncrossed her legs and rose with a grace that drew Decker's appreciative eyes.

"It was my pleasure. Life must go on. The movement is bigger than one man. We can mourn him once we fulfill his dreams."

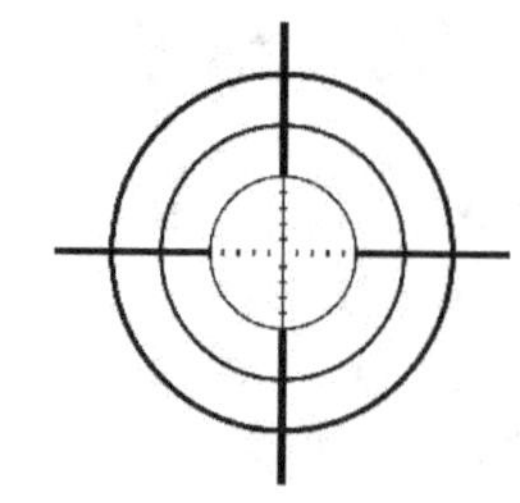

— NINE —

Piet Yorik saw Decker and Talyn to the front door where they retrieved their weapons before stepping out in the pleasantly cool night air. Their rental car, alerted by the keycard in Decker's pocket, came to life. Moments later, the softly lit mansion faded from view as they entered the winding forest lane leading back to the main Ventano highway. As soon as the darkness swallowed them, Talyn grasped Decker's hand and tapped out a message.

Assume they planted listening devices.

I'm sure they did, he replied in the same manner. *Small talk?*

No. Let's stay silent until we're in the safe house.

Decker stopped the car almost two kilometers from the safe house and sent it back to the rental lot under AI control. They would order a new vehicle from another provider in the morning. The safe house was in one of Ventano's inland suburbs, and the brisk walk along quiet streets helped both clear their minds and check for tails.

Once inside the anonymous bungalow, hidden behind privacy walls and hedges, like every other dwelling in the neighborhood, Decker retrieved his sensor from its hiding place and scanned Talyn. She returned the favor. He then switched on the machine's jamming function and exhaled noisily as he withdrew his blaster.

"Bugging our weapons? That's just low. I'm not sure whether it makes Eva and her minions better prospective DSA members or worse ones. There's a fine line between sneaky and untrustworthy."

"The question might be worthy of debate," she replied, disassembling her weapon and placing the parts on the kitchen table, "if we actually represented the Alliance. But since our job is to terminate dangerous radicals before they cross over into terrorism, it doesn't matter either way."

"True." Decker deftly turned his alien weapon into a neat line of esoteric parts. "But you were so incredibly convincing as Sherri Zadeck, the DSA's envoy plenipotentiary to Mission Colony, I could almost convince myself our orders called for the star system government's overthrow, instead of preserving it from the Freedom Collective."

"And we're still far from our goal." She ran each part of her gun past the sensor until it called attention to a stowaway in the battery pack. "Gotcha. Check your power cell, Zack. Did you notice Eva Cortez wasn't behaving like a grief-stricken widow, considering you killed her partner before her eyes mere hours earlier? She was all business tonight as if Gustav's death represented an inconvenience instead of a personal tragedy."

"I did. She could be good at masking her feelings and marching on like a committed revolutionary general."

"Eva's not much of an actress. Her anger was rather obvious. And she's no ideologically driven radical either."

"I didn't think so. Her eyes speak more loudly than her lips, and they said volumes while we talked about the future. Either she's not terribly unhappy Gustav took that final trip into the undiscovered country, or she's a sociopath so hungry for power, the lives of others don't matter."

"How about both?" Talyn asked. "Try this for a theory. Eva, backed by a few influential supporters and aides, such as your best friend Piet, was planning to set Gustav up as a figurehead first minister once the Collective took control of this star system. Even though his carefully hidden character defects make half of the criminals doing life on Parth look like jaywalkers, Kerlin was undeniably charismatic, a master manipulator capable of convincing his followers he was a sort of messiah while ignoring rumors of his unsavory predilections. The savior who'd rescue this colony from political strife. Once in power, she becomes a gray eminence, ruling from the shadows, until after a suitable period, Gustav falls ill and dies, leaving Eva as his successor."

"So you're saying I should have shot her, not him. Or rather shot both."

"We didn't know this when we were ordered to terminate Kerlin before his movement graduated from radical speech to violent action. The Political Analysis Division still suffers from blind spots thanks to the Black Sword purge. But you may get the chance to rectify that little omission."

"Do you figure Eva and Piet are a pair? I thought I sensed that vibe between them."

"Sure. She has appetites. He's a strong, healthy man who probably has fewer scruples than she does, but plenty of ambition."

"So like us, then?" Decker leered at her.

"Except you can claim a normal Marine officer's scruples and I use my pathologies for the greater good, not personal aggrandizement. Otherwise, we're exactly the same." She made a face at him. "However, I got the idea Eva's interest tonight wasn't directed at Piet, let alone you."

Decker's eyebrows crept up in amusement.

"Really? How interesting. Pathologies calling out to each other? But as long as our newest best friends bought our act and believe we're of one mind, I'm happy." He passed his blaster's power pack in front of the sensor and nodded. "Mine is bugged as well. Should be easy enough to remove though. Show me yours."

In a matter of moments, two tiny silver specks lay on a dark piece of cloth between them.

"Run them through the organic waste disposal?" Talyn asked.

"As amusing as it would be to make Piet's men listen to their toys literally go down the drain, I figure it would be best to destroy them while they're still being jammed."

"True, and I know just the way to do so."

Talyn left him sitting in the kitchen for several minutes before returning with a toolkit left in the house by the officer who bought it for Naval Intelligence use. She produced a compact laser pen.

"What we need is a suitable backstop."

"The granite countertop." Decker carefully moved the cloth and its tiny cargo into position, then watched as Talyn burned the microscopic circuits to a crisp. "And a last check," he said waving the sensor over the blackened dots. "We are clear."

"But we'll leave the jammer running, just in case."

"Of course. I wouldn't want anyone to overhear us playing radical emissary and her hard-core barbarian brute."

"I didn't know that was on tonight's menu."

"It isn't on the menu. You are."

**

Eva Cortez turned away from the darkened living room windows when she heard Piet's footsteps.

"So? Did Sherri and Corbin say nice things about us?"

She took a sip from her brandy snifter and smiled at him expectantly.

"Those two are smarter than I thought. Neither spoke a word during the entire return trip. The device we placed inside their car told us they left it near the intersection of Tenth Avenue and Salter Street, then sent the vehicle back to its home rental lot. Since the listening devices my men stuck to their blasters' power packs are single function, we don't know where they are or where they're staying. The area has half a dozen hotels."

"So few? Then they shouldn't be difficult to trace. It's residential west of Salter. Besides, your bugs will pick something up, eventually."

"I doubt it. If Zadeck and Peel were smart enough to ditch their ride, they'll check themselves for listening devices. Any decent sensor would pick up the carrier wave." He shook his head. "No. Those bugs are gone. They knew exactly how to cover their tracks."

"Which tells you something about the DSA's level of professionalism. That's reassuring, no?"

"Mannsbach didn't hide where he was staying. He simply told us to keep away. Why are these two acting differently?"

"As Sherri said, circumstances and players have changed. Gustav's death raises the stakes for everyone, including the DSA. She and Corbin can't be sure his assassination wasn't an inside job, so it's natural they would take added precautions." She took another sip while studying her chief of security. "What's bothering you, Piet?"

"Zadeck and Peel seem too good to be true, especially showing up out of nowhere so soon after someone killed Gustav."

"Or is it just they're too good, and that annoys you?"

When she saw a faint scowl deepen the lines around his mouth, Cortez sent peals of laughter echoing off walls hung with priceless artifacts.

"The difference between them and Mannsbach is..." he searched for the right word, "eerie, I suppose. Alek didn't strike me as anything other than a corporate recruiter or a sales executive with knowledge of field craft. Zadeck and Peel, however, are something more. More dangerous, more deadly, more professional. Call it what you want. They're just *more*. I can feel it in my bones."

"Don't tell me they frighten you."

"No." Yorik didn't seem offended by her insinuation. "But something's off-kilter. Sure, they know all the right things if they're genuine, they speak the right words and sound like experts in forcible government change. You wouldn't expect anything less from people representing an umbrella group such as the Democratic Stars Alliance. Yet they seemed a bit too matter-of-fact for committed revolutionaries. But since Gustav didn't take me into his confidence beyond generalities, no one can tell whether Zadeck is telling us what Mannsbach told him. And I tried again to call Alek, this time from one of our throwaway communicators, in case he was blocking me. But without success. It means we have no way of getting independent corroboration your new best friend and her gorilla really are DSA envoys even if no one's heard of them before this afternoon. And they sounded so damn glib to my skeptical ears, Eva. They were telling us, especially you, everything we wanted to hear."

"Hm." Cortez tapped the rim of her glass against her lower lip. "Then what do you suggest?"

"Take a step back and try not to fall in love with Sherri. She may seem like your type, but something tells me she's considerably more dangerous than you might think and won't let anyone interfere with her or her employer's agenda."

A pout appeared on Cortez's lips.

"Spoilsport. The one time I meet a kindred spirit and you warn me off." The pout vanished, replaced by a thoughtful expression. "Don't worry, I see your point, and in retrospect, perhaps she was subtly manipulating me. But into doing or accepting what, exactly?"

"So long as you're aware, it's fine. We continue as per plan tomorrow morning and see where it leads, but cautiously."

"Maybe I could speak with Kristy Bujold and see if the Constabulary might agree to put a tracer on them."

Yorik shook his head.

"Don't. She'll want to know why and you can't tell her, even if she is part of the patrons' circle. Besides, poor old Kristy is running around like a headless chicken because Gustav lost his to a tungsten dart. It scared everyone in the administration from the governor to the colonial council's apprentice bottle washer. They want action, any action, and they want it now."

"All right. Forget I even mentioned it. Let's see what develops tomorrow." As Yorik turned to leave, she asked, "Where did you stash that kilo of MHX? Here?"

"No. Gustav didn't want it anywhere near him after seeing the demonstration of its power."

"The beach house, then."

"Yep. It's the only other property we control that has a sufficiently secure arms room."

"Doesn't our townhouse have one?"

"Yes, but the idea of it accidentally exploding in Ventano's poshest district, killing thousands, many of whom fund our movement, terrified Gustav."

"Of course. We mustn't risk our wealthy supporters."

Cortez drained her brandy and placed the glass on a side table where one of the housekeeping droids would find it during the night.

"Did you want company, Eva, or can I do my rounds and head to bed?"

She stared at him through narrowed eyes for a few heartbeats.

"No. Not tonight."

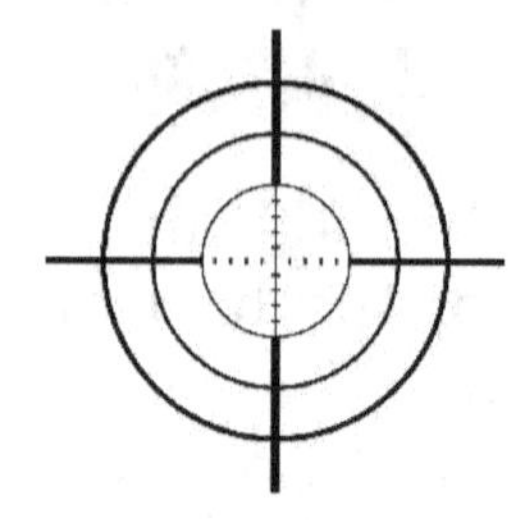

— TEN —

"Nice."

Decker and Talyn, in everyday clothes rather than the previous evening's business suits, climbed out of their new rental. The beach house, a two-story concrete, plastic, and metal structure whose outer cladding cleverly imitated wood while being able to withstand the worst gales, stood on a low promontory overlooking the Tyrellian Sea, the mostly placid expanse of water separating Mission's two largest continents, Ashima and Nanshe.

Straddling the equator, their northern and southern shores were washed by savage circumpolar currents separating the planet's temperate zone from its extensive ice caps. But here, in the shelter of the thousand-kilometer long Benden peninsula jutting out from Nanshe's northeastern corner, the climate was almost balmy.

"This place is a small fortress. I'll bet its walls can withstand small arms fire, and it likely has an extensive security perimeter and maybe even remote weapons stations hidden under the eaves. With lines of sight reaching for the horizon and little beyond scrub and widely spaced trees, you can see someone coming from kilometers away. And the neighbors, if they're so inclined, can watch who comes to visit." He pointed at a distant black cube surrounded by tiny tree-like ferns further along the peninsula.

"I prefer the wooded glen, even if it is a sniper's paradise. There's something disquieting about this open space." She gestured at the three cars parked in front of an outbuilding of similar construction to the main house. "Whoever owns this isn't shy about spending money on ground transport."

A stout metal front door surfaced to mimic dark oak, swung inward and Piet Yorik stepped out into the morning sunshine.

"You made it."

Decker jerked a thumb at Talyn.

"She'd cut out my sweetbreads if I got us lost. Quite the castle on the rock, Eva's little beach house."

"They call it Blanca's Folly after Eva's mother. She demanded her husband Sergio build them a villa far from the city, capable of withstanding a siege in case the Shrehari decide to return, back when Eva was a child. This place wouldn't hold long against determined troops, perhaps only a few minutes, but I understand it helped keep her various neuroses in check."

"Is Blanca still alive?" Decker asked

"Yes, but she doesn't come out anymore. The Cortez family now owns another, larger property further south, almost exactly on the equator, where the sand is warmer and the sea less prone to intruding cold currents from the north." Yorik gestured at the open door. "Eva is waiting for us on the seaward terrace, along with freshly brewed coffee and pastries. I'll ask you to leave your weapons at the guard post again."

Decker gave Yorik a knowing smirk and winked.

"Only if you promise our power packs won't catch another dose of security transmitted disease."

The man's laugh, a single bark, conveyed amusement with a hint of annoyance at being caught.

"Cute."

He pivoted on his heel and led them into the cool shadows of a structure whose design owed more to the architecture of bombproof bunkers than wealthy industrialists' playthings.

"I see you changed cars and rental companies, but chose the same make and model."

"Yep. Nothing wrong with the car's specs." Decker's smirk widened. "But it developed a defect last night."

"How's that?"

"An incurable desire to invade our privacy overcame the damn thing, and it broadcast our location."

Yorik's hyena-like bark echoed off the walls, but this time without the slightest trace of humor, confirming Decker and Talyn's suspicions he'd bugged their rental as well. He gestured at the man sitting behind a security console in the vestibule.

"Anton will make sure your hand artillery stays disease-free."

Decker didn't bother restraining his mirth and answered, between bouts of genuinely amused laughter, "If you say so, Piet."

After going through the same process as the previous evening, they followed Yorik through the silent house and onto a broad terrace overlooking the Tyrellian Sea's dark waters. Small waves twinkled with reflected sunshine while the warm offshore breeze was bracing and mercifully devoid of the pungent ocean smell so prevalent around Ventano's harbor front.

Eva Cortez, also casually dressed, a coffee cup in hand, turned toward them and leaned against the waist-high stone balustrade.

"Good morning, Sherri, Corbin. I trust you had a pleasant night."

"It was remarkably quiet," Talyn replied smiling warmly.

"Yeah, eerily so," Decker added with a sly grin. "*After* we finished making noise."

"Really?"

"I guess the sound didn't carry to your mansion in the glen. Pity."

Cortez gave Decker a strange look, then glanced at Talyn and smiled back.

"Coffee?"

"Please. I take it black."

"As black as her soul would be if she could actually claim one," the Marine added. "I'll take mine black as well, but only because I hate killing the taste with additives."

Talyn raised her finger and pointed at him with mock severity.

"You really are fishing for reassignment to the punishment detail, aren't you?"

"I can't help it, Sherri. My mouth has a mind of its own."

Yorik handed Talyn a finely crafted porcelain cup exuding the rich aroma of Earth-grown coffee beans.

"This smells absolutely yummy, Eva!"

"The finest blend you can find in the entire Rim Sector."

Decker took the cup proffered by Yorik, inhaled, then sipped before saying, in a contented voice, "This is living."

"Help yourselves to the petit fours, freshly baked by the beach house kitchen droid." Cortez touched Talyn's arm and nodded toward the open water. "What do you think of the view?"

"Stunning. But as I told Corbin when we arrived, I prefer the intimacy of the foothills, places like your private glen."

"As do I. Did Piet tell you what we call this place?"

"Blanca's Folly."

"Yes. My dear mother and her constant fears of a Shrehari invasion. Never mind she wasn't alive during the occupation or even had family members living in this star system at the time. But my father rarely says no to her."

"Or to you?"

"Oh, he's said no to me more often than I can remember. I wasn't daddy's little girl. Quite the contrary. That role still belongs to my younger sister Alexandra, while the role of heir apparent belongs to my older brother Carlos, also known as C.C. by our social circle. I was stuck finding my own way in the world." The hungry stare of a hunting predator briefly tightened her features. "Any siblings, Sherri?"

"None. And no living parents either. I'm the perfect orphan. Alone in the galaxy but for my friends and colleagues."

"She has me, and I'm all she needs," Decker interjected, earning a dirty look from both women.

Yorik gestured at him with his cup and nodded toward the other end of the terrace.

"Let's leave our bosses to it."

"Probably safer that way."

When they were out of earshot, Yorik asked, "How did you know we bugged your car and weapons?"

Decker shrugged dismissively.

"It's something I would do without hesitation. The car was a no-brainer. I'd want to know where those annoying newcomers from Cimmeria spend the night, and what sweet little nothings they whisper into each other's ears. Sticking listening devices to our blasters' power packs wasn't any more difficult to guess. They're not immediately visible and can leech off the cells to stay operational for days. Except without a re-transmitter, like the multifunction device you put in our car, they aren't much use so far from their base unit. Next time, you should send a mobile unit to tail your subjects from a discreet distance."

After a moment to digest Decker's words, Yorik said, "Noted. For a former Marine Corps combat engineer, you seem well versed in surveillance techniques."

"Bust your hump for an outfit like the DSA long enough, and you learn all sorts of things."

"Yet the DSA isn't even a year old. How does that compute?"

"Sherri and I worked for one of its founding organizations on Cimmeria. Don't ask me which one. We're not allowed to discuss life before the Alliance." Decker took a healthy mouthful of coffee and swallowed. "While the brass talk privately, why don't you show me the MHX brick? Get that done before they ask."

"Sure. Why not?" Yorik and the Marine drained their cups and placed them on the serving table. "Gustav stored it in what we call the arms room, a hardened vault two stories below the surface originally meant to be Blanca Cortez's rabbit hole in case of attack."

He led Decker through a gleaming, almost antiseptically clean kitchen, past a charging alcove where housekeeping droids waited in silence and down a bare hallway ending at a door that wouldn't seem out of place in a starship's airlock. He laid his palm against a matte gray screen set into the wall hard against the jamb.

A virtual keyboard appeared before his eyes and he entered a code with fingers dancing too quickly for Decker's eyes. Hidden mechanical latches fell clear with a muffled sound and the door swung outward, revealing a circular metallic staircase disappearing into the promontory's living rock.

The shaft was lit at regular intervals by glow globes attached to the walls. It ended on a landing opposite another armored door twin to the one above. Yorik again placed his hand on a matte gray screen before entering a code on the virtual keyboard. After another set of mechanical sounds, it too swung outward. Beyond lay a long corridor pierced by steel doors set at regular intervals, three to each side.

"This was, at one time, a fully serviced apartment with space for the Cortez family and supplies to last several weeks.   Now, they store items with too much sentimental value for disposal but not enough monetary value to overcome sentiment in that room." He pointed at the far door on their right. "The three on the left are used for weapons, explosives, and ammunition."

"And the other two?"

An evil smile pulled up the corners of Yorik's mouth.

"Prison cells.   Down here, no one can hear you scream, and there's no escape."

Decker put on an appreciative expression.

"Convenient. Do you use them often?"

"Once or twice in my time as chief of security. People presenting a threat to the Collective, Eva, or Gustav. The MHX is stored in that one." He pointed at the furthest door on the left. "If you'll follow me."

After one last handprint and security code, they entered a chamber almost ten meters square filled with rows of mostly empty metal shelving. The few small crates in evidence bore the markings of mining explosives. Save for one, prominently displayed by itself.

The size of an ordinary travel bag big enough for toiletries and a change of clothes, the box bore no markings, though Decker hoped the actual brick was still inside the shielded wrapping applied at the time of production.   It would bear the name of the manufacturing plant and the ammunition depot that subsequently took possession.

"Help yourself," Yorik said, pointing at it.

Decker picked up the smooth, silver plastic box and quickly found the release with his fingers. It split in half, like a clamshell, exposing a smaller brick inside a black bag nestled among material designed to fool any but the best military-grade sensors into thinking it was only an innocuous carving. He lifted the brick from its cradle and opened one end of the bag so he could glance inside.

To his relief, he saw the characteristic dull green wrapping common to every explosive compound produced by Armed Services-owned factories. A quick shake and the MHX-19 sat in his open right hand, looking no more deadly than a ration bar. He stared at the manufacture and depot markings, committing them to memory, before peeling back the wrapper at one end, where someone had already done so.

It was indeed MHX-19, better known as Mayhem. The compound glowed with that peculiar, almost buttery color and felt slick to the touch. He raised the brick to his nose and inhaled. Burned almonds. There could be no doubt this was the genuine article, capable of destroying the entire colonial government precinct in a fraction of a second.

"Happy?" Yorik asked from the open doorway.

Decker carefully repackaged the compound and placed the silver box back on its shelf.

"Ecstatic." He turned to see a dubious expression on Yorik's face, one that quickly vanished as he stepped back into the corridor. "I'll tell Sherri."

Once back in the stairwell, Yorik asked, "So that's it? A look, a touch, a damn sniff? You can tell it's the DSA's MHX-19 just like that, without a proper scanner?"

"Yep. Just like that. When you know what the telltales are, it's not wormhole science."

Talyn and Cortez seemed deep in conversation when Decker, Yorik on his heels, returned to the terrace. His partner glanced up at him long enough to see a confirming nod. The Mayhem was here.

Before they managed three paces, Yorik stopped and tilted his head to one side. Decker gave him a questioning gaze only to see the man's face harden as he stared back, eyes colored by deep suspicion.

"Sorry. I need to take this. Grab another coffee and enjoy the view." Yorik vanished into the kitchen once more.

Instead of following the suggestion, Decker walked to the far end of the terrace and studied the beach house's eastern facade, wondering what could call Yorik away from his duties as host to the DSA's security representative.

Several minutes passed before he returned, grimmer than ever, and Decker, by now on high alert, noticed one of the guards, weapon drawn, and keeping to the shadows just inside the kitchen door.

"Sorry to interrupt." Yorik addressed himself to Eva and Sherri though Decker knew his announcement encompassed him as well. "I'm afraid I bring worrisome news."

"What?"

Cortez sat up and put her cup on the patio table. She sounded annoyed at the interruption.

"Since I was worried about his welfare after yesterday's events, I sent my men to check up on Alek Mannsbach this morning. They entered his apartment a short time ago. He appears to have died in bed of natural causes. Or at least they couldn't find any marks on him. Based on body temperature, he passed away sometime yesterday afternoon, and we know he was alive when Osric brought him news of Gustav's death."

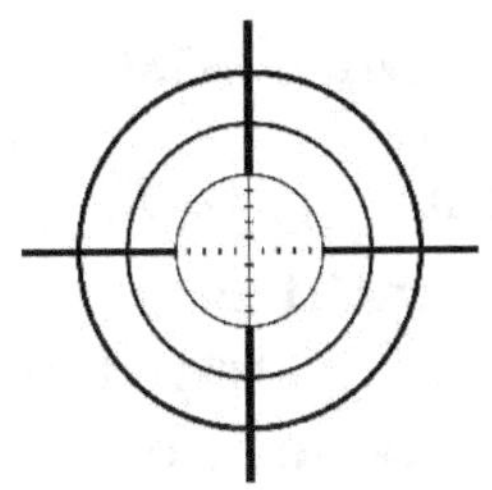

— ELEVEN —

Yorik's eyes went back and forth between Decker and Talyn, looking for a telltale reaction to his announcement.

"I beg your pardon?" Talyn asked in a tone half puzzled, half-indignant as she stared at Yorik with an air of incomprehension. "What are you talking about? Alek was fine when I spoke with him shortly after your man Floros announced Gustav's death. And what do you mean entered his apartment?"

"Yes, please explain yourself, Piet," Cortez said in a soft voice.

"The clothes Alek wore the last time he met with Gustav the day before yesterday are missing as is his ID and sidearm," Yorik continued as if he hadn't heard her. "Someone returned his rental car to the agency yesterday afternoon. The apartment looks as if it's been freshly cleaned by experts. I could go on, but I'm sure everyone sees that something's not right. Gustav dies yesterday before lunch. Alek dies a few hours later. Then Sherri and Corbin show up. Sherri claims to be Alek's boss, taking over the negotiations and talking a good game. But she and Corbin seem rather more concerned about the MHX-19 Alek gave Gustav than the nature of the discussions to date."

Decker, hands in his pockets, strolled over to where Yorik stood, facing Eva and Talyn, both still seated.

"What are you trying to imply?" The latter asked.

"That we killed Alek," Decker said, stopping behind his partner's chair. "And that we might be involved in Gustav's assassination. It's true you know. We terminated Alek. Or to be more precise, since it's not considered polite in our circles to claim a kill if there's no blood on your hands, Sherri did."

While Yorik watched Decker like a predator eying his next meal, Eva stared at the Marine in shock.

"Why? Why would you kill your own man?"

"Alek was weak, and that weakness threatened the DSA's plans to bring the Mission Colony Freedom Collective under its umbrella."

"Pardon?" Eva's eyes blazed with undisguised incredulity. "You'd kill someone for that? What sort of people are you?"

"The sort who clean up their messes before things get out of hand," Talyn said. "Unfortunately, I can't say the same about your organization."

Decker made a face.

"Indeed. Gustav saw the DSA's offer as a way to tighten his grip on the Collective and make a play for absolute power in this star system, ideology, citizens and followers be damned."

"So?" Eva asked. "Isn't that what the Alliance wants — friends running the entire Rim Sector?"

"We want allies, not quasi-independent satraps. Gustav, master persuader that he was, somehow either convinced Alek to play along or bought him off. He would pay lip service to the DSA's principles and priorities, take the MHX and the money, then make himself sole master of the Mission system. As I said, Alek was weak. Either the promise of wealth and power overcame his loyalties or Gustav found a way to compromise him. Considering your late husband's morally and legally objectionable proclivities, I lean more toward the latter explanation. Especially since Gustav was protected by other perverts and could easily throw Alek to the wolves if he stepped out of line. It's a story as ancient as humanity itself."

Yorik's eyes lit up with sudden understanding. He pointed at Decker.

"You're the sniper. I knew it. That Falkenberg Longbow isn't a weapon for an amateur. But a man your size, strength and military experience? I'll bet you're able to shoot the balls off a fly at a thousand meters."

The Marine pulled his hands out of his trouser pockets and clapped.

"Bravo. Well done. And yes, Gustav needed to go. He was a huge liability for the movement. We don't mind people whose definition of fun is a little out of the ordinary, but not when it makes them vulnerable. If Gustav had been allowed to seize power, his appetites would have spun out of control, with disastrous results. Hiding the odd body after a night of pleasure gone overboard when you're merely the charismatic leader of a radical group is one thing. Trying to do the same when you're Mission Colony's first minister? You can imagine the outcome."

"He would have exercised self-control," Eva growled, though her eyes told Decker she was in no way convinced by her own words. "Piet and I would have made sure."

"No." Talyn shook her head. "His sort is convinced they're beyond retribution, especially after they keep getting away with their crimes thanks to official corruption or friends with similar appetites in high places. They're incurable short of a mind wipe. A few months in power and his facade would slip, or the friends with similar appetites would find the temptation to blackmail him irresistible. The DSA can't afford allies whose weaknesses threaten established plans."

"So you simply went ahead and murdered him."

"There was no alternative. The Freedom Collective is important for our expansion in these parts, but not under Gustav. Corbin did what the DSA deemed necessary, making you the Collective's new leader, and Mission Colony's next first minister. You're a much better choice for this star system and us. Besides, if you examine things with clear eyes, you'd know Gustav's downfall would have destroyed everyone in his circle."

A thoughtful expression replaced the anger on her sculpted features, but Yorik wasn't having any of it.

"This is bullshit, Eva. I don't know what game they're playing, but it won't end well for anyone. Best we stop this right now. Corbin deserves a shot in the back of the head for murdering Gustav, and Sherri earned one for ordering his assassination. If they actually represent the Democratic Stars Alliance, which I doubt, we should let their superiors know the Mission Colony Freedom Collective isn't joining their little scheme unless it's as equals. In the meantime, we reset our timetable and adjust our plans to account for the MHX-19's terror factor."

Decker gave Yorik a questioning glance.

"I thought you weren't ideological."

"This isn't a question of ideology but power. Ideology is for useful idiots who volunteer to storm the barricades."

"Can't argue with the sentiment. However, killing us won't help you seize power. On the contrary. The DSA's reach is long and its patience for dissenters limited. You didn't believe we acted without authority, did you? Gustav's status was questionable even before we left Cimmeria. His attempt to suborn Alek simply confirmed our superiors' thoughts he might need replacing. Tell me with a straight face you're sure Gustav Kerlin would have made a viable first minister."

Yorik scowled in reply but remained silent.

"See," Decker continued, "even you know terminating Gustav improved things, especially for Eva."

"It did," Cortez said. "But his plan, as you summarized it last night, is fundamentally sound — with me at the helm." She stood and walked over to Yorik. "I'd rather not surrender my liberty of action to a newcomer like the Democratic Stars Alliance, or anyone else. Piet, be a dear and turn them into *desaparecidos*. Wipe any evidence they and Alek ever set foot on Mission."

Yorik raised his hand to shoulder height and half a dozen men, armed with vicious looking but legal needlers, emerged from the beach house. They formed a semicircle around them, weapons pointed at Decker and Talyn.

"This place is surrounded by remote weapon stations, so please don't try to run," Yorik said. "You'll only die tired."

"I thought that was my line," Decker replied, smirking. "You know, me being a sniper." He laid a hand on Talyn's shoulder. "I was right last night. I should have shot Eva along with her pervert of a husband. They're quite the team."

Talyn picked up her coffee cup and took an unhurried sip before saying, "You might seize power without our help, but I doubt you'll keep it long enough to enrich yourselves, let alone your families. The DSA considers betrayal a capital crime and punishes the perpetrators accordingly. Are your relatives ready to die for your mistakes? How about your friends?"

Yorik dismissed her statement with a scornful snort.

"The DSA won't find any evidence Alek Mannsbach or either of you ever set foot on this world. Alek's presence is already being erased. My men will make his body and belongings vanish while friends inside the government will delete his name and particulars from the arrivals control records. By noon today, Mannsbach will be a non-person.”

Talyn placed her cup on the table, stood and walked to the parapet, tracked by three of the needlers. She gazed at the water for a few seconds, then turned and leaned against the warm stones.

“You won’t be able to make every trace of us vanish. We left enough evidence and daily reports behind to point the finger at Eva. Better to end this futile revolt against reality now, before you forfeit your lives.”

Her reminder he didn’t know where to find their base of operations brought Yorik up short, but only for a moment.

“As clichéd as it may sound, we have ways of making you talk, Sera Zadeck. We’ll find your rabbit hole and sanitize it, and my friends in the administration will erase your presence from the official records as well.”

“Oh? It’s Sera Zadeck now?” She asked in a mocking tone. “Whatever happened to Sherri? Aren’t we among equals here, friends?”

Yorik turned to his men instead of replying.

“Take them to the cells, one in each, and secure them for questioning.”

Decker’s contemptuous laugh echoed off the beach house’s walls.

“Please. Do you think the DSA would send out operatives who weren’t conditioned against interrogation? You’ll get nothing from us. We’ll die without saying a word and leave enough evidence behind to condemn everyone here. Remember what happened to Gustav? That’s your future unless we walk free.”

“I let you walk and then what?” Cortez asked.

“You let us walk out of here with the MHX, and we’ll declare the negotiations a failure,” Talyn replied. “The DSA will find another way to exert its influence on Mission Colony and leave you alone. No harm, no foul.”

"I don't believe you, darling. You're not the type to let bygones be bygones."

"How do you figure?"

"You and I, we're so close to being twins under the skin, it's deliciously scary, and I carry grudges forever. No deal. Get going, Piet. If they die before giving us the location of their safe house, so be it. The lovely Sherri and her sniper have a date with that pod of pseudo-pliosaurs cruising over the offshore deeps." Eva's smile held all the chill of Mission Colony's eternal icecaps. "Don't worry, my dear. They'll eat you in two bites, maybe three, so it's over rather quickly."

"If they don't die under interrogation."

"We will," Decker said with an air of unconcern. "So you might as well shoot us now and save yourself the trouble of hauling our bodies up from the subbasement. Your guards don't seem like they're strong enough to deal with my carcass."

"They can always chop it into quarters," Eva replied. "And on that note, goodbye. I'm sorry it has to end this way, Sherri, but I'm sure you understand. We might have become good friends in another life. Sadly, this is the one we're living."

She turned on her heels, passed through the cordon of armed men, and entered the beach house.

"Alright. We can do this in two ways. You can let my guards shackle you and walk to the cells under your own power, or we'll lay you out cold and drag you down the staircase. Alternative number two means you'll wake up in severe pain and it'll only go downhill from there."

Decker pulled his hands out of his pockets, stuck out his arms out, and put his wrists together.

"Tie us up. We'll walk, thank you very much."

Talyn imitated him moments later.

"Tell me, Corbin," Piet said as two of the guards came forward, each with shackles in his hands, "how does it feel watching someone's head explode through a good old-fashioned optical sniper scope?"

The Marine grinned at him.

"There's no feeling quite like it. Shame you won't get a chance to try. Your destiny is to become pink mist, not be the sniper. Unless you'd like to correct my mistake and use the Falkenberg Longbow on Eva. I might even hire you afterward. We can never find enough good men willing to do whatever is necessary. Otherwise, I suggest you make sure your affairs are in order, Piet."

"Big words from someone about to die." He gestured at the nearest guard. "Take them to the cells and search them, Ben. And keep your hands off Zadeck. Gustav's gone, which means no more playtime."

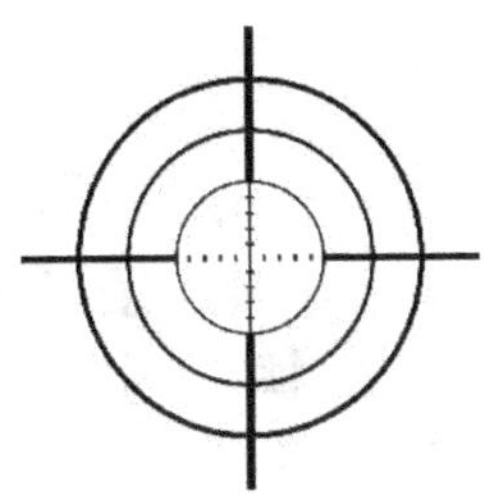

— TWELVE —

As Piet Yorik watched his men shove them into a single file, Decker and Talyn exchanged a brief glance. After years together, the Marine knew she would understand he'd improvised a plan the moment he saw things were about to go pear-shaped. Her eyes asked when. His counseled outward docility but warned her to be prepared.

As Decker hoped, their escort numbered only three men, more would be unwieldy due to the narrow spiral staircase — Ben at the front, one between Decker and Talyn, and the last one behind her. Both operatives could feel the barrel of a needler in the small of their backs. Ben led them through the kitchen and into the same bare corridor Yorik used earlier.

He stopped by the closed door, unlocked it and glanced over his shoulder to make sure his colleagues were ready. Then, he took the stairs at a slow pace, attention focused on his feet rather than the prisoners.

The moment Decker stepped off the upper landing, he no longer felt the needler's barrel, proof the guard behind him was also splitting his attention between the prisoner and the stairs. They made their way down wordlessly, the Marine and his partner by all appearances cowed.

But when Ben was only two steps from the lower landing, Decker stumbled and slammed into him. Both fell, the guard grunting in pain and surprise.

Decker rolled to one side and reached for the holstered needler, knowing he had mere seconds before the next in line stitched him with tiny projectiles. His shackled hands seized the weapon's butt, and he wrenched it free while continuing the roll until he lay on his back beside the downed guard.

He opened fire moments before the second guard's reactions caught up and turned his face into a bleeding pincushion. He toppled over but not before sending a spray of shards to break against the wall. Decker barely managed to raise his arms and protect his face from the tiny, stinging debris.

When he looked up at the stairs again, he saw Talyn, the third guard's gun in her hands, step aside, and send him to join his comrades on the landing. He too was unconscious and bleeding from a dozen pinpricks on his jaw and neck. The takedown was over in seconds. One guard was stunned, but conscious, the others were out for however long it took to shake off the knockout drugs.

Decker pushed himself into a crouch and stuck the needler's barrel into the point man's ear.

"Cooperate, and I won't blow out your eardrum before performing an improvised lobotomy."

Ben nodded once, still unable to process what just happened.

"Shackles release?"

"Right-hand thumbprint," he mumbled in reply.

Talyn took the last few steps to the landing, crouched across from Decker and held out her shackled hands at the edge of the prone man's reach.

"You will release her," Decker said. "Try anything else, and I turn you into a drooling moron."

"Yeah, yeah." He stretched out his right hand and grasped the manacles. They opened with a soft click and fell away.

Talyn immediately stuck her gun's barrel into the guard's other ear.

"Now my partner."

When his hands were free, Decker grabbed Ben by the shoulders and yanked him to his feet.

"Open the arms room door. No funny business otherwise, it's lobotomy time. Cooperate, and we won't kill you or your friends. We merely want to recover something that doesn't belong to Eva or Piet and leave."

"Take it easy, man. I'll do whatever you want. Piet's not paying me enough for this sort of shit." He pointed at the gray panel by the doorjamb. "Can I?"

Moments later, the latching bars pulled back, and the door swung outward. Decker pushed Ben into the arms room.

"Open the cells." When Ben gave him a questioning look Decker said, "Where the hell else am I supposed to store you and those two sleeping uglies? Open the cells."

He complied, and after checking both rooms, Decker motioned at Talyn to switch places with him while he dragged the two guards into one of them. Then, Decker pointed at the explosives storeroom and said, "Now open that one."

"Can't."

"Can't, or won't?"

"Piet is the only one other than Eva or Gustav who has unrestricted access."

"That's too bad." Decker raised the needler and fired. Red spots appeared on Ben's cheek. He grunted once before collapsing. "I suppose I should have shot him in the cell."

"Indeed. Is the MHX behind that door?"

"Yep." Decker dragged Ben into the cell and dropped him beside his colleagues. "But Piet will want to interrogate us himself, so he'll be here soon. Everything is falling into place as ordained by fate."

"Let me ask you this, Big Boy, if Piet hadn't let his paranoia go ballistic, how did you figure we'd get our hands on that MHX brick?"

He shrugged.

"No idea. But I would have thought of something in due time."

She walked up and down the corridor, studying every nook and cranny.

"Why are there no surveillance sensors? If they'd bothered to wire this place into the house network, a dozen of Ben's friends would be crawling over us right now."

"I noticed the same thing when Piet brought me here to commune with the Mayhem. But it stands to reason. No sensors mean no chance of anyone seeing Gustav or Eva's victims meet a sad end and recording the event to earn extra money via blackmail."

"Their weakness is our opportunity."

"Exactly. This job would be a lot harder if the opposition only recruited honest, upright people."

"Congratulations on improvising yet another harebrained scheme. For a moment or two, I wondered whether you'd lost your ever-loving mind by coming clean on Alek and Gustav."

"If it's stupid, and it works, it's not stupid." Decker sketched a mock bow. "Make sure you mention this example of my stellar ability to adapt and overcome on my next performance evaluation."

"We're not done yet, Mister Wonderful. There's still the small matter of recovering the MHX and making our escape."

"Not to mention sending Sera Cortez into that big sleep where she can reunite with Gustav and suffer torment for eternity. I should have shot her instead.

Gustav wasn't about to become the first minister without little Eva and her twisted soul."

"Not to mention that. What does your stellar ability to adapt and overcome think we should do when Piet finally joins us?"

A hungry grin lit up the Marine's face.

"We pull one of my favorite maneuvers, the ambush. I'm sure he'll show as little interest in a needler lobotomy as Ben did."

**

"Has Ben reported back yet?" Yorik asked the man at the security console as he re-entered the beach house foyer after seeing Eva Cortez off.

Anton shook his head.

"No. Maybe he and the guys are having fun with that Zadeck woman. She's not bad looking for her age."

"I sure as hell hope not. She's also damned dangerous for her age. I'll be in the arms room for the next hour. Prepare the boat. When I'm done, we're dumping them in the usual spot."

"Sure thing, boss."

Yorik stopped by his office, one of the ground floor bedrooms he'd re-purposed when Gustav hired him, and took an interrogation kit from the locked cabinet hidden inside the walk-in closet. He also pulled out a box of lethal needler loads, illegal as hell on Mission Colony, and swapped them for the nonlethals he'd carried all morning, in case Zadeck and Peel didn't die under interrogation.

The staircase door was agape when he entered the hallway from the kitchen, and he listened for any sounds that might tell him Ben and his colleagues were amusing themselves with the prisoners. Sometimes Gustav would allow a favored few to enjoy sloppy seconds before they dispatched his latest playthings, something Yorik didn't condone because it was bad for morale and discipline.

Woe betides anyone who abused prisoners without his permission now that Gustav was gone. And good riddance. Eva could be cruel, though never merely to amuse herself. But he heard nothing.

Once on the bottom landing, he saw the arms room and the first cell also standing open, while the second cell door was closed save for a small crack. There was no sign of his men. Invisible fingers crept up the back of Yorik's neck. He drew his needler and held it loosely at his side, barrel pointing downward before he entered the arms room corridor and looked into the cell.

Sherri Zadeck, its sole occupant, sat in the metal chair bolted to the floor, arms behind her back, a muzzle patch over her mouth. She stared at him with terror-filled eyes while making undecipherable sounds which increased in volume and pitch at an alarming rate.

Yorik suddenly sensed a presence behind him and tried to turn. But a powerful hand wrenched the needler from his grip while another weapon's barrel was jammed into the small of his back hard enough to draw a gasp of pain.

When his eyes turned back on Zadeck, she was standing, mouth uncovered, pointing a gun at him. Yorik froze in surprise and during those few seconds, whoever was behind him, Corbin Peel being the most likely candidate, stuck the weapon into his right ear.

Then, a voice growled, "Unless you like your brains scrambled, I suggest you do nothing more than breathe until I give you permission to move."

"What do you want?" Yorik asked in a whisper.

"The MHX. What else? Open the explosives room, and you might walk away from this reasonably intact. You're just a hired gun, paid to obey orders. Don't fall on your sword for someone like Eva Cortez. She's just as likely to order you killed as take you to her bed."

"That's what you want? The Mayhem."

"Yep. Can't leave the stuff in the hands of a wacko like your Eva. So here's the deal. I'll drag you to the door and you'll unlock it for me. Then, you take Sherri's place in the cell, we lock it and leave. Is that something you can live with? Because if not, you'll die."

Talyn walked over to Yorik and ran her fingertips along his jawline.

"I'll add one caveat. Eva needs termination, with extreme prejudice. Where is she right at this moment? Upstairs, in her suite?"

"No." Yorik quivered as he forcibly kept his head from moving side to side. "She returned to Ventano, to the townhouse. Eva doesn't stick around when there's wet work on the menu."

"Plausible deniability." Talyn took one step back. "Why am I not surprised? Eva has fewer morals than an alley cat. Her marrying Gustav Kerlin should have been a clear sign."

She gestured at Decker with her head.

The Marine tossed Yorik's weapon to his partner. Talyn caught it by the barrel, tucked the guard's needler in her pocket, and checked the loads in Yorik's gun.

"Lethal darts, Piet? I'm disappointed."

"But not surprised, right?" Decker seized Yorik's collar and spun him around until he faced the explosives' room door. "Open it."

When he didn't immediately obey, Decker pushed the needler's barrel against his ear hard enough to elicit a gasp of pain.

"Okay, okay." Yorik placed his palm on the reader, then entered the code, and the lock sprang open. Decker pulled him back, turned, and shoved him past Talyn into the open cell.

She indicated the metal chair. "Sit, sunshine."

"You know what?" Decker's voice boomed across the hallway.

"No, I don't know what. Why do you always ask that question? I'm a professional assassin, not a mind reader."

"I just had an idea you'll love."

"Judging by your enthusiastic tone, I'm not so sure. Things always turn way too interesting when you're excited."

"And they will again."

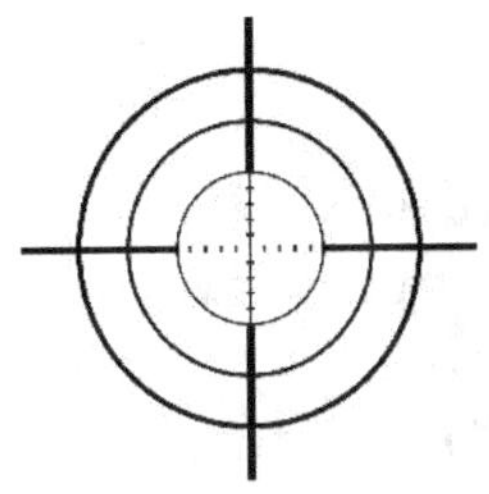

— THIRTEEN —

"I found a box of detonators that'll work with the MHX-19. By the way, that's bad form, Piet. You always store detonators and explosives separately. And I thought you were a professional."

"We did con him into shackling our hands in front of us, rather than in back," Talyn said. She gave Yorik a disappointed smile. "That made taking out your men considerably easier and quicker. Next time, you should restrain your eagerness to slap on manacles, especially when folks offer their wrists voluntarily."

An angry sneer twisted Yorik's face. "You'll pay for this. Mark my words."

"Doubtful, but if it makes you feel better... What were you about to propose, Corbin?"

"That I play the good explosive ordnance disposal man and blow this Mayhem in place. It'll save us from lugging it back to Cimmeria."

"A bit of a waste, no?"

"Fine. You can carry the brick in your bag. But consider this. We're about ten meters below ground, in a hole surrounded by granite. That means when the MHX blows, most of the explosion's force will shoot upward rather than outward, limiting collateral damage. As a bonus, it'll vaporize the Cortez family's bunker and remove an eyesore from the landscape."

"And you'd like to see what a kilo of Mayhem can do in the real world instead of watching simulator results."

"That goes without saying, honey. You know me. Making stuff go boom is my second favorite hobby, right after making you—"

Talyn cut him off. "Let's not embarrass poor Piet with a description of our intimate habits. His stomach may not be strong enough." She turned a cruel gaze on her prisoner. "Or are you a voyeur along with all your other perversions, Piet?"

"There," Decker said. "I rigged the detonator along with a timer. Nice inventory, Piet, even if you don't know squat about proper storage. Now to finagle an anti-tamper device, in case someone decides to be a hero instead of running for his life."

"You want to let these sad specimens escape when they're guilty of aiding and abetting Gustav and Eva's myriad crimes? When they intended to kill us and feed our bodies to ravenous reptiles? Are you turning sentimental in your old age?"

"I'm not a cold-blooded assassin, darling. I prefer to give even the scummiest of scumbags like Piet a fighting chance."

"Why?"

"To feel better about my life choices. The urge comes from owning a soul. Aha! That should do nicely. A few more minutes and we can blow this joint, in both meanings of the word."

"Tell you what. I'll shoot Yorik. That way he won't feel a thing when the MHX turns Eva's beach house into a crater."

"A true angel of death, that's what you are."

Talyn turned her head to blow a kiss across the corridor. As she expected, Yorik chose that moment for an attempt to recover his weapon, but before he could take more than two steps, she fired a dozen tiny darts into his torso.

He skidded to a halt, glanced down, surprise writ large on his face, then up at her again before collapsing under the effects of the fast-acting neurotoxin.

"I believe they call this being hoist on one's own petard," she said to the dying man at her feet. "If you'd been carrying legal, non-lethal loads, you might merely wake up in a few hours with a nasty headache. Say hi to Gustav for us. Don't worry about Eva. She'll join you soon."

"What are you on about?" Decker asked in a distracted tone.

"Piet went out fighting." Talyn knelt beside the dying man and rifled through his pockets. She found nothing more than an identity wafer, which she kept.

"You enticed him into trying for his gun, didn't you?"

"I did. And he loaded it with neurotoxin-coated darts. Perhaps he committed suicide."

Decker chuckled.

"Suicide by assassin. Cute. There, I'm done. Any preference for the timer?"

"Your call. Just make sure it's enough to let us get away from ground zero."

"Thirty minutes should do the trick. What about Ben and his sleeping buddies? They won't come to for another hour or more."

She didn't immediately answer. Instead, he heard her open the other cell door, then the weapon in her hand coughed three times.

"Problem solved. The bastards aren't sleeping anymore."

"Why?"

"Because they were the sort who'd rape their female prisoners if Piet didn't tell them otherwise."

"Ah. Right. Of course. Should I ask about your intentions for the rest of the guards?"

She stuck her head into the explosives storage room. "Don't you already know the answer?"

"Fine. Do what you feel best. There, the timer's set."

He joined her in the corridor and slammed the door shut, cutting off anyone without the right palm print and access code.

"As a man once said, the die is cast. Thirty minutes until detonation."

He glanced into both cells, finding three dead guards in one and their equally dead security chief, crumpled in a heap, eyes staring sightlessly at the wall, in the other.

Decker raised a hand as if holding something. "Alas, poor—"

"Don't," Talyn growled as she slapped him.

"Don't what?"

"Say it.

"Say what? *Alas, poor Yorik! I knew him, Horatio; a fellow of infinite jest, of most excellent fancy*? That's what you don't want me to say? Fine, I won't."

She gave Decker a look of utter disgust.

"Sometimes, you can be such an asshole."

"That's one of my many talents." He blew her a kiss. "But if it's only sometimes, I must be slipping. Come on. If our car's gone, thirty minutes will buy us just enough time to leave the danger zone."

They encountered the first of the remaining guards in the kitchen. Talyn felled him with Yorik's gun before the man could open his mouth.

"That makes four, plus Piet," Decker muttered. "We saw six on the terrace, not including Anton, which means there are at least three left. Did you want to hunt them or can we recover our gear and bugger off?"

"With any luck, the survivors will stick around and find themselves blown into orbit."

Anton half rose from his chair when they entered the vestibule. Talyn shot him in the face without warning.

He fell forward, face hitting the console before slumping to the floor.

"Five down."

They recovered their own weapons but kept the captured needlers. Decker glanced at the surveillance console.

"Looks like three of them are sleeping."

"They'll get one hell of a wakeup call in," she glanced at her timepiece, "twenty-five minutes."

Decker was first at the front door. He stopped abruptly.

"Shit. Our car's gone. One of Piet's boys must be taking it back to the rental lot, in keeping with the general plan to make us non-persons."

"I bet Anton keeps keycards to their speeders in his desk," Talyn replied, turning back to the console. "Choose which of the two you want."

"The Nostromo Overlander looks nice. Armored too. Probably the one Piet uses."

"He no longer needs it." Talyn stepped over Anton's body and rummaged through the drawers beneath the bank of video displays. "Where are you? Aha! Here we go. How about we take a car each?"

She tossed a keycard at him.

"Sure."

To his relief, both vehicles came to life at their approach. They reached the main road, almost seven kilometers away, in a matter of minutes. Decker pulled the Overlander off to one side and climbed out.

"You're bound and determined to watch, aren't you?" Talyn asked as she joined him on the large flat stone he'd turned into his viewing bench.

"Why pass on the chance to learn more about MHX-19's effects? Call it professional development if you want. We know where to find Eva, so there's no hurry."

"On the contrary, we need a berth on the next ship headed for Cimmeria. The idea that there could potentially be hundreds of kilos of the stuff in DSA hands chills me to the core. Especially if those maniacs are handing it out to whack jobs like the Mission Colony Freedom Collective, which was, until yesterday, run by a guy whose extra-curricular activities make most perverts seem like normal, law-abiding people."

"If you're chilled, I'll warm you up." Decker wrapped his arm around her and squeezed. "Fortunately, he received the death penalty for his crimes, thanks to yours truly. Gustav won't be diddling underage kids anymore, or murdering anyone who crosses him."

"Sure, yet you have to wonder how many Gustav Kerlins are out there?"

"Probably quite a few. The universe is filled with awful people. But one thing at a time, right? Once Eva's out of the way, we need to call home, report on this DSA whose existence everyone seems to have missed and tell them about an unknown quantity of MHX-19 going walkabout. I memorized the factory and depot markings, so at least they can launch an investigation. We should also suggest a direct action unit from the 1st Special Forces Regiment be sent to Cimmeria. If they don't screw around and put them on a fast starship, it could show up a few days after us. By then we might have found where the rest of the MHX is being kept, along with whoever is running this Democratic Stars Alliance.

"Since we both agree it's probably another Coalition scheme to cause political chaos, the boss should bless us with everything he can. As far as I know, the Cimmerian Gendarmerie doesn't have an anti-terrorism task force, and if the DSA problem is interstellar, it'll be ours to solve anyhow. Maybe you can rope in your friend from the Constabulary Professional Compliance Bureau when we land on Cimmeria. I doubt the

Coalition has suborned one of the last incorruptibles and I don't want to risk approaching anyone at Sixth Fleet HQ, in case it still suffers from a Black Sword infestation or worse one from the *Sécurité Spéciale*."

"Agreed. You're getting good at this, Zack. I'm impressed."

He stared at her in mock dismay.

"You took this long to be impressed by my abilities as a black ops ninja? I'm hurt."

A blinding flash of light near the water's edge robbed Talyn of a reply. White like nothing else in the universe, it blotted out the sun, the sky, and the surrounding landscape. Seconds later, the rumble of a planet splitting asunder reached their ears while debris rose in the air like a geyser of solid matter, seemingly reaching almost to the edge of the atmosphere. Talyn's first reaction, after regaining her senses was to glance at her timepiece.

"Five minutes early."

"Aye, but what power. Didn't that look almost like an antimatter device?" Decker stared at where the beach house once stood with a rapt expression on his face. "Either Piet's timers were screwy, or one of the guards with access to the storage room met my anti-tamper device."

Then, the debris, flung hundreds of meters up, reversed direction Most pieces were the size of a pea, but many approached that of a human head, and a few were even big enough to crush the vehicles parked behind Decker and Talyn's improvised bench.

The grassy landscape in a two-kilometer radius around what was now a steaming hole turned into a surface dimpled and scarred by a thousand craters. Within moments, the waters of the Tyrellian Sea rushed in to fill a new cove where Blanca's Folly once stood, returning the promontory to its primal state.

"That was, um, wow." For the first time since he and Talyn joined forces, Decker found her at a loss for words. "There's nothing left."

"If the explosion's main force hadn't been directed straight up thanks to the MHX brick being at the bottom of a ten meter deep, granite-lined pit, you and I probably wouldn't be speaking right now. Imagine a bomb fifty or a hundred times more powerful going off at the heart of a city."

She looked up at him with an appalled expression.

"We need to stop those DSA maniacs."

"Stop, disarm and execute. Preferably in that order." Decker stood, brushed the dust from the seat of his pants, and offered Talyn a helping hand. "Then we find their sponsors and do unto them. But after we finish cleaning up Mission Colony. How about finding Eva and telling her she no longer has a place where she can count seashells on the seashore?"

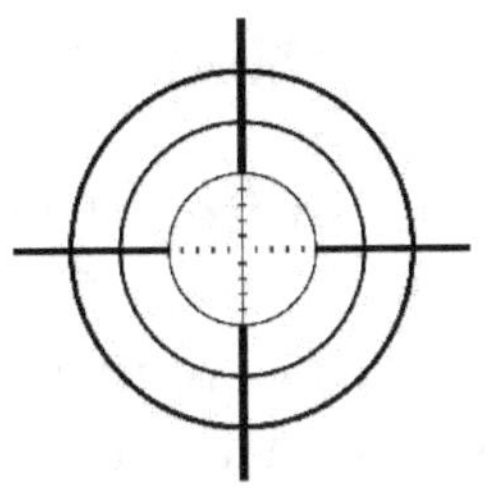

— FOURTEEN —

Decker and Talyn heard laughter in the hallway before the sitting room door opened. Women's laughter, times two. Eva Cortez had finally called it a night and come home. With someone, a complication they didn't need. The agents exchanged a glance. He grimaced, and she shrugged as if to say, collateral damage is often inevitable. Decker nevertheless indicated the needler with non-lethal loads in his hand, one of the two taken from Piet's guards, telling Talyn to let him shoot the other woman. She acquiesced with a nod.

The door swung inward and Eva Cortez, head turned to look behind her, waltzed in, a rosy glow on her cheeks. Upon noticing her unexpected visitors, she came to a sudden halt. Her face lost its color as her lips parted. The second woman stepped around her and also stopped, but with an air of curiosity rather than fear. Decker groaned in dismay as he pointed his gun at her.

"Good evening, Eva," Talyn's mouth twisted into a predatory smile. "And you must be Assistant Commissioner Kristy Bujold, the 24th Constabulary Regiment's commanding officer and Mission Colony's chief of police, as it were."

Talyn raised Piet's needler and gestured at a pair of imitation regency chairs in front of the sofa she and Decker occupied.

"Please sit. And take note, this weapon is carrying lethal neurotoxin loads. Yes, Commissioner, I know they're illegal," Talyn added when she saw Bujold's eyes harden. "Weapon and ammunition belonged to the late Piet Yorik, Eva's former head of security. I'm more partial to plasma weapons. When you shoot someone through the head or heart, they die instantly." When neither of them moved, Talyn snapped, "Sit! And close your mouth, Eva. The yokel look doesn't suit you."

"What — how..." Cortez obeyed almost instinctively.

"Who the hell are you?" Bujold demanded, a little slower to comply.

"We *were* Eva's friends and business partners until she decided to go it alone and ordered our murder."

"Sherri Zadeck and Corbin Peel," Cortez said in a weak voice. "But you're supposed to be dead. The beach house, Piet, everything is gone. A meteorite strike, they said."

Talyn jerked her thumb at Decker.

"Not a meteorite, honey. Blame the big guy. He found toys that go boom in your dungeon and couldn't resist playing with them. Unfortunately, one of those toys was Alek's present to your late husband. Sorry."

Bujold turned to Cortez. "Who are these clowns, Eva?"

"People who wanted to make her dreams of planetary domination come true, for a piece of the action," Decker said. "Except she took what we offered and tried to cut us out. And by us, I'm referring to the organization we represent, people who don't appreciate betrayal and never learned the meaning of the word forgiveness. Your presence here complicates things somewhat, Commissioner. It would have been best if you'd gone home instead of succumbing to the lure of Eva's bed."

"Why?"

"Because you're now utterly compromised. You were at the mansion when Gustav, a radical with known perversions died, and now you'll be found here, where Eva, the Freedom Collective's black widow, met her end. I'd say a team from the Rim Sector's Professional Compliance Bureau will speak with you shortly."

"How did you get in?" Bujold's voice rose in frustration, while Cortez, undone by finding them in her sitting room, seemed to have become mute.

"How? Simple. The butler did it." Decker smirked. "I kid you not. He let us in. As you well know, Commissioner, the human link is always the weakest in any security system. Employing only droids and AIs is safer, but I suppose the allure of a live human catering to her every need was irresistible. He's alive, by the way, but will suffer from a thunderous headache when he wakes up, and then from a second one when he finds himself minus a job and without references. As will you."

His right index finger twitched once, and a line of tiny red dots appeared on Bujold's neck. She barely had time to understand what just happened before slumping into the chair, out for several hours.

"Eva, Eva, Eva." Talyn shook her head. "You must be this star system's queen of bad life choices. All we wanted was the MHX-19. If you'd hadn't ordered Piet to kills us, we wouldn't be here, and you'd be making out with Kristy while dreaming of a glorious future."

"Why..." Her voice came out as a croak. "Why the MHX?"

"It belongs to the Armed Services. No one outside the Fleet, such as the DSA, should even know it exists, let alone pass it out to every scummy little wannabe revolutionary group along the Rim like your lot. In large amounts that stuff is a weapon of mass destruction. A shame you didn't see what a single kilo did to Blanca's Folly."

"If you're not DSA, who are you?" Cortez whispered as fear drove out every other emotion.

"We're Fleet operatives, tasked with eliminating terrorists such as the Mission Colony Freedom Collective before it can cause untold civilian deaths."

"Fleet?" She seemed unable to process the information.

"Big Boy here is a major in the Marine Corps, and I'm a Navy commander. Between us, we've killed more people than you could ever imagine, each more than deserving of his or her fate."

"What do you want from me?"

"Your life. My partner should have taken a second shot to kill you right after he blew Gustav's head away. But we didn't know you were more than just a pretty adornment on a dangerous demagogue's arm."

A faint spark of defiance hardened her heretofore-slack face.

"Even if I die, the movement will continue."

"Perhaps, but as an ineffectual talking shop. Your followers are, in the aggregate, useless, like most radicals and salon revolutionaries. And if one of them shows signs of becoming the next rabble-rouser with a plan, like Gustav or you, we'll be back. Any last words?"

"Fuck you."

"I doubt that will make the latest Oxford book of famous quotes. But then, you are a grubby little bitch with a limited intellect." Talyn raised her gun and fired a volley of lethal darts into Eva Cortez' face. She gasped, twitched, and then slumped over.

Decker stood and reached out to touch her throat. After a moment, he said, "Dead. I believe that concludes our business on Mission Colony."

"Just one more thing." Talyn walked over to Assistant Commissioner Kristy Bujold and wiped Piet's needler on her clothes. Then, she wrapped Bujold's hand around the butt and placed her index finger on the trigger, before letting the weapon go so that it fell to the floor naturally.

"Nasty." Decker made a face at his partner. "Even though forensics will figure out right away Bujold didn't kill her lover, it'll make sure the PCB conducts an internal affairs investigation without you tipping it off."

"I thought we might circumvent the lag time between here and Cimmeria and encourage her executive officer to think about the rules governing the suspension of a commanding officer for possible involvement in a murder. From there, it's a much smaller step to finding out Bujold was either taking bribes or being blackmailed into supporting Kerlin and Cortez.

"Or sleeping with a known political foe of the Commonwealth's colonial administration, which someone might interpret as being contrary to her oath."

"That as well. How long before Bujold wakes up?"

"Four hours max. If you want to call it in and make sure the responding constables find this scene as is, I suggest we raise the alarm as soon as we're a few blocks away, then dump the burner."

"Don't forget to take Eva's ID. Waste not, want not."

They left the townhouse's front door open just a crack, to allow first responders easy access and walked back toward the downtown core at an unhurried pace. Once within sight of Founder's Plaza, Talyn called the police emergency node and told the dispatcher a story about one dead and one unconscious victim at twelve-eighty Boll Avenue, the unconscious victim bearing an eerie resemblance to Assistant Commissioner Kristy Bujold. Knowing dispatch would ping Bujold's communicator and find it at that precise address, Talyn shut off the burner, pulled out the power pack, and disposed of both in separate garbage containers.

Thirty minutes later, a bus left them near Salter Street and Tenth Avenue. From there, it was a comfortable walk to the safe house and one last night on Mission before boarding the tramp freighter *Thebes*, due to land at daybreak, inbound from Merseaux and lifting off six hours later for Cimmeria.

Their coded subspace message to Fleet HQ, attention Commodore Konstantin Ulrich, was already on its way across interstellar space via the system's civilian relay. Though the code was unbreakable, it pointed the finger at Naval Intelligence agents operating on Mission Colony, but since they would leave in the morning, it didn't matter. The Freedom Collective was defanged, hopefully harmless for a generation if not forever, and unable to commit acts of political violence.

The next morning, Ned Sarkin and Lena Taryen, who bore only a superficial resemblance to Corbin Peel and Sherri Zadeck, presented themselves at the security gate leading to *Thebes'* landing bay and bought passage to Cimmeria from the bored purser's mate on duty. They offered the sort of untraceable cred chips favored by starship captains skirting the outer edges of both the Commonwealth and the law and were allowed to board with no questions asked.

A few hours later, flat on their backs in the bunks of their private, albeit spartan cabin, they left Mission Colony. But it was without knowing what transpired from the previous night's anonymous call to the Constabulary concerning Eva Cortez and Kristy Bujold's misadventure at the hands of a person or persons unknown.

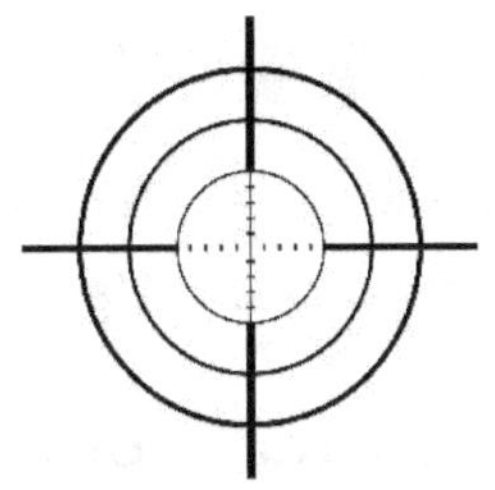

— FIFTEEN —

Decker's eyes snapped open, his mind shifting from the soft, ethereal comfort of sleep to a state of full alertness in a fraction of a second. Something had roused him. A change. He listened carefully, lying on his bunk in the darkened cabin aboard the tramp freighter *Thebes*. They were six days out of Mission Colony after a trouble-free escape and a boring trip.

He immediately sensed that Talyn, occupying the bunk above him, was also awake. After years working as a close team, closer than most, he recognized the change in her breathing pattern.

"What is it?" She asked

He checked his internal clock.

"We should be past the heliopause and FTL on the last leg to Cimmeria by now, but we're still running sublight."

Talyn didn't ask how her partner knew. Most people slept through the brief transition nausea that gripped humans when a starship jumped to hyperspace or dropped out of it, but not Zack. Besides, she knew by now that his hearing quickly became attuned to the sounds of any ship in which he traveled, and every one of them sang a different song when it was moving faster than light.

A soft, almost inaudible thump reached their ears.

"That's the main port side airlock opening," he said. "Something latched on to us. It's what woke me. We're being boarded."

He didn't need to add that someone boarding at the edge of interstellar space, during the ship's night, when all passengers were in their cabins, meant one thing only. Decker sat up and donned his boots before retrieving his Shrehari blaster from the narrow shelf above his head.

They'd left the captured needlers on Mission, hidden in the safe house's basement armory. The one that once belonged to Piet Yorik was now a murder weapon and could be traced. Lethal neurotoxin traces were notoriously difficult to eradicate entirely from a needler's magazine, chamber, and barrel.

He shrugged on his shoulder holster, checked the blaster, and shoved it into place under his left arm. Then, he quickly strapped the Pathfinder dagger to his left forearm, donned his leather jacket, and stood.

A lithe shadow dropped from the top bunk with no more noise than a falling leaf and asked, "Ready?"

"Ready. Do you think this is for us?"

"Possible, but doubtful. No one back home knows we're traveling on this reject from the starship graveyard; the division's custodian didn't issue our current cover identities, and the only one on Mission still alive who knows about us is Kristy Bujold. And she thinks we're the Zadeck and Peel comedy duo, not a pair of unemployed mercenaries called Sarkin and Taryen."

The Marine grunted. "Nothing's foolproof. We become more paranoid, and our enemies merely get more inventive."

"If someone made us, it didn't come from an as-yet-undiscovered traitor in the division. I trust the commodore's instincts. If he's convinced we smoked out every last Black Sword and *Sécurité Spéciale* mole, then we did. Maybe it isn't a pirate raid."

"You're thinking a personnel or cargo transfer someone doesn't want the authorities to notice? Possible, I suppose. But Cimmeria isn't exactly an example of tight import or immigration controls, so why bother?"

Decker tried the door, and when he found it locked, presumably by an override from the ship's bridge, he dug a multi-tool from his jacket's inner pocket and quickly pried open the controls. Disabling the automatic mechanism took only a few seconds, allowing him to open the door just wide enough to stick his head out.

"Clear," he whispered in a voice so low only Talyn could hear.

He listened again, and this time heard cautious footsteps coming from the metallic spiral staircase a dozen meters to the left of their cabin. Crewmembers or passengers wouldn't take such care to muffle their sounds. The muzzle of a scattergun, level with Decker's eyes, poked out of the shaft and he pulled his head back into the cabin. If the being at the gun's other end stepped off the landing and onto this deck, he, she, or it might spot the partially open door. But closing it now would definitely attract the wrong kind of attention.

Decker made the hand signal for 'armed hostile,' followed by the one for 'wait.' He felt her briefly touch his hand in acknowledgment. The soft footsteps sounded closer now, indicating the intruder was in the passageway outside their cabin and headed toward them.

Ignore or strike? They might be undercover intelligence operatives, but Decker remained a Marine, a Pathfinder, one of the elite with combat skills honed fighting pirates, corsairs and marauders along the Commonwealth frontier. The being with the scattergun out there was his natural enemy: scum preying on innocent, defenseless travelers.

He sensed the intruder closing in on their end of the corridor. More muffled sounds came from the stairwell. Scattergun's winger? Decker realized he and Talyn had stopped breathing.

The nearest footsteps stopped a few doors short of their cabin. Soon after, the second set, which had also stepped off the metallic staircase and onto this deck, came to a halt as well. Talyn pressed something in Decker's hand. A small sensor.

He closed his fist around it, pulled a thin, flexible, translucent wire from a recess at its top with his other hand. Then, he carefully fed the tip of the cable, a probe, around the doorjamb while looking at the sensor's small screen.

Two humans, wearing light armor and full-face helmets over black, mercenary-style battledress, both armed with scatterguns, stood in front of a cabin three doors down and across the corridor. Decker couldn't see their faces, but by their shape, they were male, a little shorter than he was, and less bulky.

One of them held a small device in his hand. When he flicked his wrist to show the other intruder something on its screen, the man briefly exposed his skin, but it was enough for Decker to spot a telltale tattoo.

He reached back to grasp Talyn's hand and tapped out 'Howlers.' It was one of the many nicknames given to members of a criminal organization notable for their ability to avoid incarceration — the much feared and even more reviled Confederacy of the Howling Stars. Involved in almost every illegal activity known, so long as it was profitable, Howlers also carried out wet work and other unsavory activities under contract to Naval Intelligence's enemies.

Piracy, however, had been off limits ever since a group of disaffected veterans of the Shrehari War started the

Confederacy seventy years earlier, and for an exceedingly simple reason. The penalties for piracy, if caught red-handed, were severe and immediate, thanks to an intolerant Navy acting as judge, jury, and executioner.

Confederacy chieftains were, in their own way, business people who weighed risks against rewards. For example, it was easier and considerably safer to suborn spaceport stevedores or squeeze starship captains for protection money than steal cargo or take hostages for ransom in deep space.

Two armed and masked goons preparing to invade a passenger cabin meant this was an abduction for hire. Decker searched his memory for the faces of that cabin's passengers. Two women. One had kept her appearance carefully hidden the few times she'd left their quarters, though judging by her hands, she was several years younger than Talyn.

The other, also in her late forties, perhaps even early fifties, seemed to be a bodyguard of sorts or a duenna. Her eyes held that special watchfulness though she didn't move like a predator. Whenever they entered the passengers' saloon, the pair remained aloof, speaking with no one, taking their meals with boot camp speed and then vanishing again.

Decker tapped out *abduction* on Talyn's hand, followed by *do we stop it?*

The sound of a cabin door being forced open lent urgency to his question.

Your call, Talyn tapped back. She nudged him with the barrel of her blaster, smaller than Decker's Shrehari hand artillery but no less deadly in the hands of a professional assassin. It was her signal authorizing Decker to shoot and kill as necessary.

He stowed the sensor and drew his gun before whispering, "Near," indicating he would take the closest target while relying on her to drop the other, then, "Go!"

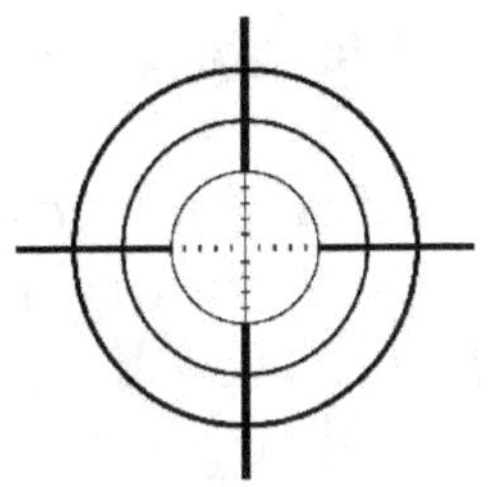

— SIXTEEN —

Talyn yanked the door wide open, and Decker stepped out into the corridor, blaster held up at eye level, barrel settling on the first Howler's unarmored neck. Talyn, quick as a flash, was out behind him, aiming at the second would-be abductor.

"Freeze or die, assholes," Decker snarled, his face contorted into a mask of rage that promised unrestrained violence.

Two helmeted heads turned to the right, eyes behind transparent visors widening in surprise. Then, almost simultaneously, the cover man's gun barrel came up just as the door kicker tilted his head to one side in the natural and unconscious motion of someone with a helmet radio opening a link.

As if connected by telepathy, both operatives fired at once, the sneeze of Talyn's smaller blaster drowned out by the basso cough of Decker's alien gun. Neither of the intruders stood a chance. Not against a Marine who qualified as an expert marksman on every small arm in the Fleets' inventory, and then some. Even less against one of Naval Intelligence's designated assassins with more kills to her credit than she cared to remember.

Each of the Howlers took a single, deadly hit in the narrow strip between the top of the breastplate and the bottom of the helmet chin guard, where a battledress tunic collar was the only protection. Good enough against scattergun pellets, needler darts, chemically propelled bullets or bladed weapons, but not sufficient to stop a blaster's super-heated round.

The Confederacy of the Howling Stars enforcers died almost at once, their windpipes and spines severed. They crumpled to the deck one after the other with a dull thump. Decker, hoping neither had time to sound the alarm but keeping his ears alert for any fresh footsteps coming up the metal staircase, knelt beside the door kicker's body.

He took the man's scattergun and searched him while Talyn did the same with the other. While his hands dug into pockets, the Marine's gaze turned to the partially open cabin door his downed target was forcing moments before he died. Beyond it, a pair of hard eyes watched him from the shadows — the presumed bodyguard or duenna. His assumption was proved right moments later when he saw the shape of a wicked needler in her hand.

He raised his chin at her. "You — try to lock that door again. Or even better, take your companion and hide in our cabin. These clowns aren't alone, and their buddies will come looking to see what's taking so long. They know where you're berthed, and that means you need to move."

The woman seemed to hesitate, then her face and the needler disappeared, though Decker heard urgent whispers coming through the narrow opening. He turned to Talyn, now standing with the cover man's scattergun slung over one shoulder and his helmet hanging from her left hand. She raised it to waist level.

"These brain buckets aren't keyed to their previous owners. If your plan is to repel the rest of the Howler boarding party, take his. It might fool them for that one second we need to fire the first shot."

The duenna stuck her head through the door and studied both agents for a few seconds.

"Who are you?" Her voice sounded like it came from the bottom of a stone crusher and her accent from the deepest corners of the frontier.

"Concerned citizens with an allergy to pirates, Sera," Talyn replied.

"Pirates?" Her eyes dropped to the door kicker, now lying on the floor helmetless. "That tattoo running up his neck makes him a Jackal, and they don't do piracy."

"No fan of the Confederacy, then?" Decker hefted the helmet and grinned at her.

She looked up at the Marine again with a suspicious expression.

"Who are you, really? Concerned citizens usually can't manage throat shots at three meters on the first try."

"When we're not concerned citizens, she and I are soldiers of fortune," the Marine replied. "It's your luck we're light sleepers and happen to bunk across the hall from you. Now if you'll excuse us, I'd like to carve a few more notches in my blaster's grip. My partner here, who hates late night shenanigans, needs to unleash her bad mood on someone and I'd rather it wasn't me. Are you taking our cabin?"

The woman nodded once. "We probably should. Temporarily."

"Good. I had to fiddle with the lock, but I'm sure you can fix it and make yourself secure. If you need a drink, there's a bottle of high octane, low-quality stuff pretending to be whiskey on the sideboard. Help yourself and offer your client a dram."

"What makes you think she's my client?"

Decker tapped the side of his oft-broken nose with an extended index finger and grinned.

"Call it a hunch. When we return, the recognition signal is vee for victory. You know it?"

"Three quick knocks, a pause, one knock."

He gave her thumbs up, then pulled the helmet on.

"Time to rumble."

Door kicker's brain bucket was a basic model, available at any surplus store in the sovereign star systems. Comms, heads-up display with basic telemetry and limited night vision, radio and protection against direct hits from anything smaller than a twenty millimeter round. Though without an armored neckpiece as support, whiplash from the impact of solid projectiles might be enough to kill the wearer. Or at least give him a killer migraine. If Decker had his druthers, he wouldn't bother with the helmet, but it was camouflage, and an easy way to eavesdrop on enemy communications.

"Main airlock?" Talyn gestured toward the spiral staircase.

"You mean take their shuttle and wait in ambush for the rest?" When she nodded, he smirked. "I'm gratified to see my lovely apprentice has mastered the fine art of fucking with enemy boarding parties."

"What can I say? You're rubbing off on me, honey." She blew him a kiss through the open helmet visor

"In more ways than one. But since I'm your plasma catcher along with everything else, decent or otherwise, please step aside and let me lead the way." He glanced back at the bodyguard, now staring at them with an expression bordering on disbelief and winked. "We're actually nuttier than we sound, but that always seems to work in our favor."

A faint, high-pitched guffaw reached his ears from somewhere behind the bodyguard, but he ignored it in favor of holstering his blaster to brandish the late door kicker's scattergun.

"Once more unto the breach, dear friends, once more."

"Go," Talyn growled, "before I shout *Cry God for Harry, England and Saint George.*" She shook her head in despair. "Now he's got me doing it too."

But Decker, as light on his feet as a professional dancer, was already in the stairwell, making no more noise on the metallic treads than one of the ship's cats, those four-legged, merciless killers Talyn found endlessly fascinating. Especially after witnessing the final moments of a successful vermin hunt. With a shrug, she followed him, her own footsteps just as quiet and assured.

Nothing came through their helmet radios, not even the faintest crackle, and Decker mentally congratulated the soon to be late Howlers on their communications discipline. Few non-Fleet boarding parties could work without incessant chatter, most of which was unnecessary and only a result of nerves because when ordinary humans felt anxious, they generally flapped their lips. When Marines felt uneasy, they stayed quiet, found a target, and applied the rules of engagement.

Decker stopped on the landing one deck beneath the passenger accommodations. The main port side airlock was on this level and approximately ten meters aft of the stairwell, just before the shielded bulkhead separating *Thebes'* engineering section from the rest of the ship. Crew quarters and the bridge were in the other direction, toward the bow, separated from this section by airtight doors, while the stairs ended on a level further down, at an airlock leading to the cargo hold.

He fed the translucent sensor probe around the bulkhead and was gratified see four gangsters, two forward and two aft, keeping the kidnapper's withdrawal route clear. But their posture and the way they held their weapons seemed relaxed enough to suggest they expected no opposition. An inside job, then. Or someone persuaded *Thebes*' captain ahead of time to cooperate.

Talyn touched the back of his hand with her fingertips. *How many?*

Decker flipped his hand around so he could tap out a reply. *Four. Two on the left near the airlock, two on the right. They're not expecting trouble. I take left, you take right. Shoot to kill. When they drop, we rush the airlock and take their shuttle.*

She nodded once, pushed the slung scattergun out of the way and drew her blaster again, imitated by Decker. The latter held up three fingers, then slowly folded them one by one. When the last vanished into his massive fist, the two operatives stepped out of the stairwell, back to back and raised their weapons.

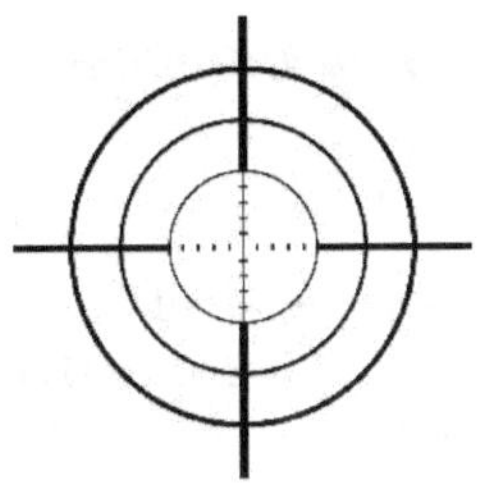

— SEVENTEEN —

The four Confederacy enforcers, alerted by movement coming from the stairwell and expecting their comrades, were slow to react, even though Talyn was visibly smaller than the gorilla whose helmet she wore. They turned toward Decker and his partner with expectant looks behind open visors. Those expressions quickly turned to disbelief when they noticed themselves staring into the barrels of two wicked-looking blasters, one of which could pass for a hand cannon.

Decker's first shot obliterated a goon's nose and flash-fried his brain. He collapsed like a deflated balloon. The next one, snapped off with a slightly less steady aim, landed partially on the side of the second Howler's helmet, spattering droplets of molten composite and plasma on his face. He fell to his knees, flailing about in agony and Decker's third shot missed completely, digging a divot in the far bulkhead. The fourth shot, taken with more deliberation, put the screaming man out of his misery.

Meanwhile, Talyn dispatched the pair by the forward doors with two well-placed rounds each, double-tap style, confirming her status as one of Naval Intelligence's deadliest shots. They dropped to the deck with a dull twin thump.

"Clear," she said in a low voice, pitched for Decker's ears only.

"Clear," he replied in the same tone as he prepared to launch himself through the port side airlock's inner door. At that moment, the radio came to life, and a male voice demanded someone give him a situation report.

The Marine plunged through the opening, hunched as low as possible, his blaster held out before him, ready to fire, but the airlock itself was empty. The outer door, however, gave onto the inside of a small craft, a sublight shuttle mated to the freighter's side. It framed the anxious face of a man holding the same type of scattergun as the rest.

Decker checked his step, fired once at the Howler, then without waiting to see the result, crashed into him with his shoulder, throwing the body across the shuttle's passenger compartment. Fighting to regain his balance, he stumbled aboard, turned his head left, then right, to orient himself and find the cockpit. If his latest kill wasn't the pilot, there was an eighth gangster still alive and dangerous.

A hard body slammed into Decker from just outside his field of vision, and he careened into the opposite bulkhead, dropping his blaster under the force of the impact. He turned to face his opponent in time to see a knife flash between them.

With no time to roll out of the way, he raised his left arm to block the Howler's stroke while reaching out to grab his wrist with the right hand. The blade bounced off his synthetic leather jacket's sleeve, but the force of forearm meeting forearm sent a shudder up to his shoulder. Decker's fingers wrapped around the offending hand as the man, using his greater leverage forced his knife's tip every closer to the Marine's left eye.

Then, a blaster coughed. The goon's muscles twitched once before turning to jelly, and his body draped itself over Decker. Grimacing at the stench of burned flesh, he pushed the remains off and climbed to his feet.

"You took your sweet time."

Talyn shoved her gun back into its shoulder holster and made a face at him.

"If that's the thanks I get for saving your life, you can find a new partner, darling."

"I was handling the situation."

"Looked like you were close to losing an eye, if not more."

Decker looked at the dead Howler. Talyn's shot had neatly severed his spine just below the shoulder blades before frying his heart.

"He wasn't exactly small, was he? Stupid gangster, though. If he and his buddy over there," Decker pointed at the crumpled form in the far corner, "bothered to wear the same armor and helmets as their colleagues, this might not be over yet."

"Or if this last one hadn't been afraid to damage the inside of his shuttle with gunfire instead of pulling a knife, you and I might not be talking right now."

Decker gave his partner a rueful shrug.

"True. I should have figured there would be at least one switched-on goon in the bunch. I just didn't think it would be the shuttle pilot."

"When you're running an unindicted criminal organization, you make sure the switched-on foot soldiers are in charge of the expensive gear, Big Boy. What's our next move?"

"Fly this junk heap back to its mothership, which can't be more than a hundred klicks away, and turn the tables on them?"

"Fun as that sounds, we risk *Thebes*' captain taking fright and buggering off without us. Then, if the Howlers try again before entering Cimmeria orbit, unlikely as that might sound, we won't be there to help your damsel in distress. And I want to know who she is, why she's traveling incognito with a bodyguard who seems able to give a good account of herself, and most importantly why the Confederacy of the Howling Stars is after her."

"You think there's a national security angle to this?"

Talyn snorted.

"We're in the Rim Sector. Everything has a national security angle out here. Besides, Howlers trying to pull a deep space kidnapping is a federal case, and in the absence of a duly sworn Constabulary officer, it's one for the Navy. I'm a Navy officer, and you're my Marine Corps muscle."

"This has to be more than just you satisfying your curiosity, Hera. What gives?"

"Call it instinct. Something smells distinctly rancid to my finely honed paranoia. It may be nothing, but we can't take that chance, and our orders give us plenty of latitude."

"You're the boss, boss. But let's not forget why we're headed for the Rim Sector's sparkling capital. I doubt this incident is connected to the lovely folks we terminated on Mission or their asshole buddies on Cimmeria who will join them in terrorist hell. How about we drag the bodies into this garbage scow, cast it off and send it home on automatic with a pink bow and a love note?"

"*You* drag the bodies. *I* will figure out how this crate's controls work. It's called division of labor based on individual strengths."

"Meaning I'm your beast of burden once again." Decker snapped off a mock salute. "I hear and obey, oh Angel of Death."

Talyn gave him the rigid digit before vanishing into the shuttle's cockpit.

******

"Funny how the ship's crew stayed really quiet throughout this," Decker said. He and Talyn stood by the airlock's porthole and watched the Howler shuttle move away from *Thebes* toward its unseen mothership. "They must have watched via the surveillance cameras."

"Or someone ordered them to shut the cameras off on pain of eternal torment until after the abduction. You can't testify to something you didn't see, let alone record."

"But if they watched, I'd say the captain won't be our number one fan right now. Screwing up a Howler operation makes us the ultimate persona non grata aboard."

Talyn's shoulders twitched in a dismissive shrug.

"So we take control of this garbage scow. You and I can stay awake until we dock at Valerys Station. But it won't come to that. Either no one saw a damn thing, or if they did, this incident never happened."

Decker glanced up at the deckhead and said, "I know you little buggers are watching, so here's a hint. Go FTL on that final leg to Cimmeria's hyperlimit and everyone will be happier. Otherwise, I might pay your bridge a little visit..."

When neither of them felt the characteristic nausea caused by a starship shifting between the normal universe and hyperspace, the Marine made a face.

"Looks like you're right once again."

"You should be used to that. How about we talk to the damsel in distress and her duenna? And don't tell me you aren't impatient at seeing that bodyguard again. She must have caught your eye somehow because I don't recall your inviting folks to sample the duty-free rotgut all that often."

"Do I see the old green-eyed monster raising its head?" He leered at his partner.

"You might recall that I'm not capable of feeling normal emotions, jealousy included. And I'll grant you the duenna has a little *je ne sais quoi.* We dark angels usually do."

Decker laughed.

"Okay. Whatever. Let's go check in on our protégées. By the way, did you really rig the shuttle's fuel cells to blow the moment its airlock is opened?"

"Of course. I need my bit of entertainment as well. Let's hope they bring it into their shuttle hangar first. That ought to put the entire ship out of action."

"Nice." He wrapped his arm around her shoulders and squeezed. "The apprentice is truly surpassing the master. And it serves the bastards right." Decker released Talyn and nodded toward the corridor. "Shall we?"

Once out of the airlock, he slammed the inner door shut and spun its emergency locking wheel until it could move no more. "There. Next time they try, they'll need to cut their way in."

"Unless insiders leave the barn doors open again."

"Not after we invite Captain Whatshisname to our quarters for a friendly chat."

"Kreipe."

"Ah, yes. Hanno Kreipe. That conversation should be interesting."

"Or we make like nothing's happened, find out what's going on, and keep an eye on our two friends until we dock at Valerys. Discretion being an operative's best quality, in spite of the fireworks on Mission Colony."

"Spoilsport."

They wound their way up the spiral staircase with as little noise as before. The only evidence of the drama on the passenger deck less than ten minutes earlier were two faint, rust-colored stains where the corpses lay before Decker hauled them to their shuttle.

Everything seemed as it should in the middle of the night watch. Doors were shut, even that of the women's cabin. Decker approached theirs and rapped his knuckles on the panel three times in rapid succession followed by a pause and then a single knock. A crack appeared between the door and its jamb, and a gimlet eye stared out at them.

"We sent the boarding party home to mother," Decker said. "There were eight of them. No survivors."

Astonishment briefly flashed in the bodyguard's single visible eye.

"It was thirsty work," the Marine continued. "My partner and I need a pull on that bottle of rotgut. I hope you left us some. Then, we'll discuss why we had to repel boarders instead of getting our full night's sleep."

The woman stepped back and allowed the cabin door to open fully. Tall and wiry, she wore a dark, loose, single piece garment liberally festooned with pockets. Short brown hair streaked with gray topped a seamed, narrow hatchet face dominated by hard dark eyes that missed nothing.

Now that he saw the bodyguard with fresh eyes, especially with the way she held her needler though its barrel pointed downward, Decker knew she was someone like Talyn or him.

Her charge, on the other hand, seemed to be the odd one out. The woman sat on Decker's bunk, wrapped in a dark robe, her straw-colored hair covered by a silk scarf that framed a pale, forty-something face dominated by a strong chin and a hawk nose. Pale blue eyes beneath eyebrows so light they appeared silvery in the cabin's harsh illumination studied Decker with equal measures of curiosity and caution.

A pang of anguish twisted his guts when he met her gaze as memories long suppressed bubbled back to the surface. Whoever she was, the woman before him bore an eerie resemblance to Avril Ducote, his long-dead partner, gutshot by pirates hired to abduct and sell him into slavery as revenge for Walker Amali's death.

Talyn pulled the door shut, then leaned against it, arms crossed, while Decker took a healthy pull from the bottle of amber liquid sitting on a sideboard to help shake off the disturbing sensation he faced Avril's fraternal twin. Yet in their time together, she had never mentioned any female siblings. He wiped his lips with the back of his hand and handed the bottle to his partner.

"Throwing out the trash always leaves a bad taste in my mouth, especially when I don't know why we did it. Would either of you care to comment?"

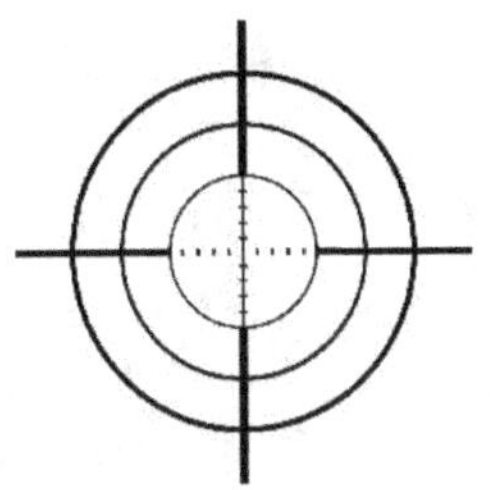

— EIGHTEEN —

When neither answered right away, Decker said, "Allow me to start with the introductions. I'm Ned Sarkin, and she's Lena Taryen. We're Fleet veterans turned hired guns."

Something in the deadly duenna's eyes told him she put as much credence in the veracity of their names as in a Howler's honesty.

"What's the point with using names?" She asked. "Surely you don't expect me to tell you who we really are? Not after this? For all I know, you might work for the opposition too. Or for someone else who'd like to cause us harm."

"Fair enough. You realize Captain Kreipe was in on it, right? He was either bought off or threatened into letting goons board and take you between FTL jumps. That means this isn't over. And very shortly, the rest of the gang will be aware it failed when they recover their shuttle and it blows up in their faces."

The woman's right eyebrow crept up. "You booby-trapped their shuttle?"

Decker jerked a thumb at Talyn.

"She did while I put the Howler corpses on board. It's headed back to the mothership under the control of its AI, which my partner reprogrammed. If Kreipe doesn't jump us out of here before the shuttle makes it home, the bastards might try again, and if that happens, we won't enjoy the element of surprise. So maybe we should get to know each other a little better, because whether or not you like it, Lena and I stuck our noses in your business, and you're damned lucky we did. As my partner keeps telling me, I'm cursed with this knight in shining armor complex, and that's now been placed at your service."

After a long silence, during which the duenna's eyes went back and forth between Decker and Talyn, she inclined her head.

"Very well. I will override my suspicious mind and trust my instincts, which are telling me you're one of the good guys, *Ned Sarkin*." Her tone left no doubt she didn't believe it was Decker's real name for one second. She gave Talyn a hard glance. "On the other hand, I can't read you, *Lena Taryen*. But that also tells me something. I'm just not sure what." Another pause. "The name's Gudrun Mariano. I'm a minder, as you've no doubt guessed by now. Strictly freelance."

"And your client?" Talyn asked.

Mariano's chuckle, though grim, wasn't completely devoid of humor.

"Now that would be telling. Even a freelancer is bound by the Personal Security Services Guild rules, and that means only the client may reveal his or her identity, not the minder. And my advice to her before you came back was don't. For our purposes, you may call her Maggie."

"Okay." Decker drawled out the word as he half sat on the sideboard. "Welcome to our cabin, Gudrun and Maggie. Now that we're a happy bunch of fresh acquaintances here, would you mind telling us why the Confederacy of the Howling Stars was so keen on offering you a ride? I presume they were after Maggie and not her heavily armed governess."

"As a matter of fact, I do mind," Mariano replied. "Telling you could unmask my client's identity."

"The goons already know her identity," Decker pointed out in a reasonable tone, "and your itinerary. Otherwise, they wouldn't have been able to set up the abduction attempt. Someone told them your cabin number and bought off the captain. A pirate raid at the edge of interstellar space, near a frontier star system, or as frontier as this part of the Rim gets nowadays, is a perfect way to make someone disappear."

Mariano studied the Marine with renewed interest.

"Hired guns? Why is a smart, deadly merc like you not under permanent contract with one of the better PMCs?"

"Wanderlust and a deep distrust of faceless corporations. What happens when we reach Cimmeria? I doubt the Howlers will try again while we're on final approach after the in-system jump, not within sight of Valerys Station, meaning the next chance at grabbing your client will be after *Thebes* docks."

"Arrangements have been made for us there," she replied in a confident tone. "You need not concern yourselves with our fate."

"What if those arrangements are as deeply compromised as your journey aboard *Thebes*? Perhaps there's a mole in the outfit that hired you to mind Maggie."

"Why do you care about the fate of two strangers?"

"Lena and I dropped eight Howlers for your sake. Not that ridding the galaxy of those amoral assholes wasn't pleasant in and of itself, but it means we have a certain interest in ensuring our efforts weren't in vain. A righteous kill is a terrible thing to waste."

"Let it be, Ned," Talyn said. "Sera Mariano is well within her rights to keep Maggie's identity and everything else about her contract confidential. If she feels sure the rest of their journey will be without incidents, who are we to pry?"

Decker exhaled noisily.

"Okay. Never mind my caring nature. Would you like to switch cabins for the rest of the trip?"

Before Mariano could answer, a soft chime wafted through the air, followed by the soothing female voice of the ship's AI.

"Please prepare for the transition to hyperspace. We will jump in one minute."

"I guess the Howlers won't be trying again out here. We'll return to our quarters after the transition, but thank you for the offer."

"Feel free to change your mind and impose on us at any time before we part ways on Valerys, Sera Mariano."

The minder inclined her head by way of acknowledgment. Three soft chimes sounded again, sending her to sit beside Maggie while Decker sat more firmly on the sideboard and Talyn braced herself in the doorframe. Nausea came and left with its usual abruptness.

"I guess we'll never find out if your booby-trapped shuttle did a number on the Confederacy ship," Decker remarked as he stood. "Shame. I'd have liked to witness that."

Mariano and her client also climbed to their feet. "Our thanks for everything you've done," the former said.

Moments later, Decker and Talyn were alone in their cabin once more. The Marine took another swig of whiskey.

"You know who Maggie the Mysterious reminds me of, right?"

"I noticed the pained expression in your eyes. The resemblance to Avril Ducote is remarkable, but it's not her. Avril died long ago."

"Sure." Decker took another sip. "But seeing Maggie's face still drove a knife through my gut. Metaphorically speaking."

"Drinking more of that will do just as thorough a job on your stomach." She took the bottle from his hand and placed it on the table. "However, I might know Maggie's real identity."

"That quasi-eidetic memory of yours again?"

"Yes and no. Along with looking like Avril's long-lost kid sister, she also bears a family resemblance to a man who's rather infamous in certain circles."

"Her father's a mobster?"

"It depends on your point of view, I suppose. But if I'm right, it raises a long list of questions and gives precious few answers."

"Turf war between the Confederacy and another gang for supremacy in the Rim Sector, perhaps?"

Talyn shook her head.

"No. Not unless the Deep Space Foundation suddenly decided to engage in retail-level criminality instead of making its profits through influence peddling."

"Louis Sorne's pretend not-for-profit? Didn't it stop operating when Sorne was indicted, thanks to your Constabulary friend?"

"Sadly, no. The firewall between Sorne's business interests and the Foundation allowed it to escape scrutiny, in part thanks to a sympathetic judge who was either overly naïve or venal. I should imagine the Constabulary is still trying to find an opening, but if Sorne's friends in the Senate are running interference, it'll take a brave Chief Constable to choose that hill for a potentially career-ending death match."

"So who is she?"

"Maggie? How about Magda Annear, daughter of the late Ryker Lubben, a wealthy dilettante with more ambition than ability, and Nerys Annear, Cimmeria's senior Commonwealth senator?   Lubben died a few years ago in what the Cimmerian Gendarmerie ruled an accident though not everyone agreed at the time. However, before his untimely passing, Lubben, among other activities of note, chaired the Deep Space Foundation's board of directors at the behest of his lifelong pal, Antoine Hakkam, the Foundation's president and chief executive officer.   It gets better. Hakkam is also Magda's godfather."

"Wait a minute.   I thought Nerys Annear was one of the good politicians.   How did she fall in bed with the best friend of a skunk such as Hakkam?"

"No idea, but they split up years ago, well before she was elected to public office."

"Why would the daughter of such a powerful mother be traveling incognito? Are you sure it could be her?"

Talyn nodded.

"The family resemblance is so strong I wonder why they didn't give Maggie a new face to go with the cover identity, and not just because of Nerys Annear. Hakkam must be collecting new enemies on a regular basis nowadays, considering he runs Sorne's empire while the old man is in custody.   Mind you, Sorne is probably still issuing orders from his prison cell."

Decker's snort was loud enough to wake the dead three decks below.

"Cell?   Try a comfort suite.   Rich fucks like Sorne receive the deluxe treatment in an idyllic place where they can meditate on the mistakes that brought them there. And plan on how they'll screw everyone over the next time. Magda Annear, huh?"

"That's what I don't understand."   Talyn reached for the whiskey and took a modest sip.   "The Confederacy rarely engages in kidnapping on its own account, which means someone hired them for this job. Perhaps people who want something from Antoine Hakkam and the

Foundation, or from Senator Annear. Or the Annear family conglomerate."

"Isn't that a rather long list?" Decker dropped into the lower bunk and kicked off his boots. "Considering how much those Deep Space bastards have been interfering in planetary politics. Didn't we decide they were among the possible offworld instigators behind the Scandia putsch attempt?" The Marine's face suddenly lit up with understanding. "Oh."

A smile softened Talyn's thoughtful expression.

"Oh, indeed, darling. Sorne is desperate for a seat at the Coalition's grown-up table, and the Foundation is his tool to ingratiate himself with the top leadership. Since Senator Annear is a firm supporter of sovereign star system rights, she's one of the Coalition's main political enemies in the legislature."

"Then who hired the *Sécurité Spéciale*'s occasional wetwork specialists to kidnap Maggie? Did the SecGen's thugs and the Coalition part ways, or did they stop using the Howlers as subcontractors?"

"Not that we know." She sat beside him. "Did you consider it could have been a false flag operation, an abduction team made to appear like Howlers, in case someone saw them?"

"That's called living dangerously if ever the Confederacy finds out." He saw the gleam in her eyes and sighed with resignation. "Let me guess. You've become determined to find out what this Maggie business is about. Don't forget our main job, find the rest of the MHX, and put every last terrorist wannabe out of business before civilians die in job lots."

"I'm not forgetting. My instinct tells me there could be a link. We already figure the Coalition is in some ways connected to if not actively backing the Democratic Stars Alliance."

"Or is the DSA's creator."

She nodded.

"Sure. And if Maggie is Magda Annear, then she's connected to both the Deep Space Foundation, which we believe supports the Coalition's goals and Senator Annear who opposes them. Does she favor one over the other, or is she opposed to either?"

"If she's in her mother's corner, an abduction attempt by Howlers makes perfect sense. Coerce the senator into backing away from her vocal pro-star systems stance."

"Then, there's Magda's estranged husband, Pavel Yagudin."

Decker's eyes widened by a few millimeters.

"Of Yagudin Industries?"

"The very same. He's apparently apolitical, almost puritanically so. Yagudin's sole interest is running his zaibatsu, and he'll work with anyone who helps him increase his reach and wealth," Talyn replied, using the ancient Japanese term for an influential family-owned industrial and financial conglomerate.

"Sometimes, I can't help wonder how you know all this."

Talyn tapped the side of her head.

"I read everything that crosses my desk when we're between missions and once stored up there, I never forget it. Besides, Sorne and I almost crossed paths on Aquilonia Station, so I've kept an interest in local affairs."

"Or is your interest more closely related to the affairs of your Constabulary bent cop hunter?" Decker gave her a knowing glance. "You certainly seem to have developed a fascination with someone you used as a dupe."

"I've not heard a certain Marine complain about his turn as my dupe lately."

"You know I'm not one to bitch and moan, although you still owe me plenty of penance for past misdeeds.

But if you're nice to me right now, I'll consider it another down payment on that particular debt."

Talyn rolled her eyes.

"And we're back to your favorite topic. How does that always happen?"

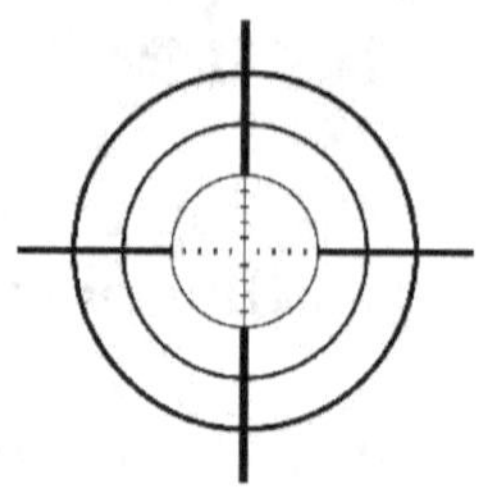

— NINETEEN —

Breakfast in the saloon, only a few hours after the abortive kidnapping attempt, seemed surreal even to an operative with Decker's long experience of strange situations. Everyone behaved as if nothing occurred shortly before *Thebes* went FTL on her last leg to Cimmeria. And for most of the passengers, nothing *had* happened.

Since the crew, other than *Thebes'* purser did its best to ignore them, Decker couldn't even gage their reaction to the night's deadly events. If anyone other than the watchkeepers knew. Talyn might be right, and surveillance of the affected areas could have been shut off, leaving the bridge blind and blissfully ignorant of doings on their own ship.

Gudrun Mariano and her client remained no-shows by the time Decker finished his third coffee of the morning, and he wondered whether a quick knock on the cabin door might be appropriate. They still faced at least five hours in FTL, with several more traveling sublight afterward, before entering orbit and docking at Valerys, Cimmeria's sole civilian station. The two women couldn't stay secluded that long without eating. But Talyn vetoed the idea.

"If we want Mariano's trust," she said once they were back in the privacy of their own quarters, "we need to give them space. I know her type. The more you try to help, the less they want it. Push hard enough, and things can become dicey."

"You know her type?" Decker stretched out on a bottom bunk still in disarray from a bout of debt-collection, hands joined behind his head. "Does that mean she plays for your team?"

"Could be." Talyn climbed into the top bunk. "I didn't sense there was much beneath the outer shell, other than a fixation on her duty toward Maggie. She certainly feels no affection for her client, or seems capable of doing so."

"You would know your own kind better than I do."

Talyn's next words faded away unspoken when the sound of hard knuckles rapping on their door echoed throughout the small cabin. It opened before either of them could answer or climb to their feet, the lock overridden by *Thebes'* captain, Hanno Kreipe, who barged in a pair of armed bosun's mates on his heels. Dark-haired, dark-eyed and with a dark, curly beard framing a worn-out face, he gave both operatives a black stare.

Decker sat up, hand automatically reaching for his blaster before relenting when he found himself staring up the barrel of a scattergun. Talyn dropped from the top bunk and faced Kreipe with a bland expression. "What can we do for you, Captain?"

"You're coming with me to the ship's brig."

"Why? We've done nothing to call for an arrest."

"Oh?" Kreipe's scowl set his beard aquiver. "I'd say you two are guilty of murder."

Decker chuckled.

"Did those Howler jackasses complain before we jumped? If they were Howlers and not pretending." He glanced at his partner. "I guess your present didn't deliver the intended effect, honey."

"Up." Whatever else Kreipe was about to say became a strangled exhalation when he suddenly found the cold, hard muzzle of Talyn's blaster pressed against his forehead.

Decker let out a low whistle.

"You sure can move, my dear. Even I didn't see that draw. Of course, now we face a standoff."

She turned a smile as cold as interstellar space on *Thebes'* captain.

"Sure, but I can keep a bead on my friend Hanno until we dock," she replied in a business-like tone. "Or your lads with the guns could try something stupid, and I fry what little brains are rattling around in that thick skull. As my partner will tell you, I'm a qualified starship pilot, and he's no stranger to the engine room, so we don't need you or your minions to reach a safe harbor. What's the story, Hanno? Did the Confederacy of the Howling Stars buy your gambling debts from some Scandian casino and propose an amnesty if you let them board *Thebes* and abduct a passenger? Or do they have a video of you doing nasty things to an underage Verdanian hermaphrodite?"

The burst of fear in his eyes told her she'd come close to the mark with the insinuation of blackmail. Or perhaps it was merely her mention of the notorious crime group's formal name.

"You know," Decker said, "good old Hanno's not the sort to bugger Verdanians. It's debt-related. I'll wager my next contract on it. And since he owns *Thebes*, foreclosure means he no longer has a home, a job, or a reason to live. Same goes for the crew, right boys?"

He grinned at the two bosun's mates, now standing uncertainly behind Kreipe, unable to bring their weapons to bear on Talyn since the captain's overfed bulk shielded her.

"Let me guess," Talyn said, ignoring her partner. "The moment we dock, a squad of Howler goons masquerading as stevedores will come aboard and take us to one of the unoccupied lower decks for summary execution. That way, the little fiasco at the heliopause becomes ancient history. But since they didn't get their target, no debt forgiveness, and no peace of mind while you sail this assemblage of spare parts across the Rim. The way I see it, you lose again."

"Hanno could still be a winner." A dubious expression crossed Decker's face. "Not by much mind you, but staying alive when a psychopath has a gun pressed against your forehead isn't much different from a ten million cred lottery jackpot."

Talyn's dead eyes caught Kreipe's increasingly terrified gaze, and she tilted her head to one side.

"Maybe he doesn't want to win on our terms."

"But I'm sure his expendable crewmembers aren't so eager to become lost souls floating in the galactic ether for eternity." Decker's blaster materialized with the same speed as Talyn's. "What do you say, boys? Do we call this a draw? No names, no pack drill?"

"Perhaps we won't be terminating anyone today. I think Hanno understands the magnitude of his mistake."

Thebes's captain, after a moment of hesitation, fluttered his eyelids as a sign of acknowledgment, since he couldn't nod with Talyn's gun barrel still pushing against his increasingly sweaty skull.

"Do you think Hanno understands we can tear through his crew in the same way we put paid to the boarding party last night if we decide he won't let us step off this ship by our own free will?"

A dubious expression crossed the Marine's face.

"I'd say there's a fifty-fifty chance, considering half of all humans are below median intelligence, and nowadays they give just about every idiot command of a civilian FTL-capable scrap heap. Of course, if Hanno backs down, that leaves the question of how we make sure he plays it straight with us between now and our arrival at Valerys. Let's see, this tub has a crew of what? Two dozen? That means odds of twelve to one. Eight to one if our newest buddy Gudrun joins in. It should be enough to seize *Thebes* and space anyone who resists. What do you say, Hanno? Are you going to be a smart guy and stop buggering around? We'll be out of your hair in a few hours. Pleasing the Howlers surely isn't worth giving up your life and that of your crew."

"Perhaps he fears them more than he fears us," Talyn suggested.

"Could be. But we're here, and they're not." Decker paused and his face lit up as if a brilliant idea had just struck him. "I know. When we dock at Valerys, you and I can take the goon squad when it comes aboard to fetch us. That way we solve both our and Hanno's immediate problems with the Howlers. What do you say, Hanno?"

Kreipe's reply came out as a faint rasp. "You're both fucking crazy."

"That's because insanity beats any other alternative. You should try it. Creative madness might help avoid stumbling into this sort of problem again." Movement in the corridor behind the two bosun's mates caught Decker's eye. "Our friend Gudrun heard the commotion and she's drawn her weapon. Eight to one odds it is."

A satisfied grin spread across Decker's face.

"Here's the deal, Hanno. My partner and I will step off this ship unmolested along with our friend Gudrun and her companion. That means you go back to your bridge and make sure no one bothers us in the meantime. If Howlers make it aboard before we leave, the three of us will redecorate your passageways in mid-twenty-sixth century *art nouveau* splatters. But disposing of the bodies becomes your problem. Consider last night's cleanup a onetime favor."

"I still think we should kill him," Talyn said in a voice devoid of emotion. "Weaklings of his sort are apt to pollute the gene pool and it's filthy enough already."

"She's not wrong, Hanno." Decker gave him a commiserating look. "And in our partnership, unfortunately for you, she's the boss. And the designated psycho. So here's what I suggest. Forget any this ever happened. Go back to running the ship, bring us to Valerys, and thank whichever deity you worship that we let you live. Does that sound good?"

Kreipe didn't immediately answer, but his Adam's apple bobbed a few times as he swallowed. Then, he croaked, "Deal."

Decker waved his blaster at the bosun's mates.

"Back to your duty stations, boys. Once I no longer see your ugly mugs, Hanno here can offer a prayer of thanksgiving while he goes back to the bridge."

After another searching glance at Talyn, Kreipe said, "Leave."

Both men backed out of the cabin, still covered by Gudrun Mariano's weapon, and vanished. Half a minute later, the duenna nodded once, confirming they'd left the passenger accommodations deck. Talyn lowered her gun with a disappointed sigh.

"Why are you always so reasonable," she asked her partner.

"Last night was a week's worth of killing for both of us, honey. You know too much death only fuels your inner demons and I can barely deal with them now."

Kreipe cautiously backed away from Talyn.

"Once I put you ashore, you're barred from ever stepping aboard *Thebes* again."

Decker blew him a kiss. "We love you too, Hanno."

When he was gone Mariano tucked away her gun and stepped into their cabin's doorway.

"What was that about?"

"I figure just before this tub jumped, Kreipe received orders to arrest us from the goons who tried to kidnap Maggie and hand us over to a delegation of their friends upon docking."

The duenna grimaced.

"That means we might come across an unfriendly reception committee as well."

"You would have whether or not they wanted us."

"Do you think Kreipe will call his buddies once we drop out of FTL?" Mariano asked.

"Guaranteed," Talyn replied. "But on a station like Valerys, they can't risk a shootout, so if we get off before they react, we should be fine."

"And if not, we send a few more of the damned jackals to hell, where they can serve as Satan's newest virgins."

The Marine holstered his gun and stood.

Mariano's eyes went from one to the other.

"Who are you?"

"Guns for hire, nothing more."

A humorless laugh escaped Mariano's throat.

"Really, Sera Taryen? I've been in the private contractor business for over twenty years, and pros of your caliber don't come around every day. Why is it I've never heard of you two?"

"We always insist on a non-disclosure clause in our contracts. Employers don't talk about us, and those who cross us don't live long enough to spread the word."

"So I noticed."

"Don't worry about who we are," Decker said. "Instead, let's concentrate on planning our escape, but not here. I suggest we spend the rest of the trip in the saloon. Hanno is less likely to try anything cute in a public compartment."

Mariano seemed to consider the suggestion, then shook her head.

"Don't misunderstand me, but why should I trust you? Maybe the piracy attempt was a sham so you could get close to us."

"A tad expensive in foot soldier lives, no?"

"I think Gudrun means whoever wants Maggie could have hired them as a throwaway diversion, and we're the real threat."

Decker considered Talyn's explanation before giving her a grudging nod.

"Twisted, but possible. Listen, Gudrun. Do as you think best, okay? My partner and I will set up shop in the saloon, backs against the wall, and we'll be the first off this ship at Valerys. You're welcome to join us or not. If you don't, good luck. Once we leave *Thebes,* you won't see us again."

"A contract on Cimmeria? Or just passing through?"

Talyn gave her a cold smile.

"Sorry. Our non-disclosure clause also forbids us from discussing the matter. But thanks for your help with Kreipe and his men."

"My pleasure."

Mariano dipped her head in an abbreviated bow and vanished into the corridor. They heard her cabin door open and close again a few seconds later.

Decker grabbed his small travel pack and slung it over one shoulder.

"Shall we?"

"You seem remarkably unconcerned by the possibility that Mariano will reject our offer of protection."

"They all come back to Zack for help. I'm one of those people everyone trusts. As it happens, I expect Gudrun and Maggie on our six when we disembark."

She gave him a mock-disgusted glare.

"Don't trip over your ego, buddy."

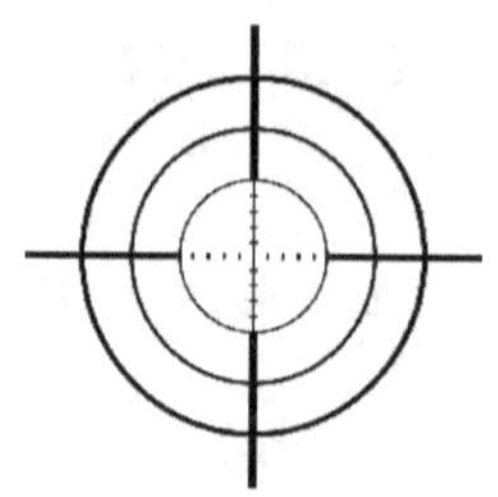

— TWENTY —

Decker and Talyn were the first passengers at the airlock and watched through the portholes as a short gangway tube extruded from the docking arm. It latched on to *Thebes'* hull with a muffled clang. Moments later, the red warning light by the airlock door shifted from red to green, showing the tube was pressurized.

Their remaining hours aboard the freighter had passed without further incident and without glimpsing Mysterious Maggie and her deadly duenna. However, just as the bosun's mate standing by the airlock unlatched the inner door, both women came out of the staircase, travel bags in hand.

They and the operatives exchanged silent nods. More people trickled down the stairs behind them, but for many passengers, Cimmeria wasn't the final destination.

Thebes' outer airlock door released its grip with a soft sigh and pulled inward before sliding to one side. The passage to the station proper was mercifully empty. Decker stepped off without further ado, glad to be away from the ship's stench of treachery and failed dreams.

The moment he emerged on the scuffed deck, his eyes were drawn to the compartment's sole occupants, a trio of blue-uniformed police troopers from the Cimmerian Gendarmerie. Two men and a woman, equipped with slung scatterguns as well as their sidearms, studied the

Marine through emotionless eyes as he headed for the exit, trailed by Talyn, Mariano, and Maggie.

Once out in the passageway leading to arrivals control, Decker glanced over his shoulder at Talyn.

"Did you notice?"

"If you mean the unexpected Gendarmerie presence, looking ready to repel boarders, then yes. Maybe they're running a high alert exercise, or they received word that suspicious characters might transit through Valerys and don't know on which ship."

He grinned at her.

"Other than us, you mean?"

She bumped him with her elbow, but it was in good humor. They followed lit arrows on the deck and found themselves herded through the passenger arrival control gates. Here too, the Cimmerian Gendarmerie seemed to patrol in greater numbers and with more than the usual police equipment.

"You visited this place last," Decker muttered as they lined up. "Was this place suffused with such a paranoid vibe back then?"

"No. But I wasn't paying much attention at the time."

He chortled.

"You, not paying much attention? Sure."

The holographic, wholly artificial immigration control officer beckoned him to step forward. Decker placed his ID wafer on the reader and gave the sim a smile which it didn't return. At least in that respect, the AI didn't differ from its human counterparts.

"Purpose of your visit to Cimmeria, Ser Sarkin?"

"Tourism."

If an artificial projection could sound and appear skeptical, this one was it.

"Really?"

"Come to visit the old battlefields from the Shrehari War. My great-grandpappy was a sergeant in the 11th

Marines back then. Spent the occupation making hit-and-run attacks on the boneheads. Killed himself a fair number before they packed up and left."

"Your occupation, Ser Sarkin?"

"Security consultant. I'm between contracts, hence the vacation."

He must have seemed sincere to the AI's lie detection algorithms, one of the many things they taught at Camp X, the Fleet's Spook School on Caledonia. The sim nodded once.

"Welcome to Cimmeria."

Decker picked up his ID wafer and tucked it away, knowing they'd added his biometrics to the immigration database. Or rather Ned Sarkin's biometrics. The red rectangle at his feet turned green, inviting him to cross over into sovereign Cimmerian territory. He found Talyn on the other side, waiting for him. She nodded at Mariano and her protégée, walking away with a pair of soberly dressed women who resembled the duenna in many ways.

"A known reception committee, judging by the exchange of recognition signs. You can stop worrying about their falling to more Howler tricks. Not that they'd try with the added police presence on Valerys."

"And you're losing the chance to figure out what, if anything, is happening."

Talyn gave him a philosophical shrug.

"It was never more than a notion, considering our main purpose on Cimmeria."

Decker's eyes narrowed as he watched the small knot of women merge with Valerys Station's foot traffic before disappearing around a bend.

"Unless this is Maggie's final destination, they're heading for the shuttle hangar. Why don't we travel with them just a little longer?"

"Why not?"

They fell into step side-by-side, their eyes watching everything and everyone, alert for any peril, and soon caught sight of Mariano and her colleagues escorting Maggie. But it quickly became obvious no one from an organization savvy enough to escape indictment would try anything illegal in full view of the frequent Gendarmerie foot patrols.

As they entered the station's main promenade, a large news display caught Decker's eye. He inhaled deeply before muttering, "Holy fuck."

An image of widespread ruin filled the largest of the screens. It appeared as if someone or something vaporized an entire mountainside, leaving nothing but a blackened crater.

Vegetation surrounding the epicenter smoldered, sending black, greasy tendrils heavenward. Here and there, along the edge, Decker could barely make out the angular shapes of what had once been human constructs, now shredded by whatever struck them.

A news presenter wearing the quasi-androgynous face of a sim materialized to one side.

"These are the remains of the Silfax Mining Complex at the heart of the Uttara Kuru Mountains, five hundred kilometers south of Archeron. It was, until today, one of the largest of its kind in the entire Rim Sector. The Cimmerian government confirms that around oh-nine-thirty local time this morning, a massive explosion destroyed the extensive installations, including the mine itself, the refinery, the administrative precinct, and the company town. An anonymous source within the Cimmerian Civil Protection Agency said although rescue efforts are ongoing, it is unlikely anyone on the surface survived.

Under a best-case scenario, the two hundred and fifty miners underground at the time of the explosion might be the only ones left alive. It means over three thousand people — off-duty miners, refinery and support workers, and their families, including almost five hundred children — were killed. Authorities are declining to speculate whether the explosion was accidental or the result of sabotage."

"Accidental, my ass," Decker muttered with barely restrained fury. "I'll bet this is the DSA's handiwork, using a few dozen kilos of MHX. We got here too damn late. The massacre of innocents has started, and that means I'm hoisting the black flag."

Talyn, her ears attuned to Decker's moods, put a calming hand on his shoulder.

"Agreed. But don't go berserker on me. We still need to question anyone we capture alive. Mission Colony and Cimmeria aren't the only Rim Sector star systems targeted by the DSA."

Decker's exhalation fell just short of a sigh.

"Don't worry. Ask first, shoot afterward. I know the drill. But we can't keep our current operational profile. Not anymore. This is bigger than two undercover Special Operations Division agents, now that someone's committed mass murder."

"You're sure there's no possibility of it being an accident? A reactor failing catastrophically for example?" The Marine gave her an irritated glare, so she raised her hands in surrender. "Fair enough. Explosives are your area of expertise."

"If they have a visual of the moment it happened, I'll know for sure."

"The only way to access anything substantive about the incident is through official channels, Zack. They'll lock this one tight if they even so much as suspect an act of terrorism, including visual records other than the image over there."

She jerked a thumb at the news display.

"Going through official channels means someone will ask us questions we don't want to answer, such as how we obtained information about subversive activity on Cimmeria and why said subversives seem to have a large quantity of the most restricted non-nuclear explosive known.”

A sly look slowly spread across his square face.

“Apropos of nothing whatsoever, since we’re already here, I wouldn’t mind meeting this friend of yours in the Professional Compliance Bureau and letting her know about Assistant Commissioner Bujold’s unhappy friendships. What was her name again?” He raised his eyes to the ceiling and tapped his chin with an extended index finger. “Caelin something or other? I hear she’s a real handful.”

Talyn jabbed her elbow into his ribs.

“Morrow, you big lummox. Not a bad idea. Hopefully, she’s at home and not terminating a high-ranking Constabulary officer’s career in another part of the sector. I’ll call once we’re in Howard’s Landing. And on that note...”

She gestured at the corridor leading toward the shuttle hangar.

“At least we know why there’s an enhanced police presence,” Decker said, falling into step beside his partner. “The Gendarmerie or our cousins in gray must have heard chatter on darknet radical sites while we were in transit from Mission. But with no clue as to the what, where and when.”

“Or the how. That was one hell of a blast, Zack.”

“Yep. I can only think of a few things able to cause so much devastation, and since they’re not warning folks of radioactive fallout danger, that eliminates most.”

His jaw muscles worked as he chewed on his anger.

“I want to find the evil fucks who weaponized Cimmeria’s radical idiots and wipe them from the face of the galaxy. Radicals? Hell, they’re nothing more than the saddest of life’s losers, perpetual teenagers prone to blaming their failures on anyone but themselves, something that makes them embrace puerile garbage like the collectivism of the Mission Colony Freedom Cretins. We've not seen that brand of stupidity in a long time, though it was pretty popular in pre-diaspora days. And it turned into a disastrous mess every single time. The idiots could never figure out why, yet the mental retardation appears to be alive and well centuries later."

Talyn gave him a quelling glare. "I hope you got the need to lecture me on human failings out of your system, Zack. We have to think about adjusting our plans."

They turned a corner and entered the shuttle terminal just in time to see Maggie, her bodyguard and the rest of the entourage climbing aboard a small, sleek orbital craft. It was unmarked save for a registration number, but its lines exuded the aura of wealth only people with names like Annear, Hakkam, or Yagudin could boast.

"So much for riding to Howard's Landing with the ladies," Decker remarked in a philosophical tone. "That little beauty could be headed anywhere. Too bad, but we have other things to keep us busy anyway."

"Like the rather intense frown coming our way from that Gendarmerie sergeant by the ticketing counter?"

Decker's eyes shifted to one side, and he grunted.

"Those are *I got you, you sonofabitch eyes* if I've ever seen any. Do you think Kreipe or the local Howlers hung a rap on us with the plod?"

"Why not? It ensures we don't vanish into the countryside and escape punishment. The Cimmerian Gendarmerie are cleaner than most, but as my old friend Caelin will tell you, every police force has a percentage of bent cops."

"What's the plan?"

"Play along. If things go sideways, I'll call Chief Superintendent Morrow."

"Prepare that comlink address. The sergeant and his wingman are moving in to cut us off from a seat on the next shuttle."

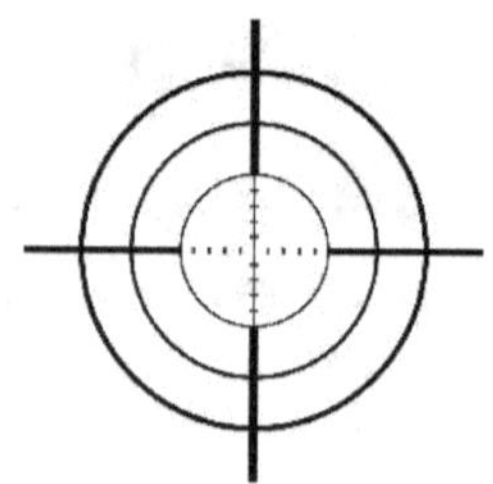

— TWENTY-ONE —

Decker turned a lazy smile on the distinctly unfriendly Gendarmerie noncom.

"Anything we can help you with, Sergeant?"

"Identification, please."

The gendarme pulled a small tablet from his equipment harness. The operatives retrieved and held out their ID wafers. He waved his reader over them and then studied its screen.

"Ned Sarkin and Lena Taryen." The man looked up.

"Yes."

"Please come with us to the Gendarmerie station."

"Why?" Talyn asked in a not particularly pleasant tone.

"We received a complaint. I presume you're armed."

"Of course. We're bonded private security consultants, as our IDs indicate."

Talyn carefully opened her jacket to show the blaster tucked under her left armpit. The Marine imitated her moments later.

"Please surrender your weapons."

"Are we under arrest, Sergeant?"

"Not yet."

"Then you have no legal cause to disarm us. My partner and I will give the Gendarmerie our full cooperation as per the professional obligations imposed by our bonds. May I inquire about the nature of this complaint?"

Caught off-guard by Talyn's reasonable tone, the sergeant studied her with eyes oozing suspicion.

"I am not privy to the particulars. They will be relayed to you at the station. My instructions were merely to detain Ned Sarkin and Lena Taryen."

"Then please lead us to whoever in your Gendarmerie detachment has the relevant information."

"There's still the matter of your weapons."

"We will surrender them if and when we're arrested, per applicable federal and star system laws. Now please take us to your station so we may clear this matter up and be on our way. Or call your supervisor." Talyn's tone remained as reasonable as before, but no one would miss the steel behind it.

After a pregnant pause, the sergeant conceded defeat with a brief, angry glare, then gestured toward the corridor leading away from the shuttle terminal.

"Follow me."

The noncom led them through a warren of passageways until they reached an airtight door marked Cimmerian Gendarmerie — Valerys Detachment. Once inside, he directed them to an interview room as bare and utilitarian as the rest of the station's service decks.

"Please wait here."

The sergeant and his colleague vanished.

Knowing they were under observation, Talyn and Decker took the two chairs on one side of the metal table and composed themselves. If the gendarmes were hoping for unguarded words between partners, they would be sorely disappointed.

Ten minutes passed before the door opened again, this time to admit a stone-faced Gendarmerie officer with a lieutenant's stripes on her collar. Middle-aged, careworn, with short dark hair and emotionless blue eyes, she reminded Talyn of Major Jon Pullar, who commanded the Aquilonia Station Gendarmerie

Detachment while she was detained there on suspicion of murder.

"Ned Sarkin and Lena Taryen, I'm Angelique DuToit. Thank you for coming without causing a fuss. I understand you declined to surrender your weapons."

"We did," Decker replied. "Tell me, Lieutenant, how many fall for your gendarmes' spiel and hand over their guns even though they don't have to?"

The ghost of a smile flitted across DuToit's thin lips.

"Only those whose grasp of the law is deficient, and that rules out pretty much anyone in your line of business, Ser Sarkin."

"Now what's this about a complaint?" Talyn asked.

DuToit took a seat across from them and placed her clasped hands on the tabletop.

"Captain Hanno Kreipe of the freighter *Thebes*, aboard which you traveled here, lodged an assault complaint against you. He alleges you attacked him and two of his crewmembers without provocation. Would you care to comment?"

The agents exchanged knowing glances. So this was how Kreipe hoped to deflect the Howlers' displeasure.

"And what evidence does he offer for this outlandish claim?" Talyn asked.

"So you deny the accusation?"

"Categorically. People in our line of business would quickly forfeit their bond and lose their livelihoods by carrying out unprovoked acts of violence on bystanders." Decker repressed a secret smile at Talyn's choice of words. She was telling nothing less than the truth, and convincingly enough for any invisible observer trained to detect falsehood even in subjects such as her. "Perhaps it might be useful if you could share the details of Captain Kreipe's allegations, Lieutenant."

Talyn's voice seemed almost hypnotically smooth and Decker wondered whether DuToit would recognize the inflection for what it was — that of a master interrogator, skilled at manipulating others into revealing more than they wanted.

"Captain Kreipe and two of his crew members accuse you of causing a disturbance aboard *Thebes* and when confronted, pulling your weapons on them."

"Does Captain Kreipe offer evidence beyond an accusation?"

Decker could have sworn a pained look crossed DuToit's eyes.

"He and his crew gave us statements."

"So no evidence." Talyn nodded as if the gendarme's response was what she expected. "Which is why we were invited to attend your station instead of being arrested on the spot. But I'm not surprised. We saw signs during our trip that Kreipe is either in league with the Confederacy of the Howling Stars or indebted to them. And since my partner and I are on the Howlers' least favored persons list, perhaps this is an attempt to take us out of the game so he can ingratiate himself with the mob or pay off a marker. If so, it's rather ham-fisted."

Surprise lit up DuToit's face. It was quickly followed by indecision. After a moment of silence, she said, "A not unreasonable deduction, Sera Taryen. Our Constabulary colleagues have long suspected Kreipe of playing footsie with the Howlers, which is why we made this a friendly interview."

"You wanted to see what sort of person our friend Hanno might be trying to screw."

"Just so. But I'm a good judge of people, and Kreipe always comes across as a slippery bugger. Yes, I've met the man before today. Then, there's the fact our intelligence on him, and his ship confirms my gut instinct. You, on the other hand, make me think of folks able to seize something like *Thebes* with little difficulties, which makes Kreipe's accusation suspect."

She paused again and studied both agents.

"I can well believe you and he clashed about something or other. Apparently, he's possessed of a quick temper and poor judgment. But since Kreipe produced no bodies or physically injured parties, it would indicate you exercised restraint, no?"

"If you didn't think he had a case to present, why ask us in for a talk, Lieutenant?"

A humorless smile appeared.

"As I said, in part to satisfy my curiosity and find out why a sketchy spacer might want to press dubious charges against his own passengers, but also to pull you two out of circulation until *Thebes* leaves Valerys. If Kreipe and his crew have a beef with you, especially something that might involve the Howlers, it's best you lie low until they're gone. If you haven't noticed yet, things are unsettled today, and we'd like to keep a lid on any potential trouble."

Talyn inclined her head by way of acknowledgment.

"We caught a newscast on the way to the shuttle terminal. What happens now?"

"Now? I'll ask you to stay here until *Thebes* cuts loose from the docking ring. After that, you're free to resume your voyage."

"Any Howler activity on Valerys?"

"Some, but since we stepped up patrols, they've been noticeably law-abiding."

"So the enhanced police presence started before this morning's terrorist attack on the Silfax Mining Complex."

Instead of replying, DuToit climbed to her feet.

"Have a safe trip. Someone will escort you back to the shuttle terminal at the right time, which shouldn't be long. *Thebes* never tarries at Valerys. Our docking fees don't suit Captain Kreipe's limited budget."

"Comes from playing the ponies without knowing how to calculate the odds."

"What makes you say that, Ser Sarkin?"

The Marine tapped the side of his nose with an extended finger.

"Hanno reeks of unpaid gambling debts. That's why he figured taking us on to please his creditors was a winning strategy. Don't be surprised if *Thebes* shows up under a different master next time around. Mobbed up body art aficionados don't take failure kindly."

"Indeed." She turned on her heels and left them to wait patiently, though they knew the invisible listeners remained at their posts.

A taciturn Gendarmerie corporal appeared thirty minutes later and wordlessly motioned them to follow him. An hour after that, they were ensconced in the cheap seats at the back of the regular shuttle linking Valerys Station with the Cimmerian capital, Howard's Landing.

As the craft nosed its way through the open space doors, Decker leaned over to whisper in his partner's ear.

"Why do I get the feeling DuToit arranged for a few plainclothes gendarmes to wait for us planetside, in case we're more than unjustly maligned private security consultants who ran afoul of the biggest crime syndicate in the Rim?"

"Because she's nobody's fool and figures suspicious strangers wanted by the Howlers showing up a few hours after the worst terrorist attack in any star system since the last war might bear watching?"

"Although they're not calling it terrorism just yet. What's the plan?"

"Same as before. Visit what used to be government house when Cimmeria was a self-governing colony and see if Chief Superintendent Morrow still thinks of me as a friend. That ought to convince the Gendarmerie their efforts shouldn't be wasted on the likes of us. They face bigger problems."

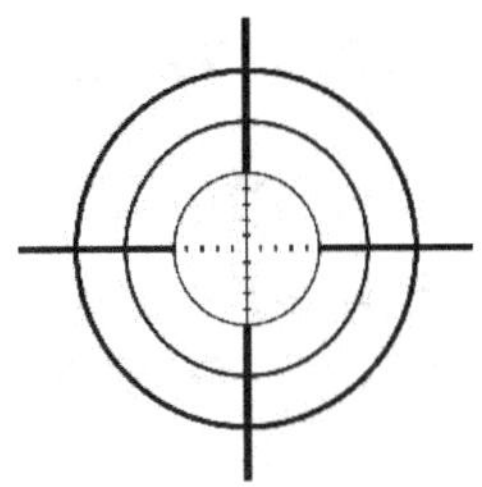

— TWENTY-TWO —

"So far, I see nothing that looks like a plainclothes cop," Decker murmured as he and Talyn crossed the Howard's Landing spaceport terminal, just two more travelers in the crowd. "But they're putting on a real show with the uniformed variety. Perhaps DuToit didn't alert her colleagues, or she did, and they figured we weren't worth it."

The police presence was even more pervasive than on Valerys Station, and more heavily armed. Gendarmes, in pairs, patrolled the arrivals halls, suspicious eyes spearing each new face with a searching stare. It seemed as if they expected the culprits for the Silfax Mining Complex destruction to be among the passengers arriving on the suborbital shuttle from Archeron, Cimmeria's second largest city, which sat on the southern shore of the Borrachas Sea.

"Sounds reasonable. On the other hand, we know the average Cimmerian gendarme isn't stupid." Talyn surreptitiously pulled a handheld sensor from her tunic pocket and aimed it at the Marine without breaking stride. "Sneaky buggers. I don't know how, but they tagged you with a tracker, Big Boy."

Decker thought back at their interaction with the Valerys Gendarmerie detachment from first to last and grunted.

"That corporal who guided us back to the shuttle terminal gave me a little tap on the shoulder as we left the station when you were walking in front of us."

"Yep. That's where it is."

"Should we remove it?"

"No. Let's allow the trackers to spot us visit their federal cousins before they lose our trace. Otherwise, who knows what the Gendarmerie will believe and how much effort they might divert from hunting terrorists. Strangers who shake surveillance with ease during tense times quickly become persons of interest. There's no point in adding needlessly to the policing burden right now since we're not here to mess with the star system government."

"For once." Decker gave her a complicit wink. "But it's kind of you to contemplate the broader situation, darling. I'm sure the gendarmes would appreciate your benevolence if they only knew about it."

"And ruin my reputation for ruthlessness? Perish the thought."

"Speaking of which, check out the two sleek-looking characters loitering by the main exit. One of them looked away real fast the moment I caught his eye."

"Maybe he thinks you're hot but is shy."

Decker grunted. "Not my type."

"That didn't stop you before when it comes to Howlers. I seem to recall a certain Ros Skillen..."

"Strictly business. Besides, I'm not quite as open-minded as you are, my dear."

"Don't I know it?" She studied the two young men out of the corner of her eyes as they neared the automatic doors. Well-coiffed with slicked-back hair, they wore designer suits and high-end shoes. Both studiously avoided staring at the operatives, a rookie mistake for watchers. "Hangers-on or probationary Howlers. They don't look like full-fledged members. Or they're not related and what happened was a false flag operation."

"Could be the Confederacy recruits a better class of goons on Cimmeria. They're carrying, that's for sure. Those fancy duds weren't cut to hide a shoulder holster."

"A lot of people on Cimmeria carry."

Decker and Talyn passed the men without paying them a shred of attention and stepped out into the warm midday air. Sunlight caressed Decker's face for the first time since leaving Mission Colony, and he let loose a contented sigh.

"Nice." He glanced around and found a public transit stop immediately to their right. "We ride in style?"

"Might as well. It'll give us the chance to study your admirer and his friend, should they be inclined to tail us."

"Want me to simper at him?"

"Knock yourself out, but I think it'll backfire. Your version of simpering would send a Shrehari Marine into convulsions."

"You wound me deeply."

A silent, automatic bus in light blue and white municipal transit colors pulled up after dropping travelers by the departures hall. Its doors opened with a sigh, revealing a clean, spare interior of molded plastic seats and bright yellow handholds. Movement behind them reflected in the vehicle's polarized windows caught his attention.

"No need to test your scurrilous assertion. Our little buddies are joining us."

They climbed aboard and sat in the first available row. The two men jumped in moments before the doors closed. Neither appeared to care the slightest bit about Decker and Talyn, but both agents sensed their interest as if the men were hunting dogs on a fresh spoor.

"Probies." Decker muttered. "Figures. Can't tail a blind man without getting made."

"To be fair, we enjoy an advantage over most people."

"Sure, but as I always say, if you're playing fair, you're not playing to win, sweetheart. Not in our line of business."

"Granted."

The bus took them along a broad, tree-lined avenue connecting the inland spaceport with Howard's Landing proper, which was strung along the shores of a broad fjord surrounded by snow-capped mountains. The fjord's mouth, facing due south, gave onto the subtropical Borrachas Sea separating Cimmeria's largest continent, Hyperborea, from its second largest, Kusan, which straddled the planet's equator. Soon after coming over a rise, they saw the city itself, spilling down a shallow slope until it petered out by the sparkling dark waters of the deep inlet.

From this distance, it was impossible to tell Howard's Landing had been almost entirely razed by the Shrehari during the final days of the war. Seventy years of peace and reconstruction had erased most of the scars. Where a rough and tumble colonial settlement once stood when the Empire's troops landed, a bustling city had taken its rightful place among humanity's brightest.

Yet Decker couldn't stop himself from superimposing the image of the devastated Silfax Mining Complex onto Cimmeria's vibrant capital and felt his stomach sink.

"I doubt they're Howlers," Talyn murmured, tearing him away from visions of Armageddon. "Wrong vibe. Too clean cut."

The Marine nodded once, acknowledging her statement. She was rarely off the mark where it concerned people. Unable to feel empathy or any connection with humanity at large, Talyn had studied others for decades so she could detect and identify social cues. It allowed her to function more or less normally and not betray her true nature, a useful skill for an intelligence agent.

"If not our lupine friends, then who?"

"No idea. They may not be particularly skilled at running a tail, but they're no amateurs either. My guess is standard-issue security consultants, but working for the wealthy set."

Decker let out a soft grunt.

"Hence the fancy suits. Friends of Gudrun Mariano, perhaps? Making sure we don't track Mysterious Maggie with the potentially serious family connections?"

"As good a theory as any."

"Meaning we keep our distance and not worry if they notice us entering Constabulary HQ, never to re-emerge."

"Give yourself a pat on the back for being smart instead of a smartass, though I'm not sure yet about making a switch. It depends on how thrilled the gray-legs are to see us."

The Marine made a face.

"If that's the criteria, we're screwed. No one is thrilled to see us."

Talyn didn't reply, and they contented themselves with watching the scenery unfold until the bus reached the outskirts of Howard's Landing where one and two-story buildings sprouted from the greenery like exotic mushrooms. These soon gave way to taller structures, though none boasting over ten floors, Old Government House, now home to the Constabulary's Rim Sector HQ, among them.

When they finally caught sight of the sweeping central plaza on the fjord's shores, at the far end of the avenue, Talyn climbed to her feet and touched a yellow panel above Decker's head. The bus glided to a gentle halt, and both agents jumped off, leaving the two young men to glare at them with annoyance as the doors closed again before they could react.

"Better luck next time, boys," Decker said, watching the bus resume its route while Talyn took her bearings.

After a moment's reflection, she nodded toward a side street.

"We'll take the long way around just in case our friends decide to backtrack."

"Why the sudden shake?" He followed Talyn into the shadows of a low-rise office building whose subdued signage advertised legal and notary services.

"Amateurs annoy me."

Her tone told Decker instinct nudged his partner into changing course. Asking for clarification was futile because she wouldn't be capable of articulating the reason. Surviving three decades as a field agent in a hostile galaxy had taught her to follow intuition without hesitating.

The moment they turned a corner to take the avenue paralleling that connecting downtown Howard's Landing with its spaceport, Talyn spotted a department store one block away and indicated it with her chin.

"We find changing rooms and turn back into our real selves. I've just decided we're entering the Rim Sector Constabulary HQ as Major Decker and Commander Talyn. Ned Sarkin and Lena Taryen have attracted more than enough unwanted attention in the last day, meaning their usefulness is over for the moment."

"Plus it'll see us past the guards and into your friend's office that much faster, since time is of the essence if the Silfax attack was merely a warm-up designed to soften the Cimmerian government's resolve."

A subdued atmosphere hung over the store. Few of the humans present paid attention to the two operatives and then only with sideways glances. Employees murmured among themselves, eyes glued to newscasts while a handful of customers shopped in a desultory fashion. Everyone seemed to focus on the worst single day's loss of life in this star system since the war.

No one appeared to notice that the man and women who exited the change rooms a few minutes later didn't resemble the pair who entered save for generalities — height, build, and hair color. Even their clothes no longer appeared quite the same.

The Constabulary HQ building, a solemn affair clad in gray stone quarried close to the current spaceport during Cimmeria's post-war reconstruction, sat like a brooding pile within sight of the fjord's dark waters. Once home to the colonial governor and administrative staff, it was vacated when Cimmeria achieved independence as a sovereign entity within the Commonwealth.

The first Cimmerian government, eager to break from the past, moved into a newly built precinct surrounding what was now the city's central plaza, a broad, grassy space dominated by the statue of R.E. Howard, who founded the colony more than a century earlier.

As they neared the capital's administrative heart, from where bureaucrats and politicians governed Cimmeria and its star system, the Gendarmerie patrols they'd seen so far gave way to squads of Cimmerian National Guard soldiers in full fighting order.

"For folks who won't officially call Silfax a terrorist incident, they sure are setting the conditions to declare martial law," Decker commented, his eyes giving the troops a critical once-over. "Those guardsmen are carrying live ammo. Either the law enforcement agencies know a lot more than they're letting on or the government is panicking."

"Bet on the former, Zack. They experienced trouble last year with those revolutionary cretins who blew themselves up before they did any damage. That was enough incentive for the prime minister to beef up the Gendarmerie's security intelligence division."

Decker grimaced.

"Which means the government figures Silfax might be an opening move with more to come unless they shut it down. If I can see a video of the moment it happened and confirm the detonation's origin, I might give them added cause to worry."

"The MHX-19?"

"Yeah, and for that, we'll need official sanction. Time to check if Chief Superintendent Morrow still loves you, honey."

"Try to remember you're a Marine Corps officer when you meet her and keep those flirtatious tendencies under control."

"Aye, aye, Commander, sir."

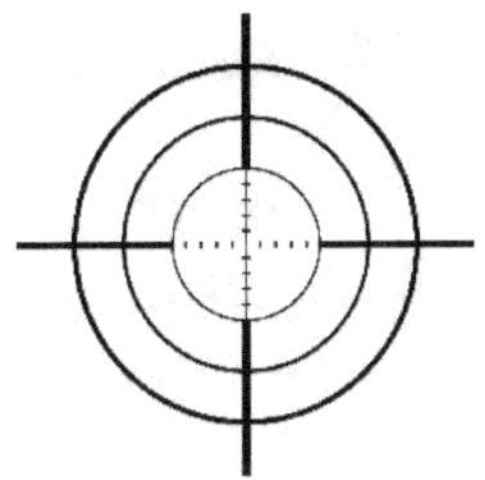

— TWENTY-THREE —

Decker and Talyn entered a spacious lobby designed to awe the hoi polloi. However, these days, it boasted nothing more than a few chairs, half a dozen displays with police artifacts, several images and paintings on beige walls, and a reception desk barring the way. A large representation of the Constabulary's crest, scales of justice balanced on the shaft of an arrow, surrounded by a laurel wreath was embedded in the white marble floor.

The sim behind the desk — an androgynous hologram showing no identifiable ethnic characteristics — rose to its photonic feet and smiled.

"Welcome to the Commonwealth Constabulary's Rim Sector Headquarters. My name is Hector. How may I be of service?"

"I am Commander Hera Talyn, Commonwealth Navy, and this is Major Zachary Decker, Commonwealth Marine Corps. We're Armed Services HQ liaison officers here to see Chief Superintendent Caelin Morrow."

"Could I see your identification please, Commander, Major?" The sim asked in an ingratiating tone.

They produced their official ID wafers.

"Thank you. I contacted the Sector's Professional Compliance Bureau detachment. Someone will come down to meet you. Please take a seat."

While Talyn composed herself to wait in one of the deceptively comfortable chairs, Decker wandered around the lobby and inspected what was in effect a mini-museum devoted to the Constabulary's history in the Rim Sector. An amateur historian himself, the Marine never missed the opportunity to increase his general fund of knowledge, no matter how esoteric or obscure a fact might be.

He was examining a set of early twenty-sixth-century submission manacles when the inner doors opened soundlessly. A rotund man with a grandfatherly face and a dark, luxuriant beard marked by a white streak over the chin ambled into the lobby at a sedate pace. His lips pulled up in a genuine smile when he caught sight of Talyn.

"My dear Commander. I thought Hector was malfunctioning when he sent word you were asking to see the chief. How are you?"

Talyn climbed to her feet and grasped his hand.

"Keeping well. And you, Inspector?"

"Tolerable, which is about the best one can say in my line of work."

"This is my partner, Major Zack Decker. Zack, meet Inspector Arno Galdi. He was Caelin's wingman during the Aquilonia business."

The Marine shook hands with Galdi only to discover he wasn't nearly as soft as he seemed.

"Inspector."

"A pleasure to meet you, Major. The chief and I always had a sneaking suspicion Montague Hobart was actually her partner, but you can't possibly be him, even with the best disguise."

Decker released Galdi's grip. "No, indeed not. The man you knew as Montague Hobart was a colleague of ours, a lieutenant commander working for the same organization as we are."

"Was?"

"He died in the line of duty earlier this year."

"I'm sorry to hear that. The chief will be as well."

"He was a fine officer and a good man. One of the best."

"An epitaph I would be proud to earn." Galdi waved at the doors behind Hector. "Shall we head to the tenth-floor dungeon, where honest constables fear to tread, let alone those of the dishonest variety? I'm afraid the chief is sitting in on a meeting of the sector division heads. It's all hands on deck right now as you can imagine." He ushered them into the corridor and indicated a bank of lifts. "Might I surmise your presence here is connected to the attack on the Silfax Complex?"

"It is, though we didn't expect a disaster of that magnitude to greet us upon arrival."

"And since you're acquainted with the chief, you thought it best to get in touch rather than stay incognito." Galdi gave Talyn a knowing look. "What do you intelligence folks call it? I believe the ancient term is coming in from the cold, yes?"

They stepped into a lift cab whose doors closed with a sigh.

"Something like that. You'll need to ask Major Decker. Unfortunately for the rest of us, historical trivia is his specialty."

Galdi turned an impish look on the Marine and said, "Really? In that case, you and I need to compare notes. I also drive my commanding officer around the bend with this sort of thing."

Talyn, recognizing she'd enabled kindred spirits to acknowledge each other, at least in her partner's quasi-obsession with history, let out a soft groan. The cab came to a smooth stop and disgorged them on a landing with two doors. One led to the building's mechanical room, the other had a sign announcing the home of the

Professional Compliance Bureau — Rim Sector Detachment.

"All hope abandon ye who enter here," Decker intoned as Galdi led them through the second door.

The inspector nodded.

"An amusingly apt quote, Major. I confess to finding Dante Alighieri most interesting.

"Through me you pass into the city of woe:
Through me you pass into eternal pain:
Through me among the people lost for aye.
Justice the founder of my fabric moved:
To rear me was the task of power divine,
Supremest wisdom, and primeval love.
Before me things create were none, save things
Eternal, and eternal I endure.
All hope abandon ye who enter here."

"Nicely done," Decker said with a broad grin. "We definitely must compare notes."

"The Almighty help me." Talyn gave her partner a playful backhander on the arm. "Don't enjoy yourself too much, buddy. We're still on the job."

"Can I offer you coffee?" Galdi asked. "I'm afraid the sticky buns are gone by now."

"I'm always up for a cup," Decker replied. "And if you can point me at a food dispenser, I'll gladly take whatever it offers."

"Good. It was either set you up in an interview suite to wait for the chief or use the break room until she comes up from the deputy chief commissioner's emergency conference. At least the latter offers a few amenities, but sadly no dispenser. However, DCC Maras isn't one to stretch things out so the chief won't be long."

"The chief," a woman's rich alto said behind them, "is back. And what's this? A Navy officer with dubious duties and a man who I suppose is her enigmatic partner, one I've heard of many times but never met?"

They turned, and Decker caught sight of a washed-out, middle-aged blond with shoulder length hair and an angular face dominated by penetrating, intelligent blue eyes. Like Inspector Galdi, she wore a civilian business suit rather than the Constabulary's gray uniform, and the Marine was struck by how much she resembled his partner, save for the hair and eye color.

"Should I be worried to see you show up on my turf unannounced?" Chief Superintendent Caelin Morrow held out her hand to Talyn while a smile more welcoming than cold tugged at her thin-lipped mouth. "How are you, Hera? I caught wind of the Scandia business a few months ago. Well done."

The Constabulary officer turned toward Zack. "And you must be the infamous Major Decker."

They shook, and the Marine replied, with a grin, "I don't know about the infamous part, sir, but that's my name and rank. If you want my serial number, you'll have to interrogate me, but I know ways of making sure it's fun."

Morrow snorted. "You come across pretty much as I thought, based on Hera's description — questionable humor included. And we can dispense with formalities, Zack. Call me Caelin."

"We were about to enjoy a cup, Chief."

"Good. Let's see if what's left in the break room is safe for human consumption. Then Hera can tell me why she landed on my doorstep. I assume your arrival isn't a coincidence?"

"Unfortunately, no."

"I was afraid of that, considering what we discussed before parting company on Aquilonia."

They entered the small lounge and Galdi made a beeline for an elaborate coffee maker whose various buttons glowed a soothing blue.

"Zack and I aren't here to pull the Constabulary into a Fleet intelligence operation, Caelin. On the contrary. We're here to help you and the Cimmerian Gendarmerie track down the animals who committed mass murder at Silfax. It just so happens that if we'd made it to Cimmeria a week or two earlier, we might have been able to prevent the attack altogether."

Morrow's pale right eyebrow crept up to her hairline.

"This, I want to hear in full detail. Grab a cup and follow me to my office. You should come too, Arno. I think Hera and Zack want more than just a shoulder to cry on because of their lousy sense of timing."

Once ensconced in Morrow's office, a sparsely decorated space overlooking the fjord, Decker took a sip of his coffee and grimaced.

"Your fancy machine needs a good reaming out if you ask me. Or termination with extreme prejudice."

"See, Chief," Galdi said with an air of satisfaction. "I'm not the only one complaining."

As if by common accord, both women turned quelling glares on their wingmen.

"Let's focus on more important matters, Zack," Talyn said. "Such as why we're in Caelin's office criticizing the Firing Squad's coffee."

Decker made a sweeping gesture with his left arm.

"Sorry. Please go ahead, my dear Commander."

"For almost a year, since before the Scandia affair, Naval Intelligence has been tracking an increase in radical darknet chatter and direct political action across the Rim. Usually, the individuals involved are little more than live-action role players content with loud protests and the occasional vandalism to make themselves feel better about their sad existences. At worst, they might give police services and militias a bit of anti-riot practice. But for it to happen in several different systems simultaneously caught our analysts' attention. The Mission Colony Freedom Collective, long a player on that star system's political scene, came into sharp focus as one of those about to reach critical mass and act on their political aims. HQ sent us to investigate, and if need be, prune the Collective back so it no longer presented a looming threat."

"I recently came across a threat assessment discussing that bunch. Led by a Gustav Kerlin and his partner Eva Cortez, right?" Arno Galdi asked.

"As of six days ago, the Freedom Collective was restructuring under new management," Decker replied. "Incidentally, you have a problem on Mission named Kristy Bujold."

Morrow's face hardened.

"So I understand. I've not told anyone in the detachment yet, but the 24th Constabulary Regiment's deputy commanding officer sent a confidential report to DCC Maras informing her he'd forced Assistant Commissioner Bujold to take a leave of absence. She was present at the time Gustav Kerlin and Eva Cortez were murdered. She also admitted to a personal relationship with both, contrary to regulations forbidding Constabulary members from befriending political figures without making a declaration to my office. Maras wants Bujold to resign quietly rather than make it a PCB case. But if she doesn't..."

Galdi grimaced. "Now there's a turn of events."

"I assume you had something to do with those deaths?" Morrow turned a stony gaze on Talyn.

"You're free to make any assumption you like, Caelin, but neither Zack nor I can comment. However, politics on Mission will shift back to where they should be now that the Freedom Collective lost its driving forces."

When Morrow didn't answer, Talyn said, "We're not bound by police rules when it comes to neutralizing violent threats. And before you mourn Kerlin or Cortez, keep in mind they were the same sort of sociopaths who murdered the folks in the Silfax Mining Complex. Evil, soulless individuals with plenty of blood on their hands already, but untouchable because others of their ilk hold positions of power on Mission. Such as Assistant Commissioner Bujold."

"Understood." Morrow's tone and the icy shimmer in her eyes made it clear she wasn't particularly comfortable with Talyn's revelations. "Please go on."

"One tidbit we discovered along the way was the existence of a previously unknown organization calling itself the Democratic Stars Alliance, apparently headquartered in this system. This DSA is attempting to unite radical groups throughout the sector under a common umbrella, to coordinate their activities."

A grim smile briefly twisted Morrow's lips.

"So we understand. As far as the Gendarmerie and our own Criminal Intelligence Division can tell, the DSA appeared out of nowhere about six months ago. It seems to have absorbed all of the radical collectives, fronts, and whatever other nonsense they call themselves on Cimmeria. Now you're telling me they're also recruiting groups in other star systems?"

"It gets worse. The DSA is handing out recruitment bonuses, a substance called MHX-19, also known as Mayhem. According to Zack, who's an expert in these things it's the most powerful non-nuclear explosive ever invented. I saw what a single kilo did on Mission."

Talyn went on to describe the destruction of Blanca's Folly.

"Zack tells me knowledge about Mayhem's existence is highly classified, and its use is subject to the most rigorous controls. In theory, not a single gram should leave Fleet ammunition depots without a flag officer's signature. Yet the DSA apparently has access to a large stockpile, since they can dole it out in kilo bricks as a way of enticing loudmouth radicals into acting on their fantasies."

"Large is right," Decker added. "If an MHX bomb destroyed the Silfax Complex, I'd say it weighed at least a hundred kilos, judging by what I saw on the newscasts. Video of the actual detonation would help me confirm whether Mayhem was responsible. It has a characteristic visual signature like no other."

"Why do I think both DCC Maras and the Director General of the Cimmerian Gendarmerie should listen to this?"

"Because you're looking at it as a cop would, but this isn't police business. Not if it involves disparate groups spread across the sector who suddenly go from the odd violent protest to a concerted campaign aimed at spreading political terror. If you'll recall, the Wyvern Accords creating the Constabulary specifically left anti-terrorism in the Fleet's hands. Has anyone claimed responsibility for Silfax?"

"No. The Cimmerian authorities haven't even ruled out an accident yet."

"Methinks they're whistling past the graveyard," Decker said. "Show me a video clip from whichever satellite was overhead when it happened, and I'll disabuse them of any remaining illusions. We need to find the DSA's MHX stash before they strike again, and in the interests of time, it means we need local help. You, the Gendarmerie, the National Guard, anyone with information."

"Zack's right. He and I usually work alone though sometimes we will call on the help of a few friends. But we can't afford to rely on our usual methods and discretion this time. I'm officially asking for your assistance, Caelin."

Morrow's eyes narrowed as she chewed on the inside of her lip. After a moment, she said, "So far, the locals shared no details with us, but I'll ask my contact in the Gendarmerie's Criminal Intelligence Bureau. You realize our colleagues in blue won't be thrilled at the Fleet sticking its nose in."

"Perhaps not, but if Silfax was the DSA's handiwork using MHX-19, the Cimmerians can expect more of the same until their government falls and the radicals seize control."

"A rag-tag bunch of starry-eyed sociopaths?" Galdi sounded skeptical. "Hard to believe."

"We think they're backed by the Coalition and stiffened by *Sécurité Spéciale* operatives in their ranks," Decker replied. "They'll already have allies inside the bureaucracy and the security services. That's how they operated on Scandia. I can't see Cimmeria being immune to the swamp creature infestation we've seen elsewhere."

"Fair enough." Galdi inclined his head. "The Chief told me everything about this Coalition back on Aquilonia. Therefore I bow to your greater experience with humanity's dark underbelly."

"There's one more item, which may or may not be related," Talyn said.

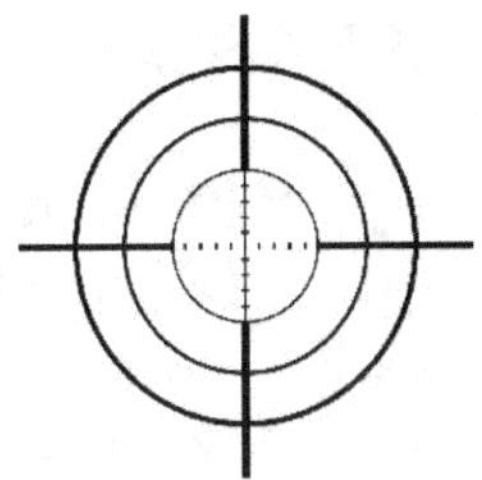

— TWENTY-FOUR —

Decker and Talyn sketched out the incident aboard *Thebes*. When they fell silent, Morrow stroked a screen embedded in her desk, and a display to her left lit up with a woman's face.

"This is Magda Annear, wife of Pavel Yagudin, and daughter of Senator Nerys Annear and the late Ryker Lubben."

"That's the one," Decker said.

"Interesting."

Morrow tapped an extended index finger on her lower lip as she studied the image.

"Isn't it? Considering her mother is one of the Outworld senators fighting to protect the rights of sovereign star systems against those who support the Coalition's goals. Not to mention her estranged billionaire husband though he has shown no political leanings Naval Intelligence could discover. I'd love to find out where she was coming from, why she's here, and why an abduction attempt by the organized crime group most often linked to our *Sécurité Spéciale* folks."

"I can't answer any of that, but Arno has a friend in the Gendarmerie who may be able to tell us where or with whom Magda Annear is staying. It might provide at least some indication. Arno?"

"Consider it done, Chief."

"If that was it, perhaps you can tell me what Naval Intelligence wants from the Constabulary?" Morrow asked.

"In the immediate, a secure link to the system's Fleet subspace relay, so we can check for messages from home and report on new developments."

"Why not go through Sixth Fleet? Admiral Kingsley's HQ is right next to the Howard's Landing spaceport."

"Rim Sector planetary governments aren't the only entities with their fair share of swamp creatures, Caelin. Right now, the only people on Cimmeria I can trust implicitly are you and Inspector Galdi."

"You mean this Coalition of yours might have people inside the Sixth Fleet command staff?"

"Almost certainly, considering what we found during the Armed Services HQ purge on Caledonia."

Morrow winced.

"I'd hate to think how many infiltrated the Constabulary."

"Consider it job security if ever your Chief Constable imitates the Grand Admiral and roots out evil wherever it lurks," Decker said, grinning.

"I prefer rooting out venality rather than treason. When we're done here, Arno will take you to the communications center and arrange a secure link under PCB auspices. That way no one will dare ask questions. What else?"

"Everything the Gendarmerie knows about the Silfax attack and the DSA as well as its predecessor groups."

"Is that it?" Morrow gave the agents a droll grimace. "I'll get you what the Constabulary knows right away. However, our Gendarmerie friends will be another matter. They're usually reasonable in cooperating with us feds, but like every planetary police force across the Commonwealth, they fear we'll take over without so much as a by your leave. And I'll have to go through our HQ liaison rather than directly. As head of the sector

Firing Squad, I have no standing in major incidents or criminal intelligence involving radical groups. The generous freedom of action I enjoy applies strictly to investigating internal affairs."

"HQ Liaison will want to know why we're interested," Galdi said. "I doubt the Commander and Major Decker will be comfortable with us revealing even the tiniest detail of Naval Intelligence's involvement, let alone how they came to be on Cimmeria at this moment."

"You're correct, Inspector." Talyn studied Morrow for a few moments, then asked, "Caelin, is DCC Maras perchance contemplating the creation of an ad hoc anti-terrorism team to help the Gendarmerie in tracking down those responsible for the Silfax atrocity?"

"She hasn't mentioned anything so far."

"You might put a word in her ear about the notion. How much do you trust Maras?"

"In what sense?" Morrow seemed puzzled by Talyn's question.

"That she's not harboring other loyalties?"

"Like this Coalition?" Morrow shrugged. "She's the only one outside of my team in the entire Rim Sector to whom I'll confide every detail of our investigations. So far, she's used nothing I told her in confidence, let alone shared it. Why do you ask?"

"Perhaps you could suggest DCC Maras forms a task force to work with the Gendarmerie and propose yourself to lead it. Justify the request by telling her in confidence that Fleet anti-terrorism officers of your acquaintance are already here and approached you directly under the circumstances because of the PCB's reputation for complete and utter incorruptibility. Maras should understand why if she's risen to deputy chief constable."

A rumble rose from Galdi's barrel chest. It took Decker a moment to identify it as laughter.

"I do believe the commander's proposition is entirely practical, Chief. And since you, I, and Sergeant Bonta have nothing on our plates at the moment while everyone else in this building is busier than the devil on a Saturday night, Maras should jump at the offer."

"That'll put you in a position to ask for whatever intelligence the Gendarmerie develops and thereby help Zack and me find the DSA's MHX stockpile before they kill more innocents."

"Why stop at being your funnel for information," Morrow replied in an acerbic tone. "Why not ask me to fly top cover over what will certainly be one of the more egregious examples of a black op carried out by Naval Intelligence?"

"If you're offering..." Talyn smirked.

"Do I have a choice?"

"Of course. But I'll remind you of our discussion on Aquilonia. What's happening here and elsewhere in this sector is part of the darkness threatening to smother the hard-won civil peace between sovereign star systems. People prepared to kill millions and deprive billions of their freedom in order to found an empire can't be stopped through conventional policing. We're standing at the edge of the abyss and what's staring back needs to die."

A heartfelt sigh escaped Morrow's lips.

"I hear you. I don't like it, but since you opened my eyes on Aquilonia, I've noticed things that make me despair about the Commonwealth's future. So has Arno."

"Sadly," the inspector said. "I recommend we go with Commander Talyn's plan, Chief. Before the terrorists let off a big one in downtown Howard's Landing. This sort of thing is beyond the Gendarmerie's experience. And beyond ours."

Morrow's eyes went from Galdi to Talyn and back.

"On one condition, Hera."

"Name it," Talyn replied.

"You and Zack come with me to see DCC Maras. No need to tell the whole story, but meeting Fleet anti-terrorism officers will help convince her. If you require top cover at some point, you'll inevitably end up needing more than I can give, and next to Admiral Kingsley, Maras wields the most federal power in the entire sector."

"Agreed. How soon can this blessed event occur? Time is not our friend."

"Wait." Morrow stroked the screen with her fingertips again. "There. I asked her adjutant for an immediate opening to discuss matters surrounding the Silfax incident privately. The DCC usually sees me right away when I bring news about a professional compliance investigation, especially if it concerns a senior member of her command. I think she'll extend that courtesy if it concerns the current crisis."

A soft chime sounded seconds later. Morrow glanced down then climbed to her feet.

"We're expected in the reception room. In the meantime, why don't you set things up for that secure link to the subspace node, Arno."

"Will do, Chief."

"Reception room?" Decker asked.

"That's what we call the DCC's office. Back when this was the Cimmeria Colony's government house, it served as the governor's reception room. You'll enjoy your daily dose of exercise walking up to her desk."

**

A harassed-looking man with the two silver, diamond-shaped stars of an inspector on his collar glanced up from a cluttered desk as they entered the antechamber to Maras' office. His gaze briefly rested on Talyn and Decker before turning to Morrow.

"Just so you understand the situation, Chief Superintendent, the DCC kicked Assistant Chief Constables Haarez and Yin out to make time for you. They're both understandably a bit miffed. May I ask who your guests are?"

"Liaison officers from the Fleet's Special Operations Command anti-terrorist unit."

The adjutant's lit up with understanding.

"Oh."

Morrow gave him a cold smile.

"*Oh*, indeed. I'm sure your esteemed Rim Sector Heads of Operation and Administration will forgive this all too necessary intrusion."

"You can enter, sir."

The door behind him silently slid aside.

"Thank you, Inspector."

Morrow led them into a room big enough to serve as a hangar for a full gunship squadron. A carved wooden desk larger than most starship cabins, backed by a dense stand of flags dominated the space. In keeping with the Constabulary's paramilitary status and its origins as the former Armed Services security branch, the imagery, decorations, and awards adorning the paneled walls closely resembled those one might find in any admiral's office.

The officer sitting behind that large desk, a stern-faced, dark-haired woman in her sixties wearing the three five-pointed stars of a deputy chief constable watched them approach with curious eyes. As if by common accord, Talyn, Decker, and Morrow came to a precise military halt in front of Maras, even though none of them wore a uniform.

"Thank you for seeing us so quickly, sir," Morrow said. "With me are Commander Hera Talyn and Major Zachary Decker of the Armed Services' Special

Operations Command. They're working on matters related to this morning's events and came to me for help."

Maras examined both operatives with intelligent eyes that missed nothing, then said, "At ease, everyone. Sit." She paused while they complied.

"Your presence in my office puzzles me, Commander, Major. Would either of you care to explain why we're talking, considering the Silfax incident happened only a few hours ago and hasn't yet been ruled a terrorist act by the Cimmerian government? Besides, this isn't Sixth Fleet HQ, nor am I Admiral Kingsley. Anti-terrorism is an Armed Services responsibility, not ours."

"Sir," Talyn began, "Major Decker and I are on a wide-ranging sweep through the Rim Sector for the SOCOM anti-terrorist unit. Our job is to pinpoint the leadership of a radical organization calling itself the Democratic Stars Alliance. We picked up a spoor on Mission Colony which led us here, but our arrival on Cimmeria coincided with the Silfax Mining Complex disaster, no more. However, we believe it was, in fact, a terrorist attack and can offer information that might lead to finding those responsible and thereby preventing more deaths."

"Okay." Maras studied Talyn with undisguised skepticism. "The Cimmerian government isn't calling Silfax anything other than an accident right now, and our criminal intelligence branch believes this Democratic Stars Alliance to be nothing more than political malcontents with delusions of adequacy. But let's set that aside for now. Why reach out to Chief Superintendent Morrow, who as you're surely aware is seized with internal affairs and reports to Wyvern? She's hardly able to help the Fleet's anti-terrorism effort. If we are dealing with such."

"Caelin Morrow and I worked together before, sir. I know her to be of impeccable integrity and one of the least likely to be suborned by the Commonwealth's internal enemies. The radical movements we've been tracing enjoy patronage in the most unexpected places and I couldn't risk compromising our operations. My partner and I intend to find the DSA and put it out of action before they destroy Howard's Landing or another densely populated area with the same sort of incredibly powerful explosive we found in the hands of DSA allies on Mission Colony."

"You think it might come to that, Commander?"

"Without a doubt. As I said, the major and I have been tracking violent political groups for months. The DSA and its affiliates are determined to overthrow legitimate governments in the Rim Sector and replace them with regimes espousing a radical — by that, you can read murderous — agenda. They believe in the philosophy of cooperate and live, resist and die."

"That still doesn't explain why you're here with Chief Superintendent Morrow."

"Considering the stakes, this situation has gone beyond what Major Decker and I can manage on our own, at least until Caledonia sends reinforcements. But we can't afford to wait. Too many lives are at stake. This is where I would suggest Chief Superintendent Morrow comes in. She can serve as the head of a Constabulary task force responsible for assisting the Cimmerian authorities and liaising with Fleet counter-terrorism. But this idea requires your blessing and your support."

"Caelin reports to DCC Hammett? She's not in my chain of command."

Hammett, the head of the Constabulary's Professional Compliance Bureau and Chief Superintendent Morrow's direct superior, was at Constabulary headquarters in the Wyvern system, several dozen light years from

Cimmeria.   It meant Morrow enjoyed a degree of independence few officers could claim, especially those below commissioner rank.

"Yes, sir. But you're in charge of the Rim Sector. Your word counts for more than DCC Hammett's when it comes to cooperating with the Gendarmerie and the planetary government."

Maras turned her gaze on Morrow.

"What are your thoughts, Caelin?"

"If we can avoid a repeat of Silfax on a larger scale, I'll agree with any scheme, sir."

"So you agree with them that Silfax was attacked and not a victim of an industrial accident?"

Morrow gestured toward Decker.

"The major is an expert with explosives, and after seeing only the newscast images of the site, he's convinced it wasn't accidental, something he hopes to confirm with live satellite images of the actual detonation."

"Yet the only way to obtain the data is through a formal Constabulary task force designated to help the Gendarmerie, correct?"

"Yes, sir."

"Shall I ask DCC Hammett for his blessing?"

"A simple memo from your office to the Gendarmerie's director general should suffice for our purposes, sir. I shall report my activities to my DCC in due course."

A faint smile softened Maras' severe countenance.

"Now we're agreed, I'll confess I was already thinking about forming an ad hoc task force like the one you proposed, though choosing which of my chief superintendents would be best suited to head it could have proved a challenge. By avoiding that decision in favor of letting someone from outside the Rim Sector's chain of command take over solves the dilemma. I'll make sure you receive every measure of support."

"Thank you, sir."

Maras turned her uncompromising gaze on Talyn again.

"I'm aware you black ops people generally put operational needs ahead of legal niceties when it's time to save innocent lives, but please remember blatant violations of Cimmerian and federal laws won't help fight folks like the DSA in the long run."

Talyn inclined her head in polite acknowledgment.

"Understood, sir. Major Decker and I are experts in the art of plausible deniability as is every member of the SOCOM anti-terrorist unit."

"In that case, we're done here. My memo will go out to the Gendarmerie and the Rim Sector branch heads within the hour, Caelin. Keep me apprised of developments as always."

"Yes, sir." All three climbed to their feet.

"Dismissed."

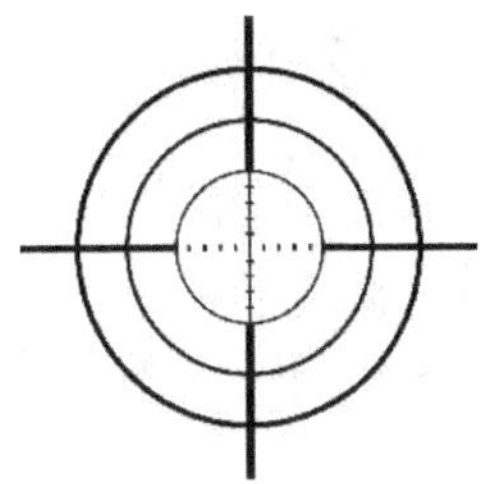

— TWENTY-FIVE —

They found Arno Galdi in a quiet conversation with Maras' adjutant in the antechamber. He looked up with a pleased smile when he caught the expression on their faces.

"I gather it went well?"

"We're in business," Decker replied.

"The communications center is ready for you anytime you want."

"How about we go there now, Arno?" The Marine suggested. "Hera and Caelin can catch up while I check for mail and report to HQ. They probably have a lot to discuss."

When Talyn gave him the nod, Decker and Galdi vanished into the corridor while she and Morrow strolled back to the lift bank for a quick ride up.

"How's your pal Monty Hobart, or whatever his name was?" The latter asked once they were back in her tenth-floor domain. A smile lit up her face. "I'd still like to thank him properly for saving my life, *after* giving him hell for trying to manipulate my investigation."

"Monty was Lieutenant Commander Garrett Montero, a career Naval Intelligence operative."

"Was?"

"He died at the Coalition's hands on Scandia during the putsch attempt. His killers didn't live long enough to face justice thanks to my partner and his friends from the 1st Special Forces Regiment.”

Morrow’s face fell upon hearing the news.

“Damn.”

“Yeah, damn. Garrett was one of the best, a rare combination of sneakiness and integrity. The Fleet gave him a funeral with full military honors. Zack and I were part of the escort carrying him to his final resting place in the Fort Arnhem cemetery.” Talyn gestured at the ceiling. “I like to think his spirit is out there somewhere watching over the rest of us.”

“I guess you truly are fighting a war.” Morrow waved Talyn into her office. “With casualties on both sides.”

“*We* are fighting a war, Caelin. Just because the Constabulary hasn’t suffered direct hits yet or at least hits you haven’t written off as something more mundane, doesn’t mean your lot isn’t among the combatants. At least as far as the enemy is concerned. Anyone who stands between the Coalition and its goals is fair game.”

“So I recall you telling me once upon a time.”

“Things have become much worse since then.”

Morrow dropped into her chair behind the desk.

“Agreed. Even Arno Galdi, ever the skeptic, sees things we never noticed a few years ago. Saying he, Sergeant Bonta and I aren’t busy wasn’t quite accurate. The three of us represent what passes for a command staff in my unit, and we are between investigations, it’s true. Yet the rest of my teams are out chasing the corrupt, venal and stupid in our ranks, and those of the Fleet, each carrying a caseload unheard of in my time with the PCB. Either we’re getting better at sniffing out bent cops, or they’re increasing in number.”

“Considering the Black Sword mess we dealt with a few months before that putsch attempt on Scandia, I’d say the latter — more of your own corrupted by our

Coalition friends and their minions. Folks like Assistant Commissioner Bujold."

"It depresses me to realize you're probably right."

"You want me to depress you further?"

Morrow gave Talyn a resigned look.

"If I say no, will you do it anyway?"

"Yes. Remember why Grand Admiral Kowalski created the Constabulary out of the Fleet's security branch last century?"

"As a replacement for the thoroughly corrupt Special Security Bureau after she ordered it destroyed."

"And for over ten years, we've been dealing with another replacement for the SSB, one which also reports directly to the SecGen's office."

"The *Sécurité Spéciale.*"

"Precisely. It would dearly like to become the SSB's anointed successor, with that unlamented organization's overly broad reach and mandate. I doubt it intends to leave any room for an independent Constabulary reporting to the Senate."

Morrow's face took on a wry expression.

"Now you've done it. I'm more depressed than I was a minute ago."

"We're in this war together, Caelin, whether or not you wish to take part."

"I know. Do you think the Silfax Mining Complex incident is an escalation in the Coalition's tactics?"

"Possibly. Even probably. The attempted coup against the Scandian government was a big step up from their usual underhanded schemes."

A soft chime forestalled Morrow's response. She glanced at her desk and nodded.

"DCC Maras just spoke directly with the Gendarmerie's director general. We should receive everything they have on the matter shortly."

"Cooperation from the locals so fast?"

"There hasn't been a suspected terrorist incident on Cimmeria since the end of the war, Hera. There's no one left in the security services who remembers those days. Our Gendarmerie colleagues are well out of their depth, and the current director general is no jurisdictionally obsessed dummy. I'm not surprised he jumped at our offer of help. Besides, he can probably see the writing on the wall concerning federal involvement, especially the Fleet's, since it owns the Commonwealth-wide mandate for anti-terrorism. Better to invite us feds into the tent now than wait until we push our way in and take over."

"A good sign the Gendarmerie already figured out this wasn't an accidental explosion. It would be nice if all planetary security services were able to think ahead in such a fashion."

"I'm sure you'll find the usual churlishness and obstruction further down the Gendarmerie's chain of command."

A sly smile lit up Talyn's serious countenance.

"That's why I bring Zack along on my missions. He's remarkably skilled at converting unbelievers and removing obstacles."

"High explosives solve many problems," a deep voice said from the corridor, heralding Decker's return on the heels of his newest friend, Arno Galdi. "Message sent. It's a bare bones report on the latest developments. But HQ replied to our earlier report and said help was coming. No mention of what, who, or when. The boss is being cagey with details, which means Admiral Kruczek's inquisitors suspect Black Sword moles in the communications system."

"What sort of help?" Morrow asked.

"If I get my wish, a full squadron from the 1st Special Forces Regiment — four hundred operators with extensive anti-terrorism training. But considering my luck, it'll be a corporal's guard with half the troops on light duties."

"That many secret squirrels? I don't know whether to feel blessed or afraid." Galdi stroked his beard. "Why not use the local Armed Services muscle?"

"As much as I respect my Army comrades of the Cimmeria Regiment, they're not trained or equipped to deal with scum who toss MHX bombs at civilians. Now if the DSA, or whoever did the Silfax job intend to storm parliament or the cabinet offices, then yeah, I'll ask Colonel Hecht for a couple of armored infantry battalions to stiffen the National Guard."

"Fair enough."

"I asked that the communications center route any reply to your office, Chief," Galdi said.

The soft chime sounded again, drawing Morrow's eyes to her desktop.

Decker chuckled.

"That can't be a reply from HQ already. My message hasn't even cleared Cimmeria's heliopause yet."

"No, it's not," Morrow replied in a thoughtful tone. "Our Gendarmerie colleagues *are* spooked. They just sent me everything they have, including the raw data, and within what — ten minutes of DCC Maras calling their director general?"

"Raw data? Does that include satellite imagery?" Decker asked.

"Let me check." Morrow perused the electronic files, and then nodded. "There's a video marked detonation. I'll put it up on the main display." She pointed at the far wall.

Galdi, Talyn, and Decker turned to face the screen. A few seconds later, an aerial view of the snow-capped Uttara Kuru mountain range swam into view. The Silfax Mining Complex sat at the bottom of an elongated bowl between two high ridges. With the satellite pickup set to wide angle, they could see most of the above-ground structures nestled at the foot of slopes covered in lush greenery.

Mine heads, refinery, administration building, and company town with shopping and recreational facilities, and the thin ribbon of the monorail linking Silfax with Archeron, where the refined metals were shipped around Cimmeria and offworld.

With breathtaking suddenness, a bloom of light so bright it might have come from the heart of a supernova, smothered everything. It faded with equal speed, leaving behind a growing black cloud that seemed to reach for the satellite's electronic eye.

Decker, Talyn, and the two Constabulary officers watched in silence until the cloud dissipated, revealing a ruined landscape which resembled nothing so much as a cooling lava field.

The Marine recovered his voice first.

"Could you return to just before the moment of detonation and run the video at one-twentieth normal speed, please?"

"You saw something, Zack?" Talyn asked.

Decker raised a restraining hand.

"Hang on for a moment."

He stood and walked to the display.

"Run it."

An impossibly white light washed out the bucolic scene with the same heart-stopping suddenness as before.

"Freeze."

"Did you slow it?" Talyn asked. "It seemed to blossom just as fast."

"That was at one-twentieth normal speed."

Galdi let out a low whistle.

"If I didn't know better, I'd say that was an antimatter reaction."

"No." Decker shook his head, eyes still glued to the display. "I'm convinced we're looking at MHX-19, Mayhem for those with a questionable sense of humor."

"How big would the device have been?" Galdi asked.

Decker looked back at the display.

"Not very. One hundred kilos or thereabouts. A standard small shipping cube would suffice for transport and camouflage. I'd say our terrorists used the monorail to bring it into the complex, hidden among a supply run, or empties returning to the refinery. Pinpointing the epicenter with any accuracy will be almost impossible. Mayhem detonates too fast for most video pickups and erases everything in a substantial circle around ground zero."

"Are you sure?" Morrow asked. "Because I have to relay your findings back to the Gendarmerie right away."

He shrugged.

"I can't see what else it might be. The visual signature is highly distinctive. You saw that single kilo blow away Blanca's Folly, Hera. Did this look familiar?"

Talyn nodded.

"It did, and that means the DSA is responsible for Silfax. This morning was the opening a salvo in their campaign to overthrow the Cimmerian government. Unless we hurry, we'll get more of these."

"And if they felt flush enough with MHX to use a hundred kilos in one strike, what does that tell you?" Decker asked.

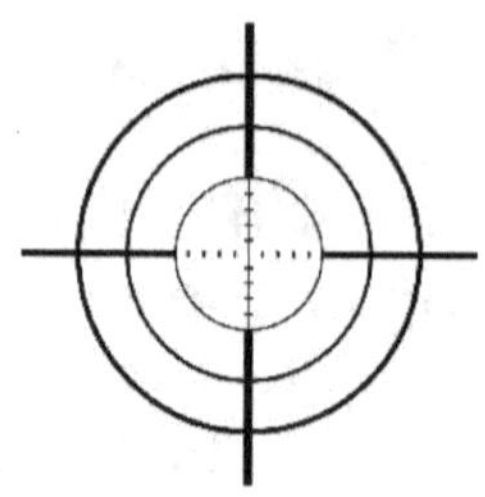

—TWENTY-SIX—

An appalled silence settled over Morrow's office. The two Constabulary officers stared at Decker with growing alarm.

"You mean there could be several hundred kilograms of that devil's mixture left on Cimmeria?" The chief superintendent suddenly sounded hoarse.

"Or more. Silfax was a test and a warning. It caused enough casualties and destruction to get the government's attention, but not quite enough to stampede it into calling for martial law and Fleet assistance right away. The next target will be an even more important node, something that'll cause a bigger shock to Cimmeria society."

"Cheerful bugger," Galdi said, scowling.

"Why has no one claimed responsibility yet?"

Talyn's chuckle sounded grim.

"Psychological pressure. The longer Cimmerian cops and politicians are in the dark about who and why, the more time they have to dream up worst-case scenarios and make counterproductive decisions. That leads to panic, and if it strikes the planet's leadership, the population will quickly sink into helpless fear. People who are afraid will do anything to ease their terror, such as forcing elected officials to negotiate with radical groups. Someone will claim responsibility, but not yet. If the bastards placed one or more moles inside the government or law enforcement, they'll be able to time it with exquisite precision."

"At least we enjoy one advantage they didn't expect. We can tell the Cimmerian authorities how it was done and who's responsible."

Talyn raised a hand with index, middle, and ring fingers extended.

"Three advantages, Caelin. The one you just mentioned, plus the fact terrorists don't know Zack and I are in play and that one of the Commonwealth's premier counterstrike units is already on its way."

Decker grunted.

"We hope. I asked for a squadron to back me in the Scandia business and they sent a troop. Not even a company but a troop."

"That was a different situation, Zack," Talyn replied. "The boss will come through this time."

"Terrorists who massacre thirty-five hundred civilians to get a government's attention frighten me. Face it. We're outmatched this time around and can't rely on local help. The boss better come through or we'll see a lot more dead children."

"He will. But back to out our advantages. I said we have three. The third is a name that can lead us to the bastards. Alasdair Malter, who traveled as Alek Mannsbach, was the DSA's envoy to the Mission Colony Freedom Collective. He gave the late Gustav Kerlin money and a kilo of MHX to join his organization. Malter's the reason we're here."

"Since both of you keep using the past tense when speaking of the dead, may I assume this individual is no longer among the living?"

"Some people don't react well to interrogation drugs," Talyn replied. "And in a field situation, we can't test them beforehand."

Morrow raised a hand.

"I don't want to know."

"As you wish. But our best bet right now is to find his friends and acquaintances. Many will be DSA members. It's the only thread we can pull on."

A soft but insistent chime forestalled Morrow's reply. She tapped the screen embedded in her desk, and the main display came to life again, this time with the image of a middle-aged, mostly bald man in Gendarmerie blue with the six stripes of a colonel on his collar.

"Chief Superintendent Morrow? I'm Alan Joubert, and for my sins, I'm the Silfax incident task force second in command. Our director general fired off a rocket ordering us to cooperate with the Constabulary. I understand you head the federal task force charged with assisting us?"

"I am, and that is my duty, Colonel. Thank you for calling so quickly and for sending over all the data on this terrible act of terrorism."

A guarded look came over Joubert's swarthy features.

"Act of terrorism, Chief Superintendent?"

"With me are experts who studied the satellite imagery taken at the moment the tragedy occurred and are formal in declaring it a deliberate act by a person or persons unknown. Are you familiar with an explosive called Mayhem?"

Joubert shook his head.

"No. It seems a rather peculiar name."

Morrow recounted, almost word for word, Decker's earlier explanation about the MHX-19. When she fell silent, the stony-faced Gendarmerie colonel asked, "May I inquire about your experts' qualifications?"

She waved at Decker to enter the video pickup's field of view.

"Good afternoon, sir," he said. "My name is Zack Decker. I'm a Marine Corps officer qualified as a

Master Gunner. Do you know what a Master Gunner is, sir?"

Joubert nodded once.

"I did a hitch in the Corps before coming home to enlist in the Gendarmerie. You're an expert on all matters involving weapons, ammunition, and explosives. But I never heard of this Mayhem, or MHX-19 which I suppose is the proper term."

"Understandable. It is one of the most restricted explosives in the Armed Services inventory."

"Yet you claim someone used it to annihilate the largest mining complex in this star system?"

"I do, sir. It leaves a distinctive visual trace at the moment of detonation. The satellite video you provided us shows precisely such a trace. Considering the Mayhem could only come from a Fleet ammunition depot despite the rigorous controls in place, I think it reasonable to assume the perpetrators didn't merely take a small sample. They'll make it worth their while."

Decker saw Joubert's face lose its color as the import of his words sunk in.

"You mean there's more of this super explosive on Cimmeria."

"If they were willing to use what I estimate was about a hundred kilos in Silfax, a relatively minor target, I'm willing to bet they still have a few hundred kilos more at their disposal."

"My God, man. Do you know what you're saying?" Joubert asked after a pause during which his eyes betrayed a series of mental calculations.

"It could be enough to level Howard's Landing and Archeron, with a bit left over for minor settlements."

"I'd like to know how terrorists obtained your damned explosive."

"That's something my superiors are already investigating, sir. But here and now, we need to find the perpetrators and make sure they can't use whatever MHX they have left."

"Easy to say, Decker — what is your rank, by the way?"

"Major, sir."

"A bit junior to be working as an anti-terrorist liaison officer with the Constabulary and planetary law enforcement, no?"

"In my line of business, the brass assigns jobs according to experience and qualification, not rank. Besides, my teammate, Hera Talyn, is a Navy commander, one grade higher than mine."

"Is she also a Master Gunner?" Joubert asked.

"No, sir. However, Commander Talyn has extensive experience tracking down violent radicals."

"I see. How did the Fleet anticipate events to the point of sending two of their anti-terrorism liaisons to Cimmeria before the Silfax atrocity?"

"We were working on something else and our arrival today is coincidental. However, due to the scope of this morning's events and the fact they might be related to our original task, we immediately contacted our Constabulary colleagues."

"I see," Joubert repeated. "And if I ask what your original orders were will you tell me they're classified?"

"No, sir. We were following up on intelligence reports that a radical organization on Mission Colony was linked to a Cimmeria-based umbrella group which recently came to our notice. Since the Mission Colony revolutionaries no longer pose a threat, our next logical step was dealing with this Democratic Stars Alliance."

"So you heard of the DSA. Good. We think it might be responsible for Silfax since it absorbed half a dozen of our own radical fronts, including at least two which we suspect were involved in recent, small-scale political violence. Unfortunately, we could never pin anything on them, thanks to their fancy lawyers."

"Let me guess, the Deep Space Foundation funded those lawyers."

The colonel gave him a surprised look.

"You're well informed, Major. Yes, the money to pay for legal expenses probably came from the Foundation, but even our best forensic accountants could not trace it back definitively."

"What happens next, sir?"

"Things remain somewhat fluid since the rescue teams are only starting to survey Silfax. No one's claimed responsibility, but that should change in a matter of hours. After that?" His shoulders twitched with a fatalistic shrug. "We must wait and see. I'll inform our team of your findings. Please be prepared to brief my superiors and possibly senior government officials on what you told me. That dangerous radicals are sitting on enough explosives to cause irreparable damage will throw everyone for a loop."

"Commander Talyn and I will do our best to find them before the worst happens."

"Good to know. Joubert, out." The Gendarmerie officer's image faded away.

"Now *that*," Decker jerked a thumb at the display, "is a worried man who doesn't know what might hit him next."

"And you did nothing to help," Talyn said.

"Perhaps not his peace of mind, but as you may have noticed, I cast bread upon the Gendarmerie's waters, my dear. News that SOCOM operatives calling themselves Talyn and Decker figured out the terrorists used Mayhem will spread beyond the bounds of whatever containment system the gendarmes put around their investigation."

Morrow stared at him in surprise.

"Pardon?"

"Our names mean something in certain circles."

Understanding lit up her pale eyes.

"Did you just bait a trap?"

"I hope so. In the event we can't find a connection between the late Alasdair Malter also known as Alek Mannsbach and the DSA, we'll need a Plan B. If this is a Coalition-driven campaign, the mere mention of my and Hera's names might sound alarm bells, considering we thwarted many of their schemes in recent years. And if our names don't do the trick, then finding out Fleet SOCOM officers are already in play could trigger a response."

Morrow nodded.

"Let the enemy come to you instead of chasing him."

"As a fallback, if the Malter-Mannsbach thread doesn't pan out," Talyn said.

"Understood. I suppose you'd like us to pull up everything we and the Cimmerian authorities have on this dead DSA envoy?"

"Please. And I'd like access to the documents section or whichever department around here generates IDs and faces for undercover police operations."

"May I ask why?"

"We'll be going after Malter's associates under assumed identities, but rather than use a set of ours, I'd like to recycle two we picked up on Mission Colony Tweaking IDs to match disguised features is easier than turning ourselves into genetic clones of the original owners."

A groan escaped Decker's lips.

"Seriously?"

"If you can come up with a better idea, I'll be happy to listen."

"What if the local nutjobs heard of Eva and Piet's passing?"

"Eva's perhaps, since the cops found her body, although I doubt news of a tawdry murder such as hers made it across the stars. Especially since the 24th

Constabulary is probably keeping the investigation under wraps due to Kristy Bujold's involvement. Piet, on the other hand, vanished in a brilliant flash of light. His body will never be found nor will his death ever be confirmed. I think Eva Cortez and her security chief will find their way into the heart of the DSA much faster than anyone else we can become in the space of a few hours."

"Provided the locals have nothing more than superficial descriptions of either."

"Considering Eva preferred to work in Gustav's shadow, and security goons rarely matter because they're interchangeable?"

"As long as this caper doesn't end up with you holding my skull while quoting a thousand-year-old play." When Decker saw Galdi's puzzled expression, he said, "The Piet I'm supposed to impersonate answered to the unlikely last name of Yorik."

Galdi's eyes lit up.

"Aha. Nice. And when he died did you—"

"He did, even though I asked him not to," Talyn said. "Can we stick with the important stuff, please? Such as the documents section? I'd like to get a move on."

"Certainly. I'll introduce you to Inspector Hartwig. He and I went through the Academy together eons ago. His lair is on the third floor."

"Zack, while I take care of our credentials, how about you play analyst and examine the Gendarmerie's data?"

The Marine made a face.

"I'd be delighted. If someone could show me to a spare workstation..." He gave Morrow a questioning look.

"The bullpen is just about empty today. Take your pick."

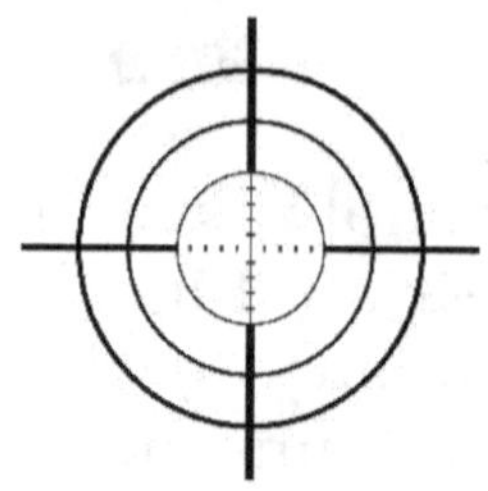

— TWENTY-SEVEN —

Decker stretched as he rose from his workstation and wandered over to the nearest window. Now that the sun had set, thousands of tiny lights marking streets, avenues, storefronts, and apartment windows studded downtown Howard's Landing. He wondered how many of the citizens enjoying a balmy evening with family or friends, or even in solitary contemplation, understood the destruction of the distant Silfax Mining Complex would forever change their lives.

With only a quick break to eat meals brought up from the officer's mess, he and Talyn had spent the last five hours sorting and grading the Gendarmerie's data. By the evening, his brain felt as if it were leaking out both ears. Morrow and Galdi were similarly occupied in their own offices. The Marine felt as if they were no further ahead in finding the DSA and its deadly stockpile.

"I need a beer, a shower, and you," he said turning away from one of the best views in the entire city. "And I'm not particularly fussy in what order."

Talyn, eyes still locked on her display, said, "I am. I'd rather not suffer the beery embrace of an unwashed gorilla pretending to be a commissioned officer. Besides, we're not done yet, so it's back to work for you."

"Slave driver."

"If anyone knows what being a slave feels like, it would be you."

"Pull out the whip, honey. I need added motivation."

"Once you've done your share."

"Tease."

"If you absolutely need a break, ask Arno where we can put down our heads for a few hours."

"Secure or terrorist bait?"

She glanced at him, eyes narrowed in thought.

"Let's go secure for tonight. It's been a long day. We can always choose a nice, easily accessible hotel room in the vicinity tomorrow. Unless we get something on Alasdair Malter or his cover identity from Arno's Gendarmerie friend between now and then."

Decker stomped to attention and snapped off a mock salute. *"A sus órdenes, mi capitán de fragata."*

"Teaching yourself Spanish now?"

"Why not? Many of the most murderous revolutionary sociopaths in pre-diaspora times spoke the language. I figure it might help me understand the terrorists' mindset."

Talyn pointed at the door with an extended finger.

"Go find us quarters for the night, Mister Amateur Historian. Before you list names and wax poetic about their gruesome ends."

"Most died miserably, like animals instead of men."

He slipped out of the room before she could launch an empty coffee cup at his head.

Decker crossed the hallway and stuck his head into Galdi's office.

"Suffering from data lock yet?"

Galdi's head came up, and he let out a weary sigh.

"Not quite, but give me another twenty minutes or so. Astounding how much they gathered in the space of eight or nine hours after the explosion."

"Most of it irrelevant."

"Yes, but one does occasionally find a nugget of gold beneath the manure pile."

"Old policeman's saying?"

Galdi shook his head.

"No. My grandfather. He was a veritable fount of folk wisdom. But it applies to detective work, or that of intelligence officers, I suppose. Can I do something for you? Or is this a social call? If the latter, you're most welcome. Misery shared is misery halved."

"As much as I'd like to hang around and kibitz, my dear partner reminded me we need a place to sleep for a few hours. Nothing fancy and preferably within a secure perimeter. We don't want to play terrorist bait in earnest until we've rested. Any recommendations?"

"You're in luck. This building has a suite of sleeping pods on the fifth floor, for personnel who need a few hours shuteye between shifts and either can't or don't want to go home. It's no worse than what you find in most spaceports or ground transport terminals. Hang on." Galdi glanced at the screen embedded in his desk and let his fingers dance. "There. Two adjacent pods reserved for you and the commander. You'll find your names on the hatches."

"Do they have a connecting door?"

Galdi gave Zack a puzzled glance, then chuckled as understanding dawned on him.

"Sorry, no. But I thought you wanted to sleep."

Decker winked at him.

"She does. Thanks for arranging quarters. I better return to work before Hera decides I'm not even worthy of a pod, let alone her charming presence."

"Isn't it a joy to work for such challenging superiors?"

"Buy me a beer, and I'll tell you stories to make your hair stand on end."

This time, Galdi laughed outright.

"Ditto, I'm afraid."

******

Decker pushed away from the desk and sighed.

"Finished with my first run through the manure pile, but I found no gold nuggets."

"Pardon?" Talyn glanced at him sideways. "What are you talking about this time?"

"Never mind. It's almost midnight. How about we find our sleeping pods and turn in?" Decker reached into the travel bag at his feet and withdrew the whiskey bottle. "After a nightcap, of course."

She leaned back and stretched her arms over her head.

"I suppose it would be the wise thing to do. I was done half an hour ago anyway and going back through some of the stuff I put aside for further review. Did our friends go home?"

"Yep. Arno sent me a message at twenty-two hundred saying he and Caelin would be back by oh-six-thirty tomorrow so they could take us to breakfast in the HQ officer's mess. It's just you, the overnight duty crew downstairs, and me." He took a swig from the bottle and sighed. "Nice. Want a nip."

She held out her hand.

"Give."

He complied, then asked, "Any insights you'd like to share?"

"Beyond the fact that whoever's responsible should under no circumstances make it to trial? Nothing of note."

"I'll do you one better." He waited until she took a swig, and then retrieved the bottle. "Unless we mete out unforgettable punishment to the sponsors of this act, it'll happen again. It's fine to wipe out the DSA, or whichever bunch of sociopaths placed the bomb, but they're the equivalent of non-player characters in virtual reality games. We never properly punished the offworld bastards behind that putsch attempt on Scandia, which is why they thought it might be fun to escalate things. We can't let the mass murder of innocents go without a response."

"The boss or Admiral Kruczek might disagree."

"Bugger 'em. We'll go rogue and ask for forgiveness afterward. It wouldn't be the first time."

"If the response you're contemplating is what I think, you might not find forgiveness so easily."

Decker took another mouthful of whiskey and tucked the bottle away.

"We'll discuss it again when the time comes, darling. For now, shower and sleep."

"What?" She smirked at him. "No lewd invitations?"

"I gave you the chance earlier. Now the only arms I want are those of Morpheus." He grabbed his bag and stood. "Downward, ho."

**

The next morning, during ablutions in the shared barracks-style washroom, Decker and Talyn attracted curious looks from Constabulary members with whom they'd shared the bank of sarcophagus-like sleeping pods.

But none seemed brave enough to question the big, taciturn man with the aura of suppressed violence or his cold, almost predatory companion. Similar puzzlement followed them as they entered the officer's mess for breakfast in Morrow and Galdi's company.

"Nice place." Decker's eyes studied the large, formal, wood-paneled common room. "It looks like the Constabulary still has a lot of Armed Services DNA in its makeup. I could almost believe myself in the Fleet HQ mess back on Caledonia."

"Some days I despair at the thought we have a few too many military chromosomes left for comfort. We'll sit over there," Morrow said, pointing at a separate table in the corner as they made their way to the buffet. "It's the most private, and since no one wants to be seen in public near Firing Squad officers in any case, we should be able to speak freely."

Once they were seated, Talyn asked, "Why do you say the Constabulary is still overly militarized? Your police regiments and battalions are often the only full-time defense force many outlying colonies can call on for protection."

"I don't mean that," Morrow replied around a bite of scrambled eggs. "It's the mindset. We're police, not soldiers. The chain of command is a necessary thing, but cops can't treat it with the same reverence as you military folks."

Talyn jerked a thumb at Decker.

"Not everyone in a Fleet uniform reveres higher ranks."

"So I understand. But investigating constables gone wrong, no matter the rank, has taught me a lot of the strays would have stayed between the lines if they were more willing to question their seniors and if necessary, act to constrain them." Morrow picked up her coffee mug and raised it as if in salute. "Don't mind me. I always thought the Constabulary needs to work harder on developing a separate culture from the Armed Services, but I'm shouting into a hurricane for all the good it does. And I've yet to finish my first coffee of the day, so..."

"She is usually a tad fierce this early," Galdi said. "A good thing when arresting a bent assistant commissioner, less so when breaking bread with friends and colleagues."

Morrow made a face at her inspector, but Decker understood the back and forth was more of a ritual than anything serious, a long-standing debate among colleagues close enough to allow themselves brutal honesty.

"Changing the subject deliberately, before I heap more opprobrium on the Constabulary because of acute caffeine deprivation, did you find anything useful in the data after Arno and I clocked off last night?"

"Nothing that'll lead us to the culprits, or even their identity. But the survey results from the site confirm Zack's conclusion Silfax was destroyed by a severely restricted explosive that should never have ended up in civilian hands, let alone those of violent radicals."

"What's next?"

Talyn shrugged before popping a ripe berry in her mouth.

"Hope your Gendarmerie contact will give us everything they know about Alasdair Malter today, and without asking too many questions," she said after swallowing. "In the meantime, we'll continue to analyze every single bit of intelligence the Cimmerians develop hoping to find an angle they missed."

"Such as Magda Annear," Decker said after finishing a healthy slice of smoked ham. "Call it a wild notion, but her traveling incognito on a tramp freighter when she's the daughter and partner of such illustrious, wealthy citizens as Senator Annear, and Pavel Yagudin seems wonky. I don't believe in coincidences, not when our favorite fake social justice organization could be involved. Maybe we should pay Louis Sorne a visit and see if that spawn of Baphomet financed mass murder. Five gets you ten he's still running things from inside his country club jail."

Morrow inclined her head in agreement.

"More than likely. I saw his true face when he ordered me killed. Sorne is pure evil, capable of anything.

Human lives are worthless to him, something he learned by cooperating with the Shrehari occupiers during his youth. And Antoine Hakkam, better known as Fast Tony in law enforcement circles, is his master's dog in everything."

"Well," Decker drawled before taking a sip of coffee, "if the motherless bastard had a hand in the Silfax atrocity, I don't doubt he'll learn a painfully terminal lesson in how worthless his own life is."

"Pardon?"

Morrow speared the Marine with a suspicious stare.

"Never mind, Caelin. I also need a good dose of caffeine before the ugly barbarian in me gets a jolt of civilization."

"May I remind both of you that there are laws, even for dealing with terrorists, radicals, and the Louis Sornes of this galaxy?"

Decker's face lit up with a wicked grin.

"Sure. I'm a great believer in justice. Natural justice that is."

"I don't think—" Morrow's communicator buzzed. She retrieved it from her tunic pocket and glanced at the screen. "Eat up. The Cimmerian prime minister's office just received a message claiming responsibility for Silfax."

"Not even twenty-four hours?" Decker shoved a last bit of egg into his mouth and swallowed. "I would have bet on another half day to let the Cimmerian government stew a little longer. Our doers must either be overly eager or on a tight timetable." He drained his coffee and stood. "Let's get to it, people."

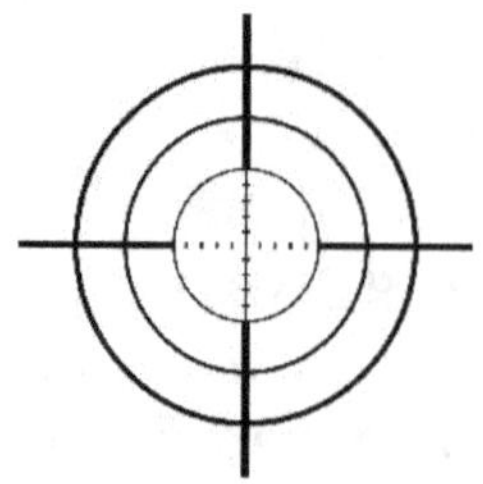

— TWENTY-EIGHT —

A woman of imposing stature, as tall as Decker but not quite as wide or muscular, greeted them on the tenth floor.

"All hell has broken loose, Chief," she said without preamble in a surprisingly deep voice.

"No doubt. Commander Talyn, Major Decker, this is Master Sergeant Destine Bonta, one of my most senior investigators. She's part of our ad hoc liaison team."

Bonta stuck out her hand.

"Glad to make your acquaintance, Commander. The chief and Inspector Galdi didn't tell us much after solving the mysterious case of the warrior's knife."

"Is that what you're calling it?"

"We give every one of our cases a fancy name. They're easier to remember that way."

The Constabulary noncom released Talyn and turned to Zack. He immediately realized Bonta was one of the few women he'd ever met who could stare him in the eye without tilting her head back. And stare she did.

"Major."

"Sergeant."

Her grip was hard, testing and Decker wondered what the others saw. They were a study in contrast, she bronze-skinned and dark-haired, he pale and blond, yet both forces of nature in their own right. The Marine briefly wondered how her powerful presence would come across in a more intimate setting. She must have seen something of that thought reflected in his eyes because a cold smile tugged at her lips.

"Charmed, I'm sure," Bonta said, giving him one last punishing squeeze before she let go. "Chief, Colonel Joubert wants to speak with you and the SOCOM officers as soon as possible."

"I thought that would be the case. My office, everyone."

While they found additional chairs in the detectives' bullpen across the hall, Morrow opened a link with Gendarmerie HQ across town. Joubert wasn't long in accepting her call.

"Good morning, Chief Superintendent."

"Good morning, Colonel. As you can see, the rest of my team and our two SOCOM liaison officers are with me."

"Hello. Well, someone finally claimed responsibility for the Silfax Mining Complex and, as expected, it was the DSA. Prime Minister Calvo received a message thirty minutes ago. It informed him Silfax was a warning shot and that if the illegitimate plutocratic regime oppressing the Cimmerian people doesn't open negotiations on a fundamental reform of every governmental institution, a second economically important target would suffer the same fate. They copied the newscasts, but we asked them in advance to hold anything they receive until we clear it for publication. So far they're complying, but the embargo won't last. And before you ask, we weren't able to trace the message's origins. It bounced around the satellite constellation over four dozen times as far as we can tell."

Decker shook his head.

"Illegitimate plutocratic regime? They sound remarkably like the bunch we went after on Mission Colony. Are all of those idiots using the pre-diaspora handbook for radical retards? The only plutocrats I see around here are probably financing the DSA."

Talyn gave her partner a quelling glance, but Joubert nodded in agreement.

"I agree, Major. It sounds terribly overwrought and centuries out of date, but here we are. When you mention plutocrats financing the DSA, what do you mean?"

"I'd put the Deep Space Foundation and its board of directors, whether they're in a country club prison or living it large on their estates, at the head of your list. But they won't be involved in the nuts and bolts of this terror campaign, nor will any financial contribution to the DSA's coffers be traced back to them. Did the DSA list the reforms it wants?"

"No. For now, they expect a public acknowledgment by the prime minister that the Cimmerian government requires a complete overhaul. The details come when Calvo agrees to negotiate."

"Of course, reform isn't actually the desired end state because anyone but the most blinkered ideologue knows no sane politician will bow to terrorist pressure," Talyn said. "Besides, groups like the DSA don't possess enough intellect to assume control over the governance of a star system, though they probably think themselves smarter than most, and their financial backers know it. In my estimation, the goal is to paralyze and then destabilize the legitimate power structure so that a savior can step in. It's the only thing that makes sense when the opening gambit is mass murder, with more of the same threatened. Radicals don't care about the oppressed, real, or imagined, nor do their puppet masters."

"It's what many of us here believe as well, Commander. By the way, did you gain any new insights from the data we transmitted yesterday?"

Talyn shook her head.

"Sorry, no. Major Decker and I intend to sift through it again this morning."

"I'm afraid you'll have to put it off for a few hours. Director General Dubnikov would like to meet you within the hour and hear about the explosive used at Silfax in person. We can do it via remote conference if you like. I know the Constabulary has the necessary holoprojection facilities."

The Marine and his partner exchanged a quick glance before the latter said, "We'll be more than happy to come over, Colonel. If Chief Superintendent Morrow can help us with transportation, we could be there shortly."

"I can," Morrow said. "And if you don't mind, Colonel, I'd like to go with them."

"Certainly. Say in half an hour? I'll meet you at the main HQ's front entrance."

"Until then."

Joubert's face dissolved, and the display returned to its standby image — a bucolic mountain scene from a world dozens of light years distant.

"I'm surprised you insisted on going to them even though he offered an alternative, Hera," Morrow said.

"A bit of goodwill goes a long way. We might have to ask Joubert for the information about Malter if your acquaintance doesn't come through, and Joubert is bound to ask questions I'd rather not answer right away. Besides, we won't entice the DSA or its backers into paying us any attention by keeping a low profile. "

The Constabulary officer snapped her fingers and pointed at the Marine.

"That's right. The bait and smite tactic Zack mentioned yesterday. Suddenly, I'm not sure I want to come with you."

"Don't worry. They won't be on us that fast."

"I certainly hope so. Sergeant, could you please call for a vehicle from the motor pool?"

"Immediately, sir. I'll even drive."

**

"Lovely." Decker slipped into the front passenger seat of a black, unmarked but visibly armored ground car while Morrow and Talyn settled in behind Bonta and the Marine. "Does it include automatic cannon behind the headlights and missile launchers in the back?"

"Nothing quite so dramatic, Major, though it'll withstand anything up to twenty millimeters for a short period, long enough to get away."

The car silently sped off through the heart of Howard's Landing where civilians, many of them government workers, made their way to work on a bright, sunny morning, still unaware of the ultimatum thrown in Prime Minister Calvo's face.

"Nice star system you have there. Shame if anything happened to it," Decker muttered to himself.

"Pardon." Bonta turned to glance at him.

"Just reflecting that there's little to no difference between organized crime and radical politics."

A soft chuckle burbled up the sergeant's throat.

"I never thought of it that way, but you're right. Maybe we need to expand the reach of the Criminal Organizations Act."

"It's a nice thought."

The car turned inland shortly after leaving the downtown core and passed through a commercial district replete with storefronts and warehouses before leaving the broad avenue in favor of a narrower tree-lined side road marked by a sign advertising the Cimmerian Gendarmerie Headquarters. After confirming identities and destination, armed sentries waved them into a hastily erected steel plate chicane cutting through the wire-topped wall that surrounded the entire complex.

"This is new," Bonta remarked as the car wound its way through the security perimeter. "The chicane and the armed guards, I mean."

"Prudent, though," Decker replied. "So long as they deploy something to keep the bad guys from coming in vertically." He pointed upward.

"I'm sure they do."

In contrast to its stately, decades-old Constabulary counterpart, the Gendarmerie HQ complex appeared so modern and sleek it might have been built last week. Three stories high, with a fluid step design wrapped around an inlaid stone parade square, it blended harmoniously with its parklike surroundings. Flags on tall poles by the main entrance provided a splash of color to liven up the walls' soothing ocher tones.

As they left the car, Colonel Joubert appeared through open doors leading to a glassed-in lobby. He raised his hand in greeting.

"Welcome. You can send your vehicle to park itself in the visitors' section."

"A pleasure to finally meet in person," Morrow replied, "though I wish it could be under better circumstances."

"Indeed. The director general is waiting in the main conference room with the rest of my team and most of the Gendarmerie's divisional commanders. We have until nine-thirty. He's expected in the prime minister's office at ten to meet with the cabinet crisis committee."

The high-ceilinged lobby matched the external architecture: pleasing curves and soothing colors, with none of the military or historically significant decorations favored by the Constabulary.

Joubert led them down a wide corridor pierced by regularly spaced doors whose sole identification were number plates centered on the panel until they turned a corner and heard the soft murmur of a dozen separate conversations emanating from an open doorway. Those conversations died off almost instantly when they entered on the Gendarmerie colonel's heels.

Joubert led them to a raised platform dominated by a wall-sized display at one end of the room. More than forty pairs of eyes followed their progress with intense curiosity. Once there, he turned toward a thin, gray-haired man with ascetic features and the four stars of a general sitting in splendid isolation at the head of the long, oval table.

"Sir, may I present the federal incident team assigned to help our investigation into the Silfax Mining Complex terrorist attack. Chief Superintendent Morrow and Master Sergeant Bonta of the Commonwealth Constabulary as well as Commander Hera Talyn and Major Zack Decker of the Armed Services Special Operations Command. Major Decker is the officer who identified the explosive compound used at Silfax. As requested, he will take us through his analysis of the attack based on the satellite imagery and answer any questions."

"Welcome." General Dubnikov's voice was deep and resonant. "Colonel Joubert told me the presence of two Fleet anti-terrorist experts on Cimmeria at this juncture is coincidental, but I'm not one to look a gift horse in the mouth. Please go ahead, Major."

While the others took chairs to either side of him, Decker asked, "Could you display the satellite video of Silfax starting one minute before the detonation? Keep it paused there until I say so, please."

Joubert made a gesture at an unseen subordinate. The wall-sized screen came to life with the now familiar aerial view frozen moments before over three thousand Cimmerians died instantly, their bodies vaporized by the force of the explosion.

"I will assume almost no one present knew about MHX-19, or Mayhem as its inventor nicknamed it before I briefed Colonel Joubert yesterday." When he saw Dubnikov and most of the other officers nod, Decker said, "In that case, I'll start by explaining what it is before demonstrating why I'm convinced someone used it yesterday morning."

"Please do," the general responded.

When Decker fell silent half an hour later, he saw nothing but grim faces around the table.

"I will admit," Dubnikov said in a tight voice, "the idea this Democratic Stars Alliance still holds several hundred kilograms of that diabolical mixture fills me with a dread I've never experienced before. Is there no easy way to detect it from a distance? We can pick up conventional plastic explosives from a kilometer or more so long as they're in contact with the ambient atmosphere."

Decker grimaced.

"Using the latest military-grade battlefield sensors programmed to recognize the stuff, perhaps from a few hundred meters, if the bastards aren't careful to keep it in hermetically sealed containers, sir."

"Could we borrow such sensors from the Cimmeria Regiment, Major?"

"They'd surely be delighted to help, however, that still leaves us without the right programming, and I don't know enough to tell a sensor what the explosive's chemical composition looks or smells like. We asked Fleet HQ to send us the technical specs, but it'll be a few days before we hear back."

"Meaning that in the meantime, we're entirely at the DSA's mercy."

"I'm afraid so, sir. If I could make a single recommendation at this point, it's to stall for time. Along with the technical specs, we also asked for a

SOCOM anti-terrorism unit, and HQ has assured me help is on the way."

"Your recommendation is noted, Major. I shall pass it to the prime minister," Dubnikov glanced down, "who expects me at New Government House shortly. Thank you.   Please continue with the question-and-answer session in my absence."

Everyone in the room stood along with him and came to attention. They stayed that way until Dubnikov and his aide left the room.

A round-faced, red-haired woman with three stars on her collar made a downward motion with her hand, and the assembled officers sat. She gave Decker a searching look.

"Since the director general did not have time to ask every question he wanted, let me do it in his stead."

"I'm at your disposal, General."

"Could you do me the favor of explaining why in any sane universe the Armed Services kept such a vile explosive in its inventory, let alone demonstrated security so lax that several hundred kilos went walkabout?"

"I'm sorry, but I cannot answer those questions to your satisfaction, sir. As a Master Gunner trained Marine, I'm aware of Mayhem's characteristics, but the reasoning that led to it being stockpiled in our ammunition depots is well beyond my pay grade. As to security, I can only surmise the moment our report reached Caledonia, every single ammunition depot in the Commonwealth found itself under physical scrutiny by the military police."

"Closing the proverbial gates after someone stole the Mayhem."

"Yes, sir."   Several pungent responses rolled over Decker's tongue, but he mercifully kept his mouth shut. Seeing the dangerous glint in her partner's eyes, Talyn rose and faced the three-star.

"Sir, if your government wishes to express its opinions on any alleged Armed Services shortcomings, may I suggest it addresses them to the relevant authorities at Fleet HQ on Caledonia. Major Decker has no more control over the stockpiling and securing of MHX-19 than you exercise over the deployment of Marine Corps Special Forces. He and I are technical experts in violent radical movements, not policymakers."

The three-star's face reddened, but agreeable nods from her peers around the table deflated the self-important display of outrage. After chewing on a few choice words, she said, "Fair enough, Commander. You and the major have our thanks. If there are no further questions, you're dismissed."

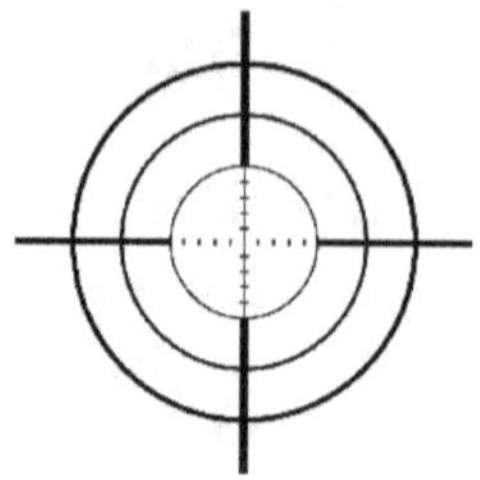

— TWENTY-NINE —

"Who was that hostile lieutenant general?" Talyn asked the moment their car's doors closed.

Morrow gave her a pained look.

"Gytha Goresson. She's the Gendarmerie's chief of operations and de facto second in command. Not only is she no fan of federal authorities, but when you think of Cimmerian plutocrats, to use the DSA's outdated terminology, the Goresson family is near the top of the list."

"Why lay into a mere major?" Talyn ignored Decker's mock-outraged snort. "Can't she differentiate between policymakers and technical experts? The rest of the assembly seems to have managed, which surely didn't do her any favors in the eyes of her peers and subordinates."

"I don't know what goes on in Goresson's mind. She might be the number two gendarme in this system, but I can't find anyone in blue with a good word about her."

"Nepotism," Bonta said without turning. "The Gorresons spend the cocktail hour with their Valerian friends at least once a week."

Decker thought for a moment, then asked, "Valerians as in Hector Valerian, Governor General of Cimmeria?"

"That family, yes. Hector is the current head though not the first to achieve high office because of good looks and an impressive family fortune."

"And Hector Valerian's spouse, Sonja Akiro is a childhood friend of Hannah Sorne as well as being on the Deep Space Foundation's advisory board."

"Oh dear," Talyn turned a disbelieving look on Morrow. "How delightfully incestuous."

"Tell me about it. Though I have no evidence, I'm sure the friendship helped that evil bastard Louis avoid hard time and spend his incarceration lording it over the other well-connected inmates at the Mill Haven Minimum Security Village. It's known as the Gilded Cage for a good reason."

Decker glanced over his shoulder at Morrow.

"How is someone like Valerian appointed as governor general anyway? I thought it took a two-thirds majority vote in parliament."

She gave him a weary shrug.

"The usual. Campaign contributions. Favors for family members. The promise of New Year's honors or a reserve commission in the National Guard for an imbecile nephew. You name it, Valerian has promised to dispense it at one time or another should he find himself the tenant of Cimmeria Hall."

"And I thought the politics around here were among the cleanest in the Rim Sector."

"Trust me on this, Major," Bonta said, "Cimmerians are as human as anyone else. The reputation for cleanliness is nothing more than fiction for the gullible, an aspiration for the painfully naïve, and a cynical fabrication by the corrupt. This star system's government has plenty of all three, never mind the electorate. Social values around here never quite recovered from the Shrehari occupation and its web of collaboration and treachery."

"You're a Cimmerian, Sergeant?"

"Mercy, no. I was born on Santa Theresa. But I've been stationed here for almost twelve years."

"Sergeant Bonta has a keen instinct for the darker foibles of human nature, Zack," Morrow said from the back seat. "That's why she's such a good professional compliance investigator."

"What the chief means is I can detect corruption from a parsec away. That's how I ended up in the PCB."

"And what does General Goresson smell like?" Talyn asked.

"Wealth and privilege, sir. She may be many things, but her family is comfortable enough that they need not soil their hands with grubby things like influence peddling."

A grin spread across Decker's face.

"Meaning they're members of the illegitimate plutocracy oppressing Cimmeria."

"Pretty much." The hint of a smile relaxed Bonta's tight expression. "According to the DSA, that is. God forbid we feds ever say a bad word about this system's elite."

Their car re-entered the Howard's Landing downtown core, and a frown replace Decker's earlier hilarity.

"Uh-oh."

"What?" Talyn leaned over to stick her head between Bonta and the Marine.

"Look at the long faces out there." He waved at the window. "Either Prime Minister Calvo called havoc and let slip the dogs of journalism, or someone sprang a leak."

"Or the DSA bypassed every single information gatekeeper when they saw their message wasn't going out to the unwashed masses," Morrow said in a resigned voice. "Either way, we can expect to see a growing sense of panic among the civilian population now they know Silfax wasn't destroyed by something accidental like a freak reactor failure."

"It'll be interesting to see how the various influencers' opinions shake out. Folks who shout the loudest for compliance with the DSA's demands or believe any attempt at negotiating a peaceful solution is treason could be in league with the terrorists' backers."

"I can understand how those advocating surrender might be on the side of darkness, but those publicly taking a hard line against negotiations?" Morrow sounded skeptical.

"Nothing destroys confidence in a government like added mass casualties and devastation because of an unyielding stance. It can be just as hard on morale for the average citizen as abject surrender."

"Heads I win, tails you lose," Bonta said.

"Something like that. If the goal is to destabilize Cimmeria by destroying the people's confidence in their leaders, thereby paving the way for a savior controlled by offworld powers, there's no way out except by annihilating the Democratic Stars Alliance."

Morrow grimaced.

"For that, we need to find them. Fast. Before Prime Minister Calvo is gored by the horns of an existential dilemma with incalculable repercussions for this star system and the entire sector."

"Which means back to the data analysis while we wait for the information on Malter. So far, it's our only avenue."

"Easy for you to say. But some of us aren't analysts. We're people of action, trained to terminate villains."

"Sorry. Once we're back in Caelin's tenth-floor dungeon, your job is to go through the Gendarmerie's data package for a second time, man of action."

******

Arno Galdi stuck his head into the corridor the moment they entered the PCB offices.

"Our unfriendly terrorists' love note escaped containment while you were making friends with the Gendarmerie, Chief."

"We figured as much," Morrow replied. "There are a lot of unhappy people walking around downtown."

"How did it go?"

"Major Decker scared the living daylights out of them, Inspector," Bonta replied. "I never saw so many appalled flag officers in a single room before today."

"In fairness, Mayhem *is* an appalling product." Galdi's eyes shifted to Decker and Talyn. "I heard back from my friend about Alasdair Malter, Alek Mannsbach, *and* Magda Annear. I'm afraid I owe him a big favor for doing this outside regular channels, which means you owe me one now."

"And we always pay our debts. What did he say?"

Before Galdi could answer, Morrow raised a restraining hand and checked her communicator.

"Hold that thought. Colonel Joubert wants to speak with us urgently."

"We left him less than thirty minutes ago."

"Nevertheless. Let's use the conference room this time." She pointed toward an open door at the far end of the corridor. "I'll link us."

The Gendarmerie officer's somber face materialized on the conference room's large main display as they entered and took seats around an oval table.

"The DSA sent Prime Minister Calvo a second message while General Dubnikov was with him, expressing annoyance at our attempt to quarantine their first one. It was the same deal as before — multiple bounces around the satellite constellation to mask the origin. They intend to set off another bomb within the hour as a sign of their displeasure and a warning to let the newscasts make DSA communiqués public with no restrictions. I sent you a copy of that message as well as the original one." Joubert's eyes turned toward Decker and Talyn, seated to Morrow's left. "Is there anything you can recommend we do to deal with this newest threat?"

Decker's face twisted into an apologetic grimace.

"Sorry, no. The only thing I can say is if it's planned as a rap on the knuckles, it won't be a repeat of Silfax in terms of magnitude."

"Why?"

"Because nudging a government in the direction you want depends on inflicting graduated doses of pain, Colonel. Death by a thousand pinpricks. Silfax was the big bang to get everyone's attention. They won't try another large-scale attack until it becomes clear your prime minister refuses to budge."

"Still..."

"I know, Colonel." Decker sighed. "We'll do our best."

Joubert's index finger shot up, stilling the Marine. "Hang on."

The sound abruptly cut out though they could see Joubert staring at someone off-screen and listing. After more than a minute, he turned back toward them.

"Surveillance satellites picked up an explosion on the Borrachas Sea approximately three hundred kilometers north of Archeron. It gave off the same visual signature as the Silfax detonation. I'll send the video for your confirmation, but what else could it be? Who sets off bombs in the middle of the ocean? At the time of the explosion, surface traffic control lost contact with an automated cargo ship, the *Valerian Theta*, bound for Howard's Landing. It left the port of Archeron four hours ago. Fortunately, there should be no casualties, since it was entirely AI-controlled with remote oversight from the Valerian Shipping Company's shore office in Howard's Landing."

Decker rubbed his chin, eyes narrowed in thought.

"If it was the promised rap on Prime Minister Calvo's knuckles, you know what that means, right, Colonel?"

"The second bomb was ready to go before even knowing about you embargoing news of their first message. The *Valerian Theta* would have finished loading cargo at the time it landed on the prime minister's desk."

"Exactly. I'll let you and your team ruminate on possible reasons why the DSA was a few steps ahead of us with this second attack. We can compare notes later. The other thing that strikes me is they likely used a standard transport container again. If you'll recall, I mentioned the strong possibility the Silfax bomb traveled in a similar casing via the monorail from Archeron."

"Meaning Archeron could be their base of operations."

"Perhaps, but I'm thinking more of a pattern in the way they deliver their devices. There's no better way to hide them than inside hermetically sealed shipping containers. Sensors set to detect airborne particles wouldn't find any traces, and you can shield the inside of a container without it being visible to the naked eye."

"Would they dare use the same protocol again?"

"If it worked twice? Why not? How many standard cubic containers are there on Cimmeria? Hundreds of thousands? How many gendarmes equipped with battlefield sensors can you field? A few hundred? Luck doesn't begin to cover what you'd need to find hidden bombs without the ability to narrow down your search. By the way, is the Valerian Shipping Company named after the current governor general's family? Or are there several rich Valerian families in this star system?"

"There's only one. Governor General Hector Valerian's brother Anson runs the dynasty's business, Valerian Industries, which includes several transportation subsidiaries. Under applicable legislation, there's a hermetic firewall isolating the GG from the company. Hector put his shares in trust, and has no standing in dealings between Valerian Industries Incorporated and any branch of the Cimmerian government, including regulatory agencies."

"I'm beginning to understand the DSA's problem with plutocrats running things around here, Colonel."

"Please, Major, not even in jest, though you'll find some who agree."

"Like the all talk, no action malcontent groups absorbed by a more militant DSA?"

"Among others."

Decker saw Morrow's signal from the corner of his eyes and said, "Pardon me for a moment. Yes, Chief Superintendent?"

"We received the satellite feed from the Borrachas Sea event. I'll play it on the secondary screen to your left."

"Thanks.   Let's see if your folks made the right assessment, Colonel."

A few minutes later, the Marine turned his head back to the main video pickup.

"The substance used was MHX-19. No doubt about it. But only a small amount. Maybe two or three hundred grams. It wouldn't take much to vaporize a surface ship in mid-ocean."

"Meaning they could have spread small amounts all over the planet, in anonymous containers, just waiting for a detonation signal."

"Could, Colonel? I think it's safe to say they did. That little demonstration was prepared ahead of time, perhaps on spec, perhaps because they anticipated the prime minister's order to hold back the release of the ultimatum or perhaps for reasons we don't yet know. But I think it's a given they prepared more."

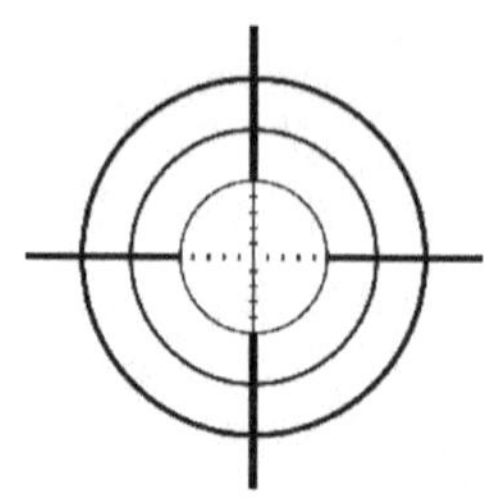

— THIRTY —

"You just love cheering people up, don't you, Major?" Master Sergeant Bonta asked after Joubert ended the call.

"Reality doesn't care about anyone's moods," an unrepentant Decker replied. "The fact they placed a bomb aboard this AI-controlled cargo ship is a pretty good hint the DSA spread devices, if not all over Cimmeria, then certainly along both shores of the Borrachas Sea. Prime Minister Calvo holding back their first communiqué was merely a pretext. It's about creating uncertainty, making everyone scared of their shadows, and pushing the government into a state of paralysis. We might well see a few more minor attacks with little or no loss of life over the next few days to keep pushing Calvo and his cabinet into the desired direction."

The Marine fell silent as a thought struck him.

"Who is Silfax's ultimate owner anyway? The records show it as a publicly traded company whose majority shareholders are other publicly traded companies. They, in turn, are owned by more companies and so on, but someone's bound to hold a controlling interest behind the scenes."

Morrow gave Decker a curious glance.

"I can ask the Financial Crimes Division if they know. Are you thinking *cui bono*? Who might profit from Silfax's destruction?"

"If the Coalition is funding this terrorist movement through local friends and hangers-on, it will make sure they don't suffer losses."

"Eliminate victims and focus on more likely suspects to sniff out the inevitable money trail that leads to the DSA." Talyn nodded in agreement. "It's not much, but anything helps at this juncture."

"So we can cross Valerian Industries off the list of terrorist financiers?" Galdi asked.

"Provisionally. One automated cargo ship, which might have been due for the knacker's yard anyway, isn't much of a loss compared to something like the Silfax Mining Complex."

The inspector caressed his luxuriant beard while he considered Decker's statement.

"So you think the Cimmerian governor general's family could be involved in something designed to destabilize the very government ruling this system under the aegis of a Valerian? Interesting."

"The Coalition's ultimate goal is to strip sovereign star systems of their independence and make them answerable to Earth rather than their citizens. Success would create a lot of opportunities for well-placed supporters to gain more power and riches, especially if they're no longer forced to contend with such inconveniences as the will of the people."

Bonta turned a smirk on the Marine.

"There you go cheering folks up again, Major."

He winked at her.

"Story of my life, Sergeant. Sit me down with a vintage Shrehari ale, and I could tell you tales guaranteed to make the most optimistic among us lose faith in humanity."

"Sadly, he's not joking," Talyn said. "And on that note, maybe Arno can tell us what his Gendarmerie contact found out about Alasdair Malter, Alek Mannsbach, and Magda Annear?"

"Magda was seen arriving at the Archeron spaceport yesterday morning aboard a privately chartered shuttle. She departed the spaceport in an aircar registered to Pavel Yagudin, who owns what they euphemistically call a hunting lodge in the Uttara Kuru foothills, so it's probably safe to assume that's where she is at the moment."

"I thought Magda and her husband weren't on speaking terms these days," Decker said.

"She could be the lodge's sole occupant under their separation agreement. Besides, Yagudin left Cimmeria a few weeks ago on business. He has interests in every corner of the sector."

"Okay." Decker rubbed his chin. "Interesting, but it doesn't tell us anything useful other than she's not staying with her mother."

"The Senate is in session, which means Nerys Annear is on Earth."

"What about Malter and his alter ego Mannsbach?"

"My friend gave me a data dump of everything the Cimmerian government has on both names. You'll like this. According to the records, Alasdair Malter died in an accident eighteen months ago. Apparently, you interrogated a corpse on Mission Colony."

Decker's eyebrows crept up. He exchanged a puzzled glance with Talyn.

"Any chance he was lying about his real name?"

She shook her head.

"No."

"I should say not. As soon as I saw Malter was long gone, I checked the biometric data you copied from Mannsbach's ID against that in Malter's dossier. It matches," Galdi said. "The story gets better. Alasdair Malter was a known member of the Cimmerian Unity Institute, one of the radical fringe groups absorbed by the DSA along with the Initiative for Democracy and the Solidarity Movement. He was an assistant professor of social history at Archeron University."

"How did he die?"

"In a climbing accident. He was part of a group, mostly Unity Institute members, on a two-week expedition in the Uttara Kuru Mountains. Apparently, Malter's lost his footing while the party was crossing one of the deepest ravines in the entire range. As he tried to recover, his safety harness failed, and he fell hundreds of meters into an underground river."

"Convenient. I suppose they never found the body?"

"Of course not, Commander. The Uttara Kuru region is an untamed alien wilderness where several dozen bold spirits lose their lives every year because of overweening ambition and unrestrained curiosity. His wasn't the first body to vanish without a trace. Based on the testimony of eight witnesses and a forensic analysis of their gear, it didn't take long for the courts to declare Malter deceased due to misadventure."

"And Alek Mannsbach?"

"He's an immigrant from Merseaux who arrived on Cimmeria about eighteen months ago, shortly after Malter's death."

"What a coincidence," Decker said in a droll tone.

"Oh, I'm not done yet, my dear Major. Would you care to hazard a guess who sponsored Mannsbach so he not only had a job upon arrival but would enjoy early admissibility for citizenship?"

"The Deep Space Foundation?"

Galdi tapped the side of his bulbous nose with an extended index finger.

"Indeed. Louis Sorne's pretend not-for-profit. Needless to say, the Cimmerian government knows nothing about Mannsbach's history before his arrival, but in the year and a half since, he's been a model citizen.   Would you like to guess his primary place of residence?"

"Archeron?"

"Right again."

"He works, or rather worked for one of Sorne's subsidiaries as a traveling sales executive, the Kusan Export Corporation."

"Not a bad cover for someone going around the sector handing Mayhem bricks and untraceable credits to radical groups who dream of revolution. Anything else on Mannsbach?"

"Other than he left Cimmeria one month ago for Mission Colony and hasn't returned, no. I'll give you everything I received from my friend so you can peruse it at your leisure."

"We can peruse it during our flight to Archeron," Talyn said. "Zack and I need to become Eva Cortez and her personal goon, Piet Yorik. They're on Cimmeria because things went sideways on Mission Colony. We'll approach Mannsbach's boss at the Kusan Export Corporation and pick it up from there."

"Do you intend to apply the same interrogation techniques you used on Mannsbach?" Morrow asked.

"I'd rather use guile and worm my way into the DSA, but time is short. We will do whatever is necessary to find the MHX and neutralize the radicals."

Morrow crossed her arms and gave Talyn a hard look.

"Keep in mind that as a law enforcement officer, I cannot condone anything that would violate star system or federal law. If it becomes known we feds, Fleet or Constabulary, are subjecting citizens to illegal interrogation, or worse, how do you think the Cimmerian authorities would react? There are many ways to help push a government deeper into crisis. A serious rift between star system and federal law enforcement because the latter willfully ignored a planned violation of the former's laws is one of those.

Unsanctioned interrogation of their citizens by the Commonwealth military is about as serious as it can get for sovereign star system governments."

"Even if an incalculable amount of lives are at stake?" Decker asked in a harsh tone.

"An argument as old as humanity, Major. If we show the same blatant disregard for the law as our enemies, we lose the moral high ground and more importantly, our legitimacy in the eyes of civilians. Besides, any Constabulary member who has foreknowledge of an illegal act, such as unlawfully detaining and questioning citizens, must act lest he or she become the target of a PCB investigation. It's one thing to bandy about the notion of interrogating and terminating terrorists with extreme prejudice in idle conversation. But you're now actually planning to carry out an unsanctioned operation involving Cimmerian citizens."

"So what's the answer, Caelin?" Talyn asked, her right eyebrow cocked in question. "We wait until the Gendarmerie amasses evidence that'll stand up in court before rousting *known* enemies of Cimmerian democracy? You want to tell the families of the next victims you're sorry we couldn't stop the DSA in time, but at least we kept the moral high ground?"

Anger wiped away Morrow's usual stoicism.

"That's bloody unfair, Hera, and you know it. Cops who disregard the law in small matters end up thinking they're above it and that's when civil society unravels. You play by your rules, questionable as they might be for people like us, and we play by ours. It's best if we don't cross the lines separating us because once we do, there's no turning back. What happened on Aquilonia was something I don't care to repeat. I often questioned how I can keep heading the Rim Sector detachment of the Professional Compliance Bureau after letting myself be roped into signing off on the fiction you created. As a result, I'd rather not find myself in a similar position unless it's *in extremis*, and since we cannot, as yet, even exercise jurisdiction over the Silfax and *Valerian Theta* incidents, we're not close to that point."

She paused and took a deep breath before continuing.

"I hereby counsel you to avoid breaking Cimmerian and federal laws. Should you nonetheless do so, the Commonwealth Constabulary will disavow any knowledge of your intentions and cooperate with Cimmerian authorities in the investigation and prosecution of any crimes."

"In other words, don't tell me what you intend and don't get caught." Decker nodded once. "Gotcha. Could we impose on you to book us flights on the next suborbital run across the Borrachas Sea?"

Talyn climbed to her feet.

"Caelin, seeing as how the Gendarmerie implemented heightened security measures, would it be possible to obtain credentials under our cover names, allowing us to pass through their controls with our sidearms?"

"Will your sidearms be used to commit unlawful acts?"

Decker raised his right hand and said in a solemn voice, "I swear my gun is for self-defense only."

Morrow studied Zack's guileless face before giving him a grudging nod.

"I'll make the necessary arrangements right away. And the credentials will be in your real names, with rank and branch of service identifiers, not in whatever cover names you might plan on using to cover your tracks. You can become Cortez and Yorik once you're in Archeron."

Talyn inclined her head.

"Fair enough. Thank you. There's one more favor I'd like to ask, Caelin."

"Yes?"

"In case Zack and I go silent for whatever reason, we still need a way to stay informed of events and communicate with you. Something like a dead drop."

"If you'll allow me, Chief," Galdi said. "An encrypted node on the darknet, something idle searchers won't find. I can set one up in a matter of minutes. You'll be able to access it from anywhere, given the exact address and passcodes."

Morrow glanced at her inspector with eyes narrowed in thought.

"I suppose it makes sense. Go ahead, Arno." She turned back to Talyn. "And I'd like to ask for something in return."

"Sure."

"I assume your communicators come from the Naval Intelligence equipment stores?"

"Yes. Dual function. Anyone without the codes to access the classified part will think they're no different from civilian versions."

"Can the spy half send a location signal to the Navy satellites orbiting Cimmeria, one that the bad guys can't decode?"

"Yes, although anyone with the right gear will notice that signal even if they can't make out what it is and where it's addressed."

"Turn it on and show me how to query the satellites."

"Are you worried about us? Don't be. We're used to operating without backup."

"Humor me, Hera."

"You'll need to connect with Sixth Fleet HQ's downlink node."

"We already have access to it."

"In that case..." She fished out her communicator and tapped its screen with her thumb in an irregular rhythm. "There. Done. I've sent you the identifier."

"Zack as well, please."

"Roger, that."

Morrow's communicator chimed once again. She gave it an irritated glance, then her eyes widened by a fraction.

"Prime Minister Calvo's office is calling. I'll put in on the main display."

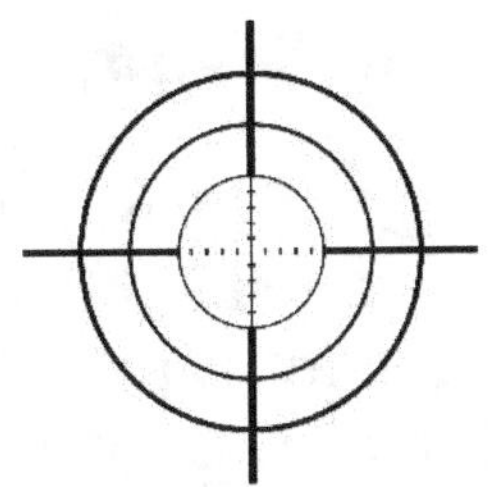

— THIRTY-ONE —

A young woman's grave mien replaced the Constabulary arrow and scales of justice. "Chief Superintendent Morrow, my name is Kamille Filteau. I'm one of the prime minister's aides. He wishes to speak with Commander Talyn and Major Decker. Are they available?"

Morrow zoomed out the conference room's video pickup.

"As you can see, they're with me."

"Thank you. Please stand by for the prime minister."

Filteau's face dissolved and the Great Seal of Cimmeria briefly took its place before the star system's head of government appeared.

Matthanias Calvo bore a striking resemblance to the images Decker once saw of statues and bas-reliefs showing ancient Athenian politicians. Gray-haired and bearded, with a shiny, high forehead, sharp nose, thin lips, and forceful, deep-set eyes, he struck the Marine as someone able to separate lies from the truth. He wore a somber expression.

"Thank you for making time to speak with me. Chief Superintendent, I'm aware our Gendarmerie doesn't always play nice with your people, but those of us in the know appreciate your sense of duty." His gaze turned to Talyn. "Commander, I can't adequately express how glad I am that fate brought you and your colleague to our planet at this time of turmoil." Finally, he locked eyes with the Marine. "And you must be Major Zachary Decker, the explosives expert."

"I'm not sure about the expert tag, sir. But I can distinguish Mayhem from Compound Mark Twenty-Two."

"I won't even ask what this Compound Mark Twenty-Two might be. General Dubnikov speaks highly of the briefing you gave the Gendarmerie's senior leadership earlier, and that's enough for me."

"The general is most kind, Prime Minister."

"He's also a good judge of people. A steady stream of generals, bureaucrats, and aides has briefed me ever since the Silfax Mining Complex vanished beneath a massive fireball, but none of them seemed to know a damn thing until you showed up."

"We're at your entire disposal, sir. Ask, and we'll do our best to answer."

Calvo let out a soft snort.

"That's the first time a federal official ever said anything of the sort in my hearing."

"We don't consider ourselves federal officials in the bureaucratic sense, sir," Talyn replied. "Major Decker and I are officers in the Commonwealth Armed Services, sworn to serve and defend without limitations."

The Cimmerian prime minister raised a hand by way of apology.

"Of course. I'm sorry."

"What would you like to know?"

"So far, I've heard little more than the sum of my advisers' fears. We are not used to violent radicals, terrorists, or insurgents in this star system. Cimmeria has been mercifully peaceful since the Shrehari withdrew after the armistice back when my father was a young man. What has transpired since yesterday morning is beyond our experience. And more to the point, beyond the Gendarmerie's and the National

Guard's experience. Granted, our homegrown radicals seem to have multiplied in the last two or three years even though we enjoyed a remarkable degree of civil peace for decades, but this sudden violence is inexplicable. Malcontents are a fact of life even in the freest societies, but they rarely use restricted military-grade explosives to demand what they call social justice."

"Certainly not the Mayhem compound, sir," Decker replied, "but Commander Talyn and I have seen an escalation of tactics by various radical groups across the Rim Sector in recent months. Though none as extreme as what we saw at Silfax or the preplanned detonation which destroyed the *Valerian Theta*."

"And that is one of my questions, Major. How does a group such as the Democratic Stars Alliance obtain an explosive compound so powerful the very knowledge of its existence is classified as top secret by the Commonwealth Armed Services?"

"Once we find the answer to that question, sir, we will know who needs termination with extreme prejudice," Talyn said.

"*Lex talionis*, Commander? An eye for an eye?"

"Special Operations Command's unofficial motto, sir. The Second Migration War's mass killings enshrined the principle of permanently removing perpetrators of atrocities from the human gene pool."

"An understandable sentiment, even if it runs contrary to many legal principles that served humanity well over the centuries."

"That's because we dispense justice, sir," Decker said, "not legalities. Too many innocents die when we tiptoe around the fact that there are people who simply need killing before they murder more innocents, such as those responsible for Silfax."

Calvo inclined his leonine head in acknowledgment.

"I understand the sentiment, even though the idea of capital punishment dispensed extrajudicially disturbs the lawyer in me. But I didn't call you to debate the philosophical differences between laws devised by human beings and natural justice, interesting as the subject might be. You said you didn't know how the DSA obtained this Mayhem. Did it perchance come from a Fleet ammunition depot on Cimmeria?"

"No, sir." Decker shook his head. "Neither the Cimmeria Regiment nor the Sixth Fleet hold it in their inventories. It's kept in maybe half a dozen places across the Commonwealth and Cimmeria isn't one of those."

"You sound terribly sure of that, Major."

"I'm a Master Gunner, sir. Explosives are one of my specialties."

"So someone brought this devilish compound to our star system as part of a plan aimed at destabilizing my government."

"Yes, Prime Minister. And if the stuff is properly packed and hidden inside a shipping container, it's virtually undetectable by routine customs scans."

"But it implies the DSA enjoys support from offworld allies."

"Almost certainly, sir," Talyn replied. "Major Decker and I came to Cimmeria because of information we obtained on the DSA and its activities while investigating violent subversives on Mission Colony."

"Did you terminate them with extreme prejudice?" A sardonic smile curled Calvo's lips. Before either operative could answer, he raised a restraining hand. "I withdraw my question."

"I'll answer nonetheless, sir. We prevented them from carrying out the sort of indecency visited on Cimmeria by the DSA.

"Too bad you didn't make it here quickly enough for a repeat performance."

"Regrettably. But our superiors will soon be aware of the Silfax attack. We sent a subspace message shortly after meeting up with Chief Superintendent Morrow's team yesterday. They'll track the Mayhem theft as fast as the laws of interstellar physics allow, which could give us a second avenue toward finding the DSA."

"And how do you intend to help us find them from this end, Commander?"

"If you don't mind, Prime Minister, for operational security reasons, I prefer not to answer. Radical movements often plant sympathizers within the establishment who escape notice by the police and security services."

"Understood."

"Rest assured we will do everything in our power to track these DSA clowns and give them a one-way ticket to Beelzebub's domain," Decker said. "It's what Commander Talyn and I do for a living. And we've become rather good at it."

"In that case, could you tell me what this is supposed to accomplish, I mean once we ignore the asinine revolutionary language? It has to be more than just getting rid of our parliamentary system which is, I admit, at times weighted in favor of the elites."

Talyn and Decker exchanged a glance. Then she said, "Sir, we believe the DSA is sponsored by a secret faction with powerful friends on Earth. This faction is intent on removing star system governments which resist the idea of undoing the treaty that ended the Second Migration War."

"Centralizers."

"Yes, sir, though the term imperialists might be more apt. They don't think of a republic the way we understand it."

Calvo let out a long, exasperated sigh.

"Are these people mad? Don't they remember that billions died the last time Earth tried to impose its will on sovereign star systems?"

"Some of them do, but like every generation of reformers, they refuse to attribute past failure to the fundamental unsoundness of their ideas, preferring to blame a flawed implementation."

"The last bunch didn't do it right," Calvo quoted in a bitter tone. "That well-worn rallying cry to justify reviving every lousy socio-political ideology humanity ever invented. You're not filling me with glee, Commander."

"Sorry, sir. But back to your question, this shadowy faction has been trying for years to install sympathetic regimes throughout the Rim Sector, since it is the most vulnerable and in certain respects the most politically volatile. Once the Rim is under the control of their fellow travelers, they can expand to more stable sectors and eventually place every single star system under Earth's direct control."

"Turning our decentralized republic of equals into a de facto empire." Calvo shook his head.

"Precisely. Until now, attempts at subverting governments have been covert, a shadow war of sorts. Using a terrorist group and shocking violence such as what Cimmeria experienced yesterday is a new tactic. An escalation, if you wish."

"In what universe do they expect terrorists to take over running this star system?"

Decker scoffed.

"They don't. The DSA are useful idiots whose only job is to pave the way for a strong leader promising to quickly suppress them and restore order. After you and the Cimmerian parliament walk off, stage left. It's not a new idea by any stretch. Many of history's worst tyrants seized power after destabilizing legitimate governments by encouraging radical front organizations to sow the sort of chaos that makes governing impossible. Terror is merely the most direct way to create political chaos.”

A frown creased Calvo’s broad forehead.

“But if you’re correct, who would the strong leader be in our situation? I can’t think of anyone with enough stature on Cimmeria willing to betray our citizens in such a despicable manner.”

“No one believed the tyrants I mentioned just now capable of betraying their people right until the moment they did so, sir. We will do what we can to uncover who’s behind the DSA, however finding and securing the MHX-19 must take priority.”

“Understood.” Calvo’s eyes slipped to one side for a moment. “I won’t take up any more of your time. Thank you for everything and good luck.”

The display went dark before anyone could reply.

“I don’t think our conversation will help him sleep better,” Decker remarked.

“But it might make him hesitate before blithely resigning to appease terrorists.”

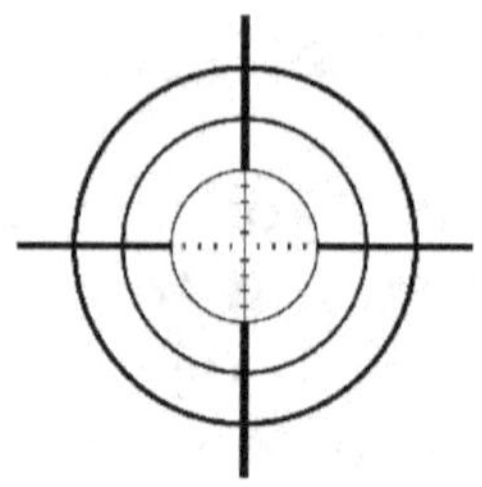

— THIRTY-TWO —

"That was quite a discussion with Caelin right before the prime minister called us," Decker said once they recovered their bags and weapons after passing through the spaceport's security checkpoint. The credentials Morrow provided worked as intended although the gendarme who passed them through seemed puzzled that Armed Services officers were carrying Constabulary-issue permits endorsed by his own organization. "Though she was suspiciously quick in granting your request to roam Cimmeria gun in hand with the proper credentials."

"Were you lying when you swore your sidearm was for self-defense only?"

"No. When's the last time I used them to execute bad guys as in one shot to the back of the head instead of during a firefight or to repel an attack?"

"Precisely. And Caelin could sense you were telling the truth. Remember, she's used to ferreting out bent cops who know every single dodge. She may not be a human lie detector, but I'd bet on her every time."

"Which is why you let me swear we'd be good. No one can figure out whether you're being straight or blowing smoke."

"Being a soulless assassin has its disadvantages."

He turned a toothy grin on her.

"Do tell."

She stopped to look into a souvenir shop window, one of many storefronts bordering the spaceport's main concourse and absently used the reflection to brush her hair with extended fingers.

"Thought so."

"What?"

"Youngish woman, alone. Long black hair, dark jacket, looks like a wide-eyed, inoffensive university student. She's doing better than the pair from yesterday. I only noticed her now, but that face crossed my line of sight as we were leaving Old Government House."

Decker let out a disconsolate grunt.

"I never even twigged."

"Let's not linger. I don't want to spook her yet." They stepped off again, headed for the suborbital departure wing. "The real test will come when we board our ride. Arno made the bookings less than an hour ago, so theoretically, our little friend should hit a snag if she can't visit Archeron with us."

"Unless her lot has a hook inside the booking system and received an alert for the names Talyn and Decker. Don't Louis Sorne and his circle of friends own most of the civilian transportation network on Cimmeria? She could have a reserved seat next to ours."

"Possibly. Or she'll hand surveillance off to someone waiting for us at the other end."

"Too bad. She's sort of cute."

"Since when are petite twenty-somethings to your taste?"

"One can show appreciation for the human form without making it sexual, my dear." He nodded at a nearby spaceport bar. "Let's take a ringside seat and see if they serve Shrehari ale while we watch petite and twenty-something figure out how to keep eyes on us while remaining inconspicuous. Our flight isn't leaving for another hour."

They took a table overlooking the concourse and Decker found a middling vintage Shrehari ale on the menu, but at an extortionate price.

"It truly is a universal constant," he remarked after they ordered their drinks and paid via the tabletop interface.

"What is?"

"Spaceports, airports, and seaports across the Commonwealth and throughout history taking advantage of a captive audience to overcharge at a rate that would make most loan sharks' eyes water."

"A good thing the taxpayer is covering our costs."

"I love the unaccountable black ops fund almost as much as my ale." When he saw her amused expression, Decker added, with a leer, "But not as much as I love you, my darling."

"Our tail overpaid for lousy coffee." She nodded toward a cafe further along the concourse. "I'd love to know who's covering her tab. A shame we promised Caelin we'd behave lawfully."

"Only as Decker and Talyn. If our newest friend accompanies us to Archeron, we can switch names and faces, and take her into a dark corner."

A serving droid approached with their drinks. Purplish, foaming Shrehari ale for him, a gin and tonic for her.

Decker raised his glass. "Here's to us, riding the storm once again."

"I thought you *were* the storm."

"Okay, here's to you, who will once again ride the storm tonight, in the privacy of our hotel room."

"Work before pleasure."

"Please. It'll be nightfall by the time we land. Doctor Zack prescribes rest and relaxation in our third-rate fleabag inn. Work can start tomorrow morning. I'd rather not stumble around a new city in the dark. Not if we're still being tailed."

"I thought we desperately wanted the bad guys to try and take us."

"That was the old plan. Since we have names and addresses, I'd rather stay on the offensive."

"Ditto. Just seeing if we agreed." She took a sip of her drink and made a face. "Overpriced crap indeed. I bet they distilled this gin yesterday and then filtered it through the dirty socks of the sapient being who brewed your ale."

An air of disgust twisted Decker's face.

"Thanks for that visual." He took a healthy swig of his ale. "At least this stuff is the real thing."

Thirty minutes ticked by in companionable silence while they nursed their glasses and occasionally checked on the dark-haired woman whom Decker dubbed 'Undergrad.' Finally, he swallowed his last mouthful and stood while Talyn kept an indirect gaze on their tail.

"She reacted to your movements, Zack. I think it confirms our suspicions."

When they strolled by the cafe, Undergrad studiously ignored them, but she was on her feet even before Decker and Talyn turned off the main concourse for the suborbital departures section. A few minutes later, they saw her enter the lounge for the Archeron flight and take a seat near the gate, looking like just another traveler.

"Doesn't seem fazed," Decker muttered as he and Talyn stood by the windows, watching ground crew droids prepare the sleek, delta-winged hypersonic aircraft for its short hop across the Borrachas Sea. "Almost as if she's taking our flight legitimately. Maybe I might get lucky, and she'll sit beside me. Then I can charm her with my wit and find out everything we want to know.”

“Or you could try to regain your grip on reality, Big Boy. You may be my type, but you’re not everyone’s cup of tea.”

In the end, Undergrad spent the flight sitting two rows behind Decker and Talyn. A man of the same general appearance and age, a relative perhaps, greeted her in the Archeron spaceport arrivals hall, and she vanished, leaving them to scan their surroundings for whoever might be picking up the tail.

**

“Did we totally misread things?” Decker asked as they stepped out of the Archeron spaceport and into the early evening air.

He took a deep breath, savoring the moist warmth after Howard Landing’s more spring-like air. Though the star system’s capital also sat on the shores of salt water, albeit further north, the underlying aroma of a planet’s aquatic life cycle seemed much stronger in these subtropical latitudes.

It tickled the Marine’s nostrils with scents both eerily familiar and hauntingly alien. The purplish peaks of the Uttara Kuru Mountains, some still showing the remains of last winter’s snow, reared toward the darkening sky south of Archeron’s soft glow.

“It would be a first. Someone else took up the tail. We simply need to exercise patience and discover who. I believe you mentioned a third-rate fleabag hotel...”

“Which we won’t use. If they, whoever that is, saw our shuttle reservations, they’ll know about the hotel booking as well. I suggest we make a clean break here and now.”

"My thoughts exactly." She reached up and patted his cheek. "You're becoming well versed in the fine art of suspecting everything and everyone."

"Didn't someone say even paranoids have enemies? I can't recall who offhand."

"I'm sure she must have been a wise woman."

An automated bus pulled up, and they joined other travelers in climbing aboard for the short drive into Archeron proper. They stepped off on the harbor front promenade and chose a down-market restaurant at random.

There, Decker and Talyn ate a quick meal, paid, then used the guest washrooms to transform themselves into convincing facsimiles of Eva Cortez and Piet Yorik before exiting via the restaurant's back door.

They strolled through downtown Archeron for almost an hour, alert to any signs of someone tailing them until Decker spotted a likely hotel close to the commercial seaport.

"Do you think it looks seedy enough for a pair of offworld revolutionaries on the run?"

"Provided it's managed by humans and not creepy holograms with suspect programming, I'm willing to try."

"Carbon-based hoteliers aren't any more trustworthy than the photon-based sort. Not if dodgy owners or organized crime are involved. Whoever's behind this one's reception desk could just as easily finger us to the wrong people." He wrapped his arm around her shoulders and squeezed. "But that's what keeps our lives interesting, sweetie."

"Would you believe just once I'd like to enjoy a few days without looking over my shoulder?"

"No."

He led her through the Blue Heron Inn's tired automatic doors and across a lobby which would have benefited from a complete makeover at the turn of the century, if not earlier. Here, the aroma wafting off the Borrachas Sea combined with that of ancient furniture, carpeting whose original color was lost to history and walls impregnated by decades of neglect, giving birth to a fusty odor oddly apt for the establishment's rundown atmosphere.

A bearded man with sagging jowls and sad eyes looked up from the reception desk and watched them approach. His slightly unkempt appearance, casual clothes, and aura of existential fatigue fit the surroundings to a tee.

"My name is Edgar. Can I help you?" He asked in a low, almost lethargic voice.

"A room for the night."

"Then you're in luck. I offer rooms for the night, the week, or the month. One bed or two?"

"Depends on the size of your beds."

Edgar gave the Marine and his partner an owlish stare.

"I think you'll be satisfied with the size of our beds." He named a per night price and asked, "How will you be paying?"

Decker dropped a few cred chips on his desk.

"One night, no questions asked or answered."

"Avoiding questions is the house's specialty. No names, no pack drill." When Decker gave him a hard look, Edgar shrugged. "You seem like someone with a military background." He swept up the chips and pocketed them, tapped a screen embedded in the desk, then said. "Room five-oh-one. I keyed the lock to your faces. Enjoy your stay."

Edgar's eyes turned back to the reader in his lap before they took a single step toward the lift.

"Not an overly obsequious character, is he?" Decker asked when the lift doors closed. "I wouldn't be surprised if he's tripping on something not quite legal."

"It's still better than a chatty, overly inquisitive AI when you're looking for a no-tell hotel."

The lobby's particular scent didn't extend to the fifth-floor hallway, nor room five-oh-one, which enjoyed the less than spectacular view of an office building between the hotel and the water's edge. Decker gave the room and attached bath a once-over with his sensor while Talyn performed a visual check, then thumbed on the jamming function.

"It's clean," he announced.

"Ditto."

"Since I saw no one trying to tail us, I think we might have made a clean break."

"More than likely."

Decker shrugged off his jacket, placed his blaster and knife on one of the night tables, and kicked off his boots.

"Since it seems like we're about to enjoy a rare night without worrying about work finding us, how about a little game of spy who loves me?"

**

A female version of Edgar sat behind the reception desk early the next morning — gray, worn-out, and disinterested. She didn't look up as Decker and Talyn crossed the lobby and left, never to return.

The sea's aroma seemed no fresher in the golden glow of Cimmeria's rising sun than it did the previous evening. Native avians, searching for sea creatures lured to the water's surface by human activity, circled ceaselessly overhead, calling out to each other with extended chirps that seemed alien to their ears.

Longshore workers, many munching on sandwiches and carrying steaming coffee cups, ambled along the water's edge, preparing for another day of work loading and offloading the automated cargo ships connecting settlements strung out along the southern shores of Cimmeria's northern continent and the north shore of Cimmeria's southern continent.   Thanks to their vaguely disreputable appearance, no one gave Decker and Talyn a second glance while they searched for a restaurant offering breakfast this early in the morning.

"Is it wrong to feel relieved I'm no longer fettered by my true name, rank, and serial number, and the legal restrictions that come with them?" The Marine asked.

"Depends on who you're talking to. Caelin and her folks might think you strange, but I agree. Playing the legitimate, law-abiding SOCOM officer felt uncomfortably constraining."

"We're hunters, my dear. Barely tamed wolves, not sheepdogs. We can play nice with the latter, but our instincts demand we rip the Fleet's enemies apart on our terms."

Talyn's gentle laugh echoed between them.

"My, but you've changed. Weren't you once proud to be the sole sheepdog among Naval Intelligence's wolves?"

"When the opposition uses your only child as a hostage to advance their filthy schemes, it awakens atavistic instincts that demand the ruthless application of violence, not the niceties of attorneys, juries, and judges."

"I'm not sure whether I should be pleased or dismayed. Your role was always to be my anchor, the one to keep me from slipping into the dark corners of my mind after losing my last few shreds of humanity. What will become of me — of us — if you get lost in your own dark corners?"

"It won't happen. There's still a line I can't cross."

She glanced up at her partner's face and understood it was better if she didn't ask about that line.

"Breakfast?"

A hungry grin replaced Decker's solemn expression. He patted his stomach.

"You bet."

"And we need to find a public access terminal so I can check the dead drop."

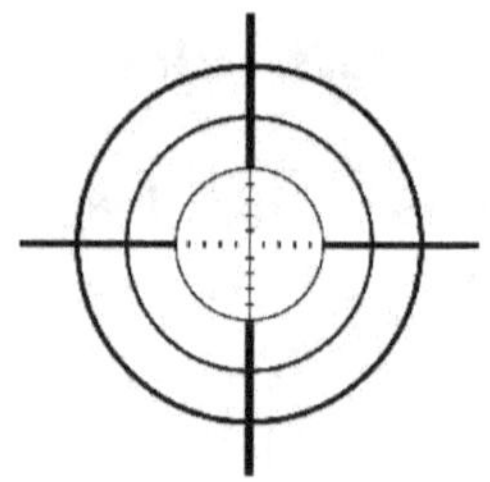

— THIRTY-THREE —

"Whatever drug these DSA fools are taking, I want a hit," Decker said, reading over Talyn's shoulder.

They were in a privacy booth at the back of a public communications node close to the harbormaster's imposing waterfront command center.

"Demanding Prime Minister Calvo and his government resign after asking the governor general to dissolve parliament and appoint a council of national salvation? There's a word for that."

"Chutzpah. But it's devilishly brilliant. Think about it. Once this ultimatum becomes public, and it will thanks to yesterday morning's warning, his time as prime minister is over no matter what. Either he refuses and bears responsibility for the next mass murder, which means he'll be forced out anyway, or he accepts and consigns Cimmerian democracy to the wastebasket. They're giving him until tomorrow noon."

"Twenty-eight hours from now. I'm not sure it's long enough to find the head of the DSA snake and cut it off." Decker let out a heartfelt curse under his breath. "This operation is turning into another fucking stampede."

"As Napoleon Bonaparte said, ask me for anything but time."

"Sorry. Can't help you. It'll take whatever time is necessary to be greeted with open arms as fellow Democratic Stars Alliance travelers on the road to a victorious revolution across the Rim Sector."

"Today, Cimmeria, tomorrow the galaxy. And then the whole damned universe." Talyn raised a clenched fist. "Caelin also found the Silfax Mining Complex's ultimate owner. Bronwen Annear, chief executive officer of Sorbonne Holdings Limited, sister to Nerys Annear, Cimmeria's senior Commonwealth senator and aunt to Magda Annear, who we saved from probably fake Howlers."

"This operation is racking up more Annears than can be explained by mere coincidence."

"Perhaps." She logged out of the dead drop and erased every track leading to it. "Take us to our revolutionary comrades at Kusan Exports, Pathfinder."

"It won't be hard. The address is a few kilometers south of downtown." Back on the harbor front promenade, he looked around to orient himself and check for suspicious behavior. "I think—"

A brilliant flash on the seaward horizon killed whatever Decker was about to say. The throaty rumble of an explosion followed seconds later.

"Mayhem?" Talyn asked.

He nodded.

"The DSA reminding Calvo they're not playing tiddlywinks. I wonder whose ship that was and whether it carried any crew or passengers."

A lugubrious howl erupted from the harbormaster's building, smothering any attempt to speak. Almost simultaneously a swarm of drones covered in flashing red strobes shot up from the roof and headed out over the water.

The siren died away shortly after they left for the port for Archeron's central square to find a bus going in the right direction.

Half an hour later, they found themselves in front of an unremarkable three-story stone building that could easily pass for a wealthy individual's townhouse rather than corporate offices. A discrete sign by the opaque glass door said 'Kusan Export Corporation.'

When they climbed the short flight of steps leading up from the sidewalk, a holographic head materialized before them.

"Welcome. How may I help you?"

"My name is Eva Cortez, and this is Piet Yorik. We're visiting from Mission Colony and are here to speak with Alek Mannsbach's superior about Alek's trip to our home planet," Talyn replied.

"Do you know who this Ser Mannsbach's superior is, Sera Cortez?" The androgynous voice asked with perfect politeness.

"If I did, I would have asked for him or her by name, wouldn't I. The matter is urgent and concerns the Mission Colony Freedom Collective."

"May I scan your identification?"

"Certainly." Decker and Talyn held up the purloined ID wafers, suitably tweaked to match their biometric data.

"Thank you."

The door swung inward, revealing a small lobby furnished with half a dozen office chairs, two side tables, and a small refreshment machine. Another opaque glass door with a smaller corporate sign led into the bowels of the building.

"Please enter and make yourselves comfortable while I inquire."

The fake Cortez and Yorik took chairs facing each other and waited in silence, knowing they were under intense scrutiny. Gustav Kerlin's partner appearing on Cimmeria a little more than a week after his violent death and two days after the DSA began its deadly campaign to force out the government would be as unexpected as it was suspicious.

Finally, the inner door slid aside and an unprepossessing, middle-aged man in a neat business suit entered the lobby. His receding hairline, thin lips and sunken cheeks gave the impression of a career bureaucrat who spent too much time at work.

"Good day. I'm Hadar Wilborg, Kusan Export Corporation's head of marketing. Alek Mannsbach works for me." Wilborg didn't offer his hand although he studied Talyn with inquisitive, deep-set eyes. "What can I do for you?"

"I'm sorry to be the bearer of bad news, Ser Wilborg, but Alek Mannsbach died a week and a half ago on Mission, within hours of my husband Gustav's untimely demise."

"Oh, dear." Wilborg nodded at the inner door. "Please accept my deepest sympathies, Sera Cortez. Why don't we discuss this in my office?"

The decor was middle-grade corporate, the artwork no more than mass-produced reproductions and the furniture functional. Not ostentatious, but comfortable, befitting one of Louis Sorne's many companies. Wilborg's office sat in the southwest corner of the former mansion's second floor. By Decker's estimation, it was the most desirable one, an indication he was more than just Kusan Exports' head of marketing.

Wilborg gestured at a pair of chairs in front of his desk, a modern wood and steel construct exuding all the charm of a starship orbital dry-dock. "Please tell me everything. Alek was a valued colleague and a good friend."

"As you know, Alek and my husband were negotiating a merger between our respective organizations."

"More of a business arrangement under our leadership, but please continue."

"Ten days ago, a sniper assassinated Gustav at our country house, during a party thrown in honor of our friends and supporters."

Wilborg nodded.

"News of his death reached us through the subspace network, but with no details about the cause."

Talyn gestured toward Decker.

"Piet Yorik's men found the weapon in nearby woods a few hours later. Tell him."

"A Falkenberg Longbow seven-millimeter railgun with unpowered Hammer Optics sights," he said. "Expensive, incredibly accurate, a professional assassin's tool of choice. I also found a chameleon ghillie suit, another high-end piece of equipment. There's no doubt it was a targeted killing. The murderer escaped even though the 24th Constabulary Regiment cordoned off the area with commendable speed."

"How utterly horrible. And Alek?"

"Considering the importance Gustav placed on the negotiations with Alek, I sent my men to his apartment the same day. They found him lifeless in bed, unclothed, no marks on the skin, no visible wounds, but what he wore the previous day was missing, and the apartment showed signs of a professional sanitizing job. I think they poisoned him via a dermal patch, but we'll never be able to prove it."

"What happened to his body, Ser Yorik?"

"We disposed of it before the cops found out. Since no one on Mission other than our organization knew of Alek, the authorities won't miss him."

Wilborg considered Decker for a few seconds.

"Sad, but it's probably best under the circumstances. Alek had no family other than us here at Kusan Exports." He turned his attention back on Talyn. "Since you're aware of the negotiations, can I assume you also know about the monetary grant and our gift to your Collective?"

"I know everything, Ser Wilborg. Upon my husband's death, I became the leader of the Mission Colony Freedom Collective. The grant is safe, but unfortunately, someone tracked down your gift in the vault beneath my family's beach house and destroyed both. A rather large inlet on the southern coast of the Benden peninsula now sits where the property once stood. Piet and I were in Ventano, dealing with certain matters vital to my taking the reins from Gustav. At the time of our leaving Mission, preliminary conclusions by the authorities appeared to favor an undetected meteorite strike."

"Why come to Cimmeria and Kusan Exports?"

"I was forced to leave Mission Colony, so my corpse didn't end up rotting beside Gustav's. Someone doesn't want to see the Freedom Collective join forces with you and they'll kill to prevent it. This wasn't just your normal politically motivated violence. God knows every star system experiences its fair share these days. I don't know who hired a professional assassin to murder my husband, but they scare me. Why am I in your office? Simple. To warn you about Alek's suspicious death and continue the discussions he and Gustav started. Perhaps by aligning our business interests with yours, I'll have a better chance of surviving long enough to achieve the Collective's goals."

"And you don't know who committed these terrible crimes? Could it be personal rather than political?"

"No. Gustav had few enemies and none with the motivation or the money to hire a top-tier offworld assassin. Since Alek died on the same day under suspicious circumstances, I'm sure both were killed because of the proposed rapprochement between our organizations."

Wilborg, fingers tapping a soft tattoo on the desktop, seemed to ponder her words.

"I'm not sure it's in our best interests to pursue the proposed arrangement, Sera Cortez."

Talyn sat up, an air of incomprehension tightening her features.

"What do you mean? We're the only organization on Mission Colony capable of achieving our common aims."

"With Gustav Kerlin gone, I doubt the Freedom Collective will keep its nerve. I think it might be best if we forget about establishing ourselves on Mission for now."

"You forget I took over to continue our work, Ser Wilborg. Gustav and I did everything together."

"No doubt, but fortunately for you, I'm not in charge. While you were waiting in the lobby, I spoke with our chief executive who wishes to see you in person. However, I shall take certain understandable precautions beforehand."

The door behind Decker and Talyn opened framing the young woman they'd dubbed Undergrad at the Howard's Landing spaceport the previous day. She held a scattergun in her hands, its menacing barrel pointed at them. When they glanced back at Wilborg, he'd moved to one side, leaving her with a clear field of fire.

"Our scanners in the lobby detected your weapons and communicators. Please remove them from their hiding places with exquisite slowness and place them on the desk."

Decker gave him a disgusted look.

"Is this how you treat offworld allies? Forget about these people, Eva. We can seize Mission Colony without their help. It'll just take a little longer."

Talyn laid a restraining hand on his arm.

"Relax, Piet. Ser Wilborg is simply taking the same precautions you would if offworlders you never met before showed up unannounced at one of our homes."

Another woman entered the office and took their travel bags, careful to avoid blocking Wilborg and Undergrad. They heard her rummage through them.

"Only a change of clothes and toiletries, sir," she said after a minute. "Scans show nothing else."

"Look for hidden or shielded compartments."

"You won't find anything." Decker scowled at him. "Because there's nothing to find."

"Perhaps. Now please place your weapons and communicators on the desk. Otherwise, we can't take you to our chief executive."

Decker and Talyn exchanged glances, and the former nodded once before holding his jacket open to show the Shrehari blaster under his left arm. He withdrew it with two fingers, then pulled up his sleeve and carefully unstrapped the sheath on his forearm before producing his communicator. Talyn followed suit.

"That's everything we're carrying," she said.

"Impressive nonetheless. Where did you get the hand artillery?"

"It's a bonehead gun," Decker replied. "And the dagger is from my time in the Fleet. I won both off a Pathfinder in a poker game years ago."

"Army or Marines?"

"Military police."

"Interesting civilian career choice."

"You meet every sort in the private security business. I'm good at my job; otherwise, Eva wouldn't keep me around."

"Didn't do much for Gustav, though."

"A professional-grade sniper with a long-range railgun is almost impossible to stop."

"I suppose." A faint smirk crossed Wilborg's face. "Convenient for Sera Cortez from what I understand about the late Ser Kerlin."

Talyn smiled.

"Let's just say he had his faults and leave it at that. The Collective will thrive under my leadership."

"We'll hold on to your weapons and communicators for now, if you don't mind. Only people who are fully vetted can bear arms in the chief executive's presence."

"I do mind," Decker growled.

"Piet. Stand down. We'll do as Ser Wilborg wishes. Remember why we came to Cimmeria."

"Yes, Eva."

Wilborg glanced from one to the other, then nodded at the woman with the scattergun.

"Lead us to the car, Collette. We're taking a ride into the countryside. Allyson, bring our guests' possessions, please." He gestured toward the door. "If you'll follow Collette."

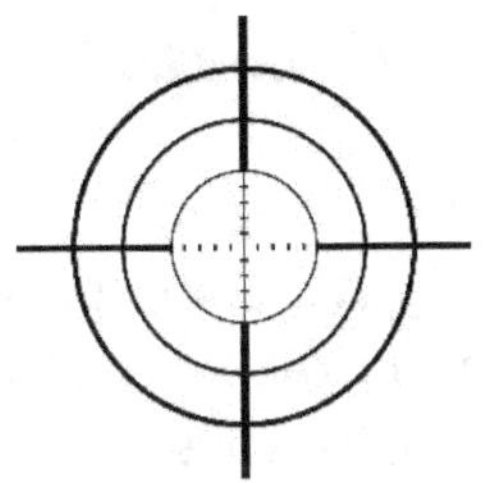

— THIRTY-FOUR —

A lift swept them to an underground garage where a large, beetle-shaped ground car waited. Collette invited Decker and Talyn to take the front-facing seats, then settled across from them alongside Wilborg, scattergun loosely held in her lap. Allyson, carrying their weapons and bags, took the driver's seat. When she switched on the power plant, all doors closed and the windows turned an opaque black.

"We keep the chief executive's current location strictly confidential," Wilborg said by way of explanation when he saw their reaction. "What visitors don't know, they can't inadvertently disclose to hostile parties."

"That makes eminent sense," Talyn replied.

The car silently sprang into motion and climbed a steep ramp before reaching ground level and the exit leading to a back street. Unable to see, Decker could only estimate the distance based on perceived speed and elapsed time. The number of turns in either direction decreased after less than ten minutes, indicating they were beyond Archeron's city limits.

Just under thirty minutes later, he felt the car slow, turn right, and stay at that speed for a bit longer before coming to a halt. The windows lost their opacity, and the rear doors opened, allowing the fresh aroma of native Cimmeria plant life to tickle Decker and Talyn's nostrils. It confirmed the Marine's guess they had driven well out into the countryside.

Wilborg climbed to his feet.

"Welcome to the lodge. Colette will guide you to the guesthouse and your rooms. Our chief executive is extremely busy this morning. I'll let her know we arrived and see when she's free to receive you."

"And our stuff?" Decker asked as he followed the man out.

"We'll hang on to your weapons and communicators, but Allyson will return your bags in due course."

"After subjecting them to an in-depth scan, no doubt." He looked around and whistled softly. "You call this place a lodge? It looks more like a small castle, or a gussied up bunker complex."

They were parked on a polished stone plaza bordered by three granite-clad buildings with steep copper roofs. The main house, three stories tall, boasted a set of metal-studded wooden doors aged to look as if someone plundered them from an old Earth fortress.

Windows, flanked by what Decker suspected were fully functional armored shutters painted a dark green, pierced the facade at regular intervals. The two lesser buildings flanking the main house, each only two stories high, seemed equally hardened against a peasant uprising or perhaps a party of drunken Shrehari Marines from the imperial occupation force, although the latter were long gone.

Decker exchanged a glance with Talyn.

"Who owns this pile?"

"You'll find out in due course." Wilborg pointed at one of the smaller structures where a door stood open. "The guest house is over there. Your rooms offer every conceivable amenity though I'm afraid we must confine you to your suite for now. Please make sure our guests are comfortable, Collette. I must report to our leader."

With that, he walked away, heading for the main house.

"Come with me please," Collette said, scattergun now slung over one shoulder.

The building's interior appeared modern and streamlined, almost like that of a luxury hotel, in contrast to its quaint, almost dated exterior. Decker and Talyn saw little more than a corridor with cream-colored walls and tasteful images of Cimmerian landscapes. One of the many doors stood open, and Collette waved them into what was the suite's living room.

She indicated two inner doors, also open.

"You're free to choose either bedroom or both. Each comes with an ensuite. You'll find refreshments in the pantry. As Hadar said, you're confined for now, so there's no point trying to leave the suite. The windows are sealed, and I'll lock the door when I leave. Do you have any questions?"

Talyn shook her head.

"We'll be fine, thanks."

The young woman turned on her heels and left. As promised a soft mechanical snick seconds after the door slid shut proved it was locked. Decker and Talyn examined the three rooms and both ensuites in silence. They found video pickups in each and gave the hidden watchers long stares.

"We have a voyeurism problem," Decker announced once he and Talyn met again in the living room. "Unless you want to give this mysterious chief executive's security detail a show, we should keep things decent."

"So I noticed. It's comforting to know our allies don't stint on security measures."

"Meaning we did?" Decker slipped out of his jacket and tossed it over a chair. "Gustav was particular about where I could place surveillance nodes."

"Particular or peculiar?" Talyn asked with a smile. "It's just as well. If a visual record of his proclivities ever becomes public, it would kill the Collective. But that will change once we return home."

**

"The resemblance to Eva Cortez is remarkable."

"It is," Hadar Wilborg replied, watching the live video feed from Decker and Talyn's suite. He stood alongside his superior in her second story private office with its wall-sized display. "And the identification chip registered as being issued by the Mission Colony government. His too, though we weren't able to secure images of Piet Yorik as a basis for comparison. Are you sure someone murdered Cortez the evening before your arrival there?"

"Assistant Commissioner Bujold certainly seemed to think so when I spoke with her. The attending constables found her unconscious beside Eva's body, knocked out by a needler. Someone also shot Eva with a needler but using lethal darts. Bujold fingered a man and a woman calling themselves Corbin Peel and Sherri Zadeck as the likely culprits. They were waiting for Eva in her townhouse living room. But I doubt the police will find either of them. Professional assassins will have left the star system under another identity."

"Cortez was in a relationship with a senior Constabulary officer? I don't know whether to be worried or impressed. Did Bujold describe the suspects?"

"She did, but they'll be wearing different faces by now. The man was, large, muscular, and square-faced, in his late forties, with short dark hair and the aura of a military veteran."

"A description that could easily apply to Yorik." He gestured at Decker's image. "Other than the hair."

"The woman was in her fifties, lithe, also dark-haired, but shoulder length, with unremarkable physical features, but Bujold called her a predator."

"Like Cortez, then, but not quite as striking."

"Both also resemble the mercenaries who boarded *Thebes* at the Ventano spaceport, the ones who saved me from abduction by fake Howlers. They shook the tail Gudrun's team put on them with almost insulting ease and vanished somewhere in downtown Howard's Landing, never to be seen again." Magda Annear touched her communicator. "Gudrun, join me in my office, please."

"Collette said our guests reminded her of people she'd seen recently. Let me call her. Perhaps studying them at a remove might trigger her memories."

"Too many resemblances in too short a time," Annear said in a soft tone, eyes switching from Decker to Talyn and back. "If that's not Cortez, her companion isn't Piet Yorik either."

"Bujold knew nothing of his status?"

"No, but if those two killed Eva, they'll have done the same to her security chief."

"And thereby decapitated the best choice as our ally in the Mission system, making it useless to our near-term strategy."

The door opened behind them.

"What can I do for you, Sera?"

"Look at the people Hadar brought in and tell me if they seem familiar."

Gudrun Mariano approached the display and carefully studied each of them in turn.

"Their faces are unfamiliar, but his size and build remind me of the one who called himself Ned Sarkin. The woman?" Mariano shrugged. "She could be anyone."

"Such as Sarkin's companion, Lena Taryen?"

"Certainly, Sera. Do you think it's them?"

"Perhaps. But Sarkin and Taryen were false identities as well. I'm sure of that." Annear tapped an elegant fingertip against her lips. "If I wasn't aboard *Thebes* and didn't speak to Bujold, we might well be treating her as the real Eva Cortez. Because of our tame assistant commissioner's involvement, information on Cortez's murder was kept closely held. We might not have found out until well after accepting her as the real Eva."

"Ah, Collette, there you are." Wilborg glanced over his shoulder when he heard footsteps in the hallway. "Come in and feast your eyes on our impostors. You said they seemed familiar. Perhaps observing them in a quiet setting might jog your memory."

Several minutes passed in silence while both Collette and Gudrun Mariano mentally stripped the prisoners of their current outer shells.

"I'm about to make a gut call," the former said, turning to Wilborg. "The big guy eerily reminds me of another large, strongly built man, that Fleet anti-terrorism officer I followed from Howard's Landing yesterday. Allyson lost track of him and the woman near the Archeron harbor front."

Annear's eyes lit up.

"It makes sense now. Kerlin's assassination by a railgun-equipped sniper, Cortez's murder at the hands of a man and a woman who left Bujold alive. Another man and woman, deadly pros beat off the abduction attempt aboard *Thebes* without knowing who I was and promptly vanish less than an hour after landing. Who appears the same day with no one noticing their arrival on Cimmeria? A pair of Special Operations Command anti-terrorism experts tripping over themselves to help those Gendarmerie idiots. They also vanish, this time shortly after arriving in Archeron. And now, a reincarnated Eva Cortez and her goon show up on

Kusan Exports' doorstep. I bet they interrogated and killed Alek on Mission Colony. It's the only way to connect him with you, Hadar."

"So you believe we hold — what the hell are their names again?"

"Major Zack Decker and Commander Hera Talyn," Collette said.

"Thanks. You think the big guy is a Marine Corps major and she a Navy officer? The two who miraculously showed up on the day we began Operation Cerastes? And that they're responsible for knocking the Mission Colony Freedom Collective on its ass?"

"I'm well past the point of believing in coincidences. There's an easy way to tell whether he's the same one who fought off my husband's hired thugs aboard *Thebes*. Right after the attack, he got a good look at my face. I saw something strange in his eyes. Shock, perhaps. As if I reminded him of someone dear or dearly departed."

Mariano nodded.

"I saw that as well, Sera. The woman too though her reaction wasn't obvious."

"And if they are Fleet operatives? Do we kill them and dump their bodies into a ravine?" Wilborg asked.

"Heavens, no. They can be immensely useful."

"If they're Fleet, Sera," Mariano said, "they'll be conditioned against interrogation, which means any attempt to use drugs will cause their deaths. Torture will do the same, but not as quickly. And with a much bloodier mess."

"I wasn't thinking of interrogation." Magda Annear's smile sent a cold shiver up Wilborg's spine. Not for the first time he questioned Louis Sorne's wisdom in putting his considerable wealth and influence behind her plans to transform Cimmerian and Rim Sector politics. "For one thing, I want to see how far they'll take the masquerade. Notice how calm and unworried they appear?   Rather interesting under the circumstances, no?"

Wilborg glanced at the display again.

"That behavior is precisely what worries me. Ordinary people don't take imprisonment with such aplomb. If they're SOCOM officers, they'll be superbly trained fighters, capable of using their hands as deadly weapons, and experts at escape and evasion."

"The guest house is locked tighter than a maximum security prison, Hadar. Besides, I don't intend to place myself within arm's reach. Or do you place such little faith in the security team Louis' people provided?"

Since Mariano and Collette Chaskel were still within earshot, Wilborg shook his head.

"Of course I trust our security. It's the finest money can buy on Cimmeria. But I'd rather avoid risks at this juncture. Who else but you can challenge Calvo and his administration effectively once the chaos we're unleashing makes their weakness and incompetence clear for all citizens to see?"

"Your concern for my welfare is touching, Hadar. But even SOCOM officers can't do much if they're locked up. No one's ever escaped the guest house."

"Experience is no predictor of future performance in this case, Magda. Our previous guests were of a more innocuous variety."

A faint tap on the doorjamb drew Wilborg's attention.

"Yes, Allyson?"

"I finished examining their things. Her weapons are high-end but fairly common. Anyone with enough money can buy them. His dagger is a genuine Pathfinder blade, and the blaster came from a Shrehari weapons manufacturer. Both communicators were made by Cavani Electronics and haven't been modified in any way I can detect, but I pulled the power packs anyway.   Scans of their bags reveal no hidden compartments, and the IDs were not tampered with.”

“That our equipment can tell.”

“Of course, Ser Wilborg. It’s a well-known fact among private security firms that certain branches of the Armed Services enjoy a technological advantage over almost everyone else in the Commonwealth.”

“Thank you, Allyson.” He turned to Magda.

“What are your intentions?”

“Invite them for lunch in the guest house dining room, as if they remain valued associates. But feel free to take every precaution you consider necessary.”

“My first precaution would be to ask whether face-to-face is necessary, Magda.”

“Oh, yes. I need to know whether they’re the same pair Gudrun and I met aboard *Thebes*.”

“And you’re hoping for a reaction when the one who calls himself Piet Yorik sees you again, this time in radically different circumstances.”

“Just so. It would confirm I’m correct and our guests are impostors. Bring their personal effects to the dining room as well.” She touched a set of controls, and six images appeared on a secondary display, three men, and three women.

“Remarkable how they can change their outward appearance at will. But you cannot disguise certain things.”

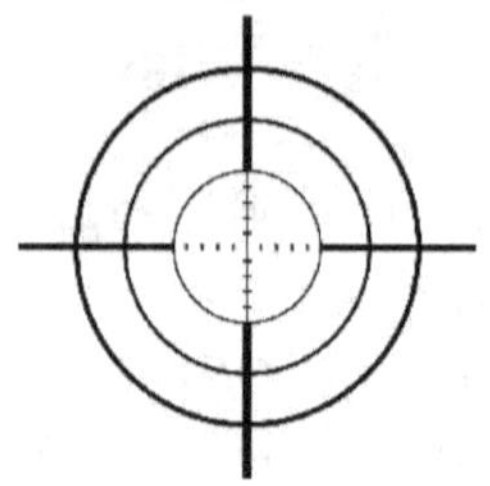

— THIRTY-FIVE —

Knuckles rapping on the doorjamb and a polite, "Chief," yanked Caelin Morrow from her absent contemplation of the Howard's Landing waterfront. She swiveled her chair around and gestured at Master Sergeant Bonta to enter the office.

"What's up?"

Bonta grimaced.

"It could be nothing, but since we're talking about Super Spooks One and Two, I thought you should know."

A faint smile crossed Morrow's lips at hearing Bonta's nicknames for Talyn and Decker, though she hadn't yet figured out who was One and who was Two.

"Let's hear it."

"The location signal from their communicators cut out abruptly a few minutes ago. This morning, the Navy satellites tracked them from the Archeron harbor to Kusan Exports. It stayed there for about half an hour, then left town via the main south road before turning off onto a secondary well beyond the outer suburbs until they reached the country lodge belonging to Pavel Yagudin and Magda Annear. Shortly after that, the signals vanished."

Morrow leaned forward and placed her elbows on the desktop, hands joined.

"Isn't that interesting? What do you think?"

"I don't have enough data for an informed opinion, Chief. But considering Magda Annear is the niece of Bronwen Annear, whose corporation owns Silfax or what little is left, I find it hard to fathom she would be involved with the DSA in any fashion. Silfax's destruction cost the Annear family hundreds of millions not to mention the casualties."

"Then why did the satellite lose contact with both of their communicators?"

"They went rogue?"

Morrow nodded.

"With Hera Talyn that's always a good possibility. But then there's the small matter of Magda traveling aboard *Thebes* when she can afford the best suite in the most luxurious starliner."

"Maybe Arno and I should dig into Sera Annear's life; find out if she's been keeping the wrong company."

"Good idea. See if you can trace her recent travels as well."

"What about Decker and Talyn?"

"We keep an eye on the satellite feed for fresh location signals and wait."

"At some point, we have to tell Colonel Joubert about this fresh development, sir."

"And that our two vaunted anti-terrorism officers are running an undercover operation in the Gendarmerie's jurisdiction without Cimmerian approval or oversight, not to mention that they're currently at a residence owned by Senator Annear's daughter and son-in-law? Let's wait until the Super Spooks call us with concrete evidence."

"Yes, sir. Keep in mind we'll need to ask our Gendarmerie contact for their dossier on Magda Annear, and considering who she is, they'll be reluctant to admit they even keep a dossier, let alone share it with us feds no questions asked."

"Understood."

**

"It looks like Magda Annear's been a bad girl," Bonta said when she and Galdi entered Morrow's office shortly before lunch.

The image of a laughing Annear and smiling Louis Sorne, Cimmeria's most infamous financier and opponent of star system sovereignty appeared on the main display.

"This was taken by the Howard's Landing Herald during the Locarno Conference two years ago, not long before Sorne became a guest of the Cimmerian correctional system. They seem rather chummy, considering Magda's mother and aunt Bronwen loathe him."

A thin smile tugged at Morrow's lips.

"It speaks well for them."

"Plenty of more or less honest politicians, financiers, industrialists, and senior bureaucrats from every star system in the Rim Sector attend the annual Locarno Conferences," Galdi replied. "As they'll be doing later today when this year's edition starts with a cocktail party. They glad-hand each other, put on insincere smiles, and pretend they don't consider everyone else a bunch of damned crooks. It's a self-congratulatory festival for those in the Rim Sector who presume to control our destiny."

Morrow snorted.

"Please, Arno. Don't hold back. Tell us what you really think."

"Locarno Conference pictures are innocuous, sure," Bonta continued. "Though it's telling neither Senator Annear nor her sister Bronwen attend them, even when the Senate is in recess and Nerys is on Cimmeria instead of Earth. They keep excellent attendance records, by the way. Louis Sorne only skipped Locarno once he became an inmate although Fast Tony still shows up on behalf of his boss and the Foundation. But there's more."

The image faded away, replaced by another one, showing Magda in deep conversation with Sorne.

"This one comes from our Financial Crimes Division, taken during the investigation that led to the evil old goat's conviction. They took hundreds, showing Magda and Louis in various restaurants or strolling along the fjord. More than can be explained by mere social calls among peers."

"Did Financial Crimes open a dossier on Magda?"

"No, Chief. They looked but found nothing suspicious to hang on her or Pavel Yagudin, who never attended the Locarno Conferences. Whatever Magda's dealings with Sorne, they weren't related to the shenanigans that put him away."

"I don't believe in coincidences, Chief." Galdi grimaced as he scratched his luxuriant beard. "We know Sorne's been meddling in political affairs across the sector and our Naval Intelligence friends think he wants to become the Coalition's main man along the Rim. Why would the daughter of a Commonwealth senator known for defending sovereign star system rights be consorting with a man opposed to everything her mother believes in?"

A new image replaced that of Annear and Sorne dining in one of Howard Landing's most expensive restaurants, this one of Magda and a thin, dark complexioned, gray-haired man. They were in deep conversation.

"Fast Tony." Morrow made a face.

"Antoine Hakkam is her godfather and Magda sits on the Deep Space Foundation's board of directors. This comes from the Howard's Landing Herald again — last year's Foundation annual general meeting."

"Why do I get the feeling Nerys and Magda might no longer be on speaking terms?" Galdi wondered. "Or Bronwen and Magda for that matter."

"Any other unsavory acquaintances?"

"I'm not sure about unsavory, Chief, but she also seems friendly with Titus Termoli, our favorite zaibatsu's Rim Sector Executive Vice President."

Morrow suppressed a groan.

"It figures ComCorp would come into the equation."

"Termoli's another habitual attendee at Locarno, but Magda also dines with him at least once a month."

"Did Financial Crimes pick up on that?"

Bonta nodded.

"When they were looking for evidence Annear might be complicit with Sorne. She also has occasional dealings with people lower in the Deep Space Foundation's food chain and those of Sorne's various businesses, and ComCorp. But no one who's come to our or the Gendarmerie's attention. One last item of note, Magda retained Sorne's company, CimmerTek Security Solutions to provide bodyguards. But according to my Gendarmerie contact, if rumors are true, she has a small mercenary company at her disposal, most of them operating from the hunting lodge south of Archeron which is reputedly a small fortress. And that's it, Chief."

"What did you find, Arno?"

"Two things. First, our Magda's quite the traveler, and second, she cleaned out Pavel Yagudin in their separation agreement. Painfully so."

"Why would she clean him out? The Annears are as wealthy as the Yagudins."

"Yes." A sly smile split Galdi's beard. "But from what my Gendarmerie contact told me, Magda's relationship with a mother obsessed by politics was never particularly good, and she fell out of favor with Bronwen after her father's death over a dispute about the provisions of his will. The falling out, apparently, was of epic proportions with Magda threatening Bronwen's life. As a result, without easy and unrestricted access to the Annear fortune, she had little besides Yagudin's money to finance her lifestyle."

"Right." A thoughtful frown creased Morrow's forehead. "I see the outline of a picture."

"You and me both, Chief," Galdi replied. "And judging by the look on her face, our good sergeant is also seeing it."

"What about the travel, Arno?"

"Until about eighteen months ago, she left Cimmeria once or twice a year, mostly with Pavel on business trips around the sector. Then, shortly after they separated, she took a long trip to Pacifica on one of the White Star liners, *Cymric*. Of course, her booking said Pacifica, but she could have left the ship at any other port along its route. Confirming it would take weeks. Soon after her return from Pacifica, she did the Rim Sector circuit twice, but on various freighters, such as *Thebes* and *Xenophon*. Again, finding out where she stepped off would take weeks, but *Thebes'* stop before Mission Colony on the latest run was Merseaux and before that, Scandia."

"Hmm." Morrow sat back and studied Magda Annear's image. "Do we know why she split up with Pavel Yagudin?"

Galdi shook his head.

"No. But Financial Crimes believe Yagudin and Sorne to be bitter rivals beneath the apparent cordiality. Their differing views on political matters might play a major part in that."

"Political views and fundamental values, if you ask me," Bonta said. "The Yagudins, Pavel included, enjoy a well-earned reputation for integrity. Louis Sorne, wouldn't know integrity if it bit him on the rear end."

"So I understand." Morrow's fingers briefly danced on the tabletop. "I'd like to see a timeline. When did Magda first become chummy with Sorne and Termoli? When did she join the Foundation's board of directors? That sort of thing. Add in her travels and the familial difficulties with her aunt, mother, and husband. And anything on Hakkam's role as her godfather."

Bonta nodded.

"Give me a few minutes, Chief. I'll throw what we know up on the screen."

"Are you thinking Magda fell into Sorne's orbit and at his urging, offered herself to the Coalition because she became disenchanted with her family?" Galdi asked. "Considering her profile on Cimmeria and her access to the sector's power brokers, she'd be one hell of an asset. Who would suspect Senator Annear's daughter of conspiring against the Cimmerian government on behalf of offworld interests?"

"Who indeed? Yes, that's my working theory right now."

"You understand what that means, right?"

"I do. Hera and Zack could have walked into a trap as evidenced by their location signals vanishing at Magda's lodge. Our friends may be masters of disguise, but they're hardly perfect, and she saw them in person only a few days ago aboard *Thebes*."

"Or even more recently via video as their real selves if she has people inside the Gendarmerie or the government. Didn't Hera leave word this morning at the dead drop she thought someone followed them from Howard's Landing? We call her and Zack Super Spooks in jest, but two against fifty of CimmerTek's best, mostly veterans of various police, military or mercenary organizations?"

"I know, Arno. We can't blithely go to Colonel Joubert with this information, in case his team is compromised."

"If he'll even entertain the notion Magda Annear could be on the enemy's side. She's hardly what one sees when picturing murderous radicals determined to overthrow a legitimate, democratic star system government."

"Which is precisely the point, I suppose, if she's to be the designated savior who'll put things right after Calvo asks the governor general to dissolve parliament and call for a government of national salvation." Morrow exhaled noisily. "Besides, DCC Maras won't let us mount an operation against the lodge, not even surveillance, without Gendarmerie approval, never mind buying into my theory."

"Chief, I drafted a rough timeline based on what the inspector and I dug up so far." Bonta nodded toward the display.

"It's no smoking bomb crater," Morrow said after studying the results of Bonta's work. "And completely circumstantial, but I'm sure something happened to Magda Annear shortly after her father died."

"Agreed, Chief. But what can we do with this information? As you said, neither Joubert nor DCC Maras will see it as anything more than speculation. Magda is one of Cimmeria's leading citizens."

"Pray our Super Spooks can talk themselves out of whatever trap might have caught them."

"Or that their promised backup gets here before it's too late."

Morrow abruptly looked at her communicator.

"Colonel Joubert is calling. I'll route it to the main display."

Bonta's timeline faded away replaced by the Gendarmerie officer's face.

"Good afternoon, Chief Superintendent." Joubert wore the expression of a man overtaken by events.

"Colonel. To what do we owe the honor?"

"Director General Dubnikov has questions for Commander Talyn and Major Decker. Could I speak with them?"

"I'm sorry, but no. They're following up on an idea and are incommunicado at the moment."

"What idea would that be?"

"They didn't say."

A frown creased Joubert's high forehead.

"Where did they go and when will they be back?"

"The where is Archeron. When, I don't know."

"That's very inconvenient."

"Is there anything we can do?"

"Thank you, Chief Superintendent, but no. If you hear from them, please call me. I'm heading to Locarno within the hour."

"Oh? The annual conference? It's still on, even under the circumstances?"

Joubert nodded.

"Yes, it is. More than half the participants come from every system in the Rim Sector and arrived before the DSA began its campaign. Besides, the organizers see a cancelation as yielding to terrorism, and that isn't on. But it means a tripling of security. The Gendarmerie canceled all vacation leave, and Prime Minister Calvo placed the National Guard's rapid reaction units on active duty. As of this morning, Locarno is the most heavily defended spot on Cimmeria. I'll be the anti-terrorism team's liaison with the joint Gendarmerie and National Guard Locarno Conference protection task force."

"I see. Try to enjoy yourself nonetheless. It's blessed with some of the most spectacular scenery on the planet."

"Thank you, Chief Superintendent. Goodbye."

Joubert's image faded as the display returned to standby mode.

Morrow exchanged a puzzled glance with Galdi.

"What do you figure that was about?"

"Couldn't say. Perhaps the added duties imposed by the conference is causing just a bit of unneeded stress."

"Or his people noticed Decker and Talyn taking a flight to Archeron and he called with a bullshit excuse to confirm the sighting," Bonta proposed.

Galdi and Morrow stared at the sergeant for a few seconds.

"Why use an excuse instead of asking outright?" The latter asked in a thoughtful tone.

Galdi made a dubious face.

"He didn't want it to seem as if the Gendarmerie's been tracking Commonwealth officers?"

"Possibly."

"I'm curious. Why didn't you use the occasion to mention Magda Annear in passing, Chief? Open the conversation and feel him out? She's a regular Locarno attendee, one with a high public profile."

"Something held me back, but don't ask what that was, Arno." She paused, chewed on her lower lip for a moment, then said, "Please see if we can access one of the Navy satellites in geosynchronous and put eyes on Annear's hunting lodge."

"What do I say if they want to know why?"

"Tell them it concerns an ongoing federal investigation, and I'm asking under the applicable memorandum of understanding between the Armed Services and the Constabulary."

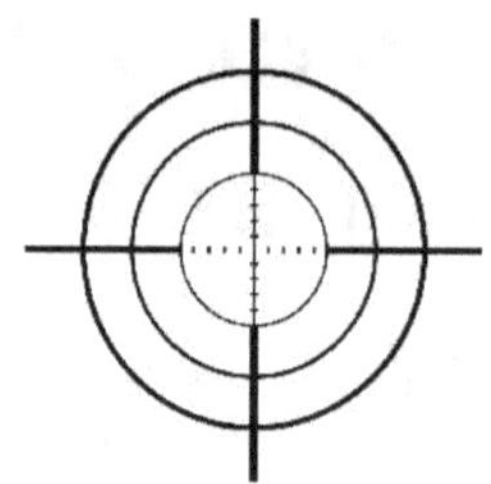

— THIRTY-SIX —

Collette, this time unarmed, entered the suite after a perfunctory knock on the door shortly after thirteen hundred hours.

"Our chief executive invites you to the midday meal."

"How kind," Talyn replied. "We accept, of course."

"The dining room is at the end of the hall. Please follow me."

She turned around and, after a last glance over her shoulder, led them to a room as big as their entire suite. A table with four place settings but easily capable of accommodating twenty occupied its center, beneath a long, rectangular lighting fixture made of stained glass joined by thin copper molding. A settee group occupied one corner, near a bank of floor to ceiling windows overlooking the distant Uttara Kuru range, while a wet bar occupied another.

Allyson stood by a side table near the bar where she'd laid out their weapons, communicators, and bags. But when Decker came toward her, she raised a restraining hand.

"Only once I receive permission to return your belongings. Please help yourselves to a drink instead."

According to Decker's internal clock, almost twenty minutes passed before Hadar Wilborg entered and joined Allyson. Then, the woman who bore a haunting resemblance to Zack's lost love, Avril Ducote, swept in and headed for them, eyes locked on Zack's. It took every bit of his willpower to stay impassive, but something in her gaze told him he'd failed.

"Good afternoon. I'm Magda Annear, chief executive of the Democratic Stars Alliance. Welcome to my lodge." She offered Talyn her hand. "You must be Eva Cortez, of the Mission Colony Freedom Collective."

"I am." Talyn nodded at her partner. "And he's Piet Yorik, my head of security."

Annear gave Decker a polite nod. "Ser Yorik." Then she turned back to Talyn as if dismissing him as a bit player. "I heard of Gustav Kerlin's tragic death at the hands of a professional assassin, Sera Cortez. Please accept my deepest sympathies."

"Thank you and call me Eva."

"Do you know who carried out the deed? Political rivals? Or was it a personal grudge?"

Talyn shook her head with an air of regret.

"No idea. It could be either. Gustav made several enemies over the years. But my inclination is to call it political since someone blew up the kilo of MHX-19 Alek Mannsbach gave us and thereby destroyed our beach house and its immediate surroundings."

"Most unfortunate."

"I'm hoping the colonial administration deems it a meteorite strike, but we left before hearing any official declaration on the matter."

"And made good time. You arrived here when? Yesterday or the day before? The ship I was traveling in briefly touched down at Ventano spaceport two days after Gustav's death, and I arrived only the day before yesterday."

Annear put on a quizzical expression and paused to let Talyn explain how they reached Cimmeria from Mission Colony.

"We have friends in the interstellar shipping community, Magda. One of them, who prefers to remain anonymous because of his business dealings, did me a favor and pushed his drives as hard as he dared."

"Your anonymous friend wouldn't be someone with a penchant for body art, perhaps?"

Talyn let a smile briefly cross her lips.

"I couldn't possibly comment."

"Funny, but I figured you might say something of the sort. Fair enough. Everyone is acquainted with people who'd rather stay in the shadows."

Annear's gaze dropped to the items on the side table. She reached out, grasped Decker's Shrehari blaster, and examined it from every angle.

"Now where did I see this unusual weapon before?"

"They're not uncommon among Marine Corps and Army veterans," he replied. "A trophy rechambered for our power packs and ammunition. You might have seen them carried by security personnel over the years."

"No. It was quite recently." She put it back and picked up Talyn's blaster. "This one seems familiar as well."

"It's a model in widespread use," Talyn said, "easily obtained from any weapons dealer. I bought mine in Ventano,"

"Still... I glimpsed weapons identical to these in the hands of mercenaries who called themselves Lena Taryen and Ned Sarkin a few days ago. They saved me from abduction while *Thebes* was crossing the Cimmeria system's heliopause, so I suppose I owe them a debt of gratitude."

Annear glanced up at them, looking for a hint of something, but both operatives met her gaze with impassive eyes.

"I gather I'm not the only one with unidentified enemies," Talyn said. "Any idea who yours are?"

"Not a clue, unfortunately. My saviors thought they might belong to the Confederacy of the Howling Stars."

Annear gestured toward the dining table. "Shall we sit?"

"Confederacy? I'm not sure about that."

Wilborg caught Talyn's eye and indicated the chair facing Annear while he and Decker sat across from each other.

"Why?"

"My friends in the shipping community are related. Let's just say they wouldn't go after those working to reform the Rim Sector's politics. It wouldn't be in their interest."

Annear spread the cloth napkin across her lap and nodded with a thoughtful air.

"My thoughts, if not exactly, then near enough. Still, they would have succeeded without the mercenaries' prompt intervention."

Serving droids filed into the room from the door behind the wet bar, each bearing a plate.

"Our first course. This is native smoked Red Piscis, a fish analog similar to Earth salmon. I'd love to hear your opinion about its delicate taste. Enjoy."

When Decker sat back, his plate cleared of every last morsel, Annear asked, "How was it?"

"Lovely. Best thing I've eaten since leaving Mission."

"I'm so glad. Might I ask you a personal question, Ser Yorik?"

"Sure." Decker picked up his wine glass and savored a sip of the Cimmerian Grigio while the droids switched out their plates. "We're all friends here."

"When I entered the room, earlier, I noticed something in your eyes. Recognition, perhaps? Could I ask what it was?"

Decker's sigh wasn't entirely feigned.

"You bear an uncanny resemblance to someone who was once very near and dear. She died many years ago."

"I'm sorry."

He made a dismissive gesture.

"I've traveled many light years since. The heart heals. If not completely then enough to continue living."

"Indeed it does. Might I inquire about her?"

"Sure."

Decker thought he felt Talyn tense beside him, a warning to reconsider revealing his innermost thoughts. But the Marine's instincts told him neither Annear nor Wilborg believed they were the Mission Colony Freedom Collective's leaders in exile.

A bit of honesty might help dispel their doubts. Besides, fighting the urge to find out if there was a link between the woman in front of him and the one living in his memories was a lost battle.

"You're almost the spitting image of a long-dead merchant starship captain by the name Avril Ducote. I spent some of my happiest moments with her."

Neither Decker nor Talyn was prepared for Annear's reaction. She leaned back and stared at them, as if robbed of speech.

After a moment, Annear asked, "Avril? Are you saying you knew her?"

A confused silence smothered the dining room.

"Who was Avril Ducote to you, Sera Annear?" Decker finally said with a faint catch in his voice.

Annear fixed a stare on him.

"My half-sister. We shared the same father. Avril is the product of a relationship predating his marriage to my mother, one that happened far from the Cimmeria system. I never met Avril, and she never knew about me, but our father kept in touch until she reached her majority. According to him, we resemble each other to the point of seeming like fraternal twins. Or rather resembled if she's dead. How did you come to know her and what happened?"

"After retiring from the Armed Services, I worked as a starship security officer for a few years before settling on Mission Colony. I met Avril on Pacifica after my ship was paid off. She hired me, and it turned into more than just a working relationship. We became pair-bonded. One day, years ago, pirates wrecked and boarded our ship *Demetria* out near the Coalsack sector. We fought them, but Avril took a large-caliber round in the gut and without immediate medical care..."

Decker shrugged helplessly, the pain of loss still shining in his eyes.

"They took me captive and abandoned Avril in deep space. I eventually escaped but found no mention of *Demetria* or her fate anywhere. News of the attack never made it to Lloyds, and they simply wrote her off as lost, cause unknown."

"That's awful," Annear replied in a soft voice after digesting his words. Decker sensed she believed him. "I can understand your reaction when you saw me earlier."

"But what an amazing coincidence," Talyn said, "that Piet would find his lost love's half-sister."

"I'll tell you about an even bigger coincidence." Annear briefly looked over Talyn's shoulder. "The folks who saved me aboard *Thebes* a few days ago reacted in the same manner as Piet did when they saw my face for the first time, especially the one who called himself Ned Sarkin. What are the odds I'd run across two large, powerful men, Armed Forces veterans now in the private security business, who seem startled by my resemblance to someone they once knew?"

"Perhaps this Sarkin fellow recognized you as Magda Annear and was surprised to find a wealthy woman, daughter of a Commonwealth senator, traveling in a rundown frontier trader," Talyn suggested.

"No. I got the impression Sarkin saw a ghost when he entered the cabin, not a minor Cimmerian celebrity slumming it with the interstellar hoi polloi." Annear took a sip of wine, eyes resting on Decker once more. "Perhaps Avril had a partner before you, Ser Yorik."

"Could be. We didn't talk much about our respective pasts."

"Don't ask, don't tell. Not a bad policy, I suppose, if one has things to hide. But twice in the space of days is an incredible fluke, no? Of course, I don't believe in coincidences. Things happen for a reason."

"Funny, I wouldn't take you for an adherent of determinism," Talyn said.

"I'm not. However, if you trace related events, even those who seem only superficially connected, sufficiently far back to their root causes, you can't help but notice inevitable linkages." Her mouth twitched. "Would you like to hear my theory on why two different men reacted in the same way at the sight of my face within a short period? I'll tell you right now it's not because I'm an extraordinary beauty. Far from it."

"Do tell."

"Occam's razor, my dear Eva. They're not different men."

The two officers sensed movement behind them.

"No sudden gestures, please. Collette and Allyson have both of you in their sights. Needlers with non-lethal darts, but it'll still be a nasty wakeup call."

"What's the meaning of this, Magda?"

"We can drop the pretense now that I satisfied my curiosity. You're not Eva Cortez, my dear, and I doubt your gorilla is Piet Yorik or Ned Sarkin for that matter, which means you're unlikely to be Lena Taryen. I arranged this meal merely to find out why my face seems to trigger a reaction in him. But please, finish your meal. There's no point in letting good food go to waste."

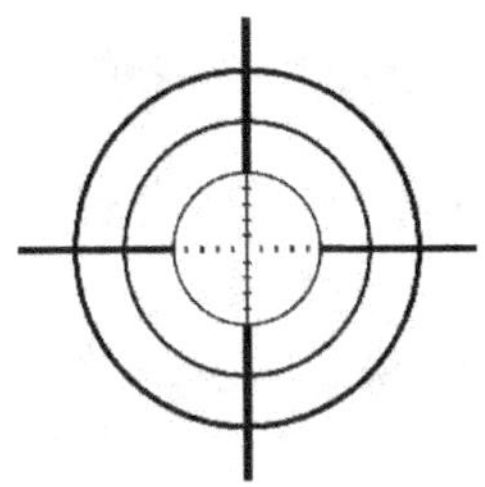

— THIRTY-SEVEN —

Magda Annear swallowed the last bite of her torte with evident relish, then dabbed at her lips with her napkin. The rest of the meal had passed in strained silence though she frequently glanced at her guests with amused eyes.

"Wonderful, as always. A good human cook is worth his weight in rare metals." Annear took a sip of coffee. "Do you know what's so ironic about the present situation?"

"That the daughter of Nerys Annear is mentally unbalanced?" Decker asked in a friendly tone, winking at her.

"How impolite." She glared back. "You're a guest at my table. Try to show a modicum of manners."

"Guests aren't forced to eat while needler-armed thugs keep a bead on them. But please go ahead."

"If not for my learning of Eva Cortez's death from Assistant Commissioner Bujold during *Thebes'* layover on Mission Colony, I might have accepted you two as the real deal."

"So she's your friend in the colonial administration. I wasn't aware Kristy played for several teams. Unfortunately, you'll need to replace her," Talyn said before raising a delicate coffee cup to her lips.

"That's right," Decker chimed in. "Bujold's career ends as soon as a Professional Compliance Bureau team arrives in Ventano. The Constabulary frowns on its senior officers playing more than just footsie with people like Kerlin and Cortez."

Annear made a dismissive gesture. "Corrupt cops are easily replaced. But those aren't the only ironic things. Your impulse to save me from the fake Howlers aboard *Thebes* was equally felicitous. If I'd never encountered Ned Sarkin and Lena Taryen, I might have been less suspicious when you showed up on Hadar's doorstep this morning. But you obviously didn't expect to see me again under these circumstances."

"Fake Howlers?" Decker pushed his empty plate away and sat back. "Would you care to explain?"

A feral smile curled Annear's lips.

"Satisfy my curiosity, and I'll satisfy yours."

"Why?"

"Gudrun Mariano tells me they condition SOCOM officers against interrogation. The only way you'll answer questions is voluntarily, correct?"

"And you figure we're SOCOM now? How do you manage that sort of mental gymnastics?"

"Oh, please. Commander Talyn and Major Decker traveled to Archeron in pursuit of a lead, and then vanished. The next morning, Eva Cortez and Piet Yorik show up at Hadar's office."

Annear waved her fingers at them.

"You're obvious skilled at disguises, but I've seen you once too often, most recently on video from the talk you gave the Gendarmerie's senior staff yesterday. Studying side-by-side pictures of Ned Sarkin, Piet Yorik, and Zack Decker turned out to be highly educational. Some things can't be hidden without prosthetics or surgery. Yes, the people waiting for Sarkin and Taryen at the Howard's Landing spaceport took pictures. Not because I suspected you might be SOCOM, but because I wanted to know why you looked at me as if I was a ghost."

She turned her eyes on Talyn.

"You were more difficult to match with Lena Taryen and Hera Talyn, but then your physique is rather common and less noticeable. Not being a natural beauty is helpful in your line of business, isn't it?"

Talyn shrugged.

"You're free to believe what you want."

"I don't merely believe, Commander, I know. Did you murder Gustav Kerlin and Eva Cortez? Kristy Bujold said Kerlin's assassination was a professional job."

Decker exchanged a brief glance with his partner signaling he would end the charade, then said, "Talk to us about the fake Howlers we killed, Magda, and we'll tell you."

He took another sip of coffee and smacked his lips.

"Excellent stuff. Better than what Eva served, and she was no slouch in the luxury department."

"Okay. You're aware of my husband's identity, right?"

"Pavel Yagudin," Talyn said. "One of those rare business tycoons with a conscience."

"I'm not sure Pavel knows what a conscience is, but his survival instincts are impeccable. He and I split up approximately two years ago because he didn't agree with my forging closer ties to Louis Sorne and his friends on Pacifica and Earth."

"Smart man. I'd dump a psycho who willingly cozies up to power-hungry maniacs. Not just dump but..."

Decker pointed his index finger at Annear and mimed pulling a trigger.

"You and Pavel seem to share the same barbaric views, Major Decker. Or should I call you Zack? He somehow found out I was touring the sector in recent weeks to prepare my allies for the day of reckoning. I'm sure you're aware of how important the personal touch can be. Don't ask me how Pavel found out. The attack on *Thebes* wasn't the first attempt by his tame mercenaries, but it would have been the first to succeed absent your intervention."

"Everyone makes mistakes. Why was he after you?"

"To renegotiate the terms of our separation from a position of strength, far from Cimmerian courts. He has friends in select Rim Sector star systems more sympathetic to his position."

"How did you know they weren't real Howlers?"

A contemptuous smile briefly flashed across her face. "Because we own the Confederacy."

"Who's we?"

"That's a new question. Time for you to answer one of mine. Did you murder Gustav Kerlin and Eva Cortez?"

Talyn jerked a thumb at Decker.

"He killed Gustav. I did Eva. I should have done Bujold as well, but we're not cleared to terminate corrupt Constabulary personnel. Who is the *we* holding a mistaken belief it owns the Confederacy?"

"A group of enlightened politicians, industrialists, financiers, government officials, academics, and other like-minded people. We want to replace the Commonwealth's rotten political foundations with stronger, better leadership and help humanity become the dominant species in this part of the galaxy. And for that to happen, we must put an end to the squabbling between fractious star systems and Earth."

"I heard of them." Decker looked up at the ceiling as if dredging his memory. "They call themselves the coven — no, the conclave or the constipation, something crappy like that."

"The Coalition, Major," Annear replied a dry, biting tone.

Decker snapped his fingers and pointed at her.

"Right. The Coalition. And you think those sad sacks own the Confederacy of the Howling Stars? You're hilarious, Magda. Has anyone ever told you that? Don't mistake them doing the Coalition's bidding in exchange for money as anything more than a purely contractual relationship. No one owns the Howlers."

"And yet we do." A sly smile briefly creased her features. "She who can destroy a thing controls it, and if she controls it, she effectively owns it. Am I correct, Commander Talyn?"

"How did that come about?"

Annear wagged a finger at her.

"Ah. An answer for an answer. I told you who we are. Now tell me what you expected to achieve by visiting Hadar at his Kusan Exports office and posing as Eva Cortez and her muscle."

"Burrow our way into the Democratic Stars Alliance so we can find and secure the MHX-19 before you kill more innocents."

"We killed no one, Commander. My dear aunt Bronwen received a warning in time to evacuate Silfax, including the shift underground. She ignored it as she ignores anyone who isn't either useful or obedient."

"Let me guess, she thinks you're neither of those things, right?" Decker gave her a cocky smile.

"Are you always this tiresome, Major?"

"Sadly, my partner is just warming up," Talyn replied. "It gets worse. How did the Coalition impose its will on our Howler friends?"

"I don't know, and that's the truth, but they assured me we control the Confederacy's leadership to the point where disobedience means instant death. As I said, if you can destroy something, you control its destiny. My turn again. You weren't expecting me as the DSA's chief executive, were you?"

"Considering you're the daughter of a Commonwealth senator known for supporting star system sovereignty against centralization by Earth? No."

Magda's face momentarily tightened at the mention of Nerys Annear.

"My mother is entirely devoid of vision. She and the other Outworld senators stand in the way of progress."

"My turn," Decker said. "When and where is the next bomb due to go off? I'm guessing this won't be a pinprick such as yesterday's and this morning's automated ships. As a bonus question, do you hold a grudge against the Valerian family as well? Or is destroying its shipping merely a coincidence?" A pause. "Then again, destroying one of the Annear family's most important properties helps deflect suspicion away from you, so perhaps attacking Valerian assets is also meant as a distraction."

He caught Hadar Wilborg's reaction out of the corner of his eyes the moment he spoke the Valerian name. It wasn't much, but the quick sideways glance at Magda spoke volumes.

"Thought so," Decker said. "Hera, if we accept the theory that this mayhem — pun intended — is to pave the way for a savior who'll head a government of national unity with the blessing of the Honorable Hector Valerian, Governor General of Cimmeria, then I would suggest the lovely Magda intends to be the next prime minister. Does that sound about right, Magda? Not that it'll work. Your life is rapidly coming to its end. I figure thirty-five hundred counts of first degree murder at Silfax are worth several death sentences."

"Do you think I would stop at thirty-five hundred, Major? That was merely the beginning. If Calvo doesn't concede tonight and ask Hector to dissolve parliament, the next bit of encouragement will be much deadlier."

"Why? Did you put your remaining MHX into a five hundred kilo bomb buried beneath R.E. Howard's statue?"

An unexpected burst of laughter escaped Annear's lips.

"That would be interesting. I never liked the government precinct's unimaginative architecture. But doing so strikes me as overly dramatic. I'll need the machinery of government to rule Cimmeria, so bombing the capital is out. No. I'm afraid many prominent families will shortly suffer a devastating blow, enough to encourage their support of a new regime capable of suppressing these maniacal Democratic Stars Alliance radicals throughout the Rim Sector. No one likes radicals, Major, free, democratic, or otherwise. Not even me."

"What happens to your supporters?" Talyn asked. "The true believers you co-opted into the DSA? You know, those who genuinely want the political reforms that remove, or at least minimize the influence moneyed families exert on the democratic process?"

"You mean the useful idiots? I don't really give a damn, Commander. If humanity is to reach its full potential, it cannot be burdened with those motivated by sloth or envy rather than a desire to surpass themselves for the betterment of everyone. Once I seize the levers of power, they'll vanish, either into the woodwork voluntarily or into the ocean, dropped from a shuttle, if they insist on pushing their foolish notions."

"You have to admire the DSA's severance program for sheer ruthlessness," Decker said giving his partner a knowing look. "And I thought ours was overly harsh. Dropping dissidents into the sea without parachutes from ten kilometers altitude? Sucks to be a revolutionary cadre once your usefulness expires, doesn't it? You'd think the starry-eyed morons would learn from history because it has always been thus. Still, I'm having a hard time faulting Magda for wanting to rid Cimmeria of social parasites, though I'd rather see them find meaningful work than an early grave. But that's the radical outlook, I suppose. Remind me of the cure for cognitive dissonance, Hera?"

"A shot through the heart of the closest Coalition critter."

"Right." He grinned at Annear. "My sort of remedy."

"I hope you enjoy taking it as much as you like dishing it out, Major."

"Why? You plan to kill us?"

"Me? Heavens forbid. Why should I get blood on my hands? But the Gendarmerie might find it necessary to kill a pair of offworld terrorists by the name Cortez and Yorik. Alas not before they commit the DSA's next act of mass murder, once that will touch the Rim Sector's most powerful families."

A ferocious smile transformed the Marine's expression.

"Be careful, Magda, darling. Every time you strike me down, I shall rise up more powerful than ever."

"Oh dear." Annear's face scrunched into a mask of amused skepticism. "How dramatic. It almost sounds like a line from some third-rate holostory."

"Don't discount the big guy because he likes to quote ancient history. Many have tried to kill him over the years. None succeeded."

"A combination of luck and skill, no doubt?"

"No." Decker's smile turned into demonic leer. "Hell didn't want me then. It still doesn't want me now."

"How do you know?"

"Ever had the devil perch on your shoulder and whisper you can't resist the storm?"

Annear thought about it for a few moments.

"Once or twice, I suppose. If you mean that metaphorically."

"Want to guess what I reply?"

She glanced at Talyn.

"Should I ask, Commander?"

"Humor him. It's easier that way."

"Okay, I'll bite. What do you say to the devil?"

"I *am* the storm." The Marine's fiendish laughter filled the dining room like a living presence. "Hell's too damn scared to let me in."

"How droll. I suppose there's no chance you're destined for heaven, is there?"

"Of course not. Even if they offered me admittance, I'd refuse because I can't face an eternity without indulging in my favorite sins of gluttony and lust. But go ahead and try to use us as scapegoats. It won't work."

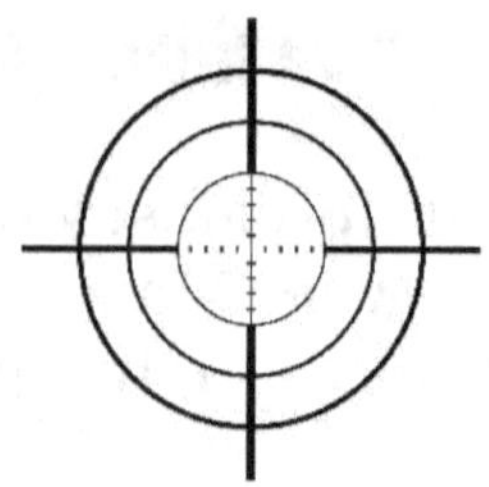

— THIRTY-EIGHT —

Hadar Wilborg turned a skeptical look on Annear. "Are you sure that's wise, Magda? We should drop them into one of the bottomless ravines in the outback and be done. Remember our timetable. Changing the plan now won't help."

"Listen to him," Decker said. "The more you complicate your scheme, the easier it'll be for us to gum up the works."

"I'm not changing the plan, Hadar. Instead of the authorities tracing tonight's big bang to a couple of DSA supporters, I'll let them blame our guests, initially under their Mission Colony Freedom Collective identities. But imagine what will happen once we leak the fact that undercover Fleet SOCOM officers, working with the DSA, are responsible for tonight's devastation. One cannot buy disruption of that nature for love or money." She turned a sickening smile on Decker. "And you'll be reunited with my half-sister while doing us a favor. A win-win proposition, no?"

"Please reconsider," Wilborg urged. "These are dangerous people. I doubt our folks on the inside will approve of the added risk. Stick with the planned sacrificial goats and let me dispose of them."

"Enough," Annear snapped. "We're taking them with us instead of the designated fall guys. I'm sure our security team can contain two prisoners until the time comes. They're SOCOM officers, not invincible demi-gods."

"Well... Actually..." Decker winked at Annear.

She stood abruptly.

"Prepare them for travel. We leave in half an hour. I must be in Howard's Landing by sixteen hundred and you in Locarno by eighteen hundred."

A knowing expression crossed Talyn's face.

"That's right. The annual Locarno Conference starts tonight. You plan on flattening the entire town along with five hundred of the Rim Sector's most influential people?"

"Slightly less than five hundred, Commander. Not everyone arrives in time for the opening cocktail party."

"Let me guess. The Coalition supporters who usually attend made it publicly known they don't plan on getting there before tomorrow morning."

Annear gave Talyn an ironic round of applause.

"Well done, Commander."

"Satanic." Decker nodded with mock approval. "Eliminate your natural opponents by massacring them in job lots. It puts the fear of God into their families and organizations and opens the way for more Coalition influence. As a bonus, you can blame everything on the Democratic Stars Alliance."

"Not only the DSA, Zack," Talyn said. "The Gendarmerie's senior leadership as well for having failed to prevent the incident, the Constabulary for being useless and the Fleet for letting hundreds of MHX-19 bricks go walkabout. Who dreamed up this operation, Magda? You? It seems both more ruthless and more effective than any other Coalition operation we foiled."

"I wish I could take full credit, but Louis Sorne is the one who came up with this idea and sold it to our friends on Pacifica. I'm merely responsible for planning and carrying out its implementation."

"Friends on Pacifica being the Amali family and their acolytes?"

"You know them?"

"Better than they would like. What did the current family head do for you?"

"Sadoc Amali's people gave us the MHX. They also provided help in creating the DSA and spreading its influence over Rim Sector radical groups so rapidly."

Wilborg cleared his throat.

"It's perhaps best if you don't reveal too much, Magda."

"You're afraid they'll escape? Who would believe them even if they managed such a feat?" She glanced at her timepiece. "The bomb is already in place, and good luck finding it."

"Please, Magda. No more details."

"Oh very well. You take the joy out of being an evil genius, you know." Annear gave Wilborg a vexed glance. "Get them ready to travel."

She turned on her heels and left the dining room.

Moments later, another woman with the same demeanor as Collette and Allyson entered, carrying a set of wrist and ankle restraints. The latter were of a type allowing the wearer to take regular steps but locking the moment he or she attempts to move any faster. Wilborg produced a small needler from inside his jacket and pointed it at them.

"Hands on top of your heads, please. Stand when Fiona says so."

"If we're going to die anyway, why should we cooperate like a pair of rookie troopers?" Talyn asked.

"Because you'll wake up in the suborbital shuttle's cargo compartment and experience the worst migraine you can imagine before facing execution like a pair of mangy rats. Cooperate, and you can fly in a padded passenger seat, watch the scenery go by and walk to your deaths like proper Armed Forces officers.”

Decker and Talyn exchanged looks. Her use of his code name, Rookie Trooper, was a question. Act now or play along? Singing out the last line of a *Blood on the Risers* verse would trigger an immediate attack on their captors, but he merely shrugged before placing his hands on his head.

“I’ve always been partial to walking.”

“Me too,” she answered, imitating him.

Wilborg’s eyes momentarily narrowed, as if suddenly beset by doubt at their apparent willingness to go along.

“Make no mistake. If we find it necessary to shoot or even kill you, it won’t change the outcome a single bit. We’ll mutilate your bodies so that previous gunshot injuries aren’t noticeable.”

“Leaving a beautiful corpse has never been one of my ambitions,” Decker replied. “But I’d like to see Locarno before dying. I hear it’s one of the sector’s prettiest towns, a throwback to those of old Earth’s European Alps before the diaspora. A shame you intend to vaporize it.”

“Locarno is a symbol of the old ways, Major Decker, and most conference attendees are firm partisans of the status quo which keeps humanity chained to its star systems instead of finding a fresh destiny in the wider galaxy.”

“Great.” The Marine rolled his eyes at Talyn. “Another true believer. I think when everything is said and done, I still prefer power-hungry cynics like Magda.”

“Stand,” Fiona ordered. Decker climbed to his feet, eyes still resting on Wilborg.

“What do you mean power-hungry cynics like Magda? She believes in our greater destiny as much as anyone.”

"Sorry, Hadar, old chum. Magda believes in Magda. She'll toss you aside the moment your usefulness ends, just as she intends to dispose of the DSA by throwing it into a black hole. What you face here — hang on. Let's let the young lady do her thing."

Fiona knelt beside him, put on the ankle restraints, and stood again. She tried to reach for Decker's left wrist, but his height put it out of the shorter woman's reach.

"Hands."

Decker lowered his arms and held them out, fists clenched, wrists almost touching. After a moment of hesitation, she clapped one side of the manacles on his left wrist and secured the other on the right, effectively hobbling the Marine hand and foot. Then she did the same to Talyn, who offered her wrists in a similar, helpful manner.

"As I was saying," Decker continued, "Magda glommed onto Louis Sorne and his dreams of becoming the Coalition's grand master in the Rim Sector so she could get back at her mother and her aunt for real or imagined slights. Absent those, I think she'd be following in the elder Annear's footsteps and either preparing for a senatorial bid or taking over one of the family's subsidiaries to succeed Bronwen as head of the zaibatsu one day."

"Bullshit. You can't psychoanalyze someone over lunch." Wilborg's vehemence sounded slightly forced to Zack's ears.

"She's a psycho all right, and you know it. No one in his or her right mind plans and carries out the murder of thousands as a way to become prime minister. Do sane people call their supporters useful idiots and plan to kill them if they don't fall in line after they find out the truth? That's weapons-grade cynicism right there, buddy. If I were you, I'd look at leaving this star system on the next transport."

"Forget it, Zack. Hadar has a thing for Magda. Not that she'd ever consider him as anything more than a hired hand, one without Pavel Yagudin's wealth and good looks."

When he saw the growing fury in Wilborg's eyes, the Marine chuckled. "Another direct hit. See, we're what you would call students of human behavior. It's a useful skill in our line of business."

Instead of replying, Wilborg nodded at Fiona.

"Take them to the suborbital and make sure they're secured. Magda won't tolerate any deviation from the timetable today. Collette, bring our guests' weapons and bags. We'll leave them with their bodies."

Brilliant subtropical sunshine greeted them on the plaza where a sleek, vertical takeoff suborbital aircraft, a rich person's toy, had replaced Wilborg's ground car.

"Pretty." Decker studied its lines and realized it was armed beneath almost imperceptible blisters. "Must cost as much as I cumulatively earned in pay since enlisting thirty years ago."

"More. Thirty years of your pay and mine combined, multiplied by fifty," Talyn replied. "I'll bet this beauty is registered to Pavel's zaibatsu and was a tax write-off when he bought it."

"Why does evil always live in luxury while those of us who fight for truth, justice, and humanity's survival are stuck traveling in steerage class?"

"Because we serve the Commonwealth while evil is funded by third-party contributions, most of them either untraceable or tax deductible."

Decker climbed into the suborbital flyer.

"Speaking of cynics. You and Magda would make a fine pair. Now this," he added, looking around, "is what I call proper living. Too bad its owner won't do much more of that. And look, there's our old buddy Gudrun

Mariano at the controls. Hi Gudrun! Didn't know you could pilot one of these things."

Mariano's expression remained blank as if Decker and Talyn were no more than unimportant cargo. Fiona pointed at Decker, then at a single seat on the starboard side.

"You. There."

He sat and waited until Collette fastened him to the seat with practiced ease. She repeated the same exercise on the port side with Talyn.

"Let me guess. We're not the first prisoners you transported in this thing. What happened to them?"

"None of your business," Wilborg replied.

"And what happens to us if we need to make an emergency water landing?"

"You drown. No matter what happens today, you won't live long enough to see another sunrise."

"Keep telling yourself that, buddy."

Wilborg, along with Fiona, Collette, and Allyson took seats around them, strapped in, and waited.

Precisely thirty minutes after she left the dining room, Magda Annear, now wearing an elegant, yet practical dark business suit, climbed aboard, gave her prisoners a quick and silent once-over, and joined Mariano in the cockpit. Seconds later, the door slammed shut and thrusters began to whine in preparation for takeoff.

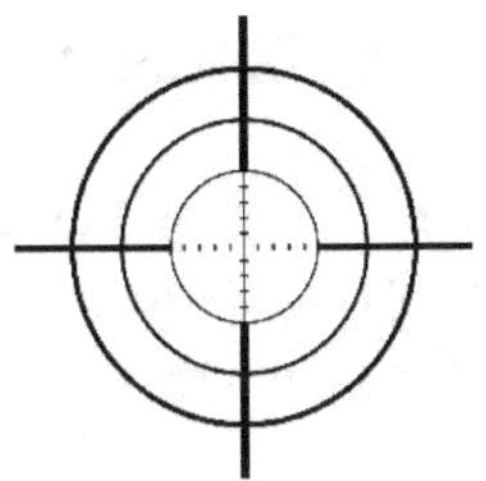

— THIRTY-NINE —

Bonta stuck her head into Morrow's office after a perfunctory warning knock.

"Chief, the Navy gave us access to its satellite constellation just in time to witness a suborbital flyer taking off from Magda Annear's hunting lodge. I checked with traffic control and its owner of record is the Yagudin zaibatsu."

"So they filed a flight plan?"

"Yes. No choice if you're entering controlled airspace. The flyer's final destination is Locarno, with an intermediary stop at the Howard's Landing spaceport."

"Locarno?" Morrow sat back and stared at her blank display. "Is Magda attending the conference? Why the stopover and where are Decker and Talyn?"

"If you want, I'll go to the spaceport and see if anyone gets off."

"Please and make sure Arno's up to speed."

"Roger that, Chief." Bonta withdrew her head and vanished.

Morrow thought for a moment and then touched the screen embedded in her desk. She counted to ten before Maras' adjutant answered her call.

"What can I do for you, Chief Superintendent?"

Though the inspector's tone was carefully neutral, she saw suspicion in his eyes, as if he was wondering what fresh hell the head of the Rim Sector's Professional Compliance Bureau intended to unleash this time.

"Is the DCC attending the Locarno Conference?"

Her question clearly surprised him.

"As a matter of fact, she's leaving at seventeen hundred today."

"Ask her if I can tag along. I promise to behave. I'll even put on my uniform if she wishes."

Morrow's offer to wear a uniform caught him by surprise. He stared at her for a few heartbeats as if searching for a catch. PCB members almost always worked in civilian clothes, except for the most solemn of occasions such as regimental funerals, because not wearing rank badges helped prevent overly unpleasant situations when investigating and arresting officers of higher rank.

"The DCC will wish to know why."

"Locarno has come up several times in the last two days during our investigation, and perhaps by accompanying the DCC, I might be able to look around without attracting attention."

He didn't reply right away and she pictured the gears spinning in his head.

"Is the DCC putting herself in danger by heading to Locarno, Chief Superintendent?"

"Not that I'm aware of, but people of interest are known attendees."

"Do you mean the high and mighty of the Rim Sector might be working with the DSA?"

He sounded incredulous

"Again, not that I'm aware of. But since Locarno came up more often than we can explain by mere coincidence in the last thirty-six hours, it's become pretty much our only lead." When he hesitated, she added, "Just ask the DCC, please, Inspector. If she says no, I won't mention it again."

"Very well. Wait one."

His image faded from the office display.

Morrow swiveled her chair to look out over a subdued city, wondering what made the two Naval Intelligence officers shut off their tracker beacons at the country residence of a prominent woman now on her way north aboard a luxury flyer. The chime of an incoming call startled her a few minutes later.

"Morrow."

"What's up, Caelin?" DCC Maras asked without preamble. "You never offered to wear a uniform in exchange for a ride with me, which is why we're talking. I always figured it would take a direct order from DCC Hammett before anyone saw you in service grays."

"A notion, sir."

She explained what they'd uncovered about Magda Annear's acquaintances and movements before telling her how Decker and Talyn ended up at Annear's lodge, where their communicators' tracking signals vanished. Finally, she mentioned the suborbital flyer and its flight plan.

"Why do I think the Gendarmerie isn't aware of this?"

"Because our Naval Intelligence cousins are operating under trust no one rules."

"Do you agree with them?"

"Yes, sir. They've come to believe certain wealthy and politically connected offworld interests might be using the DSA as a front. These people are the furthest thing from wide-eyed revolutionaries with a special dislike of illegitimate plutocratic elites, and may well have allies inside the Cimmerian government."

Maras exhaled slowly.

"Wonderful. You'll find plenty of wealthy and politically connected offworlders in Locarno, that's for sure. My aircar leaves from the roof at seventeen hundred. Wear your service grays and bring an overnight bag."

"Yes, sir. Thank you."

"On the way there, perhaps you can explain what your friends mean by these mysterious offworld interests. If that won't violate any confidences." Maras cut the link before Morrow could respond.

She stood and walked over to the office closet where she kept a uniform and what Decker would call a bug-out bag, just in case she didn't find the time or the inclination to go home and change. It was a protocol observed by most plainclothes Constabulary members, including her PCB crew, even though she couldn't remember off hand the last time any of them wore grays.

A quick check confirmed the uniform remained impeccable inside its protective sheath, the calf-high boots still shone, and her bag contained everything needed for a few nights away from Howard's Landing.

After a brief internal debate, she opened her gun safe and took out a small caliber, police-issue blaster, spare power packs and magazines, and a polished black gun belt, suitable for wear with the high-collared service tunic. On impulse, she stowed a less formal shoulder holster in her bag.

"Did someone order a regimental funeral or are you testifying at a court-martial?" Inspector Arno Galdi asked, standing on the threshold of her office door.

She turned away from the wardrobe.

"I'm off to the Locarno Conference with DCC Maras, and service grays are apparently the dress of the day for Constabulary attendees."

"Got a bee in your bonnet, Chief? Magda Annear and her entourage? Bonta told me about the suborbital flyer and its flight plan."

"How does the old saying go? Once is happenstance?"

"Twice is coincidence and three times means we crank up a new inquisition. I'd offer to watch your back, but my grays shrunk in recent months."

"Someone needs to stay here anyhow, Arno. In case a SOCOM unit appears in orbit looking for Super Spooks One and Two. Or the Super Spooks suddenly materialize on our doorstep."

"You don't believe that. Otherwise, you wouldn't have sent Sergeant Bonta to the spaceport."

Morrow shook her head.

"No. My gut tells me Decker and Talyn are aboard that flyer. But I don't know whether it's as Magda's putative allies from Mission Colony or as prisoners."

"And Locarno?"

"No idea. Yet."

"The DSA's next deadline is noon tomorrow, which means you should enjoy a quiet evening hobnobbing with the most rarefied of the sector's upper crust. It'll give the corruption-chasing cop in you a chance to observe her prey in its natural habitat while sampling top quality hors-d'oeuvres."

"You almost sound jealous, Arno."

Galdi's chuckle sounded like a volcano preparing to erupt.

"Perish the idea, Chief. Finger food that would make me put on service grays and indulge in mindless small talk with the obscenely wealthy has yet to be devised by humanity's finest chefs."

**

Morrow was adjusting the black, collarless shirt she wore under the service tunic when her communicator, sitting on the desk, chimed for attention. She'd already donned gray trousers with black senior officer's stripes on the outer leg seams and stepped into the calf-high boots.

"Accept the call." The communicator chimed again, in a different tone, to show the connection was live. "Yes?"

"Bonta, Chief.   We're in a conference call with Inspector Galdi."

"Good.   It'll save me repeating the conversation. What's the word?"

"I used my credentials to mix in with the aerospace terminal crew.   Annear's flyer rode into one of the general aviation hangars.   I talked my way inside and got a good view of Magda Annear disembarking. Alone. But I also managed a quick look through the flyer's open door and spotted a man who resembled Major Decker's cover identity as Piet Yorik.   Based on what little I saw, they appear to have shackled him to his seat. No sign of Talyn, but I only had eyes on a small section of the flyer's interior.   Magda walked out the front door where an unmarked ground car picked her up."

"Unmarked, as in no registration plate?"

"Affirmative, Chief.   The only cars around here without regular plates belong to—"

"The governor general's official motor pool."

"Precisely.   From what I saw, it was of the armored and armed variety, not just a normal staff car."

"Where are you now?"

"Tailing it in my vehicle.   So far, we're on the right itinerary for Cimmeria Hall."

"Why is Magda visiting Governor General Valerian instead of continuing on to Locarno for the conference opening cocktail party?"

"Because she intends to travel there tomorrow with Valerian for his keynote speech?" Galdi asked. "They're known to be chummy."

"Lovers?"

"I doubt it, Chief. Magda's not his sort of human."

"Oh. Never mind, then. What about the flyer?"

"I asked the terminal crew to let me know what it does, and they called just now. It lifted off and headed north with clearance to Locarno."

"Why send Decker and Talyn to Locarno, especially if Sergeant Bonta is right and they're in shackles?"

"That is today's ten million cred question," Galdi said. "Might I suggest the moment Sergeant Bonta confirms Magda enters the Cimmeria Hall compound, she zips back here, changes into service grays and rides up front with DCC Maras' pilot? There's just enough time."

"You figure I'll need backup."

"Call it a gut feeling, Chief. Better safe than without a winger at your side."

"Okay. I'm sure the DCC won't mind a Constabulary non-commissioned officer who looks like someone from a recruiting poster in our party. I'll let her adjutant know."

A rumbling chuckle came over the link.

"Sergeant Bonta is indeed impressive in uniform. If it weren't for the fact she arrests bent cops instead of taking down dastardly crime lords, I'm sure the Public Affairs Branch would make her an offer she can't refuse."

"Nice to know my superiors see me as an adornment to the PCB. I should be there in twenty minutes."

"Anything else?"

"No, Chief."

"See you then. Morrow, out."

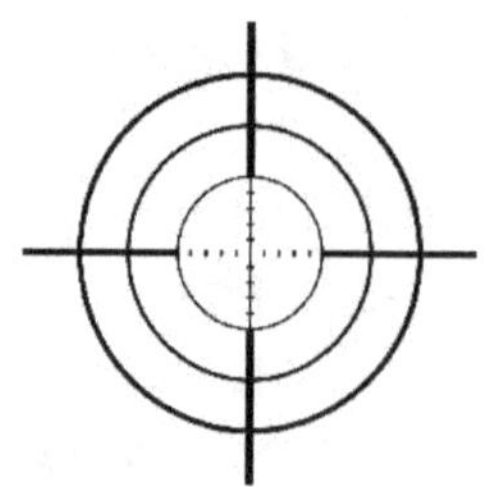

— FORTY —

"You should wear the uniform more often, Caelin," Deputy Chief Constable Maras said as she returned Morrow and Bonta's crisp salutes when they joined her on the rooftop landing pad. "That impressive ribbon collection on your left breast might remind everyone else around here you're a hell of a good cop who's seen and done more than most. Or in earning combat Pathfinder wings as a Constabulary liaison officer, more than anyone in my HQ. I could say the same about you, Sergeant Bonta. There are few master sergeants in my command entitled to wear so many awards."

"But I was smart enough to avoid jumping out of perfectly good shuttles from low orbit," Bonta replied, chuckling. "That's a distinction the chief can keep."

"No doubt." Maras turned to Morrow again. "Although Sergeant Bonta's addition to the Constabulary delegation adds a certain panache, you didn't give Paul any explanation why."

"Sergeant Bonta thinks she saw one of the Fleet officers, Major Decker, aboard Magda Annear's flyer when it briefly touched down at the Howard's Landing spaceport this afternoon. He was wearing a cover identity and appeared to be shackled. I can only assume Commander Talyn was also aboard. The flyer will have reached Locarno by now, minus Magda who is enjoying the governor general's hospitality at Cimmeria Hall."

"Along with several conference attendees who don't intend to partake in tonight's social event." When she saw curiosity in Morrow's eyes, Maras smiled. "Paul keeps track of everyone invited to Locarno on my behalf. Call it self-preservation. A few always try to buttonhole me around the buffet table and I'd rather no one sees me in their company. Forewarned is forearmed."

"Then why go, sir?"

"Because like you, I answer to a higher power on Wyvern. The Chief Constable wants the sector's most senior officer to attend and show the flag. It's why we're in uniform."

"Understood."

At that moment, the rooftop hangar's door rolled aside, and an armed and armored Constabulary aircar rolled out, engines already whining in preparation for takeoff.

"We're using one of the heavies, sir?"

Morrow studied the sleek, dark gray craft with its visible gun blisters.

"I have little choice. With the current situation on Cimmeria, I either take this one or travel in an armored ground car. Regulations don't allow me to use regular staff cars, flying or otherwise, while the threat level is elevated and I don't want to spend three hours on the highway."

The car stopped when its rear compartment door was precisely level with Maras. The door moved to one side, and a cheerful voice said, "Express flight to Locarno. Please make yourselves comfortable. Sergeant Bonta, your seat is up front with me."

Once the car lifted off, Maras turned curious eyes on Morrow, sitting across from her.

"Care to tell me what's really happening, Caelin? Commander Talyn and Major Decker aren't SOCOM officers, are they?"

A faint smile tugged at Morrow's lips.

"They are, but not from the conventional end of special operations. If there is such a beast. I suppose under the circumstances, you're entitled to an explanation, need-to-know be damned. Both are Naval Intelligence officers and belong to its Special Operations Division. Hera calls her group the blackest of black operators. But they often work closely with SOCOM direct action teams."

Maras snorted.

"Figures. I'll bet they've been five steps ahead of the Gendarmerie and us on this DSA matter, but didn't want to share."

"Sadly, no. Otherwise, they wouldn't be traveling aboard Magda Annear's suborbital flyer shackled to the seats."

"Are you saying the younger Annear is part of this mess?"

"If Hera and Zack are in her power, then I'm afraid so."

"But she's exactly the sort of person this Democratic Stars Alliance professes to hate."

Morrow took a deep breath, conscious she was about to violate Talyn's confidences, but as instinct told her long ago, Maras was one of the good flag officers.

"Did you ever hear of an organization calling itself the Coalition, sir?"

"No. And judging by your expression, I'll probably regret asking what it is."

When Morrow finished explaining, Maras let out a long, noisy exhalation.

"If you weren't one of the least excitable officers I ever met, your story would strike me as pure fantasy."

"Are you saying I'm unimaginative, sir?" Morrow asked in a mischievous tone. "I suppose you mean it as a compliment."

"I meant you're not prone to flights of fancy, as you well know. What does this Coalition want?"

"I can only assume their goal is a government which will bend its knee to Earth. Considering the current Cimmerian members of parliament speak as one in support of star system sovereignty, no matter the political party, they hope to replace Prime Minister Calvo and his cabinet with outsiders once the governor general dissolves parliament."

"And the DSA is a Coalition front?"

"A fall guy. Hera and Zack's theory is Valerian will call for a government of national unity once Calvo resigns tomorrow, and a designated savior will head it, someone capable of promptly shutting down the DSA threat. Who better than the person actually running it?"

"Diabolical."

"That's what Arno Galdi said."

"But how can this Coalition hold influence over Cimmeria's future in the long run? Surely once the danger is past, they'll elect a new parliament and install a fresh cabinet."

"I don't know, sir, but they'll have thought of it. According to Hera, the Coalition has sympathizers and operatives holding some of the most senior government positions across the Rim Sector and elsewhere in the Commonwealth, along with access to the SecGen's own security intelligence service. Remember the purge on Scandia after the failed putsch earlier this year. The head of their National Guard, opposition politicians, deputy ministers, the chief of police — every one of them a Coalition supporter, though no one openly identified them as such."

Morrow paused before asking, "Could your adjutant give Inspector Galdi the list of Locarno invitees, including those staying at Cimmeria Hall tonight instead of attending the cocktail party?"

"You think they might be Coalition sympathizers and operatives?"

"I'm looking at every possibility, sir. It's something Hera would ask."

"Hang on." Maras produced her communicator, tapped out a message, and tucked it away again. "Done. Galdi will get the list shortly."

"Thank you."

"This seems rather far-fetched."

"Don't I know it? I felt the same way you feel right now when I first met Hera Talyn during the Shrehari envoy assassination case."

"The warrior's knife, I believe you nicknamed it for the files?"

"Yes."

"Let's hope we won't stumble across murder most foul in Locarno."

**

Inspector Arno Galdi's office communicator beeped with enough insistence to yank him from an intense contemplation of the list provided by DCC Maras' adjutant. He stabbed the controls embedded in his desk.

"Galdi."

"HQ communications center, sir. Sergeant Yee. Chief Superintendent Morrow left instructions to inform you if any outside caller asked for her."

"Indeed."

"Someone aboard a Navy ship by the name *Mikado*, recently arrived in orbit, wishes to speak with her."

"I'll accept the call in her stead."

"Yes, sir. Wait one."

Galdi put the names of the Rim Sector's wealthy and powerful out of his mind while he composed himself to deal with what could only be Talyn and Decker's backup. The cavalry coming to the rescue. Except he couldn't tell them much.

His office's main display sprang to life, but instead of a naval officer in midnight blue with gold rank insignia on his collar, he found himself staring at a hard-faced civilian.

"I'm Inspector Arno Galdi of the Professional Compliance Bureau's Rim Sector detachment. Chief Superintendent Morrow is on the move right now. I gather you're here at Commander Talyn's behest?"

"Major Henrik Boldt, Number 6 Company, B Squadron, 1st Special Forces Regiment at your service. We have orders to contact Chief Superintendent Caelin Morrow in case we can't raise either Commander Talyn or Major Decker upon arrival."

"My chief is on the way to a resort town called Locarno, north of Howard's Landing, for a conference involving the high and mighty of the Rim Sector. It's an annual thing. From what little we know, individuals we think belong to a terrorist organization called the Democratic Stars Alliance took Commander Talyn and Major Decker as prisoners. Our last sighting of them was aboard a private suborbital flyer also headed to Locarno. It has since landed."

"I see. Would you be able to brief me on what, exactly is happening in this star system? The last report I saw before leaving home was sent by Commander Talyn from Mission Colony and contained precious few details save for Cimmeria-based radicals holding large quantities of MHX-19."

"May I assume you know what MHX-19 is, Major."

"You may. Nasty stuff that shouldn't be going walkabout. It's the main reason SOCOM sent an entire company as a backup for everyone's favorite operatives this time."

"In that case, let me tell you what transpired since Commander Talyn and Major Decker showed up on our doorstep two days ago."

**

Morrow stowed her communicator and gave Maras an apologetic grimace.

"Sorry about that, sir, but if you harbored any last doubts Commander Talyn, Major Decker, and I were indulging in a bit of mass psychosis, Inspector Galdi's latest news should dispel them. Fleet HQ appears to consider the situation rather dire. A company of Special Forces operators aboard a Navy ship entered orbit just now, with instructions to place themselves at Major Decker's disposal. They're to carry out any operation he considers necessary for the retrieval of the MHX-19 and the destruction of the Democratic Stars Alliance, even if it violates the general laws, regulations, and protocols governing star system sovereignty."

Maras raised her eyebrows in surprise.

"Dire indeed. And I suppose they may do so without even consulting the admiral commanding Sixth Fleet, let alone Cimmerian authorities?"

"That's apparently up to Commander Talyn and Major Decker. They're operating under direct orders from Armed Services HQ and are solely answerable to the Chief of Naval Intelligence."

"Your friends seem to enjoy a remarkable degree of freedom. Now, why does that concept seem familiar?" An ironic smile twisted Maras' lips. "Perhaps that's why they reached out to you upon arrival."

"Could be, sir. Since we first met during the Aquilonia matter, we've helped each other out several times, mainly with information."

"And what will these Marines in orbit do if neither Talyn nor Decker is available to issue orders, considering you believe them to be captives?"

An air of pained uncertainty settled over Morrow's features.

"Arno put that very question to the company's commanding officer. In their absence, he'll ask me for instructions."

"Is it wrong that I'm somewhat relieved you're not in my chain of command?"

Morrow chuckled.

"No. But I'm sure DCC Hammett will have a few choice words for me when I finally tell him what I've been doing instead of chasing bent cops. Mind you, once this is over, we need to discuss the Bujold matter. Even if we let her retire instead of prosecuting, I'm sure you'd still like to know how a regimental commander got mixed up with the wrong crowd."

"I would, but Kristy going wrong doesn't exactly surprise me. She always—" Both of their communicators chimed at once. "What the..."

Morrow was the first to answer hers.

"What's up Arno?"

"Three new explosions, Chief. One took out most of the automated cargo sorting facility in the port of Archeron, another destroyed the docks in Quimper and the third took out the Kosala tide turbine complex. No word yet on casualties, but the economic damage will surely be in the hundreds of millions, if not worse. Notice a pattern, Chief?"

"Every single terrorist incident so far happened on Kusan or on the Borrachas Sea. The DSA hasn't touched Hyperborea yet. It either means their main base of operations and ammunition dump are there...”

“Or they want everyone to focus on the southern continent while they prepare something even nastier up here.”

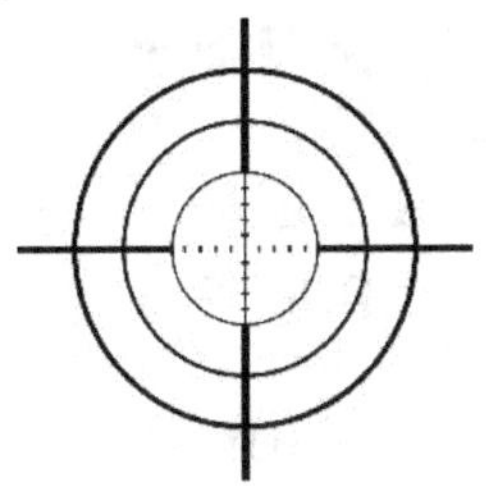

— FORTY-ONE —

"Stunning scenery," Decker remarked as the flyer made its final approach to Locarno.

Nestled at the bottom of a verdant alpine valley, the town was built as a leisure destination for those with both money and time to spare.

Its founders wanted to replicate a pre-diaspora Earth resort featuring half-timber houses and chalets, charming little hotels, and a convention center capable of hosting the most rarefied conferences. The general effect, however, struck Decker as overdone.

"Shame you're about to obliterate everything," he continued, "but I suppose you can't reform the Commonwealth without wiping out a few landmarks. Where did you put the bomb? Under the convention center?"

"For the last time, shut up," Wilborg growled.

Decker had kept up an almost constant monolog during the trip, asking questions without answers, commenting on everyone and everything, trying to rile his captors into making mistakes once they landed. Talyn, on the other hand, had spent the trip in stony silence.

"Did you have any friends while you were growing up, Hadar?" Faced with Wilborg's stony silence, Decker said, "I guess not. And you won't make any now. Unless, of course, you stop this nonsense and release us when we land. Showing us to the bomb will make sure we put in a good word for you at your sentencing. It might make the difference between twenty years in a labor colony and life on Desolation Island, which generally ends up being a lot shorter than twenty years. Nasty too. Ask me how I know."

Wilborg glared at Decker before saying, "Thankfully, once I deliver you to our people in Locarno, my work is done."

"You're not sticking around for the fireworks? Can't say I blame you."

The flyer abruptly shed most of its forward momentum and rode its thrusters for the last fifty meters until settling on the tarmac with little more than a soft bump.

A traffic control droid trundled up and led them into one of the hangars lining the paved strip. Moments after the flyer's tail cleared the opening, a set of panels slid across it, cutting off the late afternoon sunshine. They came to a gentle stop, and the pilot unlatched the cabin door.

"Keep them here," Wilborg said, climbing to his feet. "I'll make sure the welcoming committee is ready to receive our scapegoats."

He left the aircraft, returning a few minutes later trailed by an all too familiar figure wearing an equally familiar uniform.

"Who the hell are they, Hadar?" Colonel Joubert asked.

"Magda's last minute change of plans. What can I say? She's the boss, and I'm not in a position to contradict her."

The Gendarmerie colonel studied Decker and Talyn in turn, a frown creasing his forehead.

"Names?"

"She's carrying the credentials of one Eva Cortez, Mission Colony citizen and leader of its Freedom Collective. He's carrying those of Piet Yorik, her security chief. Their IDs might be genuine, but we know Cortez is dead and presume Yorik was killed as well. Those two are Fleet operatives. You might recognize the names even if you don't recognize the faces. Commander Talyn and Major Decker."

"What?" Joubert's voice rose by an octave while his eyes threatened to bug out. "Has Magda gone completely around the bend?"

"She went around the bend long ago, Colonel," Decker said. "But I'm disappointed to see you crewing her ship of fools, although it explains a few things."

"Magda thinks blaming the Locarno operation on offworlders Cortez and Yorik, who'll be subsequently unmasked as Talyn and Decker, Fleet officers, will help increase tonight's chaos and ease her assumption of power."

"An unnecessary embellishment. How did you come to capture them?"

"We walked right into Hadar's office this morning," Decker said. "And lunched with the lovely Magda Annear at her country estate."

"Shit." Joubert turned to Wilborg. "What the hell was Magda thinking? You should have shot them back at the lodge. Think about it. They didn't stumble into your office by accident. I found out just before leaving Howard's Landing that their Constabulary friends from the Professional Compliance Bureau were quietly inquiring about Alek Mannsbach, his Alasdair Malter incarnation, and Magda."

"I told her it would be best to kill us at the lodge but did she listen? No. You're working for someone with serious mommy issues, folks. And that won't end well. It never does. We know about her plans except for the Locarno MHX bomb's location. Do yourselves a favor and back away. Let us disarm it and arrest Magda. It's the only way you'll enjoy another sunrise."

"As you can see, Colonel, he's full of wind and fury with no substance behind it. I'll be happy to see him in your hands." Wilborg gestured at Collette. "Transfer the prisoners."

Collette stood and offered Joubert a small control tablet.

"Please apply your thumbprint to assume control of their shackles."

"I'm curious. How can a senior Gendarmerie officer contemplate killing hundreds of people?" Talyn asked in a conversational tone.

Joubert's shoulders twitched with a dismissive shrug.

"Third-rate politicians with no vision, profiteers with no conscience, social manipulators, and assorted sociopaths? I consider it cleansing the Rim Sector of those holding us back."

"What about the townspeople? Surely they're innocent bystanders in this vendetta?"

"Gone on paid holidays elsewhere for the duration of the conference, courtesy of Cimmerian taxpayers." He pressed his thumb against the tablet and then took it from Collette's hand. "There."

"What about your Gendarmerie men, the National Guard troops, and all those civilians working at the conference center? Are they to become collateral damage?"

"Sadly, Major, it's an inevitable sacrifice for the greater good. I'm sure you're familiar with the concept."

"Did you ask them whether they agreed?"

"Do you ask cattle whether they consent to enter the slaughterhouse?"

Decker turned to his partner.

"You know, the general attitude of Magda's minions is really getting up my nose."

"If Joubert, our buddy Hadar, and the others were nice people, they wouldn't do her bidding."

"Time to step off." Joubert pulled a large-caliber blaster from the black, shiny holster at his hip and gestured toward the door. "You first, Major."

"Don't forget their things." Allyson handed him both travel bags.

A man they'd never seen before waited on the hangar floor, weapon at the ready. He wore what Decker liked to call the security consultant role-playing costume. Black trousers tucked into combat boots, black tactical vest over an equally black roll-neck sweater and opaque glasses. He carried an example of the snub-nosed carbine favored by private military corporations and likely wore both a throat mike and an earbug.

"Couldn't corrupt a few gendarmes, Joubert?" Decker asked, giving the silent goon a dismissive glance.

"He probably works for CimmerTek," Talyn said. "Just like Collette, Allyson, Gudrun and every other goon-for-hire we've seen."

"CimmerTek. Right. Louis Sorne's bunch. A senior police officer such as you associating with rent-a-cops of dubious quality? What's the galaxy coming to? I understand they made a hash of trying to replace your lot as station security on Aquilonia."

"Were you born tiresome, Major, or did they teach it in basic training?"

"Ouch." Decker winced. "Kudos for being wittier than Hadar Wilborg, even if that isn't hard to do."

The silent man in black pointed at an open door.

"In there? Sure. Tell me, Colonel. How do you intend to blame obliterating Locarno and killing most of the sector's elite on us?"

"Why do you care? You'll be dead by the time it happens."

They entered a room furnished with only a few chairs and tables. Behind them, the flyer came to life once more while the hangar doors reopened, then the sound faded as it backed out onto the tarmac and lifted off.

"Sit. We'll be here for a while," Joubert said, pointing at the chairs against one wall.

Talyn and Decker obeyed while keeping their eyes on the treasonous Gendarmerie officer.

"Do you mind if I run a few scenarios past you?" Decker asked.

"Yes. Now shut it."

"You probably didn't have many friends growing up either, just like Hadar Wilborg, and as many chances of making up for that lack before you die. But I'll run a scenario by you anyway, since you can't afford to blow my head off just yet. Shortly after Locarno goes up in a great ball of fire at the height of the opening cocktail party, you'll call Gendarmerie HQ telling them you're in the neighboring valley and just killed two suspects last seen racing away from the convention center. They not only refused to stop for an ID check but shot at you. When forensics examines our bodies, they'll find traces of MHX-19 on our hands and conclude we're the mass murders everyone has been looking for. How am I doing so far?"

"Judging by the look in his eyes," Talyn said, "you're scoring ten out of ten."

"Don't you just hate dealing with amateurs? In what universe will anyone believe that explanation?"

"Shut up, Major."

"That's what Hadar said."

Joubert dropped their bags on one of the tables and watched them for a moment as if weighing a decision.

"You look like a man wondering whether one CimmerTek goon and a police desk jockey are enough to watch two SOCOM operatives," Decker said. "Why didn't you bring more people?"

"Because Wilborg was supposed to deliver a pair of DSA stooges, pencil-necked zealots without the training or gumption to fight their way out of this. Had I known about you two, I'd have brought additional muscle."

"Of course. Dear Magda making decisions on the fly and telling no one ahead of time. I always hate it when my boss does that."

"I can hear you, *Major*." The intense irritation in Talyn's tone caused Joubert to stare at her for a few seconds.

Then, he upended Decker's bag and shook out its contents. The Shrehari blaster landed on the metal tabletop with a thud, followed by the Pathfinder dagger. Joubert held both up.

"Nice. This should be enough help confirm your identity as a SOCOM officer after I shoot you."

"No one will believe we're responsible for the atrocity you're planning."

"They'll believe it long enough to generate added chaos. A lie travels light years while the truth is still putting on its boots." He placed the weapons to one side, then emptied Talyn's bag before examining her blaster and stiletto. "Not quite as distinctive, but it doesn't matter. I'm beginning to think Magda made the right decision in reassigning the role of scapegoats."

"Hurray for Magda."

Joubert picked Talyn's communicator from the pile and studied it.

"Disappointingly ordinary. The sort anyone can buy from a vending machine. I expected something a little more high speed, low drag, as you people like to say."

"Who says it's ordinary under the skin?" She replied.

"Oh?" Suspicion clouded his gaze.

"Undercover work means our tools are disguised as well."

"Are you telling me there's a military-grade communicator inside this shell?"

He shook the device.

"Certainly. In his too." She nodded at Decker.

"How do you access the hidden functionality?"

Decker chuckled.

"I bet he's thinking of adding our talkies to the evidence pile and goose that lie into traveling a little faster. Guns and blades are nothing beside genuine classified Fleet-issue communicators keyed to their owners."

"Won't do him much good if they're not properly unlocked. Try to force them, and the insides self-destruct, leaving nothing more than a lump of fused electronics, impossible to identify as Fleet-issue."

"How do you unlock this?"

Decker and Talyn exchanged looks, then the latter said, "Go pound sand, traitor."

After a moment of hesitation, Joubert tried to switch the communicator on, without success.

"It needs a power pack, genius." Decker rolled his eyes in mock derision. "Although it won't do you any good."

Joubert searched through their belongings until his hand closed on a thin stick. He found a matching slot on the communicator's side and slammed it home.

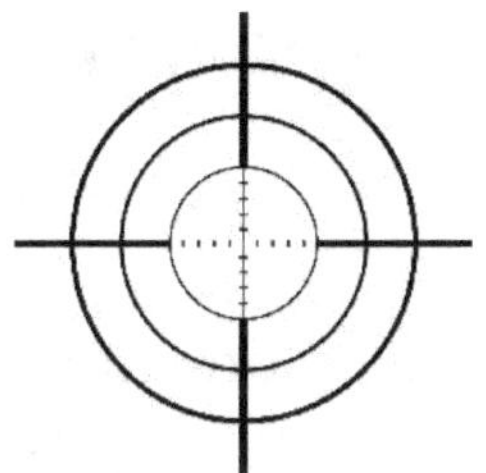

— FORTY-TWO —

"Here we are." Maras pointed at the valley unfolding beneath the aircar as it crossed over the last ridge and began descending toward the convention center's forecourt. "I gather you never came here?"

"No, sir. Too rich for my blood." Her communicator chimed once more. "Pardon me. It's Arno again." She held it to her ear. "Yes?"

"Chief, the tracking signal from Commander Talyn's communicator came back a few minutes ago."

"Where?"

"About two kilometers from your current position. The Locarno aerospace terminal, hangar number three."

"Makes sense if they were indeed prisoners aboard Magda Annear's flyer. Let the Marines in orbit know."

"Already done. Major Boldt will land a team to investigate."

"How long?"

"An hour, give or take."

Morrow turned to look out the window. She spotted hangar three, one of five white, pillow-like structures lining the black tarmac in the distance.

"Hang on, Arno."

"What is it?" Maras asked.

"For some reason, the tracking signal from Commander Talyn's communicator is back online. If you'll recall, we lost both hers and Major Decker's at Magda Annear's lodge."

"And that signal comes from Locarno."

"Yes, sir. One of the terminal's hangars."

Maras tapped the passenger compartment's intercom.

"Please take us on a loop around the aerospace terminal at the lowest allowable altitude, Warrant Officer.

"Wilco."

"What are your thoughts, Caelin?"

"If I assume Talyn and Decker are missing persons, my first instinct is to investigate. Perhaps you could drop Sergeant Bonta and me off before proceeding to the convention center. Both of us are armed for once."

"Are you sure it's a good idea?"

"It'll be at least an hour before the Marines land, and something tells me my friends aren't here to enjoy the recreational facilities. Time may well be of the essence."

"Gut instinct?"

"Screaming. I'd be a piss poor cop if I didn't listen. There was a time, well before I joined the Firing Squad, when, as a Constabulary liaison officer, I jumped out of perfectly good shuttles from low orbit with folks like Major Decker and Commander Talyn. Those days taught me to listen whenever my gut yelled loud enough to drown out what I thought was my common sense speaking."

"Do you want me to find whoever's in charge of the Gendarmerie task force and ask them to send backup?"

Morrow shook her head.

"No. If I see the situation is beyond what Bonta and I can handle, I'll simply keep eyes on them and wait for the Marines."

"You don't trust our planetary colleagues?"

"If Magda Annear's at the center of this mess, she'll have helpers in every branch of the Cimmerian government, including the Gendarmerie. We're in a trust no one situation."

"Be careful."

"No worries. I plan on living long enough to see how many people show up at my retirement party. Besides, my winger is almost unbeatable. Sergeant Bonta won the annual Rim Sector combat shooting competition five years running now."

Maras stroked the intercom again.

"Please land us by the terminal's main door. Chief Superintendent Morrow and Master Sergeant Bonta will disembark. You and I will head for the convention center once they're off."

"Yes, sir."

After a single circuit which revealed nothing of use, the aircar swooped down for a smooth landing in front of the building before disgorging both PCB officers. With the townspeople gone and the day's conference attendees already in their rooms, the area felt eerily deserted. Morrow pulled out her service-issue sidearm and checked the power pack before chambering a copper disk. Bonta imitated her example

They made their way along the service road toward hanger number three, weapons in hand, muzzles pointing downward, eyes and ears alert for anything that might betray Decker, Talyn or the people holding them.

Morrow and Bonta reached the hangar without encountering anyone and stopped just before the first of several wide windows looking out onto the street. She briefly moved her head forward to glance inside but saw nothing more than an empty office. The next one showed another unoccupied room, this time with crates stacked haphazardly against the walls.

She crept up on the third and pulled back the moment her brain understood what her eyes saw. Talyn and

Decker, shackled, sitting on chairs against the far wall under the watchful eyes of a gun-toting man in black tactical clothing.

It took her synapses a bit longer to process the sight of Colonel Joubert of the Cimmerian Gendarmerie wearing a gold-trimmed blue uniform and half sitting on a table while he studied one of the agents' communicators. She backed away almost out of reflex and motioned Bonta to come closer.

"You found them, Chief?" She asked in a whisper, her lips a few centimeters from Morrow's ear.

The latter nodded and replied, in the same tone, "Prisoners. Shackled. One guard, one Gendarmerie officer. Joubert."

"Fuck."

"We figured the bad guys had insiders."

"What do we do?"

"Two against two. Do those odds work for you, Sergeant? If they don't, we wait for the Marines."

Morrow risked another glance only to stare straight into Talyn's eyes. She must have seen her first look through the window. Talyn's gaze briefly shifted to Joubert and back again, and then her head moved minutely but in an unmistakable nod.

"I think Commander Talyn just invited me in," Morrow whispered at Bonta.

When the sergeant nodded in acknowledgment, Morrow dropped into a crouch beneath the windowsill and waddled below toward the door. Bonta, because of her greater height, was forced into a leopard crawl to the detriment of her service grays.

They reached the hangar's roadside door without raising any alarms and stood. Bonta fished a small sensor from her tunic pocket. She stared at its screen for a few seconds then gave Morrow the all-clear sign. No active intrusion detection system.

**

"Very interesting. A fine piece of technology. Too bad it didn't do you any good."

Joubert finally placed Talyn's communicator back on the table after studying the device's hidden functions. He retrieved his gun and aimed it lazily at a spot halfway between the prisoners, elbow resting on his thigh.

Once he'd switched her device on and reactivated the tracking signal, she'd given him the means to unlock it and study the complex electronics as a way of buying time in the hope Morrow's people were still monitoring the Navy satellites. The chief superintendent's unexpected and mercifully brief appearance on the other side of the window proved she'd made the right choice.

"How about a verse of Blood on the Risers to cheer us up, Zack?" Talyn asked, warning him something was about to happen.

"Which one?"

"He counted long, he counted loud, he waited for the shock," Talyn sang in a soft voice.

"What are you talking about?" Joubert asked, frowning as he stood.

"Just a joke between fellow professionals," she replied. "You wouldn't understand."

"Why?"

Decker let out an exasperated sigh.

"Because you're not a fucking professional, mate. A pro would put a damned blaster bolt through Magda Annear's brain the moment she waxed poetic about bringing forth social justice through mass murder. Were you born dense, or did they hammer it into you during Gendarmerie officer training?"

An angry sneer twisted Joubert's face.

"You're hardly in a position to talk, Major. Walking into Magda's trap like beginners isn't likely to win SOCOM any awards for its personnel selection process."

"It wasn't exactly her trap, you know. Hadar Wilborg did most of the heavy lifting. I daresay he wouldn't be standing there like a useless lummox, kibitzing with prisoners instead of watching his six."

"What do you mean?"

"Did you really think we walked into Magda's so-called trap like a pair of beginners? We did it to find out where the DSA planned to commit its next act of terrorism. Now we know. Last chance, my friend. End this and you might survive. Otherwise, your name won't even appear on the Gendarmerie's memorial wall."

One of the room's two doors opened with a loud crash, and a disembodied voice hidden in the hallway's shadows said, "I recommend you take Major Decker's suggestion, Colonel. Drop your weapon. The same goes for you, Mister CimmerTek muscle."

"Morrow." Joubert hissed. "How the hell did you get here?"

"Drop. Your. Weapons." Bonta growled in her deep, throaty alto.

The black-clad guard raised his carbine in her direction. A soft cough came through the open door, and a small, black hole appeared in the center of the man's forehead. The back of his skull came apart in a spray of shattered bone, followed by an eruption of blood and brain matter. He crumpled to the floor almost instantly.

Decker winced in feigned sympathy.

"Ouch. Talk about a terminal migraine."

"Don't kill Joubert, Chief Superintendent," Talyn said in an urgent tone, climbing to her feet.

"Put your gun on the floor, Colonel. You heard her. She wants you alive. Take the chance to live through this. Two feds against a Gendarmerie officer, one of those feds a champion combat shooter? Your chances of surviving if you don't cooperate are somewhere between zero and minus infinity."

"My sights are on Colonel Joubert's sweaty forehead, Chief. Maybe his skin is sensitive enough to feel the caress of my targeting laser."

"You have a wonderful way with words, Sergeant," Decker said, climbing to his feet with a lurch. He held out his manacled hands. "Once you drop that gun, Colonel, how about cutting me loose?"

Joubert's eyes shifted from the darkened doorway to his prisoners and back again as he calculated his chances.

"Drop your weapon," Bonta shouted. "Do it now."

Talyn took a step closer to him fists clenched. Then another. The barrel of Joubert's gun wavered between her and the door for a second. Then he sighed and gently placed it on the table.

"All right. I surrender."

"Unshackle them," Morrow ordered.

Joubert, jaw muscles still working, nodded once. He touched Talyn's manacles, crouched to release her ankle restraints, and did the same with Decker.

The moment both agents were free, Talyn seized Joubert's left arm, forced him to turn around before grabbing and twisting his right arm into a painful lock behind his back. He bent forward until his upper body was hard against the tabletop.

"Where is the bomb?" When he didn't immediately answer, Talyn twisted harder. "I don't mind dislocating your shoulder before I get nasty. Where's the bomb?"

Joubert gasped at the pain.

"Screw you. I surrendered, but it doesn't mean I'll betray Magda."

"Are you willing to die for her, Alan? Because if we don't find the bomb, I'll order Locarno evacuated and leave you right here, wearing those restraints."

She gave his right arm another upward jerk. This time, an involuntary yelp escaped his throat.

"You wouldn't dare. Magda will own Cimmeria by tomorrow night, and I'll become the head of her new security agency. Kill me, and she'll avenge my death. If I'm alive, I can make sure you leave this star system unharmed."

"Magda cares for no one other than herself. You're a tool, just like the dead goon over there, or Hadar Wilborg, something to be used and discarded. Where is the bomb?"

Another jerk, an even louder gasp.

"The only way you're getting out of this alive is by telling me where we can find the bomb. Sure, Magda might still become prime minister tomorrow, but her term in office will be the shortest in Cimmerian history. She won't find and kill those who betrayed her. Especially if they're sitting in Constabulary cells, well out of reach."

"There's a Navy ship by the name *Mikado* in orbit," Morrow said, entering the room. "If you cooperate, Commander Talyn can arrange for your rendition to the Armed Services, which would put you completely out of reach."

Decker's face brightened at the news.

"Are buddies of mine aboard?"

"Number 6 Company, B Squadron. A troop is on the way to Locarno. They should land in about forty-five minutes."

"Do you hear that, Alan? It's over, done, finished. The Marines are landing. One company of special operators is enough to shut down the DSA and Magda's dreams permanently." When Joubert didn't answer, she said, "I suppose it's time to use more persuasive methods."

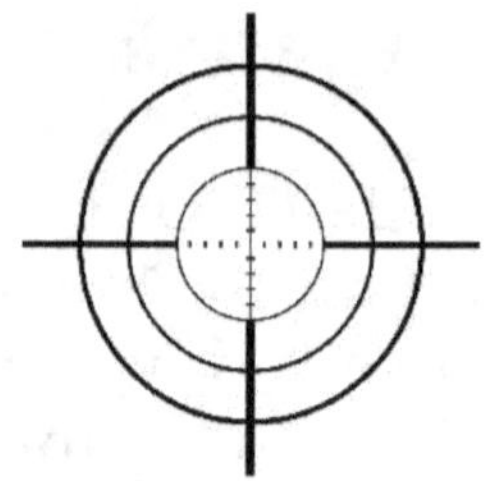

— FORTY-THREE —

"Zack, please hold him while I loosen his tongue."

They switched places, and then Talyn gave Morrow a meaningful look.

"You and the sergeant might want to go circle the hangar in case he has more CimmerTek thugs standing guard."

A stubborn look hardened Morrow's eyes.

"Sergeant Bonta and I are officers of the law, Hera. We cannot let you torture a prisoner."

"Hundreds of lives are at stake tonight, and if the attack succeeds, thousands if not tens of thousands more might die during the inevitable aftermath. Go away, Caelin. I need a few minutes with this piece of trash. He'll still be fit to stand trial for treason once I'm done, although he might be missing a few bits."

"Good Lord, Hera! The ends never justify the means. Otherwise we become just like them. If he doesn't talk, then I'll call Maras and ask her to organize an immediate evacuation."

"Maras is here?"

"How do you think we entered the restricted zone? She's a regular attendee."

"You know the panic of evacuation will give Magda and her co-conspirators almost as much impetus as a massacre."

"No time for an orderly evacuation," Joubert's muffled voice forestalled Morrow's reply. "Bomb will detonate in less than an hour."

Decker pulled the Gendarmerie officer's upper body away from the table and then slammed it down with enough force to rattle his brain. Joubert yelped again as the impact mashed his right ear into the hard metal.

"Cease and desist, Major."

"Doing what?" Decker gave Morrow an innocent stare while he lifted Joubert up and dropped him again. "Feel like telling us where the bomb is, Alan?"

"Don't you carry interrogation drugs?"

"Yes. They're hidden in my bag's shielded compartment, but there isn't enough time. And when I last used them, the subject died of cardiac arrest. Alek Mannsbach back on Mission Colony." Talyn shook her head in exasperation. "Arrest me on charges of torture if you want. But after we secure the bomb."

She picked her stiletto from the weapons lineup on the neighboring table and placed her left hand on Joubert's head to hold it.

"Keep him steady, Zack. In deference to the chief superintendent and her sergeant, I'll try to leave as little visible damage as possible. So here's what'll happen, Alan. I'm about to insert my stiletto into your ear canal. I'll stop once the tip reaches your eardrum. Then, I'll ask you again about the bomb. If you refuse to answer, I'll push a little more and pop your eardrum. The pain will be excruciating."

"Commander Talyn, I warn you."

"Go away, Caelin."

She gently caressed Joubert's outer ear with the stiletto, then, with surgical precision, fed the tip into the canal. Joubert quivered under her restraining hand while his breathing became shallower and faster.

"Where is the bomb?" She applied more pressure. "You're about to lose hearing in one ear, Alan, and for what? A sociopathic mass murderer like Magda Annear? By the time I'm done, the only way you'll regain hearing is with a bionic implant, and that means you start turning into a cyborg. Stand by for pain. Three... Two... One..."

"No. Wait!"

She eased the pressure.

"You'd better not be jerking me around."

"The bomb is in a standard cubic container," Joubert replied in an urgent tone. "The container is in the convention center's basement warehouse, to the left of the vehicle ramp."

"How do we identify it?"

"A serial number." He rattled off nine digits. "And the notation not to be opened without Magda Annear's permission."

"Pretty bold, isn't it?" Bonta asked, her eyes glued to Talyn and Joubert with an air of sick fascination.

"No one would dare touch her property, and once the bomb explodes, there won't be anything left of the convention center, let alone the container," Decker replied. "Where's your ground car, Alan?"

"Hangar. Key chip is in my right trouser pocket."

"If we don't find the bomb, my friend, the next time it won't be my partner's stiletto tickling your eardrum. Let's grab our stuff and move." Decker rifled Joubert's pocket for the chip, grabbed one of the discarded manacles, and cuffed him. "You're coming with us, sunshine."

**

The unmarked Gendarmerie staff car roared through Locarno's deserted streets under Decker's control. Talyn sat in the back with Joubert and Morrow while Bonta occupied the front passenger seat. Three cops in uniform aboard should help see them through any guard posts, even though the officer in blue had a gun pointed at his midriff, but the vehicle's registration markings seemed to suffice.

The armored National Guard troopers posted at the roadblock a few hundred meters from a convention center blazing with light in the early evening gloom merely waved them through.

"You'll find the basement warehouse ramp at the rear," Joubert said in the passive voice of someone who's run out of options.

"Who delivered the container?"

"I don't know, but Wilborg probably made the arrangements. According to the log, it arrived a few days before Magda came home. Wilborg gave me enough information to make sure everything was as it should be, and earlier this afternoon, I was able to confirm it."

"How do we get inside?"

"Wilborg provided the access code as well."

Decker followed a narrow street around the sprawling complex until they saw the sign pointing to a closed, vehicle-sized door at the bottom of an incline.

"What's the code?"

"Call up the entry for the warehouse on the car's control panel. The AI will transmit it."

Decker stopped at the top of the ramp and obeyed Joubert's instructions. The door pulled away to either side, revealing an immense space half-filled with neat stacks of varying shapes, sizes, and colors between evenly spaced pillars.

"The bomb is near pillar twelve, to our left."

"Leave the car here or drive in?"

"Drive in," Talyn replied.

Moments later, they came to a halt near the indicated pillar, and Decker jumped out after shutting off the power plant. He found the right container within moments.

As Joubert said, a sign affixed on every side forbade anyone from moving or opening it without Magda Annear's permission. It was as high as Decker, twice his width, and constructed so that one of the four sides could be removed to allow loading and unloading.

"Any anti-tamper or anti-lift devices, Alan?" Decker asked through the open car door.

"No idea, but I doubt it. Any of the warehouse employees might move it around for innocuous reasons, and a curious one might even take a peek. If it went off before tonight's gathering, the effect would be wasted."

Talyn frowned at the white cube.

"Do we risk opening it?"

"No choice."

Decker pulled out his handheld sensor and scanned the latches before popping them one at a time. When he'd unfastened the last one, he gingerly lifted a surprisingly well-padded panel to one side and peered inside.

"They packed the device into a smaller container, approximately one cubic meter in size. The outer shell is no more than camouflage and a barrier against explosives sniffers. I figure we're talking seventy-five kilos of MHX, tops, but still enough to scrape the Locarno valley down to bedrock."

He scanned the smaller box and the foam padding around it.

"Nothing to suggest the presence of anti-tamper devices on the outside, but I'm not inclined to open this one. At least not here. Does anyone know what's in the next valley to the north?"

"A wilderness preserve attached to the Locarno resort," Bonta answered. "No humans allowed during the conference."

Decker nodded.

"It'll do. Everyone out and clear the aft compartment. Hera and I are taking the bomb away from here."

"Can you manage?"

"Can you find me an exoskeleton in the next thirty seconds, Sergeant? If not, I'll have to manage."

"Don't be a hero, Major. I'll help."

Between them, Bonta and Decker eased the smaller cube from its rigid foam nest, carried it to the car, and placed it on the rear bench seat.

"How long before this blows, Alan?" The latter asked.

"What time is it?"

"Almost twenty-hundred hours."

"A little over thirty minutes."

Decker caught his partner's eye.

"You can stay here. Disarming bombs isn't your specialty anyway."

"Where you go I go." She dropped into the passenger seat. "Let's ride, Marine."

"Strap yourself in, honey. I'm about to prove even a ground car can fly with the right motivation." Decker sketched a salute at Morrow and Bonta standing to either side of the defeated Gendarmerie colonel. "Take good care of Alan. He came through in the end."

Then he joined Talyn and slammed his door shut. The car backed up at breakneck speed, bounced up the ramp and vanished into the night.

"What do we do with Joubert?" Bonta asked her superior.

"Find Maras' driver and tell him to bring the aircar around, then we head for home and stash Alan in one of our cells. But only after we're sure our friends disarmed the bomb. I'll need to tell the DCC something, and I'd rather it be good news, not something apt to cause panic."

"I'll call him. We compared notes as fellow shooting aficionados during the trip up here, so he'll play nice with us. We might as well wait in privacy and comfort."

Once they were in the back of the armored vehicle, Morrow pulled out her communicator, gave Joubert a thoughtful glance, then shrugged, and opened a link.

Inspector Galdi answered with commendable speed.

"How are things?"

"Decker and Talyn are moving the bomb away from Locarno in a ground car right now, looking for a safe spot to disarm it. As soon as they give us the all-clear, Bonta and I are flying home with a prisoner, one of Magda Annear's crew."

"I'll let *Mikado* know to call them directly and ask if there's any point in landing a team up your way."

"Please do."

"And the satellite's tracking both locator signals. They seem to be moving faster than any ground car should try in the mountains."

"Keep watching. I'd like to know when they stop and more importantly when they reverse course after neutralizing the device."

"Will do, Chief."

Twenty minutes passed in uneasy silence while everyone's eyes were glued to the jagged, black horizon where a low ridge separated the Locarno valley from its nature preserve neighbor. Galdi called once to announce the tracking signals had stopped at the heart of the preserve.

Suddenly, without warning, a white so intense it seemed to come from the heart of a supernova blotted everything out. A few seconds later, an apocalyptic rumble washed over Locarno while the ground trembled.

"Shit." Bonta turned her eyes away from the glare while afterimages danced on her retina. "So that's what Mayhem does."

The light faded at an almost incredible speed, plunging the mountains back into darkness.

Morrow thumbed her communicator to life.

"Arno, tell me you can still see their tracking signals."

"Sorry, Chief. They stayed in the same place for ten minutes then vanished a few seconds ago. Why?"

"The bomb they took from the convention center just detonated."

"Oh, God."

"Call *Mikado* and ask if they're receiving anything."

"Will do. Wait, out."

An alarm siren began to howl while additional illumination came to life, bathing the conference center in a quasi-daytime glow. Morrow's communicator buzzed with insistence. DCC Maras.

"Yes, sir."

"What the hell was that, Caelin?"

Morrow sighed.

"Something that almost blew you and the other conference attendees into the afterlife, if it wasn't for two insanely brave friends of mine who I hope weren't standing at ground zero when it exploded."

"MHX-19?"

"Yes. Major Decker figured around seventy-five kilos, enough to wipe Locarno from the map. We found it in the convention center's basement warehouse thanks to an informant. Talyn and Decker took the device into the next valley where he hoped to disarm it, evidently without success."

"So they're dead?"

"We lost the signal from their location trackers when it happened."

Maras didn't immediately reply.

"The informant?" She eventually asked.

"Under my care, sir. With your permission, I'd like to take him home aboard your aircar. Call it protective custody for now."

"Did the informant tell you who was behind this attempt to kill the Rim Sector's most influential people?"

"Yes. Magda Annear."

"What about proof?"

"Other than his word? Nothing, sir. Not yet. But there are persons of interest to question and Annear's hunting lodge to search."

"Which is properly within the Gendarmerie's jurisdiction, Caelin. We must turn your informant over to them."

"Sir, our informant is Colonel Joubert. His confession wasn't exactly voluntary, but he led us to the device."

"Damn."

"That's why I want him in our cells, out of Annear or the DSA's reach until we clear this up. The most important thing right now is for someone to tell Prime Minister Calvo he should not, under any circumstances, ask the governor general to dissolve parliament. Talyn and Decker foiled the attack that was supposed to push him over the edge and a Marine Corps anti-terrorism company is in orbit, ready to eliminate the rest of Annear's people."

"Understood. Let me see what I can do in here with what I presume are people loyal to the Cimmerian constitution and its duly elected government, if Annear targeted them for death. Take Joubert to Howard's Landing and lean on him. Names, dates, everything. Then I'll have a long discussion with Director General Dubnikov, Prime Minister Calvo, and Governor General Valerian. We'll see who squirms the most."

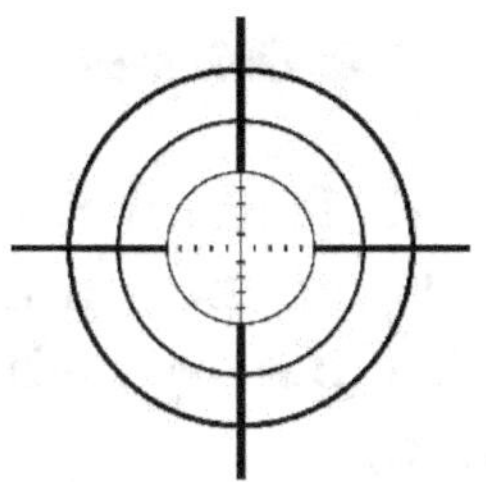

— FORTY-FOUR —

Two blurry shapes, almost indistinguishable from the background vegetation slipped through the dense, primeval Cimmerian forest without noise or leaving a trace. They soon crested a low hill overlooking the prairie-like expanse of grass surrounding the Mill Haven Minimum Security Village, known by some as Cimmeria's Gilded Cage. It housed only the non-violent wealthy and powerful who'd fallen afoul of star system or Commonwealth laws.

The larger of the chameleon ghillie-suited intruders quickly found a suitable spot overlooking Mill Haven's lavish exercise yard, almost one and a half kilometers away. He assembled a bipod-equipped Falkenberg Longbow Mark Five railgun topped by a Hammer Optics sniper scope while his companion put together a more powerful spotting telescope, also manufactured by Hammer Optics. The gun was a twin to the one that killed Gustav Kerlin and came from the armory of Number 6 Company, B Squadron, 1st Special Forces Regiment, as did the ghillie suits and the spotting scope.

Once they were satisfied their gear was ready and functional, they crawled through the last bit of undergrowth and into position, invisible to anyone more than a few meters distant, including the prison's perimeter sensor array. At least until the sniper powered up his railgun to prepare for the kill shot.

Sniper and spotter waited almost an hour for their target to leave the cottage he shared with three other inmates. Unlike the day before, when they'd carried out their reconnaissance, a younger companion accompanied the old man.

"Hakkam is with the target," Talyn said in a whisper so low only Decker could hear.

"Twofer?" Zack Decker replied in the same tone.

"Sorne's the priority. If you can't put a clear bead on Hakkam, don't try. Terminating him isn't essential at this time."

"Roger."   Decker pulled the railgun's stock hard against his shoulder and slowed his breathing. Louis Sorne's lined, sagging features filled the sniper scope.

"I've acquired the target."

Talyn studied Sorne and his companion one last time.

"You're weapons free."

Decker's thumb flipped on the power pack, and within two seconds, a green dot appeared in the scope, signaling the railgun was ready to fire. He took one more breath, released half of it, and then applied gentle pressure to the trigger.

The back of Sorne's head exploded like an overripe melon striking concrete. Decker shifted his aim until Fast Tony's swarthy face filled the scope. The Deep Space Foundation's chief executive officer seemed rooted to the spot, incapable of processing what had just happened to his superior.

"I can take a clean shot at Hakkam."

"Fire."

Another stroke of the trigger and Fast Tony joined his boss in a messy death.

Talyn took a few seconds to examine both bodies and their immediate surroundings.

"Clean and clear. We can withdraw."

They were already well away from the tree line when a lugubrious alarm siren echoed over the countryside.

This time, they didn't bother masking their trail, preferring to trade speed for concealment. Sorne was merely the latest in a long list of targets requiring termination with extreme prejudice to finish choking off Magda Annear's attempted revolution.

With Cimmeria in disarray since the unsuccessful attempt to murder Locarno Conference attendees three days earlier, it would take the Gendarmerie a significant amount of time to react. And considering the identities of the victims, Decker and Talyn doubted investigators would carry out anything more than a perfunctory search for the assassins.

They reached their rental car, parked in a secluded spot near a woodland lane before the alarm ceased wailing, and stripped off the ghillie suits. Decker dismantled the gun and stowed it in a hard case which bore the manufacturer's seal while Talyn did the same with her spotting scope. Then, they drove off at a sedate pace, two tourists taking in the sights north of Howard's Landing.

******

"Chief, you need to hear this." Arno Galdi burst into Morrow's office, trailed by Master Sergeant Bonta.

Morrow, trying to organize her notes from Alan Joubert's latest round of interrogations, looked up with an irritated grimace.

"It better be good. DCC Maras is waiting for my report. She's meeting with Governor General Valerian, Prime Minister Calvo, and Director General Dubnikov at New Government House in an hour to discuss the way ahead."

"Should be interesting, if Valerian was in cahoots with Magda."

"He's a born survivor and one of Cimmeria's leading citizens, the type able to dance between raindrops and keep dry. Now, what do I need to hear?"

"Sergeant Bonta just picked up electrifying news over the Gendarmerie's emergency band. Someone assassinated Louis Sorne and Antoine Hakkam in the Gilded Cage's exercise yard. A long-range sniper from what the Cimmerian Correctional Service is saying, possibly using a railgun."

Morrow's eyes widened enough for Galdi to notice. His rumbling chuckle filled her office.

"I think we can stop mourning Commander Talyn and Major Decker. I was wondering why *Mikado* and the Marines were no longer accepting our calls."

"And why suspected DSA activists were turning up dead everywhere," Bonta added.

"If they're responsible for Sorne and Fast Tony, then how did they escape from the nature preserve before the bomb detonated?" Morrow tapped her lower lip with an extended index finger. "Arno, can you pull air traffic control records for the hour before and after the explosion?"

"You think the Marines who were on their way that night diverted over to where we last saw their locator signal and picked them up? But why make us believe they perished?"

A spark of understanding lit up Galdi's eyes before Morrow could answer.

"Of course. Freedom of action. Neither we nor the Cimmerians would approve of wholesale terminations. Nor would Prime Minister Calvo be pleased to know about the Fleet carrying out armed operations in his star system without so much as a by your leave, never mind the extra-judicial execution of Cimmerian citizens. But if we don't even know whether they're alive, let alone leading what seems to be an extensive direct action against the DSA, we can't stop them."

"Precisely. And that leaves me in a quandary much like the one I faced on Aquilonia. Do I share what we discussed with Maras, or do I let events take their course?"

Galdi's shrug spoke volumes.

"We're talking about mere suppositions, Chief. Unless someone claims responsibility for the rash of assassinations over the last couple of days, I doubt the Gendarmerie will ever find conclusive evidence, and unless Maras claims federal jurisdiction, those deaths remain a star system responsibility, not ours."

"In other words, forget about this conversation? Is that what you suggest, Arno?"

"The DCC has enough on her plate helping our Cimmerians friends deal with the fallout so Prime Minister Calvo can keep his grip on power while Magda's sympathizers are unmasked and arrested. Or at least those who survive SOCOM's purge."

"Speaking of the devil, did our Gendarmerie colleagues ever find out where Magda went after leaving Cimmeria Hall? *If* we can believe the governor general's claim, she excused herself shortly after news of the DSA's failure at Locarno got out."

"No, Chief. Do you still want me to check air traffic control logs for the night of the explosion? It seems rather futile under the circumstances."

Morrow let out a soft sigh.

"No. Anti-terrorism is a Fleet responsibility. Whether I like their methods or not, we're in no position to gainsay them."

"Agreed."

"And I won't discuss our conversation with Maras. It would only muddy the waters even though the idea of SOCOM carrying out a *lex talionis* style operation in a sovereign star system offends the career cop in me."

"Consider us in a war, Chief. That's how Decker and Talyn look at it, and I can't find much fault with their interpretation, not when the enemy won't hesitate to kill civilians in job lots using military ordnance."

"I'm with the inspector," Bonta said. "The only thing I can think of is that miniature supernova blanking out the horizon two nights ago, and how many would die if the DSA set one off at the heart of Howard's Landing. Let Major Decker's Special Forces friends hunt those bastards down with extreme prejudice. They seem to be doing fine so far. We've not heard reports of any further explosions."

Morrow glanced from one to the other and sighed again.

"Okay. Back to work helping the Gendarmerie, folks. I'll brief Maras on the latest we squeezed out of Joubert, which I think is about the extent of what he can tell us short of letting Commander Talyn use her illegal methods."

"When do we hand him over to the Cimmerian authorities?" Galdi asked.

"Once the Commonwealth Chief Prosecutor for the Rim Sector decides whether he wants to retain jurisdiction on the grounds Joubert aided and abetted terrorism, or let the locals take him on charges of fomenting treason against the star system government."

Galdi rolled his eyes.

"Great. He'll be in our cells for the next eighteen months."

"But not our problem. Once I declare us finished, Maras will dissolve the ad hoc task force, and we return to normal duties. Joubert will belong to the Major Crimes Division from that moment on. After recent events, Maras won't feel generous enough to let Assistant Commissioner Kristy Bujold fade into early retirement. We may well be leaving for Mission Colony before the week is out."

"Praise the Almighty. I prefer our regular responsibilities, onerous and unpopular as they might be." Galdi suddenly froze and held up his hand. "I think my ears picked up something on the Gendarmerie band in my office. Give me a few seconds."

He ducked out but returned in under a minute.

"The Gendarmerie finally obtained a search warrant for Magda Annear's hunting lodge. That was the officer in charge reporting. They found a dozen bodies, every one of them shot in the back of the head, execution style, including the elusive Hadar Wilborg, who seems to have been interrogated by an expert. The place was ransacked and basically trashed, the bodies dead for at least a day, probably longer."

"Major Boldt's Marines or our friendly Super Spooks?"

"No idea, but my money's on the Marines. Whoever did it left a note saying they recovered just over fifty kilograms of MHX-19 and eight detonators, all of which are no longer on the surface of Cimmeria."

Morrow made a face.

"I believe they call that chutzpah, but it's nice of them to let the gendarmes know."

"I hope those fifty kilograms represent every last bit of the aptly named Mayhem."

"There have been no further explosions since Locarno," Bonta pointed out. "Either Wilborg told his executioners where to find every remaining bomb, or Locarno was the last one."

"We'll probably never know." She glanced upward as if to indicate the heavens. "Our answers are about to sail away with *Mikado*."

"I'll be content if Commander Talyn and Major Decker are aboard as well."

A faint buzz sounded and Morrow glanced down at her communicator. A faint smile tugged at the corners of her lips.

"If they're not yet, they will be soon."

"How do you figure, Chief?"

"I just received a message from an anonymous source. It said *I kept my promise.*"

Galdi's eyebrows shot up.

"Talyn?"

"Without a doubt. Before she left Aquilonia, Talyn promised me she would do her utmost to avoid using us as patsies again and bring me in as a full-fledged partner."

"Which she did to a certain extent."

"To a great extent, Arno. We would never take part in the cleanup phase because as much as I believe the people responsible for Silfax and the near miss in Locarno deserve to be struck from the human race, I'm a cop. I cannot do anything other than apply the law as written. Talyn and Decker are under no such moral or legal constraints."

"Thankfully," Bonta said in a soft tone. When Galdi and Morrow turned their eyes on her, she asked, "What? We each play a role in keeping humanity safe. Theirs is simply more primal than ours."

"I suppose you're right, Sergeant," Galdi replied. "As someone said long before our species spread across the galaxy, people sleep peacefully in their beds at night only because rough men and women stand ready to do violence on their behalf."

"And on that note," Morrow climbed wearily to her feet, "time to head for home. I think we did everything we could. The rest, what our SOCOM friends didn't sort out, belongs to the Gendarmerie."

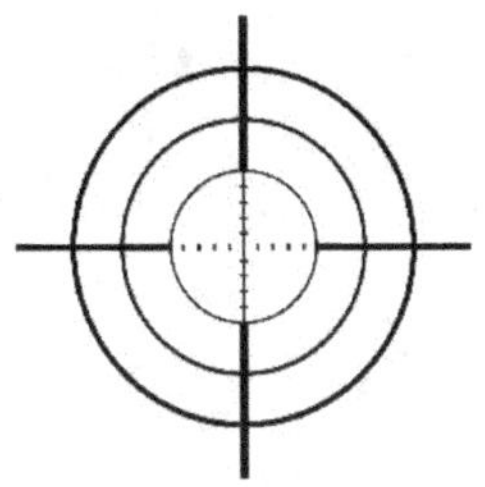

— FORTY-FIVE —

Decker glanced through the private shuttle's aft porthole when his peripheral vision caught the unlit hangar's personnel door opening.

"It's show time. Magda just entered."

"It's about bloody time. She's the last loose end now that Boldt's people recovered the remaining MHX. I'd love to know where Valerian stashed her for the last three days."

"We can always ask."

Decker rechecked his blaster, out of habit rather than need, eyes straining in the darkened passenger compartment before settling back in his well-padded seat, one of two facing the starboard door. Talyn occupied the other.

"But why?" He continued. "Judging by what *Mikado* gleaned from the Gendarmerie and Constabulary communications channels, he's not even in play. Once we send Magda to join her followers in the great beyond, our work here is done. Calvo and his cabinet can decide whether it's time for a new governor general."

The characteristic mechanical sounds of a spacecraft door unlatching stilled Talyn's reply. Then, it moved inward and slid to one side. Magda Annear climbed aboard. Preoccupied with thoughts of escape, she noticed nothing was amiss at first. Then, she touched the cabin lighting controls, dispelling the gloom. Her eyes widened in shock as she stared into the barrel of Decker's hand artillery.

"Hello, Magda," Talyn purred. "Nice of you to join us."

"You're supposed to be dead," she replied in an accusatory tone.

"And you're remarkably well informed for someone who disappeared seventy-two hours ago when her plan went sideways." Talyn pointed at the seat in front of them with the barrel of her gun. "Sit."

When she didn't move, Talyn's voice cracked over Annear like a whip, "Sit, or Zack will break your legs."

"Surely there's no need to use that tone with me," Annear replied in a voice dripping with contempt. But she obeyed, eyes searching Talyn's face for a clue to her destiny.

"What do you want? Thanks to Joubert's fecklessness and your untimely intervention, my plans failed. You win. The Gendarmerie hasn't issued an arrest warrant for me yet, but I suppose it's only a matter of time considering Hector Valerian is playing elder statesman to Calvo's avenging fury. But good luck finding the evidence and witnesses for a terrorism or treason conviction. At best, I might do twenty-four months in the Gilded Cage for attempted sedition. A vacation, nothing more."

"Ask Louis Sorne how he enjoyed his. Oh, that's right, you can't. I shot him."

"So the governor general was in on your scheme?" Talyn asked.

"Hector? He always comes out on the winning side. If I seemed a likely champion, able to suppress the dastardly DSA after they murdered most of the Rim Sector's most notable citizens, we wouldn't be speaking right now. But thanks to you, Calvo backed down from resigning and asking Hector to dissolve parliament. Don't bother trying to hang something on him. The

Valerians didn't rise to prominence by accident. Now was that all? A ship is waiting in orbit to take me — well, away from here."

"A Howler ship?"

Magda gave Talyn a feral smile.

"How did you ever guess?"

"The Navy seized it a few hours ago. Its captain told us where we could find the shuttle he sent to pick you up. Apparently, he didn't need much convincing. It's sad. You simply can't find loyal help these days, not even among the most ruthless of criminal gangs. Speaking of help, your DSA no longer exists except for a handful of scared hangers-on, and CimmerTek will need a serious recruiting drive to replenish the ranks. If it doesn't simply fold now that Louis Sorne and your favorite godfather, Fast Tony Hakkam, are supping with Satan. But I hear the funeral director business is experiencing a mini-boom this week. We also recovered the rest of the MHX-19 thanks to the late Hadar Wilborg. He turned out to be a good conversationalist during his final hours before entering the big sleep."

"And that only leaves you, honey," Decker said with a cruel grin. "The last important loose end. At least where Naval Intelligence is concerned. The Cimmerian authorities will no doubt be able to take care of the remaining details."

Annear's smooth forehead creased with a frown.

"Naval Intelligence?"

"More specifically, the Special Operations Division. We terminate folks like you who think they're entitled to change governments against the will of the people."

An unattractive sneer twisted her face.

"The people? Those bovine, flatulent heaps of protoplasm? They wouldn't know proper government if it bit them. Humanity hasn't advanced an iota since we kicked the Shrehari back into their sphere because the people would rather wallow in their delusions of adequacy instead of imitating our ancestors and claiming new worlds. The Empire's invasion unified us. Peace returned us to the atomized, weakened state we've suffered since the end of the Second Migration War. That is about to change despite the mindless herds."

Talyn scoffed.

"I'm sure your mother, who believes in constitutional government of the people, for the people and by the people is proud of her only daughter."

"My mother can go to hell. She's part of the problem and her day of reckoning will come, you can count on that. My failure here won't stop our movement. We will restore a united Commonwealth, governed by a strong Earth and capable of seizing the galaxy."

"I can think of several non-human polities who would object to our seizing their part of the galaxy."

"Too bad. The progress we champion will spread throughout the Commonwealth and beyond. We will crush those who oppose us, including useless uniformed parasites like you."

Decker studied her as if she were a strange specimen.

"Did the good senator drop you on the head as a baby? Because what passes for your brain sure seems damaged."

Annear's face tightened at the insult.

"Can we end this persiflage? You still didn't answer my question. What do you want? Do you expect me to tell you everything about our movement and its grand plan?"

Talyn raised her blaster and pointed it at Magda's forehead.

"No Sera Annear, we expect you to die for your movement and its grand plan."

A panicked expression wiped away her earlier anger. She gave Decker a beseeching look.

"Surely you wouldn't let her kill your lost love's only half-sister? Am I not the closest thing to Avril's twin?"

"You're nothing like her," he growled. "She would never think of using and discarding human beings in pursuit of personal ambition and illegitimate political power, let alone committing mass murder. Of the two sisters, she was the sane, humane, and admirable one. You're only a sad, evil, shriveled soul, using the misguided ideals of naïve radicals for your own purposes. But thanks for trying to cheapen her memory in an attempt to save your worthless life. Goodbye, Magda."

Talyn's weapon coughed once, spitting out a small, fiery ball of plasma. The bridge of Annear's nose vanished, replaced by a smoking black hole while the back of her skull erupted with flash broiled brain matter.

"Shame about the upholstery, but if Senator Annear had smothered her daughter at birth, a few thousand people would still be alive."

They left the small spacecraft's door open and walked through the late evening shadows to the spaceport's nearby naval section where an unmarked shuttle from *Mikado* waited.

"I never asked, but what was your plan if Joubert didn't turn on my communicator, thereby allowing Caelin and Sergeant Bonta to find us? Was there even a plan or were you improvising from minute to minute?"

Decker nudged her.

"Watch me."

He convulsed while white foam appeared in the corners of his mouth.

"You would have feigned a seizure? Seriously? That's one of the oldest and lamest tricks in the book."

"Our book, maybe. However, Joubert's a bureaucrat. He was probably a decent cop years ago, but no longer has the reflexes of someone dealing with tricky customers on a regular basis. I merely needed to wait until the right moment."

"And the CimmerTek man?"

"Joubert's big enough to make an excellent human shield, and while the goon had his eyes glued on me wondering what the hell was happening, you would have been able to take him."

"I'm touched by your trust in my abilities."

"It ain't so much a matter of trust but experience, sweetheart," he drawled. "I've seen you kill often enough. Do you intend to call the cops and let them know about Magda?"

"I should, otherwise the maintenance crew will get a nasty surprise in the morning."

Talyn sent one last anonymous message to Sergeant Bonta, informing her where Magda Annear's body could be found, then they climbed aboard and lifted off, the Democratic Stars Alliance and its leader gone forever.

"I'm glad this one is over," she said once the lights of Howard's Landing disappeared beneath the clouds.

"It's not over just yet, my dear." Decker patted her hand. "We still need to return the remaining MHX."

"What do you mean?"

"Let's wait until we're aboard to discuss it."

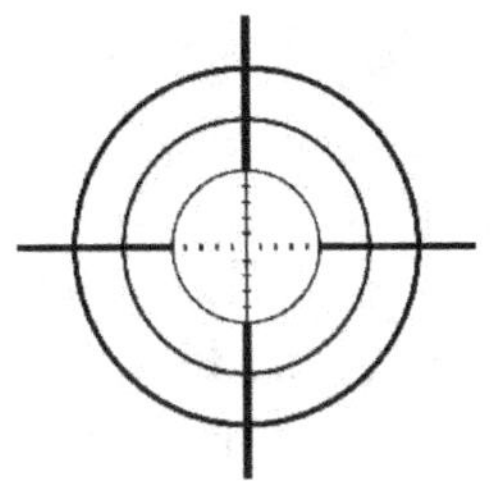

— FORTY-SIX —

Zack climbed out of the shuttle and stretched with contentment while he watched the flight of gunships carrying G Troop, Number 6 Company, land on the hangar deck, their work retrieving every last MHX-19 explosive device completed. They were the last of the anti-terrorism teams to rejoin the Q-ship.

"Welcome aboard *Mikado*, Colonel Decker." A stocky, silver-haired man in Navy battle dress with the three gold stripes of a commander on his collar stood on the yellow safety line beyond the shuttle's nose. "I'm Sandor Piech."

"A pleasure to be here, Skipper, but it's major."

"Not anymore. Orders caught up with us thirty minutes ago. You've been a lieutenant colonel for the last week. Congratulations."

"Congratulations for what?" Talyn asked as she joined her partner.

"It looks like the Commandant finally lost his ever-loving mind. I'm a lieutenant colonel."

Talyn let out an exaggerated sigh of relief.

"Excellent. Now I can dump the burden of command officially into your lap. No more standing at attention in front of the commodore to explain why my subordinate once again disregarded rules, regulations, and protocols. When he didn't blatantly violate Commonwealth and star system laws. The next time you dream up a harebrained scheme, we will switch places, and you can plead for the commodore's mercy." She winked at Piech. "Zack's not exactly a standard-issue intelligence operative. How are you, Sandor?"

"Enjoying every minute in command of this beauty. And you?"

"Since I survived another of Zack's sure-fire plans, I can't really complain."

"What did you want?" The Marine growled. "We saved hundreds of lives, recovered the remaining MHX, and put the Democratic Stars Alliance permanently out of business. Our work in *this* system is done."

Something in the way he said 'this system' gave her pause, and she eyed him with suspicion.

"What outrageous scheme is fermenting in your brain this time?"

He jerked a thumb at the gunships.

"A few dozen kilos of the Mayhem we recovered needs to be wrapped in gift paper then topped with a nice pink bow and stamped with a big red label that reads return to sender. Remember when I said the only way to stop this sort of crap is by inflicting so much pain on the bastards they'll flinch every time someone comes up with a new plot. Killing Sorne, Hakkam, and the ever so lovely Magda was only the beginning. It cleaned up this sector. Or at least the Cimmeria system. The Commonwealth has five more sectors, and that means we cut it off at the very top. We're taking *Mikado* to Pacifica, and I'll hand deliver our gift to the head skunk himself."

"Blowing up the ComCorp tower in downtown Hadley isn't a good idea. Most of the people working there don't know what their top boss is doing."

A wicked grin split Zack's face.

"Didn't I read somewhere the Amalis rebuilt their island getaway after our last visit, but newer, better and bigger than before? Possibly even made it the

Coalition's unofficial headquarters? Perhaps if I sanitize the place with Mayhem, they'll stop rebuilding."

"It's a lengthy trip, even at top speed," Piech replied in a dubious tone.

"I know. But the real question is do your orders allow you to sail that far without asking HQ for permission?"

"Zack, are you considering an unauthorized operation on Pacifica?" Talyn gave her partner a hard look.

"Do you think the commodore would let me set off approximately fifty kilograms of MHX on another inhabited planet after what happened here?"

"Ulrich? If it's in a good cause, perhaps. Kruczek? Not without Ulrich twisting his arm, and then it's only a one in ten chance he says yes."

"There you go. This is one of those times where we ask forgiveness instead of permission. And if you turn over command of our team to me, I'll assume full responsibility."

When she didn't immediately reply, he added, "You know we eventually have to take this fight to the Home Sector. Now is as good a time as any. How many thousands did Magda's DSA maniacs kill? We're damn lucky the death toll didn't climb into the hundreds of thousands, but it will if we don't smack the Coalition's top leadership harder than ever."

Talyn glanced at Piech.

"Opinions, Sandor? It may be our operation, but this is your ship. If you say no, we're returning to Caledonia, it'll be the last we hear of Zack's notion."

"My orders are to help you eliminate any threat you designate, the same orders SOCOM gave Number 6 Company."

"In that case, I name the Coalition leaders on Pacifica a clear and present danger to the Commonwealth," Decker intoned while his eyes challenged Talyn to contradict him.

When she didn't say a word, Piech shrugged. "Then I guess we're off to Pacifica, Earth's uglier, nastier, and more corrupt sibling."

Decker clapped him on the shoulder.

"That's what I wanted to hear. Let me give Henrik the good news."

"I'm sure he'll love the idea of spending a few more weeks in *Mikado*," Talyn replied with a wry smile. "Especially if you intend to do what I think and make a solo jump on Amali's island."

"He and his company just enjoyed three thoroughly exciting days hunting real live terrorists, something they don't often do. They shouldn't mind a relaxing pleasure cruise on a fine ship such as this one."

"I'm not sure I like the idea of a solo jump, Zack."

"Yet it's the only way to go. Plausible deniability. One shuttle and one jumper will not only have a better chance to get in and out unnoticed, but if our bosses vehemently object after the fact, Boldt's company will be in the clear. Besides, I'm sure both the commodore and Admiral Kruczek will approve of us limiting the number of participants in a totally unauthorized and illegal operation. And if we time it right, I could be jumping in on our anniversary."

Piech gave him a strange look.

"I first met Hera when she rescued me from Amali's private island after almost getting me killed thanks to her not particularly surefire spook plan."

"He was quite a bedraggled, waterlogged, and pitiful escapee."

"Who resented her for a long time, even after being drafted into the Black Gang."

Talyn nudged him.

"Enough of the auld lang syne, Colonel Decker. Henrik is looking in our direction, probably hoping for words of wisdom from the senior Marine Corps officer aboard. Or maybe a hint of what his future holds."

"Right. If you two fine naval officers will excuse me."

Decker crossed the hangar where Major Henrik Boldt was speaking with G Troop's leader. Both snapped to attention at his approach and saluted even though Zack wasn't in uniform. He returned the compliment with a formal nod.

"Gentlemen."

"Congratulations on your promotion, Colonel."

"Don't you mean congratulations on offering to subsidize Number 6 Company's party tonight as a way of wetting my new rank?" Decker winked at the troop leader, a command sergeant who could claim almost as many combat jumps as Zack.

"Am I that transparent, sir?" Boldt asked with a sly grin.

"When it comes to free drinks, every jumper created by God and the Pathfinder School is as transparent as glass. Are these fine young men and women the last to board?"

"Yes, sir. What happens now?"

"Did you ever visit the Home Sector's priceless progressive jewel, an open sewer by the name Pacifica?"

Boldt made a face.

"No, and for that, I give thanks to the Almighty. I met enough Marines who enlisted to escape the place, and they taught me the wisdom of avoidance."

"I have, several times. One of my visits almost ended with me turning into bug food. Ask me about it in the wardroom during our upcoming trip to the dark heart of the Home Sector. We're returning the Mayhem you collected to the people who stole it from our ammo dumps. I figure blowing their asses into orbit for messing with Cimmeria will be an object lesson they won't soon forget."

"May I assume this will be in an unapproved and unauthorized operation, sir?"

"The blackest of black ops, Henrik, *lex talionis* on a scale big enough to make the opposition think twice about trying again. And once we've delivered our message, it becomes another of those missions we never speak of again. Your unit diary will show nothing more than a few weeks spent training aboard the Q-ship *Mikado*."

"Understood, Colonel."

Decker clapped him on the shoulder.

"Good man. We can discuss the details once we're in interstellar space. After the last few days, I need a cold beer and a warm bunk."

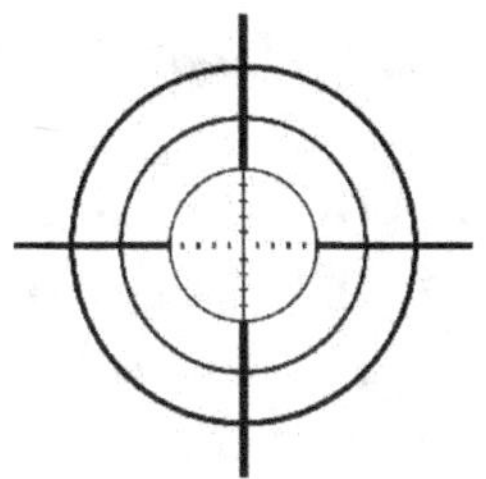

— FORTY-SEVEN —

Decker's feet touched the black sand beach where Talyn had saved him from certain death years ago. He took several steps to absorb his remaining forward momentum and then slapped the controls to retract his kite parachute back into its hard shell.

Though the sun had already set over this part of Pacifica, Decker easily recognized the spot where he almost made a last, defiant stand against Walker Amali's giant, semi-sapient insectoid soldiers, terrifying creatures capable of tearing a human being apart.

Decker made his way to the tree line where he stepped out of the chute harness after dropping his rucksack and carbine. The chute assembly vanished into a thicket of the thorny native bush he remembered only too well from his first visit where it would escape notice from any roving patrols Amali might use to secure his private island's northern shore. The equipment was unmarked, so even if it survived the explosion, no one could prove the Fleet was involved.

He swung his heavy rucksack, with its fifty kilos of MHX-19 and a detonator far more reliable than the ones used by Annear's DSA terrorists, over his shoulders, picked up the carbine and oriented himself. The day he had spent evading Amali's insectoids was indelibly burned into his memory. It meant finding the way across to the southern shore, even in the dark, would be easy. Then, he headed off at an easy lope, thanks to his battle armor's mobility enhancements.

Using the edge of a streambed and various animal trails, Decker reached the ridge running from hill to hill at the island's center in just over an hour. There, he found a familiar boulder arrangement and, more importantly, a hidden vantage point from which he could study the entire resort.

The Amalis didn't just rebuild their island getaway after the 251st Pathfinder Squadron's Warthog gunships flattened every last building all those years ago. They considerably enlarged it, turning what was once a quiet family retreat into a sprawling, albeit tiny city reserved for the obscenely wealthy. Glass and steel spires competed with marble-clad mansions while a vast reception hall and extensive recreational facilities lined the shore.

Decker could make out hundreds of men and women strolling along beautifully manicured paths under the soft light of glow globes. Others, clustered in groups, were talking, laughing, and drinking from sparkling crystal glasses dispensed by a battalion of service droids. He recognized many faces from the files Naval Intelligence kept on suspected Coalition leaders, including the thuggish features of the *Sécurité Spéciale*'s director general.

Perhaps Amali was hosting his version of the Locarno Conference, or more likely, an emergency meeting following the disastrous failure of the DSA scheme on Cimmeria and in the broader Rim Sector. The news would have reached Pacifica long before *Mikado*, now in orbit disguised as the freighter *Boudjankar*, dropped out of FTL at the Pacifica system's heliopause.

Or it could merely be another Saturday night for the rich and powerful on the first extrasolar world settled by humanity centuries earlier. Neither Decker nor Talyn counted on Sadoc Amali himself being present tonight. They designed this operation as a warning shot using the last of the purloined MHX.

But seeing so many of the enemy's senior leadership on display would make this all the sweeter. He recorded the scene for posterity and Commodore Ulrich's forgiveness before searching for the spot he'd selected based on *Mikado*'s orbital scans and his recollections of the island. It was far enough from the glittering spires to be well outside any immediate security perimeter, yet close enough to make sure Amali's resort vanished, Atlantis-like, beneath the waves.

When Decker found it, he took a last look at the party then slipped back into the woods, unseen, and unheard. The final two kilometers downhill took him longer than the entire trip from the northern shore to the ridge, primarily because of his increased caution and more frequent checks for nearby surveillance sensors. He finally reached flat ground and made his way toward a low cliff where he hoped to find a suitable fissure or even a shallow cavern to place the bomb.

This close to the resort, he could hear the soft murmur of voices, an occasional tinkle of laughter and even background music. Sounds that turned the silent enemy faces he'd observed from his previous perch into something more human and reminded him not everyone about to die was guilty of capital crimes. Perhaps not even most.

But then, the thirty-five hundred who perished in Silfax had been wholly innocent, as most of the Coalition's future victims would be. The merriment reaching his ears came from those who started this war and would keep stoking it with a growing tally of civilian casualties if no one stopped them. Decker, coarsened by years of undercover battle, hardened his heart and tuned out the noise. There was no way to sort the good from the bad this time. It would be a night for retribution, not sentimentality. *Lex talionis.*

He found a crack in the basalt large enough to hide the bomb and removed his rucksack. He knelt, opened the pack, and removed the padding that covered the detonator. A last, lengthy check proved it was functional and none of the connections had been disturbed during the shuttle's launch from *Mikado*'s hangar deck, its long glide around Pacifica, and his jump from ultra-high altitude. Decker set the timer, carefully jammed his pack into the fissure, and armed the anti-tamper and anti-lift devices.

He stood, took one last look at his surroundings, and then glanced up at the starlit sky, hoping Talyn would receive the pickup signal on his first try. One hour wasn't much time to get away from Amali Island, even with the battlesuit's propulsion system.

One last obstacle remained, however. A strip of open ground bordering the water's edge. Only a few dozen meters, but enough for some sharp-eyed guard to notice a curious blur distorting a landscape faintly lit by the resort's lights.

Decker reached the final tree line and dropped to the ground. He pushed himself out into the open, eyes and ears alert for any evidence of human or robotic activity nearby. When nothing of note triggered his augmented senses, Decker crawled through the short grass, then down the sandy shore until water lapped at his helmet.

The battlesuit, while positively buoyant, behaved more like a semi-submersible in salt water. He switched back to canned air, hoping enough remained after his fall through the upper atmosphere to last until Talyn arrived.

Once in deeper water, Decker turned onto his back and activated the suit's propulsion module. One tap and he began to move effortlessly through the water at several times the speed of the fastest swimming creature in the known galaxy. But his range was limited; barely enough to leave the bomb's immediate danger zone. After a suitable interval, he activated the suit's emergency beacon, conscious anyone scanning in his direction would notice an unusual signal emanating from the water's surface.

Forty-five minutes passed in silence. Semi-submerged as he was, Decker quickly lost sight of Amali's gleaming little kingdom, though the glow of its lights remained above his minuscule horizon, decreasing with each kilometer of distance.

Finally, a soft whine cut through the monotonous sounds of water passing over his helmet and a black shape blocked out the stars. It came ever closer until stopping to hover within arm's reach before gently touching down. Decker switched off the MHD drives and swam for the shuttle's side, where a hatch swung open to welcome him. He half climbed, half slithered on board, dripping water on the craft's metal deck.

The hatch closed with a muffled clang, and he felt the craft lift off again.

"Come here often, Big Boy?" Talyn asked from the cockpit.

Decker wrenched his helmet off and tucked it under one of the aft compartment's seats.

"Only my second visit, ma'am. How about you?"

"My second visit as well, but I seem to have picked up the same Marine again. Though he looks a lot healthier and happier than last time. It went well?"

"Outstanding, ma'am, just fucking outstanding."

"Oorah!"

Decker shook off the last droplets and joined Talyn in the cockpit.

"See, you learned something from me since our last time in these parts, even if it's only how to pronounce the Marine Corps' ancient and noble war cry without massacring it."

"How long until the premature sunrise?"

He checked his timepiece.

"Four minutes. Amali was hosting a party. Many of the worst people were in attendance, folks whose mugshots adorn our assassination wish list."

Decker rattled off a few names and approval lit up her face as she nodded.

"Nice. And ironic. They plotted to blow up the Locarno Conference. Now, we're doing it to them, with the MHX they stole from us."

"Indeed, and on the anniversary of our first meeting too, my dear. I can't help but think we somehow came full circle." He glanced at the time again. "Give us a rear view, will you?"

"Getting philosophical in your old age?" She switched the cockpit's secondary display to show the tiny speck of light that was Amali Island, now far in the distance. "Or are you regretting your life with me during the intervening years?"

"Regrets? Perhaps a couple, but you're not one of them, sweetie."

A white bloom soundlessly blotted out the night with enough suddenness to take both operatives by surprise.

Talyn let out a low whistle.

"For a reason I can't fathom that was even more spectacular than the last one we saw while flying away at top speed."

"Only innocent trees and animals died in the nature preserve. This time, few, if any true innocents were vaporized. Killing in job lots with the highest of non-nuclear explosives tends to send a shiver up your spine."

Something in his voice caught Talyn's attention. She took her eyes off the rapidly fading mini-nova and glanced at her partner.

"Let me guess. One of your regrets is becoming inured at causing so much death even though we probably saved countless lives by taking a bunch of power-hungry sociopaths off the board."

"Or we could have condemned even more to die because of what we did tonight. That's the thing with playing God when we're mere mortals. We can hardly predict first-order effects with relative certainty, especially beyond the immediate future, let along second and third-order effects." He sighed. "I could be getting too old and too tired for this business."

"We are overdue for a long furlough, and tonight should give the Fleet time to breathe while the enemy deals with its losses. The commodore shouldn't balk at granting us two or three months of rest." She smiled at him. "How do twelve weeks of intercourse and intoxication sound?"

"Right now? Heavenly." He grinned back at her. "And what will you do during that time?"

Talyn stuck her tongue out at him.

"I sure you're not the only explosives expert capable of blowing my mind, honey."

"But I'm the only one who knows your triggers." He sat back and stared at the rear view display. "That was one hell of a detonation, though. If ever the Master Gunner School invites me as a guest speaker, I'll be able to tell a classroom of attentive senior noncoms what creating a big bang is like."

"It'll remain one of your many fantasies. HQ will give this business a security classification that will forbid us from even remembering it, let alone telling anyone."

"Sadly. When future historians write my biography, they'll find my service record pretty damn flimsy thanks to all the redactions."

"They might not find mine, period," Talyn replied, "so don't feel too sorry for yourself."

Decker let out a disconsolate grunt. After a long pause, he asked, "Do you think the commodore will chew us each a new asshole for stretching the spirit of our orders beyond the breaking point?"

"Yep. If not him, then Admiral Kruczek."

"Maybe Sandor can drop us off somewhere nice on the way home so we can start our furlough a bit earlier and without that messy business of reporting back after blowing a hole into the crust of a sovereign Commonwealth planet."

"And spend the rest of our lives on the run from Commodore Ulrich's wrath? Pass. We'll take our lumps like the professionals we are."

"That's what I thought you'd say. But we're still on for that twelve weeks of I&I, right?"

"Of course. After we do our penance."

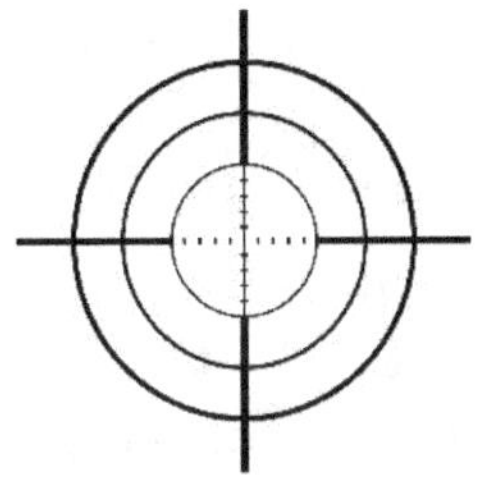

— FORTY-EIGHT —

"Enter."

Commander Hera Talyn and Lieutenant Colonel Zack Decker, she in naval blue service dress, he wearing Marine Corps black, stepped into Commodore Kos Ulrich's office and stomped to attention a regulation three paces in front of his desk. They saluted as one and held their hands to their brows while Ulrich studied them with hard eyes before returning the compliment.

"At ease." When they complied, he said, "Congratulations on your promotion, Zack. The new rank suits you."

"Thank you, sir."

"If we'd known what you two commissioned lunatics were planning before the orders were cut, I might have suggested the Commandant reconsider signing them."

"Yes, sir," Decker replied.

"Is that all you can say for yourselves? Yes, sir?" The chill in Ulrich's tone dropped the ambient temperature by another degree. "Admiral Kruczek is furious, not just at what you did without authorization but at having to lie to the Grand Admiral. We are in the business of surgical strikes and targeted assassinations, not terrorist-style bombings. The remaining MHX-19 should have come home with you."

"Sir, you saw my recording of Amali Island. We—"

Ulrich raised his hand, palm facing outward.

"I'm not done yet, Colonel.   Admiral Kruczek has ordered that I formally reprimand both of you for grossly overstepping your orders and for terminating Coalition members without authorization. I won't even mention the collateral damage, which we will never establish with any degree of certainty. I'll note the reprimands in your service records, without specifics, since your jaunt to Pacifica never happened. So far, the Grand Admiral has successfully refuted any accusations from Earth that we're responsible because he believes Admiral Kruczek's assertion Naval Intelligence never authorized the attack. Officially, we think a faction of the Coalition opposed to Sadoc Amali's handling of the Rim Sector business was responsible. At least you had the grace to avoid involving your comrades from the 1st Special Forces Regiment. Do you understand how your decision to play avenging angels almost caused fatal damage to our freedom of action?"

"Yes, sir," Decker and Talyn replied in unison.

"Ass chewing over. Sit." Ulrich pointed at the chairs facing him. "Unofficially, and I'll deny I ever said this, Admiral Kruczek wishes, and I quote, Naval Intelligence had more officers able and willing to take the fight deep into enemy territory, no matter the consequences to their careers. Well done."

Decker and Talyn glanced at each other. "Told you," the former murmured.

"We can argue about acceptable and unacceptable methods until the end of time," Ulrich continued, "but no one can argue about the results. The Coalition lost three-quarters of its most senior leadership that night, effectively ending it as a political and economic threat for the near future. Initial reports coming from our various field offices show half the zaibatsus in the Commonwealth struggling with succession issues while the *Sécurité Spéciale*'s upper ranks are in a death match to decide who becomes the next director general. I'm sure you caught wind of the Senate's bitter debates on the replacement of the Home World senators who died that night on this morning's newscast."

"Why do I hear a 'but' coming?" Talyn asked.

"Because you're one heck of a sharp agent, Hera. This was your last mission as field operatives. Your luck is bound to run out some day and the Fleet needs your services in other capacities."

Decker cursed under his breath.

"I fucking knew it."

Ulrich gave him a sharp look.

"Sorry, sir."

"Late last night, Admiral Kruczek signed your promotion orders, Hera. Congratulations. You get to put up a fourth stripe. Once we're done here, I'll call everyone together in the main conference room, and announce it formally. With the promotion comes a permanent assignment as chief of staff of the Special Operations Division."

When he noticed the disappointment in her eyes, he said, in a gentler tone, "I need to prepare my successor, Hera. The boss recently told me I'm next in line as Deputy Chief of Naval Intelligence for Operations, which leaves two years at most to make sure you're ready for this job and your first star. I don't know anyone better suited than you."

Talyn nodded her acceptance of the news.

"I exist to serve the Commonwealth. What about the Marine here?"

She jerked her thumb at Decker.

"He finally gets to go home. As much as it pains me to lose you, Zack, the experience you gained working with Hera will be invaluable when you take up your new duties as the commanding officer of A Squadron, 1st Special Forces Regiment."

Decker's face lit up with surprise.

"No shit, sir?"

"Not even a whiff. In the next few days, A Squadron will be re-designated as SOCOM's principal black ops unit, and you're the best placed to make it happen. Colonel Martinson asked for you by name when SOCOM laid the new task on his regiment. He figures you're the only Marine officer with the right combination of qualifications, experience, and professional standing in the Pathfinder and Special Forces community. Congratulations."

"Thank you, sir."

Ulrich waved his thanks away.

"You earned it fair and square, Colonel. Now, why don't we turn Hera into a Commonwealth Navy captain and then you can be off on your furlough. Martinson doesn't expect your smiling face at Fort Arnhem for at least eight weeks. It will take them that long to shift things around and prepare A Squadron for its transformation, and I've lasted without a permanent chief of staff since Manfred's death anyhow."

As they stood, Decker turned to his now ex-partner.

"It's been one hell of a ride, darling. And I'm sorry it has to end."

"You know there's regular air service between Carrick and Sanctum, right? You can be home in under an hour every Friday afternoon." When he stared at her without replying, she chuckled. "You didn't think I'd let you slip away that easily. Once I replace the commodore, I want what every chief of intelligence black ops needs — her own contingent of door kickers. Besides, my life would be dull without you."

Decker blew her a kiss.

"I love you too, Hera."

**

Later, as they were returning to their quarters via one of the underground corridors connecting the Fleet HQ complex's various buildings, Decker nudged Talyn and murmured, "Watch this."

He nodded toward a middle-aged, tired looking Marine officer coming from the other direction, head down, preoccupied with something on the tablet in his left hand.

When the officer neared them, Decker barked out, "Good morning, Captain Sarratt. And how are you?"

He looked up and at first, noticed only a Marine Corps lieutenant colonel and a Navy captain. His right hand snapped up out of reflex to salute.

A fraction of a second later, his brain processed what his eyes saw, and he recognized the man wearing 1st Special Forces Regiment badges.

Sarratt's mouth opened in astonishment while his eyes bugged out of their sockets. "You—"

It came out as a strangled sound. Then he appeared to lose his ability to speak.

"I'm doing fine as you might have noticed, Captain, thanks for asking. If you ever need a recommendation from a former Pathfinder comrade, look me up in Fort Arnhem. I'm taking command of A Squadron, 1st SFR in a few weeks. In the meantime, have a blessed day."

They left him standing in the corridor, struck mute and staring at their receding backs.

"You thoroughly enjoyed that, didn't you?" Talyn asked once they turned a corner and lost sight of Sarratt.

"More than you could ever imagine, my dear." He wrapped an arm around her shoulders and squeezed. "Life is good and getting better."

ABOUT THE AUTHOR

Eric Thomson is the pen name of a retired Canadian soldier with thirty-one years of service, both in the Regular Army and the Army Reserve. He spent his Regular Army career in the Infantry and his Reserve service in the Armoured Corps.

Eric has been a voracious reader of science fiction, military fiction, and history all his life. Several years ago, he put fingers to keyboard and started writing his own military sci-fi, with a definite space opera slant, using many of his own experiences as a soldier for inspiration.

When he's not writing fiction, Eric indulges in his other passions: photography, hiking, and scuba diving, all of which he shares with his wife.

Join Eric Thomson at http://www.thomsonfiction.ca/

where you'll find news about upcoming books and more information about the universe in which his heroes fight for humanity's survival.

Read his blog at
https://ericthomsonblog.wordpress.com

If you enjoyed this book, please consider leaving a review on Goodreads or with your favorite online retailer to help others discover it.

ALSO BY ERIC THOMSON

Siobhan Dunmoore
No Honor in Death (Siobhan Dunmoore Book 1)
The Path of Duty (Siobhan Dunmoore Book 2)
Like Stars in Heaven (Siobhan Dunmoore Book 3)
Victory's Bright Dawn (Siobhan Dunmoore Book 4)
Without Mercy (Siobhan Dunmoore Book 5)

Decker's War
Death Comes but Once (Decker's War Book 1)
Cold Comfort (Decker's War Book 2)
Fatal Blade (Decker's War Book 3)
Howling Stars (Decker's War Book 4)
Black Sword (Decker's War Book 5)
No Remorse (Decker's War Book 6)
Hard Strike (Decker's War Book 7)

Quis Custodiet
The Warrior's Knife (Quis Custodiet No 1)

Ashes of Empire
Imperial Sunset (Ashes of Empire #1)

www.ingramcontent.com/pod-product-compliance
Lightning Source LLC
Chambersburg PA
CBHW072005190726

48293CB00001B/161